THE BERKLEY PUBLISHING GROUP
Published by the Penguin Group
Penguin Group (USA) Inc.
375 Hudson Street, New York, New York 10014, USA

Penguin Group (Canada), 90 Eglinton Avenue East, Suite 700, Toronto, Ontario M4P 2Y3, Canada
(a division of Pearson Penguin Canada Inc.)
Penguin Books Ltd., 80 Strand, London WC2R 0RL, England
Penguin Group Ireland, 25 St. Stephen's Green, Dublin 2, Ireland (a division of Penguin Books Ltd.)
Penguin Group (Australia), 250 Camberwell Road, Camberwell, Victoria 3124, Australia
(a division of Pearson Australia Group Pty. Ltd.)
Penguin Books India Pvt. Ltd., 11 Community Centre, Panchsheel Park, New Delhi—110 017, India
Penguin Group (NZ), 67 Apollo Drive, Rosedale, North Shore 0632, New Zealand
(a division of Pearson New Zealand Ltd.)
Penguin Books (South Africa) (Pty.) Ltd., 24 Sturdee Avenue, Rosebank, Johannesburg 2196,
South Africa

Penguin Books Ltd., Registered Offices: 80 Strand, London WC2R 0RL, England

This book is an original publication of The Berkley Publishing Group.

This is a work of fiction. Names, characters, places, and incidents either are the product of the author's imagination or are used fictitiously, and any resemblance to actual persons, living or dead, business establishments, events, or locales is entirely coincidental. The publisher does not have any control over and does not assume any responsibility for author or third-party websites or their content.

Copyright © 2010 by Judith Rock.
"Readers Guide" copyright © 2010 by Penguin Group (USA) Inc.
Cover art: *View of Paris from the Pont Royal* by Franco—Flemish School (17th century), Private Collection/The Bridgeman Art Library; *Businessman and Monks Walking in Abbey* copyright © by Altrendo Images/Getty Images; *Italy, Lake Como, Stairs* copyright © by Diego Uchitel/Getty Images.
Cover design by Rich Hasselberger.
Interior text design by Tiffany Estreicher.

PRINTING HISTORY
Berkley trade paperback edition / October 2010

Library of Congress Cataloging-in-Publication Data

Rock, Judith.
  The rhetoric of death / Judith Rock. —Berkley trade paperback ed.
    p. cm.
  ISBN 978-0-425-23664-2
1. Collège Louis le Grand (Paris, France)—Fiction. 2. France—History—17th century—
Fiction. 3. Murder—Investigation—Fiction. I. Title.
  PS3618.O3543R44 2010
  813'.6—dc22   2010014041

PRINTED IN THE UNITED STATES OF AMERICA

10 9 8 7 6 5 4 3 2 1

The Rhetoric of Death

The Rhetoric of Death

JUDITH ROCK

BERKLEY BOOKS, NEW YORK

For Jay
Without whom, nothing

ACKNOWLEDGMENTS

It only takes a writer to create a manuscript, but it takes many people to create a book, and I am more grateful than I can say to those who have helped this one come into being. Damaris Rowland, my agent, has believed in me against all odds, taught me what I needed to know, and kept me writing. Shannon Jamieson Vazquez, my editor, has believed in Charles and his story and has been welcoming, meticulous, and every good thing an editor could possibly be to a new fiction writer.

To those who helped with research, warm thanks, indeed. Patricia Ranum generously shared her extensive knowledge of seventeenth-century clothing, and of Jesuit clothing in particular. Ryan Auer and Jeremy Zipple, S.J., also helped with information about what Charles would have worn. John Padberg, S.J., whom I think of as Charles's literary godfather, gave me essential feedback about details of Jesuit life and attitudes. Any historical or other mistakes that remain are solely mine.

Finally, to all those who have read and responded to the manuscript at various stages, my thanks for helping Charles come to life. And a special thank-you to Lydia Veliko, who saw into Charles's heart.

Prologue

JULY 5, 1686

The sun of Languedoc poured down like molten brass. As the sound of water began to murmur in the still air, the man huddled under his wide-brimmed clerical hat straightened in the saddle and sighed with relief. A few more minutes, and the Gardon River lay before him, rippling blue and green and gold beneath the Pont du Gard. "When we're across, *ma douce*," the man murmured encouragingly to his tired horse, "we'll stop and drink." As she plodded onto the bridge and the shade of the Roman aqueduct's upper level swallowed them, the man looked through the wide stone arches at the river below, wondering as he did every time he crossed, how the Romans had done it. The aqueduct no longer carried springwater to the town of Nîmes, now safely eleven miles behind him. But as a bridge, it looked likely to stand a second sixteen hundred years. On the far bank, he dismounted and led the horse upstream away from the road, around a stand of scrub oak and down a gentle slope to the water. As she drank, he looked up and down the river, listening intently. He was almost sure he wasn't being followed, fairly certain he'd gone unseen that night in Nîmes.

That terrifying night was more than a month past now, but as things were, it was foolish to be too sure of anything.

He saw no one, heard only the river's music and the mare sucking in water. The heat had stilled even the birdsong. He tethered the mare under a wide-canopied oak, well hidden from the road but in reach of rough grazing, and loosened the saddle. On a river-lapped rock under the tree, he stripped off his cassock and shook the white limestone road dust from it, dropped it on the rock, and set his flat-crowned black hat on top of it. Because anything white would show like flame against the shade, he also shed his long, high-collared, sweat-soaked linen shirt. Then, still in the black knee breeches he'd put on under the cassock for riding, he lay flat on his stomach to drink and splash his face. The cool water felt so good that he dipped his head under and came up shaking himself like a happy dog. With a grunt of satisfaction, he rolled over, pulled off his boots and stockings, and stretched his legs to let the river slide over his bare feet. No Jesuit should be this naked in public, but was he in public if there was no one to see him? Smiling wryly at his self-serving logic, he lay back on the rock and squinted at the hard blue sky, figuring the time. Last night's wine-drenched family gathering had made for little sleep and a very late start. An hour's rest out of the morning could hardly matter. He put a hand behind his head to cushion it and shut his eyes.

If a casual passerby had noticed Maître Charles Matthieu Beuvron du Luc on his shady rock, he would have seen only a young man taking his ease without a care in the world. Though Charles's left arm rested carefully across his middle, a war wound in the Spanish Netherlands having left him unable to lift it higher than his shoulder, he was good to look at, big and broad-shouldered and brimming with life. His straw-colored hair, long since grown over the symbolic little Jesuit tonsure given at first vows, was drying in thick, unruly curls, and his face was tanned to pale gold. More than a few women still sighed over the sad fact that Charles du Luc had chosen a cassock.

Seven years a member of the Society of Jesus, Charles had finished the two-year novitiate and taken first vows, the three traditional promises of poverty, chastity, and obedience. Now, in what Jesuits called the scholastic phase of his training, a long period of study and teaching, his final vows and ordination as priest were still some years off. Because he already wore the Jesuit cassock, laypeople often called him *père*, or father, but his real title was *maître*, meaning master or teacher, and his present work was teaching rhetoric, both Latin and French. Rhetoric was the art of communication, and because Jesuits believed that the body, too, should be eloquent, his teaching included directing the student ballets, which were part of the school dramatic productions. Charles had spent the five years since finishing his novitiate assigned to the Jesuit school in Carpentras, the same school he'd attended as a boy. Now, after a brief farewell visit to his family—minor Provençal nobility scraping a bare living from their vineyards deep in the countryside beyond Nîmes—he was on his way to Paris to teach at Louis le Grand, the flagship of the Jesuit schools in France.

Or on his way into discreet exile, depending on how you looked at it, he thought, wriggling into a more comfortable hollow in the rock. Far from being at ease there beside the river, he was a hairsbreadth from being a fugitive. If his cousin the bishop changed his mind . . . But he wouldn't. God send that he wouldn't.

Six weeks ago on Charles's twenty-eighth birthday, his mother's most trusted servant, old Fanchot, had ridden at a gallop into the Carpentras college courtyard, reined his lathered horse to a halt in a spray of gravel, and half fallen from the saddle.

Refusing to tell anyone else what he wanted, he'd bullied his way to Charles.

"Get gone, Maître Charles." Fanchot had gasped when they were private, and pulled a wrinkled letter from his belt. "Your girl's in mortal danger."

"Not mine anymore, Fanchot," Charles had said sternly, not needing to ask what girl. But his heart had turned over. He'd given the exhausted old man into the care of the lay brothers and gone to his chamber to read the bad news in privacy, the bad news about Pernelle, his second cousin, his first love. It was very bad news, written in Mme du Luc's native Norman dialect, which all her children had learned along with Provençal.

Dear Charles,

I write for safety in the language of my infancy. Toinot has just been with me—the cobbler's son, fifteen now, can you believe it? He brought my red brocade shoes, but really came to tell me that the parish priest caught Pernelle and others of The Religion praying in her attic last night. No rosaries, no precautions to pass the whole thing off as new Catholic convert fervor. Stupid of them, but your cousin is as uncompromising as ever. Still, she is a du Luc and we cannot turn our backs. She is imprisoned in her house, not the jail, no doubt because of the child, who is not yet two years old. Père Mazet is not a cruel man. But the Intendant has sent for dragoons. Toinot's father says they cannot be here before Saturday, so if you leave the moment you get this, you can reach Nîmes by Friday night. She is expecting you and means to go to David's family in Geneva. May the Virgin forgive me, but with things at this pass, it may be just as well that her other children died. The young sister-in-law staying with her will also go. Stop first at the convent, your sister Claire has something you will need. I will pray daily to the Virgin

that you may be safe—safe in every way, Charles, if you
understand me.

Your loving mother

Charles had stared incredulously at the letter. Last October, King Louis XIV had revoked the Edict of Nantes, the only legal protection of French Protestants, Huguenots, as they were called. Now their religion was not just heresy, but treason, and the Huguenots themselves were outlaws. They were also forbidden to leave France, since the Revocation's goal was their forced conversion to Catholicism. The penalty for trying to escape— and the penalty for helping them—was usually death. That or slavery in the galleys. Yet his mother was telling him to get two women and a child across France, across the Alps, and across the Swiss border. Never mind that the journey would take weeks and he had no plausible reason for such an absence. But if he refused, the dragoons would most likely kill his cousin. His mother would certainly kill him.

Of course, all this had begun long ago, more than a hundred years ago in France's Wars of Religion. True, much had changed since then, but France was still soaked in blood. Like most French children in the century since those wars, Charles knew the terrible stories by heart: stories full of the frenzied shouts of Protestant and Catholic mobs, the clash of arms, the reek of blood, the stench of burning, the dying shrieks of the slaughtered on both sides, the laughter of the looters who cared nothing for either side. Du Lucs had fought on both sides and their clashing loyalties had left wounds in the family, but Charles's Catholic parents, like their parents and grandparents before them, did what they could for their still-beleaguered French Protestant kin.

The king had formally forbidden using the dreaded soldiers called dragoons to force conversions, but he turned a blind eye as local officials went on billeting dragoons on Huguenot families and letting them pillage, torture, and rape, until their victims either went bruised and bleeding to Mass, or died. Nîmes, where Pernelle had lived, had been a mostly Huguenot town, known far and wide as "Little Geneva." But when its citizens heard that the soldiers were coming, they had "converted" en masse, hoping to spare their children the cruelties of the "preachers in boots." The "conversions" were only for survival, though, and The Religion continued in secret.

Charles had burned the letter and dropped the ash down the latrine. Then he'd gone to the college rector's office and begged leave to go to his mother, who was taken ill, he'd said, with what her physician feared was plague. Permission to go, but only for five days—and without the normally prescribed companion, because why expose anyone else, if it was indeed plague?—was hardly out of the rector's mouth before Charles was gone.

He'd ridden hard to Avignon, found the great bridge partly washed away by the spring floods, and taken the ferry across the Rhône. There he'd turned a little north to cross the Pont du Gard, then south again toward Nîmes. At Blessed Sacrament Convent, his sister Claire, the convent's Cellarer, had given him a covered basket. "I will pray for you," she'd whispered as she kissed him. "For all of you."

When dark fell and the *couvre-feu* bell rang, he'd made his way with a shaking heart through an old breach in the town wall, past the ghostly remains of the Roman temple, into Nîmes's tangle of tiny lanes. He'd eluded the guard at Pernelle's gate, climbed her wellyard wall, and when she'd opened the door, stepped like a man dreaming into her cousinly embrace and kiss. When she pulled back, out of his arms, he'd stood wordlessly drinking in her cloud of black hair, her onyx eyes shining with intelligence, the strong clear curves of her cheekbones.

Until that night in Nîmes, he hadn't seen her for ten years, not since the night their parents had discovered their secret betrothal. He'd been eighteen and she sixteen, both green enough to think that love could overcome anything, even their warring religions. But her parents had quickly betrothed her to a young Huguenot watchmaker, David Potier, and Charles had taken his shattered heart into the army. Now he was a Jesuit, and she was a mother and a widow, David having died last Christmas. Their paths had long diverged, their love had found other and better homes.

I didn't do it because I still love her, You know that, Charles said silently, opening his eyes and looking up into the twisted branches above his head. He said it as though Love Himself were there on the rock beside him. Charles made little difference between this kind of inner talk and prayer, letting one become the other, the way speaking could fountain into singing and settle again to ordinary talk. *I mean,* he amended conscientiously, *I do love her, but not in the old way.* Love said nothing, though it seemed to Charles that the quiet took on a certain ambiguous quality. *I am not condoning heresy,* he added firmly. *I know the danger of mistaking single truths, or angers, or plain craziness for You. But I will never believe that You want cruelty.* The river music seemed to grow louder in the stillness. *And if I'm not supposed to judge what's being done to the Huguenots,* Charles said, reaching his customary closing argument in the one-sided debate, *why did You give me a conscience?* Love continued to say nothing, as was also customary. But it was a vast, still nothing, and it calmed Charles's arguing into sleep.

He woke, instantly alert, the way he'd learned to wake in the army, sat up, and started pulling on his stockings and boots, listening intently again to the countryside. Nothing seemed to

have changed, except that a pair of ducks, a bright feathered
male and his softly brown mate, floated past, riding the river.
Sitting with a boot in his hand, Charles watched them disappear
around a bend. An old Provençal poem sang through his
mind.

> Joyous in love, I make my aim forever deeper in Joy
> to be.
> The perfect Joy's the goal for me: So the most perfect
> lady I claim . . .

He pulled on the boot, wondering if Pernelle remembered
the poem and the music he'd made and set it to, for singing to
her. He hoped Geneva would prove a true home for her, prayed
that she and her child, Lucie, and her young sister-in-law, Julie,
were safely there, at their journey's end. He still shuddered when
he thought of their miraculous flight through silent, sleeping
Nîmes. In the army, he'd earned a reputation as a scout and spy,
and that night he'd been grateful for it. Once they were away
from Nîmes, the women had passed unquestioned in the nuns'
habits his sister had hidden in the basket she'd given him, and
they'd explained Lucie as a child in their charge, now going to
live with an aunt in Orange. In Carpentras, again wearing their
own clothes, Pernelle and Julie had passed as a Catholic widow
and her maid at the convent guesthouse near the Jesuit college
where Charles lodged them. And there the Virgin made them
another miracle. A wealthy elderly widow at the guesthouse, on
her way home to her lands near the Swiss border after a leisurely
pilgrimage to shrines of Our Lady, fell in love with little Lucie
and invited Pernelle to travel in her entourage. Giddy with relief
and trying to ignore the pain in his heart, Charles had watched
the lumbering coach and its six armed outriders dwindle and

disappear into the distance. He would never see Pernelle again. Which, of course, was as it should be.

Charles shook his head, as if to shake the memories out of it, and got to his feet. The trouble with knight errantry—for a Jesuit, at least—was that, just like in the old stories, it involved a lady. And, just like in the old stories, it had set him on a journey, thanks to the long and branching du Luc family grapevine. Another cousin, the newly appointed Bishop of Marseilles, had learned what Charles had done in Nîmes. The bishop had been scandalized, but he had always had a fondness for Pernelle, and family was family. Instead of turning Charles in, he'd leaned hard on several highly placed Jesuits and gotten his rash cousin sent to Paris, as far away as possible from Marseilles and his own unblemished reputation.

Back on the dust-clouded road, Charles forced his horse into a trot. His thoughts circled back to his mother's letter. *I pray that you will be safe in every way,* she'd written. Safe from Pernelle's wiles, she'd meant, safe in his vocation. But his vocation was already in danger when the letter arrived. He rode wide around a high-wheeled oxcart, calling a greeting in Provençal to the sunburned *paysan* driving it. The man, nearly as broad-backed as his ox, glowered in silence and Charles heard him spit when he was past. A Huguenot, then, though most followers of The Religion were townsmen, not countryfolk. Charles felt the man's eyes still on his back. The *paysan* represented what was troubling Charles's vocation. The Society of Jesus wielded great spiritual and temporal power, often for good, since it usually took power to fight power's wrongs. But the Society had done nothing to stop the dragonnades and its voice had been strong among those urging the king to revoke the Edict of Nantes. Jesuits had helped bring this new wave of suffering on the Huguenots and Charles was finding that very hard to live with.

But his Jesuit life, in other respects, mostly suited him. He loved his church and its ancient ritual, revered its heroic saints, believed its shining promises. He liked teaching rhetoric, loved producing the ballets that went with it. He wanted to come as close to Love as a man could, wanted to reach God's heart. Through all his Jesuit training, in the heat of every theological argument, his deepest certainty had remained unshaken: that the beginning and end of God was Love, Love beyond human grasp or measure. For him, that trumped all other arguments. For him, cruelty in God's name was blasphemously wrong. It was as simple as that. And so, for him, nothing was simple now.

He wiped his sweating face on his cassock sleeve and squinted through the road dust at the northern horizon.

Chapter 1

JULY 22, 1686

Charles leaned at the open window, gazing hungrily at Paris spread before him. Not that he could see much more than the faint outline of roofs, it being the dark of the moon and the sky thick with clouds still spitting rain after a wet day.

A discordant concert of bells began, from the Carmelites, the Visitandines, the Jacobins, the abbeys of St.-Germain-des-Pres and St.-Geneviève, from Cluny, Port Royal, and all the other religious houses on and around St. Geneviève's hill, marking the hour and calling monks and nuns to prayers. Midnight, and the twenty-second day of July about to begin. This new day would be his first day at the College of Louis le Grand, and he'd hardly prayed since the old day's morning, hunched and shivering in the saddle as his hired horse splashed through the downpour and the last long miles to Paris. Jesuits lived together, but they weren't cloistered and didn't sing the daily offices in choir. Instead, they prayed them from their breviaries wherever they found themselves. Those at the scholastic level like himself weren't required to say the offices but they were encouraged to do so, and as the bells ceased, Charles shut his eyes and murmured Matins' opening psalm. But the approaching rumble of iron-shod wheels over cobbles scattered his silent words like blown leaves and he leaned farther out of the window to see what was happening. The smell preceding the dung cart up the hill enlightened him. And surprised him, too, because waste collectors—in places that had such amenities—usually came near daybreak. But this was Paris, everything was different. Everything seemed possible.

Below him, the small light of hand lanterns swung and flickered as a night watch squad passed, and a few candles burned in windows where Latin quarter scholars—the lucky ones who could afford candles—sat late over their books. Or over wine and argument, more likely, Charles thought, a little enviously. When he'd been a student in Carpentras, enjoying wine with his academic arguing had meant risking expulsion by climbing a wall and going to a tavern. Most arguments, and tavern wine, hadn't been worth it. This quarter, however, named for the Latin that was still the language of academic life, not only teemed with colleges—secondary schools for boys—but had at its heart the University of Paris, where older students, at least, must have more freedom—even if the wine wasn't any better. Prayers forgotten, Charles stayed at the window, unwilling to let the darkling city go from his sight.

This wasn't his first time away from the south. But nothing—certainly not the little town of Carpentras, not even his two years in the army or his novitiate in bustling Avignon—had prepared Charles for Paris. The heavy rain on this last day of his journey had brought early dusk, and it was long past Compline and dark in earnest by the time he'd ridden past the embankment where the city walls and the St. Jacques gate had once stood and joined the scattering of people hurrying home on horseback and foot. Keeping a wary eye on the fast-moving, lantern-hung coaches and carts, he'd fumbled in his travel purse for coins to give the beggars following his horse in spite of the weather and the late hour. The city had closed around him and he'd welcomed her embrace.

Now, standing at the window, he felt as though the goddess Fortuna had picked him up by the scruff of the neck and set him down in ancient Athens or Rome. As though, at any moment, the revered ancients whose works he taught would gather under his window to study him, peering into his brain, his heart, his very soul, to see if he was still worthy to pass on their learning. Romans had lived where the College of Louis le Grand stood, just as they had in the countryside where he'd grown up. From the time he could walk, he'd climbed on their ruined statues and played around the broken fluted column leaning at one corner of his father's olive grove. Part of a black-and-white mosaic plowed up in a field was tiled into his mother's kitchen fireplace. The Romans' ghostly presence had fired his imagination and helped to make him a teacher of Latin rhetoric. So strong was his sudden sense of their presence here on the hill they'd called Lutetia, that he stood up straight and smoothed his cassock. But it was the reeking cart and its pair of muttering attendants that stood below him in the street, not Cicero and the rest. Laughing at his foolishness, he reached to pull the window shut, but before he closed it, he kissed his hand to sleeping Paris.

He latched the casement, glad for its glass against the night's unseasonable chill, and closed the plain wooden shutter over it. These two little rooms were the first he'd ever had with glassed windows, since most windows in the warmer south—except in churches and grand houses—were still made of oiled paper. He turned to survey his chamber. Its roughly plastered white walls held a narrow, uncurtained bed, a backed but uncushioned chair, an age-blackened wooden chest for his linen, a hanging rail for his cassock, and a small oak table against one wall. A candle stood on a three-legged stool beside the bed and a couple of nichelike plaster shelves were built into the thick walls. The low, massive ceiling beams weighed on the small space, and he fought the urge to crouch as he went to trim his guttering candle's wick. Neither the chamber nor the even smaller adjoining study had a fireplace, and he was too cold for the fumbling process of finding his flint and tinder in the dark and relighting the candle.

He shed his cassock, riding breeches, shoes, and stockings and stood in his long linen shirt eyeing the bed's thin brown blanket. His woolen cloak was still wet, so he spread his cassock on top of the blankets, stirring the candle flame and sending shadows winging out from the crucifix hanging at the foot of the bed. He knelt, said the night prayers, gave thanks for his safe journey and this new assignment, and added prayers for Pernelle and her family. Surely, in the two months since he parted from them, they had reached Geneva. Let her—let all of them—be safe, he whispered, leaning his head on his clasped hands. Then he blew out the candle and slid between the coarse and worn flax sheets.

He woke to freezing feet and the clamor of bells. Peering blearily over the covers, he saw that his feet had neither mattress under them nor blanket over them. A common occurrence and his mother's fault. His maternal forebears were the Norsemen who'd swept down from the Viking lands long ago to leave their name to Normandy, and their blondness and long bones to future generations. Charles was still gathering his sleep-sodden wits for morning prayers and rubbing one foot against the other for warmth, when a sharp rap at the door made him draw his feet out of sight like a startled turtle.

"Still sleeping, I see." The lay brother sent the door bouncing back against the wall. He set a tray on the table and flung open shutter and casement to a flood of morning light that turned his red hair to a shock of flame. Charles grimaced. The light was as accusatory as the brother's voice. It was obviously long past five o'clock, the normal rising time in a Jesuit college.

"*Bon jour, mon frère,*" Charles said, trying to reclaim some dignity.

The lay brother, lean and wiry under the heavy canvas apron over his shorter version of the Jesuit cassock, looked to be still in his teens, a good ten years younger than Charles.

"It's half after six," the brother said. "Those bells were for first classes. But I was told to let you sleep. Since you were so late getting here." He stared down his long thin nose at Charles, who couldn't tell whether the boy disapproved of all lateness, or was simply envious of his chance to stay in bed.

"I am Maître Charles du Luc, *mon frère.* May I know your name?"

"I am Frère Denis Fabre." His disapproving gaze shifted to Charles's feet, showing again beyond the end of the bed. "Your bed is too short," he said, as though Charles had made away with part of it during the night. He turned to the table and began taking things off the tray. "The assistant rector, Père Montville, wants to see you," he said over his clattering. "Immediately."

Charles shot out of bed and hurriedly straightened its covers. "*Mon Dieu,* why didn't you say so sooner?"

"You were asleep sooner. Here's shaving water. And something to break your fast. The bread is stale. And the water won't be hot now."

"Good, fine, thank you." Charles was searching in his bag for his razor. "Where do I go when I'm ready?"

"I'll have to show you, won't I?" Frère Fabre drifted out of the room, sighing faintly.

Charles rolled his eyes, laughing in spite of himself, and dug his razor out of his bag. He shaved himself badly in the cold water and got a crick in his neck peering at his greenish reflection in the little round mirror he'd brought. He nearly choked himself trying to get quickly through the dry bread and cheese. But in spite of his hurry, he uncorked his little pot of wine vinegar, salt, alum, and honey and gave his teeth a sketchy cleaning with the end of the towel. Not something most people would have done, but another thing he had to thank his mother for. He cleaned his teeth most days, and he even washed with water fairly often, instead of only changing his linen or wiping himself down with a dry towel. He took his brother Jesuits' warnings about the likely consequences of his eccentric habits in good part and went his way, usually free of lice and, so far, with all his teeth.

He recorked the pot and pulled on his cassock. With a final gulp of heavily watered wine to dull the sting of his tooth cleaner, Charles clapped a new skullcap on his head for extra warmth and hurried into the passage. The lay brother, slumped against the wall and whistling tunelessly under his breath, broke off abruptly and was running a critical eye over him, when the door across from Charles's opened and a thick-bodied Jesuit with long, curling black hair emerged. Ignoring both Fabre and Charles, he swept toward the stairs with his Roman nose in the air.

"Your cap is crooked, maître," Fabre said to Charles laconically.

Gravely, Charles straightened it. "Better?"

Fabre nodded curt approval and loped down the stairs. After two narrow flights, the bare wooden stairs widened and became pale stone. A grand, stone balustraded curve decanted the two of them into an anteroom between the college's tall double front doors and the grand salon, where the rector, Père Le Picart, and the senior rhetoric master, Père Jouvancy, had briefly greeted Charles the night before. Fabre led Charles across the salon to another anteroom and stopped at a closed door. Before he could knock, the door opened and a Jesuit backed slowly through it.

"But, *mon père*," he was saying earnestly, "I beg you, you cannot imagine what this glorious painting would add—"

"I can imagine what our superior, our good Paris Provincial—not to mention Rome—would say about the cost," someone beyond the door said tartly. "No, and again no. I am sorry."

Pulling the door shut harder than was strictly necessary, the disappointed Jesuit muttered a greeting to Charles and clumped dispiritedly away. Fabre tapped on the door and it flew open.

"No, I tell you! Oh. Sorry, not you." The speaker's middle-aged pudding face relaxed into a beaming smile and he bowed slightly. "I am Père Montville, assistant rector here. You must be Maître du Luc. Come in, come in," he said, as Charles bowed in return. "So long as you don't want me to buy paintings. Thank you for delivering him, Frère Fabre." He ushered Charles into his tiny office. "Every Jesuit wants something for his pet enthusiasm," he sighed. "More paintings for the chapel, more telescopes, maps, books, I don't know how the bursar keeps his sanity. And when he says no, they come to me!" He waved Charles to the only other chair in the room. "And you, I suppose, will want more ballet costumes."

"But yes, *mon père*," Charles said, ingenuously wide-eyed. "And all cloth of gold, please."

"Don't even think it." Montville laughed. "Well, Maître du Luc, you are welcome to Louis le Grand! This morning we will see to the details of your life with us and get you settled in. A Jesuit college is, of course, a Jesuit college, but all have their differences, too. First, though, I must write you into my ledger of our scholastics." He thumped the enormous leather-bound book lying on his desk. "Then you will see our rector, Père Le Picart. I know you met him last night with Père Jouvancy, but he wishes to talk with you further. I think you will find that we are fortunate in our rector—though his ability to see straight into our souls and out the other side can be a touch disconcerting."

Montville laughed, but his description of the rector's perspicacity made Charles's stomach tighten, in light of his recent activities.

"After that," Montville went on, "you must go to the clothing master. Your cassock, if I may say so, is showing the effects of your journey. Do you need anything else?"

"Perhaps another shirt, *mon père,* if he has one to spare. Other than that, I think I am well supplied."

"Good. When the clothing master has finished with you, he will take you to the prefect of studies, who will work out your teaching schedule. And if, after all that, you are still standing, I will give you a tour of the school, which will end at the refectory and dinner. After dinner, you will go to Père Jouvancy." He shook his head, laughing. "Père Jouvancy is excused from dinner the last two weeks before a show, because no matter how often anyone reprimands him, he simply forgets to come to eat." Montville eyed Charles speculatively. "They have been rehearsing the tragedy and ballet since late May, you know. It's quite unusual to get a new rhetoric assistant this far into summer show preparations." He raised an inquisitive eyebrow, but Charles refused the bait. "Well, well, far be it from us to question the will of our superiors, especially when it brings us such a good gift. So. Your father's name?" He picked up a quill and opened the ledger.

Chapter 2

The warning bell was ringing for dinner and Charles's head was spinning as Montville led him back to the main courtyard after the promised tour. It had already been spinning when the tour started. Père Le Picart, a lean man in his forties with eyes as gray as the North Sea, had been less formidable than Montville had painted him, smiling gently and nodding approval as Charles answered questions about his studies and his teaching experience. But there had been unspoken questions in his cool gray eyes, and Charles had gone to his next appointment with some sense of escape. The clothing master Frère Dupont had scuttled around his dark room, searching through the piles of black cassocks as he measured Charles with his eye and shook his head at how much of him there was to clothe. When a cassock with enough hem to let down had been found, and a new linen shirt to go under it, Dupont had dismissed him to the prefect of studies, assuring him that the new garments would be taken to his chamber. Père Joly, the prefect of studies, eagle-beaked and ascetic-looking, had told Charles in the fewest possible words that he would be assisting in a morning grammar class and spending his afternoons working with Père Jouvancy to ready the ballet and tragedy. Joly had added austerely that such a light schedule was only for now, and that after the performance, Charles could expect more classes added to his day.

Then Montville had appeared at Joly's door and swept Charles away to tour the college. They'd started at the opulent chapel on the south side of the Cour d'honneur, as the main court was called, and from there Montville had chivied him over the entire property, explaining who taught what to whom and where, and where they all lived, ate, and studied. A secondary school, like all the Jesuit colleges, Louis le Grand's students ranged from about ten to twenty years old. Its syllabus of studies followed the plan laid down by St. Ignatius and was based on Latin and Greek writers of the ancient world. The general shape of the Paris college's life would be familiar to any Jesuit, but as Montville had said, each college also had its uniqueness. Louis le Grand was known as the nursery of France's great men. The college's day students outnumbered its *pensionnaires*, or boarding students, by nearly four to one. But the *pensionnaires*, the five hundred or so boys from noble and wealthy upper-bourgeois families, were its heart. It was these boys who acted and danced in the elaborate schedule of plays and ballets for a large and influential audience.

"An astronomy class?" Charles had said, peering through a window at perhaps a hundred half-grown, black-gowned boys crowded cheek by jowl on benches, windowsills and floor, listening to a small bespectacled Jesuit turning a large, wood-mounted globe of the heavens as he lectured. "Are all the classes so large?"

"No, not at all, those are day boys." Montville had shrugged. "We try not to turn any qualified boy away, whether or not he can pay. We also have a handful of scholarship boys, who live together in a *dortoir* and are counted with the *pensionnaires*. Most of the day students are Parisians. They sleep and eat at home, or in cheap student lodgings. If we hadn't been able to expand our property as much as we have, we'd have to sit them on bales of hay in the street and teach them there, like the university did a few hundred years ago. Fortunately, we've bought, stolen, won—depending on who tells the tale—a number of neighboring college properties, most of them defunct or derelict. Mans, Marmoutier, most of les Cholets. But it's taken decades, and without our Père La Chaise—the king's confessor—speaking for us at court, we'd still be arguing over the loot, so to speak. Some of it, I may say, cost us a good deal to repair. Ceilings coming down, rooms you couldn't swing a cat in, rats fighting the fleas for floor space. But on the whole good bargains, and our classes are spread over all of them. The University of Paris, our less than good neighbor across the rue St. Jacques, is sick with envying our property. And our popularity. But what do they expect? The lackwits still teach as though it were eleven hundred-something and poor Peter Abelard were on the faculty!"

The acquisitions had turned Louis le Grand into a minotaur's maze of largely old and ill-matched buildings, most built of weather-blackened stone, a few half-timbered in the old fashion, some five stories high, some only two. Blue slate roofs pitched at clashing angles sprouted a mushroom growth of chimneys and dormer windows, an exuberant roofline further punctuated with towers as ill assorted as the buildings. The largest tower, on the south side of the Cour d'honneur, had bells and its own windows. A smaller tower at the southeast corner had a bell and a clock, and a windowed hexagonal tower on the north side looked to Charles like it might be an observatory. Though what anyone hoped to see through the clouds of this northern sky, he couldn't imagine.

The mélange of buildings was honeycombed with courtyards. The vast Cour d'honneur, which opened from the street passage leading from the postern door and the rue St. Jacques, was graveled, with a few old trees around its edges shading a half dozen stone benches. The other courts were smaller, some invitingly green with turf and big plane trees, like the fathers' garden near the rue de Rheims, enclosed now on two sides by the sparkling new stone of the main college library. Montville and Charles had passed a chattering group of Englishmen leaving the garden, and Montville had explained that visitors came from all over to marvel at Louis le Grand's enormous collection of books. Then he'd walked Charles through the quiet, shady court where the *pensionnaires* lived with their tutors in private rooms and small *dortoirs*, then under a classical archway and back into the Cour d'honneur.

Now, as they crunched across the grayish gravel, Montville pointed to the range of windows reaching nearly to the ground floor on the main court's east side.

"Your senior rhetoric classroom, *maître*."

"How many are in the class?"

"Only thirty or so. We try to keep the boarders' classes smaller. And you wouldn't want a hundred boys in your ballet! The lay brothers and workmen from the Opera will build your stage out from the classroom windows. Your performers change costumes in the classroom and the windows let them come and go from the stage. We cover the whole courtyard with a canvas awning; do they do that at Carpentras? I suppose the sun is the problem there, but here it's rain. If it rains enough, though, the canvas collects puddles and sags and—well, you can imagine what happens then! You might start praying now for the miracle of a dry performance day!" Montville cocked an eye at the clouds. "Early summer was stifling," he said, as a fine rain began to spatter on their hats. "Though you'd never think it now!"

"I hope this cold and wet won't hurt the harvest," Charles said. "At home, it promised well, after too many years of drought."

"Too much drought, too much rain, always too much hunger. And too little charity," Montville said soberly.

"Much too little charity," Charles agreed. And not least because the king sees only his passion for a wholly Catholic France instead of his people's needs, he thought, but didn't say. Color and movement caught his eye and he exclaimed with pleasure at a sudden fountain of colored balls rising and falling across the courtyard.

"Oh, dear," Montville murmured, as they stopped to watch. "Poor Frère Moulin refuses to believe that we are not all panting to see his juggling. The courtyard proctor is going to enjoy this."

Charles saw that Frère Fabre, his dour nursemaid of the morning, was standing beside the juggling lay brother, gazing spellbound at the spinning balls. All over the court, heads were turning. An older student on his way to dinner dropped surreptitiously out of his classmates' double line to watch. The juggler said something to him, but as the boy moved closer, another boy ran back from the line and grabbed his sleeve. The first boy shook him off angrily. The newcomer shrugged and hurried toward the refectory, and the first boy began talking to the juggler. Fabre abruptly turned his attention from the juggling to the talk, and what looked like an argument quickly blossomed between him and the student. Charles marveled at the ease with which the juggler, looking in surprise from the student to Fabre, kept the balls rising and falling without mishap. But the bright moment the spinning balls had made in the gray morning ended as the courtyard proctor and another Jesuit bustled toward the little group. The proctor bore down on the juggler, who caught the balls and stowed them so deftly in his apron that they might never have existed. The other Jesuit upbraided the student. Fabre faded unobtrusively toward the refectory.

"Come, Maître du Luc, even if you are not hungry, I am!"

Montville steered Charles toward the court's northeast corner, where lines of boys streamed through the refectory's wide door. Its windows wore metal grids against balls and other missiles of play, Charles noticed, as he looked up at the tower clock.

"Eleven? You eat later here. The Carpentras college eats at 10:30."

"In Paris, the hours for everything get later all the time—the influence of Versailles, I always think. But our king does not have to teach boys at half past six in the morning."

Inside the building, they passed a broad staircase and turned along a right-hand passage.

"We eat with the older boys," Montville said. "The younger boarders' refectory is down the other way."

They went into an enormous room with soaring rafters, full of boys standing around closely crowded long tables covered with linen cloths. Under the eyes of their tutors and the college proctors, the boys kept their noise to a reasonably civilized level, but the room still hummed like a giant beehive.

Montville led Charles up onto the hall's dais, where they bowed to Père Le Picart, who stood waiting at the end of the dais table until all its places were filled. Charles and Montville made their way behind the professors standing silently at their places, along a wall painted in faded, old-fashioned red-and-blue checkerboards and stripes. Montville stopped at his own chair and gestured Charles to the empty place at the table's end. The rector moved to his place at the long table's center, facing the rest of the hall. Miraculously, the noise drained away like water out of a stone sink. Le Picart said a Latin grace, all crossed themselves, and chairs and benches scraped over the floor's worn, honey-colored stone.

Lay brothers set green and yellow tin-glazed basins—faience, they were called in the south—along the center of the table. Charles winced as Frère Fabre plunked a basin down beside the rector and sent a wave of steaming sauce onto the tablecloth. Charles's neighbor offered him a crusty loaf, and Charles realized that he'd seen him twice before, once when he'd come out of the rooms across from Charles's early that morning, and just now with the proctor in the courtyard, putting an end to the juggling and berating the student who'd stopped to watch.

"You are our new rhetoric man, are you not?" The Jesuit, whose thick black curls might almost have been a wig, drew a serving basin close and used the spoon ready in the dish to help himself to chicken stew fragrant with the smell of ginger.

Charles made his nod half a bow. "I am Maître Charles Matthieu Beuvron du Luc, *mon père*. And very glad to be here."

"As you should be," the man said, without smiling or introducing himself. His eyes raked Charles. "A surprising assignment for a simple scholastic. And from the south. As your accent sadly proclaims."

Charles let the rudeness about his origins and accent pass. Louis le Grand was without doubt the most coveted teaching assignment in the five French Jesuit provinces. He certainly wouldn't be here if Bishop du Luc hadn't leaned hard on the head of the Paris Province. Which, of course, was how things usually worked. Someone knew someone—and too often something—which the someone would much rather not have known, and there you were. On the other hand, of course, it might well be of no great consequence to a busy Jesuit Provincial where a lowly scholastic made himself useful.

"Being here is a great honor," Charles said mildly, pouring his small plain glass half full of wine and adding water.

"The highest honor for someone like you. I see you eat in the Italian fashion," the man said, as Charles picked up the fork lying beside a matching spoon. "Louis's style is good enough for me."

Charles's neighbor dipped his thick fingers into his bowl and carried a mound of chicken and vegetables to his mouth. A drop splashed onto his cassock, and Charles turned his head away to hide his smile at the old-fashioned affectation. The king, so it was said, still forbade forks at his table—though only at court—but even he probably ate stew with his spoon. And the Paris college, Charles knew, had used forks for a hundred years, ever since a Jesuit inspector from Rome had been appalled at the state of the college tablecloths after so many fingers were wiped on them and recommended the Italian innovation. Although from what Charles could see of the cloths on the students' tables, forks hadn't made all that much difference.

"This is good," Charles said. "Rosewater in it as well as ginger, isn't there?"

"Rosewater, yes. Old-style cooking, usually. No luxury here. But what there is, is generally good enough." The man gave him a sharp sideways glance. "Du Luc, your name is?"

Charles nodded, sighing inwardly. One of his hopes when he joined the Society had been that the noisy, glittering show of nobility would be less important. He had very quickly learned that influence was influence, and that Jesuits were as shameless as everyone else about using it.

"The Comtes de Vintimille du Luc?" his neighbor said. "Originally from Nice?"

"We are descended from them, yes."

The man's eyes narrowed and he studied Charles. "You are related, then, to the newly appointed Bishop of Marseilles. Young for a bishop. Very sound against the Jansenists, though."

The mention of his cousin made Charles's breath catch in his throat. He forced a smile and nodded. He was all too familiar with Bishop du Luc's ire toward the Catholic followers of the theologian Cornelius Jansen, whose austere piety sometimes made them seem more like Huguenots than Catholics. But the less said about Bishop du Luc, the less chance anyone would discover what had really gotten Charles to Paris.

"What do you teach, *mon père?*" he asked his still anonymous neighbor politely.

"I am in charge of the student library. We have an extraordinarily fine collection here, nearly thirty thousand volumes in our new main library. I also have the honor to act as confessor to many at court." He managed to look simultaneously down his nose and sideways at Charles. "I am Père Sebastian Victoire Louis Anne of the House of Guise."

The man rolled the syllables of his name off his tongue as though proclaiming an addition to Holy Writ. Charles choked on a mouthful of bread. Dear God, the House of Guise. Instigators of the Wars of Religion, leaders of the Huguenot-hunting Catholic League. Nearly kings of France, with the help of the League's Guise-financed army. The irony of getting away with rescuing Pernelle, only to become the colleague and tablemate of a Guise, made Charles uncertain whether to weep or toast the *bon Dieu's* sense of humor. Still coughing, Charles picked up his wineglass. Guise turned his broad back and began talking to his other neighbor.

Charles gulped wine, catching his breath, and gazed up at

the faded stars between the ceiling's wide black beams. No luxury here, Guise had said. The little yellow stars, the Virgin's symbols, did indeed need repainting. Even dull and chipped and faded, though, they comforted him. Mary's stars made him think of the glittering sky of his childhood in the dry nights of the south. Until he got too big to curl up in the stone window-seat, he'd moved his bedding there most clear nights and fallen asleep watching the sky through the open shutter, imagining that Mary had spread her star-strewn cloak over the sleeping world to keep it safe. He emptied his glass, reached for a pitcher, and drew back his hand. There was no point in trying to drown the Guises of the world in watered wine. And even if there were, he couldn't go fuddled to his first day of rehearsal.

He turned his attention to eating and watching the sea of students in front of him. In spite of the proctors' frowns, the boys gestured energetically as they talked. The black sleeves of their scholar's gowns fell back, lighting the dim room with flashes of white linen and the occasional sheen of richly colored silk. Most of the boys were European, but there were two who had to be the Chinese students he'd been told about, and several others with an exotic slant to eyes or cheekbones. As his eye wandered over the faces, he saw the handsome black-haired youth who had stopped to watch the lay brother's juggling. Charles jumped as Guise, still turned away from him, slapped the table.

". . . they serve God and their king. Souls are saved. No faithful servant of the Church—or the Society of Jesus—can deplore that."

Charles reached for a strawberry tart from the platter that had appeared on the table, and craned his neck to see who Guise was lecturing. Several places away, a hawk-nosed old man shook his head, his wispy white hair waving like feathers around his skullcap. Charles caught the word *heretic* and then the old man sat back in his chair, disappearing from view.

"Old woman," Guise said savagely under his breath.

Wanting more than anything not to talk about heretics, Charles stuffed the whole tart into his mouth, turned his head away from Guise, and pretended to be absorbed in the checker-board pattern that continued around the side wall.

"And you?" Guise demanded at his back. "Do you agree with me?"

"About what?" Charles said, around the mouthful of pastry and without turning.

"Heretics."

Hoping to give deliberate offense so that Guise would leave him alone, Charles chewed the rest of his tart and swallowed before he turned. Guise was still waiting, his nostrils pinched with anger.

"Saving souls is part of what God requires of us," Charles said evenly.

"And are you squeamish about the method, like old Dainville?"

An updraft of anger seared Charles's chest and heated his face. Squeamish? Method? Squeamish about the king's dragoons tying his uncle Jean Marc du Luc's new young wife to a bedpost and refusing to release her until she recanted her faith? While her frail newborn screamed for food? Annette du Luc had pleaded through the night to be allowed to feed the sick child. Finally, her little boy's misery was too much and before the sun rose, she agreed to become Catholic. But the baby died, worn out with sickness, terror, hunger, and wailing. Annette died, too, because she wrested a knife from a half-drunk dragoon and at-tacked the soldier who had kept her from her child. Jean Marc had been sent to the galleys. That had been more than a year ago, and no one knew whether he still lived, or even whether to hope he did, considering what everyone knew about the living death of galley slaves. Charles forced words through his anger.

"Our Savior is a God of love, Père Guise."

Guise's sculptured lip curled. "Is it loving to let heretic souls be damned?"

"Is it loving to torture them into false conversion?" Charles shot back. "Is it loving to kill children?"

Something moved behind Guise's eyes, and he gazed at Charles with new interest. "The south," he said lazily, "Provence, Languedoc, the filthy strongholds of heresy." He leaned toward Charles like a cold shadow. "Have you grown so loving to your neighbors—and your kin, perhaps—that heresy no longer troubles you? Holy Scripture commands us to 'compel them to come in.'"

"If you read further in that same fourteenth chapter of St. Luke's Gospel, you will find that those who refuse are not hunted down and tortured until they accept the invitation. More to the point, can we ever be too loving to our neighbors? Whom Holy Scripture commands us to love as ourselves?"

"And whose souls we are required to save. *Un roi, une loi, une foi*, Maître du Luc. Or has your tender heart carried you as far as treason?"

An insane desire to plunge his little table knife into Guise's well-padded ribs washed over Charles. He folded his hands tightly in his lap and studied his white knuckles.

"Consider our Jesuit rule of education," he said softly. "Our Ratio. About which we cannot possibly disagree. It directs us to make learning pleasurable. Should we not, even more, make the learning and acceptance of God's true religion pleasurable?"

Guise sat back, watching him as a cat watches a wounded

bird. "A follower of Epicurus, are you? The highest good is pleasure? How interesting."

"Epicurus held that pleasure comes from the practice of virtue. And few faithful theologians would dispute that our savior preached love and virtue."

"So love and pleasure are one?"

"Hah, Père Guise, you old dog, you should know," Montville said loudly from Guise's other side. "Corrupting our new professor already?" He leaned around Guise, smiling broadly, his eyes warning Charles to smile with him. "I hope your dinner was to your satisfaction, *maître*?"

"Very much so," Charles said warmly, profoundly grateful for the boisterous interruption.

"Good, you'll need sustenance to get through your first afternoon of rehearsals."

"Ballet!" Guise spat on the floor, narrowly missing Charles's arm. "Womanish nonsense. A waste of time and money."

"I'll be sure and tell King Louis you said that, next time I'm at court." Montville laughed, slapping Guise on the back.

"Our official plan of studies says nothing about ballet!" Guise replied stiffly. "'*Tragoediarum et comoediarum, quas non nisi latinas ac rarissimas esse oportet, argumentum sacrum sit ac pium.*' That is what it says!"

"Yes, yes." Montville laughed. "'Tragedies and comedies should be rare,' we all know what it says."

"It says *extremely* rare," Guise snapped. "And *pious.*"

"And we send reports to Rome every year and mostly they only object to the expense," Montville said, the light of battle in his eye. "For plays and ballets alike. How do you explain that?"

"The Society of Jesus is deeply in need of reform."

Montville's infectious laughter pealed out again. "You become more like our good Jansenists every day!" He leaned closer to Guise. "Is it your old sins troubling you, *mon père?*"

Charles's lips twitched as Guise grew white around the nostrils. But before Guise could answer, the rector rose for the final grace and everyone rose with him.

Chapter 3

The final grace's "amen" echoed from the walls and the professors on the dais filed silently into the passage, to be followed by the boys, table by table. Père Montville hurried Charles outside, past the lay brothers putting a dozen wooden chests down near the doors and setting their lids open to reveal game boards, chessmen, darts, toys, and pastimes for the hour of quiet recreation that followed dinner.

"Never mind Père Guise," Montville said, making for the main building's rear door. "He is a good librarian. But he suffers from the handicap of being a Guise. My advice is to do as I do, try hard to stay out of his way. Now. You will spend this hour with Père Jouvancy." He flashed Charles a sideways grin. "Though whether you will find it an hour of quiet recreation, I beg leave to doubt."

Nerving himself to face his new boss, Charles held the heavy door open for Montville and followed him into the gray day's indoor gloom. Père Joseph Jouvancy, senior rhetoric master, was as famous for his brilliant teaching and his rapport with students as for the elegant Latin tragedies he wrote. Drama in schools run by religious orders was a centuries-old tradition, but dance with it was the Jesuits' new contribution. Though King

Louis no longer danced himself, the French court had been in love with ballet for a hundred years, ever since Queen Catherine de Medici brought it to France from Italy. For persons of any social standing, dancing well was an indispensable part of claiming one's rightful place in the world. Charles, like most people, had heard the cautionary—and true—tale of the young noble who so disgraced himself by dancing badly at court that he was sent abroad by his father until the resulting scandal died down. The Jesuit college ballets trained dancers for the ballets still staged occasionally at court, and for the frequent and lavish productions at great country chateaus. Unlike those ballets, the Jesuit productions had more or less edifying themes, no female dancers and no romantic plots, yet they still attracted glittering audiences and wealthy patrons for the college.

Charles stumbled nervously as he and Montville started up a staircase toward a half-open door. Last night, as Jouvancy and Le Picart had kept him company while he ate a late supper, Jouvancy had been cordial and warm, telling hilarious stories of crises in rehearsals and performances over the years. But Charles had quickly seen that the little man was impatient and exacting, with the tireless energy of a squirrel. Now, as he reached the top of the stairs, a murmuring stream of exasperation, punctuated by thumps and the crackle of paper, poured from the half-open door to meet him. Montville knocked lightly, the murmuring broke off, and a high tenor voice called, "Come, come!"

Putting his head around the door, Montville said, "Here he is, *mon père*," clapped Charles on the shoulder and clattered away down the stairs.

Charles went in and found Jouvancy bent over a desk, scrabbling through an ill-assorted drift of books, loose sheets of paper, quills, a long curly dark wig, a cone-shaped sugar loaf wrapped in blue paper on a pewter plate, glass bottles of red and black ink, a sugar sifter, and a thick roll of wide blue ribbon uncoiling itself over the desk's edge. Even in the gray light from the tall, many-paned window, Charles could see the cloud of dust rising from his efforts.

"Yes, yes, good morning to you, too," the handsome little priest gabbled without looking up and before Charles had said anything. "I am sorry to trouble you with this nonsense, but I am sure that we are of one mind."

The sugar sifter slid off the desk and Charles caught it in midair, wondering what nonsense he was being troubled with.

"Here it is. Sit, sit. You are a sensible young man, I could see that last night, look at what he wants—it is impossible, it is an offense, just look!"

The rhetoric master thrust a sheaf of sketches at Charles and went back to his frenzied search. Charles put the sugar sifter back on the desk, removed a papier-mâché Roman soldier's helmet from a straight-backed chair, and sat down.

"Ah, here it is!" Jouvancy disappeared below the desk and straightened, holding a blond wig. "Well?" He subsided into his chair, glaring at the sketches in Charles's hand. *"Well?"*

"These are beautiful," Charles said sincerely, riffling through the big, flopping pages filled with drawings of ballet characters.

Jouvancy's fine-boned face darkened ominously.

"Though, of course . . ." Charles fanned the sketches like limp cards and frowned at them, praying that the tirade obviously about to burst forth would tell him what he was frowning at.

"Look—there!" Jouvancy bounced up again and leaned across the desk, flattening the wigs as he stabbed a finger at the drawing of a dancer wearing a clock on his head. "A messenger delivered these sketches to me at dawn. Barely dawn, I wasn't even dressed. A clock! I ask you, a monstrous black and gold clock! Are my boys tables? How is anyone to dance wearing that? And apparently it chimes—he expects poor Time to tilt his head as he dances and make the cursed thing chime!"

The harried producer fell back into his chair, shoulders around his ears, hands flung up in a gesture of utter desperation.

"Um—Monsieur Beauchamps sent these?" Charles hazarded.

Jouvancy's nostrils pinched. "Who else?"

Every Jesuit college that staged ballets hired a layman as dancing master and the great Pierre Beauchamps was Louis le Grand's. Beauchamps was to the world of dance what the pope was to Holy Church and Charles could hardly believe his luck in getting to work with him. The greatest dancing master in France, probably in all of Europe, Beauchamps had danced with the king in court ballets and had gone from strength to strength, first as Louis's dancing master, then as director of the King's Twenty-Four Violins, director of the Royal Academy of Dancing, and now dancing master for the Royal Academy of Opera. But Charles did see what the problem was. All dancers, amateur and professional, were used to unwieldy headdresses as part of their costumes. In his student days at Carpentras, Charles had danced the role of Spring with a small cage full of live birds on his head. That had been bad enough, but this clock was three feet tall. Though it would be anchored to a leather cap and tied on, it would be the rare student who could keep the thing from tipping over while making it chime in time to his steps and the music.

Jouvancy shifted in his chair, tapping a finger on the desk and scowling as though Charles were a promising pupil failing to live up to his promise.

"Mon père," Charles said quickly, "Maître Beauchamps some-times brings his Opera professionals in to dance for you, does he not? Perhaps—one of them could wear the clock?"

"I am sorry to see that you miss the point, Maître du Luc. Pierre Beauchamps is trying to alter my ballet livret. Mine! *Again.* Do I change the steps he sets the dancers? No, I do not. In my livret, there *is* no Time character. Instead, there is a beautiful minuet for the four seasons, wearing simple garlands—flowers, fruit, leaves, bare twigs—to show time's passage."

Charles smiled politely. He and everyone else had seen those same dancing seasons a hundred times. Aside from the technical problems, his artistic sympathies were with Beauchamps.

"You say Maître Beauchamps has done this before? Tried to change your livret, I mean?"

Charles knew perfectly well that this duel of wills between professor-librettist and hired dancing master was a fixture of every ballet production in every college, even without formi-dable personalities like Jouvancy and Beauchamps involved. But the more he knew about the lay of the land here, the better.

Jouvancy put a trembling hand to his forehead. "He does it every ballet," he said in a resonant whisper, and became be-fore Charles's eyes every persecuted, aging monarch in the his-tory of drama. "It is why I am as you see me, a man old before my time."

Charles bit his tongue to keep from laughing, thinking that Jouvancy, who was probably in his middle forties, could have made a fine career in Molière's company. With the sense of delivering his next line, Charles said what he suspected the rhet-oric master was waiting to hear.

"With your permission, *mon père* . . ." Wickedly, he hesitated, and Jouvancy shot him an impatient look. "Perhaps—if it would be of use—*I* could convey your judgment to M. Beauchamps and free you for other things?" Charles finished brightly.

Jouvancy let his hand fall from his face. His large gray eyes were luminous with a finely judged opening of hope.

"You?"

"Yes, *mon père*," Charles said gravely. "I would be honored to be of service." And just stopped himself from adding, "Your Majesty."

"Very well." Jouvancy's eyes gleamed with satisfaction. "It is all one to me," he added mendaciously. "Speak to him—no, inform him—this afternoon. I cannot be bothered, the whole thing is beneath me. The man must be taught that he cannot dictate in this manner to a learned theoretician. Telling him so will be good practice for you." Jouvancy grinned suddenly and came offstage. "And whether it will or not, none of these boys would be upright at the end of a pirouette with that thing on his head. But don't tell him that."

"But surely he knows?"

"Hmph. He thinks he has only to show them, shake his stick at them, yell at them, and they become gods of the dance. No matter if he is demanding that they dance on their hands in a sack. No theory, that's the trouble with Beauchamps. But he is just a practitioner, so what can one expect? A great one, I grant you that—but a practitioner all the same. The man cares *nothing* for theory."

Charles kept his mouth shut. He was all too familiar with the age-old theoretician vs. practitioner argument, but calling Beauchamps just a practitioner was like calling the pope just a priest.

"A chiming clock!" Jouvancy snorted. "The ancients would never think of anything so absurd!"

"Well, they didn't have clocks," Charles said reasonably.

"True. But never forget, the arts are for imitating nature, Maître du Luc. 'The monkeys of nature,' as our dear Père Menestrier says so well in his learned treatise on ballets. Are there clocks in nature? No, there are not clocks in nature."

"But there *is* time," Charles murmured, admiring a sketch for the Horizon's shimmering costume, half black, half white.

Jouvancy chuckled. "All right, Maître Charles du Luc. I see we will get on together. And whether we do or not, we have a ballet to present in just two more weeks. Not to mention the tragedy." He cocked his head, his eyes bright with curiosity. "Though I am pleased to have you here, I have been wondering—so late in our rehearsals, a bare two weeks before a show, is a peculiar time to acquire an assistant. Not that I am ungrateful, of course." He waited hopefully.

Smiling blandly, Charles shrugged and gave the answer he'd prepared. "My superiors decided I had been at Carpentras long enough. In addition to teaching at the school, I had also been a student there, you know."

"I see. Well, your arrival comes just as I am realizing that this production is hopeless."

"Hopeless? Do they really dance so badly?"

"No, no, thanks to Beauchamps, they dance very well, most of them. But they do not care *why* they dance. They do not care that the dance is meant to show every movement of the emotions and the eloquence of the soul shining through the body. Without that, it is nothing. Yet these wretched boys only want to show the shapely leg, jump higher than their *confrères*, and wear the richest costume. Though surely you know all that. Boys are boys, even at little Carpentras."

"True," Charles laughed. "But as long as they didn't trip over their feet and the ballet amused parents and patrons, the rector

there was satisfied." Though Charles hadn't been. Only rarely
had he come across a boy who had it in him to make what he
danced burn with beauty. "After all, the ballets are to adorn the
yearly prize-giving and provide some enjoyment for the boys
near the end of the school year, are they not, *mon père?*"

"Of course, but you are at Louis le Grand now. The king
himself is our patron, my dear Maître du Luc, which means that
he helps pay for the ballet. As well as the year's academic prizes.
Do you have any idea what those suitably bound tomes we give
as prizes cost? So the ballet must be superb, because we cannot
afford to lose the king's money! Anything less would be an in-
sult, since King Louis was such a very gifted dancer himself.
And I do not say that only because he is the king. Look."

He pointed to the wall behind Charles. Charles turned in his
chair and saw a gilt-framed painting of a half-grown boy in a
golden tonneau—a stiff, tight-waisted coat standing out over
his breeches like a very short skirt. The coat's full sleeves were
tied with yellow ribbons at elbow and wrist, and the shoes,
heeled and square-toed, sported rayed golden suns. The boy's
face was still softly rounded and his silky light brown hair curled
on his shoulders. He wore a crown with golden rays, and above
it a tall sheaf of waving white plumes.

"That is the king," Jouvancy said reverently. "Only fourteen,
dancing as France's Rising Sun in Cardinal Mazarin's *Ballet of
Night.* I was there and I tell you, it was magnificent. My father
wanted me to see the king reclaim his kingdom after the hor-
rors of the nobles' revolt—the Fronde, that was, before your
time. Anyway, the room—in the Petit-Bourbon palace—was
crowded beyond belief, and my father and I, being of little
importance, were shoved away in a corner. It was February, but
the room was stifling from the crowd, and I soon fell asleep on
the floor—I was just ten. The ballet really did last all night,

twelve hours. My father shook me awake at daybreak and lifted me up onto his shoulders in time to see our young Rising Sun come in at the east windows. Ah——" Something of the ten-year-old's wonder on that long-past morning glowed on Jouvancy's face. "It seemed to me that the sun himself had truly danced down into our midst. He did his sarabande down the room, with all the Graces dancing in his train. All around me courtiers were weeping and kneeling. Such a fine dancer he was, a beautiful dancer." Jouvancy sighed. Then he laughed and returned to the present. "Though you'd never think it to look at him now," he said, glancing down somewhat complacently at his own trim figure, "because he has become a very fine eater. Not fat, really. Just—ah—solid."

In spite of his current feelings about Louis XIV, Charles was moved by this glimpse of the young monarch reclaiming his kingdom. But he still didn't much want to talk about the king.

"What is this year's ballet called, *mon père?*"

"*Les Travaux d'Hercules*. Hercules represents Louis, of course."

Of course. So much for not talking about the king. And these labors of Hercules-Louis would inevitably include revoking the Edict of Nantes and outlawing the Huguenots, because college ballet, like court ballet, referred to real people and events. The people and events were always veiled under layers of allegory and symbol, but recognizable to the educated audience that easily read the code of Greek and Roman heroes and their myths.

"Is the ballet your creation, Père Jouvancy?"

"The livret, yes." The priest picked up the blond wig from his desk and draped it on his fist. It looked like it had caught mange from someone's lap dog. He frowned at it and looked at Charles's thick, springy hair. "Nearly a match," he murmured.

Charles involuntarily pressed his skullcap more firmly onto

his head with his left hand and winced as his old shoulder wound twinged. Yesterday's wet, cold hours in the saddle had taken their toll.

"Are you hurt, Maître du Luc?"

"Just an old war souvenir, *mon père.*"

Jouvancy studied him with a gravity Charles had not seen until now. "Where were you wounded?"

"At the battle of St. Omer."

"Ah, the Spanish Netherlands. Perhaps, then, you've come to this life as our St. Ignatius did?"

"In a small way, *mon père*. As I am a much smaller man. In the year when I was recovering, someone gave me the story of his life to read and—well—here I am." Wanting to turn the conversation, he said, "Who is dancing the role of Hercules?"

"Philippe Douté," Jouvancy said, with a worried sigh. "Our best dancer, who has longed for the starring role in the ballet since he was in the little boys' grammar class. But, I don't know why, lately he has not been as attentive as he should be. And last Friday he was so preoccupied and almost discourteous that Beauchamps threatened to replace him, even at this last minute." The rhetoric professor picked up a wide, feathered hat, put it on the blond wig, and studied the effect. The mange still showed. "Which I truly pray does not happen, because this is Philippe's last year, and he is a bright, good boy, one of our best. He is also my nephew, I should tell you, so I am not unbiased. But even though he is presently as secretive and sullen as a thwarted courtier, he is a talented dancer and a good scholar. Ah, well, sixteen is a terrible age, all teachers know that." He smiled at Charles. "Especially those, like you, who are not so very far from it."

"Twelve years from sixteen, *mon père*," Charles said, trying not to let his irritation make him sound as young as Jouvancy was making him out to be. In spite of his impressive size, people often thought him younger than he was. He supposed the time would come when he would enjoy that, but it had not come yet.

"Oh, I am not impugning your maturity, Maître du Luc," Jouvancy said earnestly. "Far from it." He considered Charles gravely. "I suppose it is your—enthusiasm, I must call it—the impression you give of throwing yourself into things, that makes one think of you as younger than you are." He eyed Charles for a moment. "As I watched you last night at your supper, I found myself thinking what a bad courtier you would make."

Panic lurched in Charles's stomach. Jouvancy was all too shrewd, and Charles could ill afford to be as transparent as the rhetoric master seemed to find him.

"Or what a good actor, perhaps?" he suggested lightly.

Jouvancy blinked. "Well, yes, that, too, I suppose. But I hope you were *not* acting and that you are indeed glad to be with us."

"Assuredly I am glad, *mon père!* Glad and grateful. I was merely pointing out another way to read the evidence—always a danger of being devoted to rhetorical logic, don't you find?"

"Yes, true, there is that."

He tried the hat on the brunette wig and Charles watched in silence, giving the tension he had created a moment to settle. Then he asked what tragedy they were playing with the ballet.

"*Clovis*—the Frankish king, you know. Though the tragedy seems hardly to matter these days, now that men use their Latin so little, once they leave school. And most women, of course, never learn any." Jouvancy's jaw set stubbornly. "But our syllabus requires Latin drama. *And*—" He stabbed the air with his wig-draped fist and the hat cocked itself at a rakish angle. "—the audience must sit through the Latin if they want to see the ballet, since we have the good sense to alternate the tragedy acts with the ballet parts. And, of course, *Clovis* has some good swordplay. That always helps hold their interest."

"Is this *Clovis* one of yours?"

Jouvancy nodded proudly.

"I look forward to it," Charles said sincerely. Europe's vernacular languages might be shouldering Latin aside in many areas of modern life, but Jouvancy's elegant tragedies were still in demand by rhetoric masters throughout the Jesuit college system. Which pleased Charles deeply, since he loved Latin for itself and the rhetoric master's Latin was exquisite.

"You'll be sick of play and ballet both before August the seventh," Jouvancy said, but his brown eyes danced. "To work, then, while your enthusiasm lasts, Maître du Luc!" He draped the wig over the sugar cone and opened the ballet livre.

Chapter 4

A bell clanged, and Charles looked up hopefully from the livret in his lap. He'd had more than enough of Hercules-Louis's anti-Huguenot labors.

" . . . And then," Père Jouvancy prattled on happily, "the ballet's fourth and final part." Ballets had parts and entrées where plays had acts and scenes. "The crown of everything that has gone before! This part's first entrée has Hercules throwing down the giants trying to scale heaven—a compliment to Louis's piety in destroying the Huguenots, of course. In the second entrée, Hercules razes Troy—that is Louis destroying the nests of heresy. Huguenot churches," he added helpfully, as though Charles might not get it.

Charles kept his eyes on the livret and said nothing.

"And the third entrée—Hercules helping Atlas hold up heaven—that is Louis defending true religion. And then the last entrée and the best!" Jouvancy's face was as gleeful as a rule-breaking boy's. "We have a new machine for that one. It's a seven-headed Hydra representing the Huguenots' false religion, and the Opera workmen have made it wonderfully dragonish and horrible! Hercules defeats the monster and sends it back to hell, as our crowning compliment to the king and the revocation of the Edict of Nantes!" Fortunately for Charles, Jouvancy rushed on without waiting for a reaction. "Then comes the trag-edy's last act and the ballet's grand finale—with both casts on-stage, of course. And after that, we have the dear old philosopher Diogenes—that's Père Montville—descending from the heav-ens with his lantern. If that cloud machine can be stopped from creaking like the gates of hell! Diogenes brings the boys re-ceiving the laurel crowns and the rest of the prizes onto the stage. And then, grace *au bon Dieu*, we can all breathe!" He threw himself back in his chair and beamed at Charles. "But we can-not breathe yet, because that was the warning bell for afternoon classes. We must hurry."

He started for the door and Charles got slowly to his feet, staring at the livret in his hand.

"Maître du Luc? Is something wrong?"

"No. That is—I beg your pardon, *mon père*, I was just think-ing." He put the livret on the desk and joined Jouvancy at the door.

"Of what?"

Charles dredged up a smile. "Of what we are readying for the stage."

"I am glad to see you take it so seriously! *Avaunt*, then, into the lists!"

He plunged down the stairs. Charles followed, thinking that, in spite of his distaste for the strident allegory of both ballet and tragedy, he couldn't hold the little priest's enthusiasm against him. He suspected that, for Jouvancy, the stage and the doings of heroes were often more real than the world beyond the college walls. The rhetoric master seemed to see the Edict of Nantes's revocation the same way he saw Hercules's labors: as a heroic story ripe for stage effects.

Outside in the courtyard, the students had put away their games and were scattering to classes. Jouvancy caught up with a group of older boys and shepherded them briskly toward the rhetoric classroom Montville had pointed out earlier. Feeling his mouth go dry, as though he were once more a student dancer about to step onstage, Charles followed in their wake.

"Your new realm, Maître du Luc," Jouvancy said over his shoulder, as they went into the weathered stone building and turned left into the classroom. The big room had the usual beamed ceiling and plain plastered walls, but its tall, small-paned windows flooded it with the day's sunless light. The students were taking battered plumed hats from pegs along one wall and hanging up their black gowns. In shirts and breeches, and wearing the oddly shabby hats, they took their places on rows of benches. Charles followed Jouvancy to the small dais, eyeing the dusty tapestry in somber browns and greens that hung behind it. The tapestry showed Socrates forced to drink hemlock by his enemies. Feeling the thirty or so pairs of assessing eyes on his back, Charles wondered if drinking hemlock might be easier than facing new students. His heart was thumping and his mouth was still as dry as the morning's bread. But this happened every time he faced a new class, and he concentrated on gathering spit in his mouth, so he could talk when the moment came.

"*Bon courage,*" Jouvancy murmured to Charles with a knowing grin and took his place behind the oak lectern.

Charles sat down in one of the platform's two carved oak chairs, but before Jouvancy could begin speaking, a boy of sixteen or so raced in. As he peeled off his gown, Charles recognized him as the boy who'd stopped to watch the lay brother's juggling before dinner. Tall and slim in his black breeches and a bright yellow silk shirt, the boy grabbed a hat and slid onto a bench, seemingly impervious to the tense silence. His fellows looked studiously straight ahead. Jouvancy fixed the boy with a long, quelling stare but, to Charles's surprise, no interrogation followed.

"Let us stand and pray, *messieurs*," Jouvancy said, releasing Yellow Shirt from his scrutiny.

Jouvancy commended their enterprise to God and the boys crossed themselves, put their hats back on, and sat down. The rhetoric master beamed at them.

"I have now the very great pleasure of presenting my new assistant and your new professor," he said. "The learned young chevalier of rhetoric, and sometime chevalier of arms, just like our dear St. Ignatius: Maître Charles du Luc."

Charles went to the lectern and the students rose. As one, they swept off their hats and executed a beautiful ensemble bow. Charles gave them a lesser bow, as his age and ecclesiastical status dictated, though he was sorry he had no hat to flourish, skullcaps being socially useless. The boys ceremoniously replaced their hats and resumed their seats. Once seated, though, they surprised Charles by plucking the old hats off again and stuffing them under the benches.

"I thank you for your most courteous welcome, *messieurs*," he said, smiling at them. "I am lately come from the Society's college at Carpentras, where I taught rhetoric and produced ballets and plays. I am most honored to be at Louis le Grand and I trust that our association will be both a pleasant and a profitable one. I know that Père Jouvancy holds you to the highest standard, in the rhetoric of the body as in the rhetoric of words. I, too, shall hold you to that standard."

He stepped back and Jouvancy took his place.

"Two weeks." Jouvancy glowered over the lectern at the rows of boys. "Two more weeks to put a perfect *Clovis* and a perfect *Hercules* on our stage. Both of which are now, as you too well know, as far from perfection as the east is from the west." His gaze settled on Yellow Shirt. "And so, from this day, you will work like demons. Or I will personally flay you alive."

Yellow Shirt stared at the floor, but most of Jouvancy's audience traded sideways looks. Some of the faces were bright with upwelling laughter, but some wore startled frowns. A few boys crossed themselves.

"Oh, for the *bon Dieu's* sweet sake, that was a simile!" Jouvancy barked. "A figure of speech! This is a senior rhetoric class and you cannot even recognize a figure of speech?"

A pink-cheeked boy of fifteen or so, with guileless blue eyes and a thatch of straight brown hair like a roof, put up his hand.

"Yes, Monsieur Beauclaire?" Jouvancy said, still glaring at the students.

"*Mon père*, would you not rather have us work like angels? That would also be a simile."

Snorts of laughter broke out and turned instantly into bouts of coughing.

"I suspect that angels take things a good deal easier than their infernal counterparts, Monsieur Beauclaire." Jouvancy's eyes were dancing now, but his expression was professorially sober. "Being sure of divine grace, you understand."

The class nodded as solemnly as a college of Cardinals. Charles grinned broadly, and Jouvancy dusted his hands together as though he and Beauclaire had clarified the theological problems of the age.

"Now," he said briskly. "The cast of *Clovis* here in front of the dais and mark out your stage. Bring your scripts. *Labors* cast, speakers as well as dancers, mark your stage there against the windows."

The students exploded in a whirlwind of movement. Benches were stacked and pushed against walls, tragedy scripts flew from piles on a side table, and the students sorted themselves into their places. The shabby condition of the hats explained itself as Charles counted fifteen ballet cast members, including Yellow Shirt, scattering the hats along invisible lines to mark out a stage with the long open windows as its back wall. Jouvancy thrust a ballet livret into Charles's hands.

"Make the speakers say their lines, and the dancers walk their floor patterns."

Charles nodded. Floor pattern, the path a dancer traced on the stage, was as much part of a dance as the steps. And that it be accurate was doubly important, given all the singers, speakers, scenery, and machines with whom dancers usually shared the stage.

"No steps," Jouvancy said, "floor patterns only. Their spacing needs work. And see that they come readily on their cues. M. Beauchamps will rehearse the steps and music when he comes. Those waiting for a cue," he said, raising his voice, "stand in your correct place and no talking. Anyone playing the fool, Maître du Luc will bring to me for flaying."

He flashed Charles a smile and hurried away to the actors at the other end of the room, obviously in his element. Clutching his livret, Charles advanced on the ballet cast, thinking that Louis's court was probably a more forgiving audience than this wary huddle of teenaged boys. He remembered only too well how it felt to face a new professor, an unknown quantity who could make life miserable if he chose. He stopped in front of them.

"You began rehearsing this ballet in May, I understand, *messieurs.* And I have only this morning read the livret. May I rely on you to help me catch up?"

To his relief, most of them nodded. The irrepressible boy with the thatched head stepped forward.

"Yes, Monsieur Beauclaire?"

"Is it true, *maître*, that you were a soldier?" Beauclaire glanced toward Jouvancy at the front of the room and lowered his voice. "A real one, I mean. Not just a church soldier."

Charles balanced for a moment on the horns of that dilemma and, in the interests of getting on with the rehearsal, took the easy way out.

"I fought in the Spanish Netherlands, yes."

Enthralled, the boys crowded closer and questions poured out.

"Were you a *mousquetaire*? Did you have a sword? Were you wounded?"

"Yes to all three. But I am a truer soldier now, you know." He said it because he was expected to say it, and because thinking of himself like that had been part of wanting to be a Jesuit. The soldier image had always hovered over the Society of Jesus, founded as it had been by an ex-soldier. But that image was irreparably tarnished for Charles now, and the word "soldier" coupled with religion made him cringe.

"How were you wounded?" someone said. "Didn't you have armor?"

"*Mousquetaires* don't wear armor," Beauclaire said loftily. "My brother is a *mousquetaire*." He frowned consideringly. "Maître du Luc, I see a fault of logic. Weapons are forbidden in the college, of course, but the church kills heretics. So why should you not be able to still carry your musket and sword when you go outside the college?"

Remembering tales of the armed and armored processions of Paris clerics during the Wars of Religion, Charles mentally awarded Beauclaire an "alpha" for logic. But he held up a restraining hand, glad for once for the rule that only questions relevant to the class should be discussed.

"You pose an interesting and important question, Monsieur Beauclaire. Our task, though, is to rehearse this ballet. You might not mind being flayed alive by Père Jouvancy, but I would, especially on my first day. So let us turn to Hercules and his labors. We will start with the prologue. Who speaks it?"

A gangling boy with fine reddish hair stepped forward, stumbled over his feet, and was saved by another boy grabbing the back of his shirt.

"I'm clumsy, me," the stumbler said equably over the chorus of laughter. He pushed his white linen shirt back into his breeches. "That's why I only get to talk, *maître.*"

His voice was a beautiful light tenor. Past cracking, Charles hoped.

"And your name?"

"Jacques Douté, *maître.*" He bowed too low and Charles put out an arm to keep him on his feet.

"Let us hear you then, Monsieur Douté. The rest of you, take your places, wherever you are when the ballet begins. Who is Hercules?"

Yellow Shirt, staring out a window as though Charles were not there, held up a languid hand.

"Step forward, please, *monsieur,*" Charles said crisply. "You are?"

Charles had deduced the boy's name. But he wasn't about to ignore more rudeness, Jouvancy's nephew or not. With an elaborate sigh, Yellow Shirt turned from the window.

"I am Philippe Douté."

Charles locked eyes with the boy and raised an eyebrow, waiting for the expected and courteous *"maître."* When it was grudgingly given, he said, "You and Monsieur Jacques Douté are brothers?"

"Cousins, *maître*," Jacques said brightly, when Philippe didn't answer. "But Père Jouvancy is only Philippe's uncle, not mine. His mother was Père Jouvancy's sister, you see, and so—"

"Thank you." Charles held up a hand to stem the tide of family history. "We will hope that Monsieur Philippe Douté dances more generously than he speaks. If Monsieur Jacques Douté gets through his speech without mistakes, we will continue with the first entrée, but without steps or music. You will enter promptly on your cue, walk the floor pattern of your dance briskly, paying particular attention to your spacing with regard to your fellow dancers, and exit. *Entendu?*"

The boys nodded that they understood and withdrew from the hat-defined stage. Jacques Douté took his place in what would eventually be a wing, downstage of the curtain. When the cast had made a pocket of stillness and silence in the noise of the tragedy rehearsal, Charles banged the end of a bench on the floor three times, signaling the beginning in the best Molière tradition. Jacques Douté tripped twice on his way to the center of the stage's width, but when he began to speak, it was with the ease and confidence of the great Molière himself. As Charles listened, he wondered if Molière, who had been a day student at Louis le Grand when he was still only little Jean Poquelin, had shown his talent even then and been allowed to act and dance. And if he had gone through a clumsy period, and what his teacher had done to train him out of it. Jacques got through his prologue faultlessly, gestured magnificently to open the invisible curtain, and was nearly run over as the Nemean lion and his suite, Hercules's first challenge, galloped onstage. The six boys paced at speed through their puzzlelike floor pattern and rushed off. Philippe Douté entered and stalked through his solo's pattern. The lion ensemble returned and wove energetically around him. Philippe barely looked at them. But whenever he faced upstage, he gazed intently out of the long windows.

Entrée by entrée and floor pattern by floor pattern, the ballet's first part ground on. The sullen Hercules/Louis was bearing down on the mythological Hesperides and its golden apples—a political allegory for coveted and prosperous Holland—when Jouvancy clapped his hands and shouted for silence. An elegant man in his fifties, in shoes with red heels and a sky blue coat and breeches, stood in the doorway. With a flourish of his beribboned, silver-headed walking stick, he swept off his wide-brimmed beaver hat and bowed. Charles caught his breath as the boys murmured "*Bonjour,* Maître Beauchamps," and bowed in return. Jouvancy led the dancing master to Charles and introduced them, Charles managed some awestruck words of greeting and admiration, and there were more bows. Then Pierre Beauchamps surveyed the ballet cast and glanced at Charles's livret.

"So we have arrived at the enchanting Hesperides," he muttered under his breath. "Would that we had, Maître du Luc. Would that we may by the seventh day of August." He turned to the students. "Very well. The approach to the Hesperides again, *messieurs,* if you please. Take your places. We begin with Hercules's solo. With music and steps. Perfect steps."

The dancers melted into position. Beauchamps's thin, stooped manservant, whose long bony face was creased in what looked like a permanent mask of worry, flipped his greasy tail of brown hair over his shoulder and opened a wooden box. He took out a small fiddle, a *violon du poche,* and dusted it with the skirt of his jacket. Beauchamps took the fiddle, tucked it under his chin, nodded sharply at the dancers, and began to play. All dancing masters were, of necessity, musicians, but Beauchamps was nearly as accomplished a musician as he was a dancer. But the stage remained empty and the music stopped.

"Philippe Douté!" Beauchamps thundered, looking furiously around the room.

The cast and Charles looked, too, but Philippe was nowhere to be seen. Heels rapping like hammer blows on the bare wooden floor, Beauchamps strode to an open window and stuck his head out.

"Philippe! Where are you? Get in here and dance before I use your guts for fiddle strings!"

"Um—he was by an open window when you came in, Maître Beauchamps," a small, slight blond boy said. "Looking out. And then—he stepped over the sill while everyone was bowing to you. He went toward the latrine. Perhaps he isn't feeling well." The boy put a hand discreetly on his belly.

The dancing master rolled his eyes at Charles. "Maître du Luc, will you be so good as to see if Hercules is in the privy?"

Charles was nearly at the door before he realized that he didn't know where the latrine was, but Jacques Douté caught up with him and pointed to the southeast corner of the courtyard.

"Through the arch there, on the left behind the screen of rose bushes, Maître du Luc." The wind whined across the court and whipped Charles's cassock around his legs. Behind him, the fiddle began again as Beauchamps drove Hercules's suite to the Hesperides without its leader. Overhead, clouds scudded past in a sky more like November than July. Half hoping that Philippe really was ill rather than playing the fool, Charles hurried through the arch Jacques had pointed out and into a smaller courtyard. Skirting the hedge of old roses, he stopped in the doorway of the long, low, wooden latrine building.

"Philippe Douté? Are you here? Are you ill?"

Birds fluttered in and out of the latrine's low eaves, but nothing else disturbed the dark, malodorous quiet. Charles took a few steps inside and was peering along the row of seats when unseen hands shoved him hard between the shoulders. He crashed to his knees and heard someone pound away across the gravel court. Charles scrambled up. Jouvancy's nephew or not, he thought grimly, this time Philippe Douté would get what was coming to him. A flash of yellow disappeared through a second narrow arch, and Charles followed it into a yet smaller courtyard, which was empty and surrounded on three sides by outbuildings. Its fourth side was a high wall with a wooden gate. The sound of running feet was loud beyond it.

"Philippe! Don't be an idiot, come back!"

The gate was locked. Cursing his old wound, Charles jumped for the top of the wall, hauled himself up with his good arm until he could get a leg over, and dropped into the narrow cobbled way that ran behind the college. The boy was out of sight, but his running echoed between the walls that hemmed both sides of the lane. Charles's long legs ate up the distance. And where the lane turned sharply left, he caught another flash of yellow and a glimpse of black hair. He put on a burst of speed and emerged into the rue St. Jacques, only to flatten himself against a building as a carriage flew past inches from his nose. Dodging the end of a ratcatcher's pole hung with pungent evidence of the catcher's skill, he darted into the street. A panting, leather-aproned man pushing a bundle-laden handcart stopped beside him and lowered the cart's handles to the ground for a rest. Intent on the hunt, Charles vaulted onto the cart so he could see over the crowd.

"What are you doing, you crazy priest?" The man pulled angrily on Charles's cassock. "Get off my cart!"

Charles overbalanced and landed in a passing group of students wearing short scholar's gowns. "Did you see a boy in a yellow shirt run past just now?" he asked breathlessly.

Smiling unpleasantly, the students closed around him and

looked him insolently up and down. Charles added the short gowns to the hostile faces and came up with the unwelcome answer that these were University of Paris students. Though new to the city, he was well aware that its university hated Jesuits in general and Louis le Grand in particular, deploring its influence, its progressive humanist theology, its modern teaching methods, its ballet and drama. Most of all, the university hated the Jesuit college's enjoyment of so much tantalizing property just across the street.

"Why do you want this boy in a yellow shirt, Jesuit?" one of the students drawled, recognizing the distinctive Jesuit cassock, which wrapped to the side instead of buttoning. "Good luck to him, he's well away from your lies."

"And what are you doing out without your priest hat?" another taunted.

Charles whirled as the second speaker plucked off his skullcap from behind and tossed it to one of his friends, who threw it into the gutter in the middle of the street. Hands twitching with the urge to thrash the lot of them, Charles planted his feet and locked eyes with each boy in turn. They seemed to register his height and breadth of shoulder for the first time and drew closer together.

"Perhaps you didn't hear me, *messieurs*," Charles said pleasantly. "Did any of you see a boy in a yellow shirt just now?"

They shook their heads.

"Then I thank you for your help, *messieurs*," Charles said, sounding as though they were all in someone's salon and still showing his teeth in what might be taken for a smile by the unwary.

The boys walked quickly away, casting apprehensive glances over their shoulders. Charles went to see if his new skullcap was salvageable. It was true that he shouldn't be in the street without his hat, but he hadn't planned on chasing a runaway Hercules out into Paris. Sadly, he surveyed his new skullcap, which rested like a funerary offering on a very dead cat and definitely was not salvageable. He left it where it was and started back to the college, zig-zagging through the traffic and peering down side streets and into shops in case Philippe was hiding somewhere. He guessed, though, that the boy was long gone, absorbed into the melee of the streets.

The cacophony that was Paris traffic—voices, feet, hooves, rattling wheels, barking dogs—beat against Charles's ears as he walked. Everyone and everything shared the square-cobbled pavement and shouting matches erupted constantly, everyone being certain that the *bon Dieu* had put the next open foot of pavement there for him or her alone. Charles wove his way among the high-wheeled, painted carriages, students in short gowns, white-, black-, and brown-robed clerics on foot and on mules, professors lost in private fogs of thought, coiffed and basket-laden serving girls, the scavenging dogs, ragged street porters with loaded wooden carrying frames on their backs, and bewigged gentlemen whose ice-white linen gleamed against the jewel colors of their skirted coats as they swept iron-tipped canes before them to clear a path. Over it all, bawling street vendors cried everything from "brooms, brooms," to "Portugal, Portugal," which sounded so warmly exotic but meant shriveled little oranges.

Charles wondered why on earth Philippe had run. Running away from the college was not a light offense. Nor was shoving a professor to the ground in the process, though now that his temper had cooled, Charles didn't intend to report that. But even without that black mark, Philippe had almost certainly lost his place in the ballet, if not in the college. Charles had seen him watching the classroom windows before he vanished, seen that his mind was anywhere but on his dancing. Had something—or someone—in the courtyard drawn him away? Jouvancy had said that the boy was bright. But he was also sixteen, and sixteen, whether bright or dull, wasn't known for its wisdom.

Charles rang the bell at the college's small postern door to the right of the formal entrance and then stepped back to look up at the carved and painted tympanum above the tall double doors. When the Jesuits opened their Paris college more than a century ago, they'd called it the College of Clermont. Now the tympanum said "Collegium Magni Ludo," The College of Louis the Great, and was topped by a crown and the royal fleur de lis, which proclaimed King Louis XIV's patronage.

A lay brother opened the postern and Charles hurried through the echoing stone-vaulted passage to the Cour d'honneur, toward the sound of Beauchamps's violin. The dancing master was still driving the harried, and now heroless, dancers toward the mythical Hesperides. With a sigh for the ephemeral allure of earthly paradises, Charles went to report his failure to find Philippe Douté.

ᕦ *Chapter 5* *ᕤ*

When Charles finally gained the quiet of his chamber that night, he was too tired even to look out the window at Paris. He stripped down to his shirt, fell into bed, and stretched out, past caring whether his feet hung over the edge. He fell asleep between one thought and the next, to dream that he was dancing a gigue while Pernelle played Beauchamps's little fiddle.

When he woke, he was curled into a tight ball and the day's first light was gray around the shutters. He said the waking prayers, yawned his way to the window to open shutters and casement, and leaned out. Across St. Jacques, the dome capping the university's new church was just visible in the growing light. The air was blessedly mild and birds poured their songs into the early quiet. A sharp rap at the door made him turn reluctantly from the window as Frère Fabre came in, sloshing water out of a pitcher. The brother set the pitcher down, rubbed with his foot at the puddle, and then glared at his wet shoe.

"Shaving will make you late for Mass." He squelched out of the room. Charles sighed and mopped up the water, shaved, and cleaned his teeth. He was tying the cincture around his cassock when a second rap on the door was followed immediately by Fabre's red head. "The Mass bell's about to go, come on, I'll show you a short way to the chapel."

Charles clapped an old, darned skullcap on his head and followed his self-appointed guide. This main building of the college had once been a grand family hotel, as townhouses were called, the Hôtel au Cour de Langres. Grandeur still lingered on the ground floor, where visitors were received. But in the century and a quarter since the Society had acquired the property, the upper floors had been reconfigured again and again to accommodate the growing college and were now haphazard mazes of small chambers, studies, cramped salons, dead-end passages, and low doorways. Fabre led Charles around corners, up and down inconsequential steps waiting like traps in dark passages, and finally down a last steep flight of stairs to a small door set into a corner.

The door opened on an echoing dimness and a soft rustling, a sound like homing birds folding their wings, as Jesuits and students gathered. At the chapel's east end, the high altar gleamed with gold and silver. Where the aisles crossed, a faux dome's painted angels and saints spilled from a tender blue summer sky, and reached their plump hands down to struggling mortals. Charles loved these joyously painted ceilings, with their message that heaven and earth could touch, that mortals could reach heaven from the earth's muddy ground. He found a place on the end of a backless bench and settled to the business of opening himself to the Mass.

When the Mass was over, the rest of the morning's business claimed him. He followed his colleagues to the small and private fathers' refectory for bread, cheese, and watered wine set out informally on the dais table. He ate his share standing beside Père Montville and successfully avoided Père Guise. Most of the talk was about Philippe Douté's flight and continuing absence from the college, and Charles found himself answering a barrage of questions about going after the boy. From there, he went to his morning assignment as assistant in a grammar class on Cicero, where he listened to eleven- and twelve-year-olds translate and corrected their efforts. At the dinner bell, he returned to the refectory to eat undistinguished pea soup and mutton stew, the pleasure of Guise's absence making up for the blandness of the food. When he arrived in the rhetoric classroom after the recreation hour, he found Père Jouvancy and Maître Beauchamps toe to toe and nose to nose. Jouvancy looked as though he had not slept.

"You are not listening, *mon cher* Maître Beauchamps," Jouvancy snapped. "Even if my nephew comes back—and pray God he does—he will forfeit his place in the ballet. You must find another Hercules."

"Another Hercules?" Beauchamps's widening smile showed little yellow teeth that reminded Charles of a fox's. "Oh, but of course!" The dancing master gestured at the room, which was filling with boys. "He grows on trees, Hercules. I have only to reach out and pluck him." He thrust his face even closer to Jouvancy's. "There is no other Hercules ripening in your little orchard, *mon père*."

"No. There is not. But you were already threatening to replace my poor Philippe because of his behavior. You have a half dozen Opera dancers who could do Hercules in their sleep, even at this late date. Be so good as to choose one and bring him tomorrow."

Jouvancy swept away to his actors. Beauchamps ground his teeth, his shoe ribbon bouncing as he tapped one of his beautifully made shoes. With a sinking heart, Charles realized that in the distraction of Philippe's flight yesterday, he had failed to address the question of the chiming clock headdress. Fortunately, Jouvancy hadn't yet asked him about it. But now was definitely not the moment to confront the dancing master.

Jouvancy led everyone in a short and uncharacteristically militant prayer and dismissed them to mark out their practice stages. Armand Beauclaire and Jacques Douté tried to ask him about Philippe, but he waved them away without answering and Charles set them to moving benches. After a brief, tense conference, Beauchamps and Charles started the cast on the Hesperides section of the ballet, beginning with the ensemble gigue for Hercules's suite.

The music began to ripple from Beauchamps's fiddle and Charles settled on a bench with a ballet livret in his lap, ready to prompt anyone who forgot his entrance and exit cues. The dancing master sawed away, stamping the rhythm on the floor when the dancers lost the beat, and yelling corrections. What Beauchamps was able to pull from the students amazed Charles. As he watched, he thought how lucky he was to live in an age when dancing had reached the very height of perfection. At once lively and dignified, it really was the true expression of the soul, as the best classical principles inherited from the ancient writers directed it should be. Arms, hands, and fingers were held softly curved, arms were never raised above the shoulder, legs never higher than a forty-five degree angle from the hip. Feet in their heeled and ribboned shoes flashed like knives in small, precise steps and jumps. Dancers pirouetted as smoothly as cream pouring from a pitcher, balanced as solidly as statues. When all went well, not the slightest sign of effort showed. Charles sighed with satisfaction.

Then he frowned and looked down at his own feet. They were twitching, sketching the gigue's steps as the dancers did them, and he realized that his body was remembering what his mind had long forgotten. Dances and their music were often passed among colleges and reused for different characters in different ballets. Between them, he and the Carpentras ballet master had taught this gigue to a suite of comets a year or so ago, in a ballet about the classical myths behind the names of the constellations. The six dancers in the suite all had the same steps, though their floor patterns differed. Charles had taught the part that Armand Beauclaire, yesterday's logician with the thatched head, now had. He winced as Beauclaire, an accomplished technician—with, apparently, no ear for music—strayed further and further from the melody.

Beauchamps stopped playing in the middle of a measure and flung his violin to his hovering servant. Grabbing a handful of papers from a bench, the dancing master bore down on Beauclaire. The other dancers exchanged resigned looks and studied their shoes.

"Your steps are perfect, as usual, Monsieur Beauclaire. But that is all that is perfect and it is not enough, as I have told you more times than I have gray hairs! Your steps are on the wrong notes. Why? You do not know the music. And you do not know the shape of the dance on the page, so you do not know your path on the floor. Though *how* you cannot know all that by now, the goddess of dance Terpsichore, she only knows." He cast his eyes up toward a classical heaven and thrust his handful of pages at the boy. "First, the music. Sing it."

Panic crossed Beauclaire's round face. "Sing?" he faltered, staring at the pages.

Each page had a line of music printed at the top, and below that, a maze of vertical lines crosshatched with what looked like the tracks of a crazed chicken. Jouvancy had told Charles that Beauchamps's pet project was a way of writing dance, which he was teaching the students to read. That, Charles guessed, was what Beauclaire was staring at so hopelessly.

"But, *maître*, I . . ."

"You sing like a donkey, yes, we know that. There, at the top, that line is the music that goes with this page of steps. As you should know by now," he sighed.

Sweat broke out on the boy's face, but he drew himself up manfully. "Would you give me the first note, please, *maître*?"

Beauchamps sang a pure and liquid note, and Beauclaire plunged into the gigue's tune like a prisoner jumping from a gangplank. Charles looked away and bit his lip. The boy really did sound like a donkey.

"No, no, no!" Beauchamps grabbed the papers away and gave them to the small blond who had suggested yesterday that Philippe might have been taken ill. The boy calmly started the melody with perfect pitch and in perfect time, his surprising treble clear as birdsong.

"There, Monsieur Beauclaire, you see? Compound duple meter. Six beats to the measure, distributed over the underlying beat of two." He beat the six on his thigh while counting the two. "You see? Come, the rest of you, join in. Not you!" Beauchamps pulled the escaping Beauclaire back from the group. "You will listen as you follow the music and read your steps on the page."

Charles listened in amazement as the boys sang the lilting melody line. Everyone who learned to dance learned to read music, of course, but these boys were musicians as well as dancers. What would happen on the courtyard stage on the seventh of August would indeed have more in common with court and professional performances than with the earnest little shows he had helped to produce at Carpentras.

"Now, Monsieur Beauclaire," Beauchamps said, with terrifying gentleness, when the singers finished. "Now let us see you put it all together."

The dancers took their places. Beauchamps closed his eyes briefly in what looked like prayer and began to play. All was perfection and Charles released his held breath, still marking the steps with his feet and singing quietly along with the melody. Then all six boys went down in a writhing tangle.

"Ow! Get off, you ass!" Indignant howls rose from the heap as Beauclaire struggled to his feet. "You go left, idiot," someone cried at him despairingly, "*left!*"

Beauchamps barreled onto the stage and grabbed Beauclaire's hand. "This is your right hand." He dropped it and grabbed the other hand. "*This* one is your left. Do I have to tie colored ribbons on them so you can remember?" He marched Beauclaire, who had clearly given up all hope, through the floor pattern again and picked up his fiddle. "Now. With perfect timing. With perfect directions. Or I may kill you."

The dejected Beauclaire looked as though that might be preferable, but he and his fellows dutifully began again. Beauchamps played and sang the tune, leaning precariously in whatever direction Beauclaire was supposed to turn. As the boys turned accurately and on the correct notes, Charles relaxed again, his feet still marking the remembered steps. Then Beauclaire did a series of small beautiful leaps in the wrong direction, two other boys skidded out of his way, and Beauclaire cannoned into Jacques Douté, who was standing offstage. The dancing master sank onto the bench beside Charles, laid down his violin as though it were his dead beloved, and put his head in his hands. A deathly quiet descended on the ballet end of the room.

"Maître du Luc," Beauchamps said into his hands. "Show him how it is done."

Charles blinked. *"Maître?"*

"You know the part," Beauchamps said without looking up. "I saw your feet. Would you rather dance it for him or would you rather I kill him? Let us hear what Jesuit casuistry has to say to that proposition."

"Please, Maître du Luc, we have never seen a professor dance, not really!" the boys clamored.

"On the other hand, we have never seen a teacher kill one of us, either," someone else said in an interested tone.

Charles wished he could disappear like Philippe. Everyone of his social class learned to dance, of course. And he was a good, even gifted, dancer, indeed had thought more than once when he was younger of running away to join a theatre company. But now he was a Jesuit, and while teaching was one thing, performing, even for these boys, was quite another. He hadn't danced—not really danced—since the ball where his secret betrothal to Pernelle had been discovered.

"Well?" Beauchamps was glowering at Charles from under his eyebrows.

"Yes—I do—I did—know Monsieur Beauclaire's part of this gigue. But you must excuse me, *maître*, you know that Jesuits do not perform."

"Nonsense. Is your Superior General going to drop through the ceiling and excommunicate you if you dance this gigue for us? You are a teacher. What I ask is part of teaching M. Beauclaire. So teach."

"But, *maître*, I can no longer position my left arm exactly as it should be and—"

"You have another arm and two legs, use those. We'll get the idea."

He positioned his fiddle and waited. Charles turned toward the front of the room to enlist Jouvancy's help. The senior rhetoric master could put a more courteous stop to this than he himself could. But Jouvancy was busy demonstrating dance's fourth position, a stance used by actors, lawyers—and most males having their portraits painted—as well as by dancers. As Charles watched, Jouvancy threw up his hands in exasperation and pulled off his cassock to stand in his linen shirt and black breeches, then struck the fourth position pose, his black stockinged legs and small feet in their low-heeled shoes turned out just so, his arms, hands, and fingers softly curved, his whole stance imbued with arresting, silent beauty. Charles shrugged and pulled off his own cassock. Jubilantly, the boys cleared the stage for him and he took up the gigue's beginning position, wondering how much he really remembered. And what Beauchamps would do to him when he reached the end of his memory.

The dancing master gave him a nod, attacked the fiddle with the bow, and they were off. Charles plunged into the gigue like a hooked fish thrown back into water. He stepped, he leapt, he flew. He balanced on one foot's tiptoe as though merely pausing during levitation. A wild joy possessed him. His feet invented effortless, flickering steps for what he'd forgotten. He pirouetted, flashing like a top as he spun. He wove a lover's knot of a pattern on the ancient floorboards and sprayed his audience with sweat as he skimmed past them. When the fiddle achieved its finish, his blood and his heart went on singing. Grinning from ear to ear, he bowed to Beauchamps, who bowed in return, though with one raised eyebrow to mark Charles's inspired improvisations.

The boys clapped wildly. As Jouvancy and his actors turned to see what was happening, Père Montville, the rector's assistant, burst into the room. For one startled moment, Charles thought Montville had come to censure him. But Montville hurried to Jouvancy and whispered urgently in his ear. Jouvancy blanched and grabbed up his cassock. Montville left as quickly as he'd come. Beauchamps and Charles looked questions at each other as Charles shrugged hastily back into his own cassock.

"Gather both casts, please," Jouvancy said as he passed them, "work on the finale, the *ballet général.*"

He rushed from the room, his cassock billowing behind him. Seeing that Jouvancy had dropped his black cloth cincture, Charles grabbed it up. "I must take him this," he told Beauchamps, and hurried after the rhetoric master.

Chapter 6

If Père Montville's news was about Philippe, Charles thought, running across the Cour d'honneur, then the news was obviously bad. He caught up with Père Jouvancy in the postern passage and handed him the cincture. Jouvancy wound it around his waist without breaking stride.

"What is it, *mon père?*" Charles said, walking beside him. "Can I help?"

Jouvancy shook his head. "It is my nephew."

He pushed his way through the postern, which was blocked by a crowd of lay brothers looking out and talking excitedly. As Charles hesitated, torn between knowing that he should go back to the classroom and wanting to know what had happened to Philippe, a hand plucked at his sleeve.

"Down there." Frère Fabre pointed at the narrow street that opened off St. Jacques almost straight across from the college. "The baker's little girl said it happened down where the rue des Poirées turns."

Charles threw a sop to his conscience, telling himself that Jouvancy might need him, and squeezed through the door into the street. Movement caught his eye and he glanced to his left, beyond the chapel's street door, where a small girl was pointing anxiously toward the rue des Poirées as a man in a baker's baglike cap held her firmly by the shoulder.

Charles followed Jouvancy into the shadows of the rue des Poirées, over its patchy and uneven cobbles toward the sharp left turn where Père Montville and Père Le Picart were bent over something hidden by their cassocks. To Charles's surprise, Père Guise was there, talking to a tall gaunt street porter with a loaded wooden carrying frame on his back. A small, round woman stood watching them, radiating indignation, even at a distance. Beyond the bend in the street, two lay brothers held back traffic, stolidly silent under a rain of abuse from riders, a carriage driver, and a dozen pedestrians, all determined to gain the rue St. Jacques without going the longer way around. Less encumbered pedestrians were starting to edge past the brothers along the house walls.

Jouvancy pushed his way through a knot of gesticulating university students and dropped to his knees between Montville and Le Picart. Charles, tall enough to see over their shoulders, hung back, wondering in confusion who the little boy lying on the pavement could be. He certainly was not Philippe, he looked almost too young to belong to the college at all. The boy lay ominously still and his eyes were closed. The rector was trying to stanch the blood pouring from a long cut on his forehead.

Not dead, Charles prayed silently. Dear Blessed Virgin, don't let him be dead. Fabre and another brother arrived at a run with a board. As Jouvancy and Le Picart carefully lifted the boy onto it, his bony little chest rose and fell in a shallow breath and Charles released his own held breath in a prayer of thanks. The lay brothers lifted the board and started back to the college.

"Go back to the classroom," Jouvancy said distractedly as he passed Charles, his eyes on the motionless child. "Keep them working. I won't return today."

Montville, on Jouvancy's heels, stopped and laid a hand on Charles's arm. "If you need help, Maître du Luc, just ask any of us. I know you've hardly arrived."

"You are most kind, *mon père*. But I'm sure Maître Beauchamps won't let me put a foot wrong. Who is the child? What happened?"

"He is Antoine Douté, brother to the silly young bravo who ran away yesterday. The boys are Père Jouvancy's nephews." He jerked his head at Guise. "And this little one is also Père Guise's godson. As for what happened here, well, it seems a little confused, but witnesses say that a horseman, probably drunk, knocked the child down."

"Who saw it happen?"

"Père Guise, for one. And that man he's talking to, the porter with the twisted nose."

Charles looked over his shoulder and saw that the poor man's nose had at some time been broken so badly that it was flattened almost against his cheek.

"The baker's wife saw it, too, the woman there in the wooden shoes. Those university fellows say they saw nothing, but you know what that's worth. I must get back, but please ask for whatever you need, *maître*."

"Thank you, *mon père*. I only hope that Philippe returns, and that this little one is not badly hurt. That looks to be a bad slice in his head."

Montville nodded, his ebullience dimmed for once. "To have these things happen to both boys—" He shook his head. "We're hoping that Philippe has simply gone home to Chantilly, but there is no word yet. Keep praying, *maître*."

Montville walked quickly toward the college and Charles went to the place where Antoine had lain. He stared thoughtfully at the patches of slightly rounded cobbles glistening with a roux of street debris, dung, urine, and last night's rain. The lay brothers had released the blocked traffic, but Charles, heedless of the stream of people, animals, and carts parting around him, protected the piece of road with his body while his eyes moved steadily out from the place where Antoine's head had been.

"What are you doing here, Maître du Luc?"

Charles looked up to see Guise glowering from under his wide hat brim. "I brought something Père Jouvancy needed, *mon père*. Like all of us, I am wondering how the accident happened."

Guise looked around pointedly. "Père Jouvancy is gone. And so should you be. There is nothing more to gape at."

"No? Père Montville said the child is your godson."

Guise's expression rippled and smoothed, like water when wind blows over it. He moved to the side of the street, and gestured Charles to follow.

"The child's name is Antoine," he said gravely. "I saw him fall. The man who rode him down was going like a demon out of hell. Oh, I know it happens all the time, but I would dearly love to get my hands on the cur."

"Was Antoine with you?"

"He was not. I have no idea how he got out of the college. He should have been in his grammar class. Why he was not, will be for his tutor and his teacher to answer," Guise said grimly. "And answer they will. No, I was coming from the bookseller's back there on the corner. Reading, as is my bad habit, as I walked." He held up a small, elaborately bound book. "When that street porter cried out a warning to Antoine, I looked up and saw the horse galloping at the child."

Charles nodded encouragingly, surprised at Guise's sudden friendly spate of words. "The rider came around the turn. I thought the horse was going to fall, it was going at such a pace. Poor Antoine tried to get out of the way, but—" Guise shook his head sadly. "To the rider's credit, he leaned down—at some risk to himself, I may say—and tried to push the boy aside. But Antoine stumbled and fell. And then the cursed man just kept going. Afraid he'd killed him, I suppose. Well, all we can do now is pray." He gestured toward the rue St. Jacques. "Will you walk back with me?"

Wooden shoes clattered on the cobbles and the woman Charles had noticed earlier pushed her way between the men.

"I saw you over there with your nose nearly on the cobbles," she said to Charles. "*You* seem to have eyes in your head, anyway. Unlike *some*." She twitched a shoulder at Guise behind her. "I must talk to you, *mon père*."

"Be off, woman!" Guise pushed her aside. "Do not waste your time on this excessively stupid woman, Maître du Luc. Her lurid tale is nonsense."

"Tale, is it?" The woman spun around and looked Guise up and down. "It's the truth and you know it, you saw it yourself! Antoine never fell, the man rode him down on purpose, I saw it with these two eyes!" She turned back to Charles, pointing at her round brown eyes as though Charles might not know where to find them.

"If you must talk to someone, Maître du Luc," Guise said, barely opening his mouth, "talk to the street porter. He is a reliable man."

He departed in a whirl of cassock skirts and Charles turned to look for the porter, but the man was gone.

"Now that there is no *man* available, perhaps you will listen?" The woman's curling chestnut hair was escaping from her white linen cap in every direction and her eyes snapped with outrage. "That priest is lying. Lying, do you hear me?" She spat over her shoulder at the place where Guise had stood. "But what can you expect from such a *mignon*?" She picked up her coarse brown skirt and mimicked the way Guise was holding his hem away from the street dirt as he walked toward the rue St. Jacques.

"*Mignon?*" Charles turned involuntarily to stare after Guise. Surely she didn't mean "darling" the way the court meant it, as a jibing name for the pretty men so beloved of the king's brother. Whatever else Guise seemed, it wasn't that.

"You want to tell me something, madame?" He hoped that Beauchamps was not keeping track of how long he'd been gone from the classroom. "I have only a moment."

"I have been *trying* to tell you something," she said severely.

"I am listening, madame."

"Well." She gave herself a small shake, like a ruffled bird. "Little Antoine comes into our shop sometimes with his brother, Philippe, and—"

"Your shop?"

"Ah, I thought so from your accent, you're new, that's why you don't know anything. We're the first shop to the right of your chapel door. My daughter Marie-Ange and I were returning from delivering bread to the boardinghouse kitchens. We're bakers, LeClerc the baker, that's us. The amount of bread these skinny students eat, you'd hardly believe it—but, there, I suppose you would. Anyway, we were walking back toward St. Jacques and Antoine was running this way, toward us. Though he hadn't seen us. Marie-Ange called out to him, but just then a man coming toward us, that street porter, shouted, and I turned and saw a horse coming around the turn and galloping straight at Antoine. I yelled out to warn him and the porter jumped out and tried to frighten the horse and make it turn. Antoine dodged—he's very fast, that little one—and I thought he was safe, but—" She shook her head and dropped her voice dramatically. "The rider swerved and went after him! And pushed him down! Antoine fell and the man kept going, if you can believe it. I sent my little girl running to the college for help and I went to see how badly the child was hurt. But that son of a pig Guise got there first and warned me off."

"The rider swerved and went after the boy? Are you sure, madame?"

"As sure as I stand here and hope for salvation!"

Charles turned to stare at the place where Antoine had fallen. "You say the man reached for him—Père Guise saw that, too. He said the rider was trying to push the boy out of the way."

"Then why didn't he try to stop the horse or turn it?" She frowned and her eyes opened wider. "Unless he was reaching out for the boy because he was trying to snatch him up and ride off with him!" She stepped closer, her eyes avid. "Another thing I can tell you, he wore a mask!"

"A mask, madame?" Charles quickly reassessed his informant, remembering Guise's sneer at what he'd called her "lurid tale."

She crossed her arms over her straining bodice. "I see you don't believe me. But I saw what I saw. I swear it. It was the kind of mask ladies wear when it's cold. Or at Carnival. But—" She looked expressively up at the sky. "—it is not cold, not today, anyway. And it is not Carnival. And he was not a lady." She eyed Charles triumphantly, as though she'd just bested him in a rhetorical display.

"Did the porter also see the mask?"

"Is he blind? Of course he did. And so did your *mignon*. But the porter will never tell you he saw it, now that your *mignon* has got hold of him." She held a hand under Charles's nose and rubbed thumb and fingers together in the age-old sign for money.

Charles's head was beginning to spin. "Père Guise gave him money?"

Her shrug nearly took her ears off. "Why did the porter run

away before you could talk to him? And Guise does not like my version of the story at all, you heard him."

"Did he offer you money to change your story, madame?"

Mme LeClerc spat again. "That object knows better than to try his tricks with me."

"Madame, Père Guise is Antoine's godfather. Why would he pay the porter to lie about what happened?"

"Why would the masked man ride the child down?"

Charles opened his mouth, then shut it. It was not the moment for a logic lesson. "Did you notice anything else about the man, madame? What was his horse like?"

"A rangy chestnut. Missing his manhood, if you know what I mean, poor thing." She dimpled and Charles suddenly realized that she wasn't much older than he was. "The horse was. About the man, of course, I couldn't say."

Charles struggled to keep a straight face, thinking that the baker was a lucky man.

"The rider's hat was pulled down low." She paused, watching the air, obviously seeing the whole thing happen again. "Plain and flat the hat was, a floppy brim, no feather. His hair I didn't notice. He looked wiry—not thin or reedy, though, he looked strong. A good rider. Not so tall, not nearly so tall as you." She looked Charles up and down approvingly. "His coat and breeches were ordinary brown. Like this." She touched her worn bodice. "The only thing good was his boots. A blackish color like burnt sugar, and they folded over at the top."

"Which way did he ride?"

She pointed toward the rue St. Jacques. "I was looking at the child, I didn't see which way the man turned."

"Do you know the street porter's name, madame? Or where I could find him?"

"I never saw him before. But you might find him on the quays, they wait there for the boats to unload."

"And you, madame, can you be found in your shop?"

"But of course. You can't miss it, as I said, it's beside your chapel door. Which is beside your little postern, in case you don't know yet. Our bakery and the bookbinder farther along are the only shops left in your frontage now."

Charles thanked her and began his farewells before he remembered that she didn't know his name.

"Forgive me, Madame LeClerc, I have not introduced myself. I am Maître Charles du Luc."

She nodded her approval of his manners and made him a small reverence. Then she frowned. "Why are you not *père*? What did you do?"

Charles burst out laughing. She sounded exactly like his mother. "Nothing, madame—at least, not in the way you mean. It takes a long time to become *père* in the Society of Jesus."

"That Guise is *père* and you're not? Pah. It's the same in the church and out, the bad ones get everything, the good ones go begging." Her face softened. "I will pray for our Antoine, *maître*."

"As we all will. *Au revoir*, madame." Head down, he walked toward the college, thinking about what he'd learned and scrutinizing the paving stones as though he'd lost a handful of gold.

Chapter 7

Instead of making speed back to the classroom, Charles went in search of Père Le Picart. A lay brother directed him to the infirmary, in a small court with a tidy garden of herbs and flowers, above the workroom where the infirmarian prepared what medicines weren't bought from apothecaries. Le Picart answered his tap at the infirmary door.

"Maître du Luc?" The rector frowned. "Has something else happened, God forbid?"

"No, please forgive my intrusion, *mon père*, I came because a woman in the street, the wife of the baker LeClerc, told me she saw the accident. But perhaps Père Guise has already told you . . . ?"

"He told me what he saw. He has just gone. But come in, the more we know, the better."

The big square room was dim and herb-scented, with wooden shutters half-closed over the windows and rush matting on the floor to muffle footsteps. The infirmarian, a bear of a man with hands the size of soup bowls, sat on a stool beside one of the dozen narrow beds, busy with a cloth and pitcher.

"Maître du Luc, this is Frère Brunet, who sees to our health."

Brunet glanced up and nodded.

"How is the boy?" Charles asked him softly.

"The head wound seems to be the only injury," Brunet said. "Except for bruises. If he wakes soon, he'll do well enough."

"Mother of God, let him wake," Charles murmured and crossed himself, watching Brunet sponge wine into the gash on Antoine's forehead to help against infection. Wine stung an open wound, but the boy's eyes stayed closed and he lay ominously still. Charles peered over the infirmarian's beefy shoulder.

"A sharp slice, *mon frère*," Charles said. "Though in the place where he fell, what cobbles there are, are rounded. And where the cobbles have come up, there's only mud. Nothing sharp that I could see."

"Perhaps the horse's hoof caught him," Brunet said, spreading a foul-smelling unguent on the cut.

"But wouldn't the injury be worse? And the flesh more bruised?"

Charles had seen men horse-kicked in battle, and most of them had gotten not only cuts and bruises, but their skulls broken in the bargain. The infirmarian's hands stilled for a moment as he considered.

"Maybe not, if it was a glancing hit."

Charles held his peace. The injury could have happened like that. He looked up to find the rector watching him narrowly.

"The baker's wife?" Le Picart prompted him. "Père Guise told me that Mme LeClerc was there, but he dismissed what she said." There was a fractional pause. "Myself, I have always found her reliable."

Charles repeated what she'd said about the masked man riding straight for Antoine and reaching out for him. But he left out her insistence that Guise had bribed the porter. He needed to be very sure of his ground before he made an accusation that serious.

"Well," Le Picart said, "the mask sounds like a tale. But if three people see a thing, especially if it is frightening, they see three different things. But *could* the man have been trying to abduct the child, I wonder? Rather than trying to shove him aside, as Père Guise thinks?"

Charles shrugged. "It must have happened so fast, *mon père*, both efforts might look the same."

"Yes. Well, the child's father will want to know as much as possible. I should tell you that Père Jouvancy—uncle to the Douté boys as I'm sure you've been told—has already left for Chantilly to fetch him." The rector's face was grim. "We sent a message about Philippe yesterday, of course. And we are still hoping he has made his way home, but we have no word yet."

Brunet finished bandaging Antoine's head, tucked the blanket snugly under the boy's chin, and sat back on his stool. "That's all there is to do for him now. Except to pray he wakes soon."

"And to pray that Philippe is safe in Chantilly." Le Picart gave Charles a brief and wintry smile. "And if he is, to pray that his father rewards him appropriately for putting us all through this!"

"I cannot understand Philippe," Brunet said mournfully, turning on his stool to look up at them. "All he's ever wanted, ever since he came here, was to be the star of the ballet! Why would he—"

Another tap at the door made them turn, and Jacques Douté's worried face appeared around the door's edge.

"What are you doing here, Monsieur Douté?" The rector strode to the door as though to shut it in the boy's face. "Go back to your classroom, we have had enough Douté disobedience!"

Jacques bowed awkwardly to Le Picart and Charles. "No, *mon père.* I mean, yes, *mon père.* Maître Beauchamps gave me permission, *mon père.* I was worried about my cousin."

"Come in, then. But quietly, do not trip over anything!"

Wavering on tiptoe, Jacques approached the bed. "He's not dead?"

"Now, now, don't be foolish, it's just a bump on the head," Brunet said robustly.

"They say he fell down in the street?" Jacques made the question sound as though Antoine was reported to have flown. "And a horse went over him?"

Charles's attention sharpened. "You are surprised at that, Monsieur Douté?"

Jacques nodded, chewing his lip as he gazed at his unconscious cousin. Before Charles could ask more, Jacques glanced at the rector, bowed his head, and prayed silently. When he finished, Le Picart drew him away from the bed, though not out of Charles's hearing.

"I asked you yesterday, Monsieur Douté," the rector said, "and now I ask you again. Do you know where Philippe has gone?"

The boy's eyes were instantly wary. "No, *mon père*, I swear it! I told you, he just disappeared from our rehearsal."

"Could Antoine have known where he went? Perhaps Antoine was going to Philippe when he was hurt?"

"I don't know, *mon père*."

"Do you know what has been troubling Philippe lately?"

Jacques's face flushed and he looked down. "Not really."

"Which means?"

Jacques brightened, as though with sudden inspiration. "Antoine, perhaps? Antoine has been homesick, you know," he said earnestly. "He's not yet even nine. Philippe was angry when his father let his stepmother send him to school, so maybe . . ."

The rector was staring at Jacques like an unimpressed cat, and the boy's words trailed into silence.

"So perhaps Philippe ran away because he is worried about his little brother here in the college? If you are going to make up a tale, do yourself—and me—the honor of making sense, M. Douté. Understand this. We are very worried about Philippe. If you develop any ideas about where he has gone or why, or if he sends you any word, you are to come straight to me, do you understand? Failure to do so will mean severe penance. Expulsion from the ballet. Perhaps expulsion from the college."

Jacques bowed his head. "Yes, *mon père.*" There was a short silence. Then he raised pleading eyes to the rector's face. "But if Antoine is worse, you will tell me?"

"But yes, of course." Le Picart's face softened and he put an arm around Jacques and turned him toward the door. "You heard Frère Brunet, we think Antoine will do well. All the same, Père Jouvancy has gone for your uncle. M. Douté will no doubt want to see you when he comes."

Jacques looked sideways at the rector. "Antoine's stepmother is already in Paris, *mon père.* If you want her, too."

"How do you know that?"

"Philippe said so. At dinner yesterday."

"Then might Philippe have gone to her? Why haven't you told us this? Where is she staying?"

"Where she is staying, I don't know, *mon père.* But Philippe would never go to her!"

"Why?"

"He hates her!"

"And why is that?"

"Because Mme Douté—he said she—" A new tide of red crept up the boy's neck. "He just doesn't like her. You know."

"No, I don't."

Sweat had broken out on the young man's face. "She— well—she kisses him," he said, keeping his eyes on the floor.

"And she tries to make him kiss her back. And other things. He told her just a few days ago, at her birthday fête, that if she didn't stop, he was going to tell his father. He wouldn't really tell his father, though, because it would make M. Douté feel like a cuckold."

Le Picart's frown was showing a new kind of worry. "Are you so sure Philippe doesn't like what she does? Some boys would, I fear."

"He hates it!"

"That is to his credit, then." Le Picart turned Jacques toward the door. "Go back to your rehearsal now," he said briskly. "Maître du Luc will come shortly." When Jacques had gone, Le Picart shook his head in exasperation. "I pray that Jacques is right and that Philippe has not run off to his very young and very pretty stepmother. I will have to talk seriously to him when we find him. That wretched girl—she's no more than that, twenty this last birthday. And Philippe will soon be seventeen. And poor M. Douté, whether Jacques is right or not! I must find out where Mme Douté is staying and make certain Philippe is not with her. And send her a message about Antoine." He grimaced. "Like Philippe, I prefer to avoid her. Truth to tell, she flirts with every man she sees!"

"You could let her husband fetch her when he arrives," Brunet said. "Because of her condition. She expects a child in the autumn, you know."

"A child? Dear Blessed Virgin, and trying to entice her stepson even so?" Le Picart sighed heavily, but a measure of relief showed on his face. "I will make her condition my reason for letting her husband fetch her. How do you come to know about the child, *mon frère*?"

"This little one was chattering one day when I mended his skinned knee." He put a hand on Antoine's forehead, grunted, and got heavily to his feet. "So, Maître du Luc," he said, "it seems you and Mme LeClerc are not the only ones wondering about this accident." His voice grew muffled as his head disappeared into the depths of a cupboard. He came back to the bed with another clean cloth and a blue pottery bowl. "My feverfew infusion," he said, resuming his seat. He dipped the cloth in the bowl and wrung it out. "He's heating a little—which is only to be expected." He loosened the blanket, sponged Antoine's face, and dipped the cloth again. "These cousins," he said, with a glance over his shoulder at Charles and the rector, "know each other very well."

"Yes, they do, Frère Brunet," Le Picart said. "And so?"

"And so Philippe is graceful, agile beyond the ordinary," the infirmarian murmured. "I've heard this little brother is the same."

Le Picart glanced at Charles, cast his eyes up at the ceiling, and folded his hands in an attitude of patience. "Yes?"

"Jacques, now, he might fall like that. Under a galloping horse. Our Jacques falls off the carpet. But I think he finds it hard to believe that Antoine simply fell."

"And you are saying what, *mon frère*?"

"I am not saying. Only wondering."

"On the contrary. You are saying that perhaps Mme LeClerc is right and this was not an accident. But why? Why would anyone want to harm Antoine?"

Brunet ducked his head. "I only wondered."

"Keep a rein on your imagination, *mon frère*," the rector said, moving toward the door and motioning Charles ahead of him. "Send me word of how Antoine does before the bedtime bell." He shepherded Charles briskly downstairs. "Thank you for coming to tell me what you learned from Mme LeClerc," he said, as they walked through the infirmary garden. "And I am sorry that this sad accident thrusts all the responsibility for rehearsals on your shoulders so soon, Maître du Luc."

Charles smiled and bowed. "I will do my best, *mon père*." But his smile faded as he hurried back to the classroom, thinking about what Jacques and Brunet had said. Too many people were "wondering." The accounts of Antoine's accident, taken together, seemed even further from making sense.

The next day, there was still no word of Philippe. Antoine was said to be better, alternately waking and sleeping. Père Jouvancy and M. Douté were presumably on their way back to Paris, less than a day's journey in dry weather. Charles and the dancing master rehearsed the two casts as best they could, Maître Beauchamps taking the dancers and Charles the actors. Beauchamps still had no new Hercules, and insisted despairingly that there was no one—but *no* one—who could take the role. Suspecting a dramatic buildup to the discovery of the perfect Hercules, Charles ignored him and concentrated on the tragedy.

When they dismissed both casts at the end of the afternoon, the third act of *Clovis* was a little smoother and Beauchamps had coerced miracles of order and memory from the dancers, even the musically dense Beauclaire. Charles was exhausted. The night before, he had ignored the bell for going to bed and stayed up until his candle burned itself out, rereading *Clovis* and planning how he would direct the actors. Then he'd lain awake wondering how Antoine had gotten the cut on his forehead. And how to reconcile the discrepancies between Mme LeClerc's report of the accident and Guise's. It seemed that he had hardly closed his eyes before the waking bell announced a new and unwelcome day.

Now, with the Compline bells about to ring, all Charles

wanted was bed and the oblivion of sleep. Instead, still dogged by his questions, he went to the infirmary to see if Antoine had remembered anything of the accident. As he climbed the infirmary stairs, high-pitched wailing met him. At first he thought that Antoine was crying, but then the wailing turned to words.

"Oh, Blessed Virgin, this child is dying! Fernand, can't you see? Oh, dear Jesu and all the saints—"

"Softly, Lisette, hush! He is not dying, he is doing very well, you heard Frère Brunet! Do not distress yourself—Lisette!" The faint sound of scuffling came through the door. "What is that thing? Give it to me!"

There was a female shriek and a male oath.

"God's teeth, madame, what do you want the good fathers to think—"

"It is only my charm, my maid gave it to me, *she* cares that I am suffering! If our baby dies, it will be your fault, give it back! Oh, why have men no feelings? St. Anne, help me!"

Charles turned quickly back, remembering what he'd heard about Mme Douté. At least he now knew that Antoine's father and stepmother had arrived and that the little boy was better. His other questions could wait. He had started downstairs, thinking with relief that Jouvancy must also have returned, when the door opened and a brief glow of candlelight brightened the antechamber outside the infirmary. Charles looked over his shoulder to see a stout, harassed-looking man hesitating at the top of the stairs.

"A word, *mon père*," the man said curtly.

Charles retraced his steps. "I am Maître du Luc, *monsieur*. How may I help you?"

"I am Monsieur Fernand Douté." The wall sconce candle cast flickering shadows on the man's pale, sagging face. "I want to speak with whoever saw my boy Philippe last."

"He has not returned home, then?"

"Not when I left. And I do not believe for a moment that he simply ran away! That is a tale told by some enemy to get him into trouble!"

"Père Jouvancy told you what happened?"

"Yes, yes, he told me, but—I simply cannot believe it. He said that some new teacher went after the boy. And who knows what happened? I want to see that man!"

Charles didn't react. "Has Père Jouvancy returned with you to Paris, *monsieur?*"

"Yes, but he insisted on continuing in my carriage to the college's country house at Gentilly."

"Gentilly?" Charles said, and then remembered that Louis le Grand had a house in a small village a day's walk south of Paris.

"He had some idea that Philippe might go there," M. Douté was saying, "since the boy has spent school holidays there. I doubt that's where he is, but Joseph—Père Jouvancy, I mean, he is my first wife's brother—wanted to leave nothing undone." Douté started to rake his pudgy hands through his hair, knocked his wig askew, and yanked it straight. He clasped his hands tightly at his full-skirted coat's straining closure. His awkward anguish suddenly reminded Charles of his own father seeing him off to war the first time.

"It was I who was sent to find Philippe, Monsieur Douté," Charles said gently. "This is only my third day at Louis le Grand. I am the new assistant in the senior rhetoric class. Philippe went over the college's rear wall and I followed him, but I lost him in the rue St. Jacques."

M. Douté's little eyes narrowed, and he released his clasped hands and took a step toward Charles. "And what did you do to him that he would run?"

"Not the smallest thing, *monsieur*, I assure you. As I said, I had only just met him."

"Yes, yes, you did say that. Forgive me." Douté lifted his hands helplessly and let them drop, his limp lace cuffs fluttering like tired birds. "It is only that—I cannot understand any of this! And Antoine—what was he doing out by himself? No one can even tell me that! Do you let these children run wild?"

"We have learned that Antoine's teacher gave him permission to go to the latrine, *monsieur*. The child must have slipped out by the stable gate. It's near his classroom. The brother at the street postern swears he never left his post, and never saw the child." Charles spread his hands apologetically. "The college is not a fortress, *monsieur*. Is Antoine better this evening?"

The father's eyes softened. "Yes. They say he will recover well."

"Thanks be to God."

Douté nodded distractedly. "But Philippe—I have called on everyone he might go to here in Paris, but no one has seen him. My God, when I sent the boys back here on Sunday—no, I am going distracted, it was a week ago Sunday—I never thought—" He pressed his lips together and shook his head.

"Sent them back after your wife's birthday fête, you mean?" Charles said, remembering that Jacques had mentioned the fête when he came to see Antoine in the infirmary.

"Yes. They don't come home often, but the thirteenth was their stepmother's first birthday since we married, and we celebrated with a small family fête. I particularly wanted them there. So they will know her better."

"I see. Did Philippe seem—worried about anything while he was there?" Charles said carefully. "I only ask because Père Jouvancy mentioned that lately the boy has seemed—distracted."

"Yes, Père Jouvancy told me that. But I can't say I've noticed much. Only that on the evening of the fête he was somewhat sullen, and refused Mme Douté her birthday kiss. And he was rude to Père Guise. Count yourself fortunate that you will never know the shame discourteous sons bring on their father! In the end I had to box Philippe's ears to remind him of his manners." M. Douté tried to smile. "Well, we all know what youth is. And Père Guise can be very—definite, shall we say, in his opinions. Young men are not always patient with that. But he has long been a dear family friend, and is godfather to Antoine. He was Adeline's—my first wife's—confessor, and Philippe and Antoine have known him all their lives. Père Guise is nearly as distraught as I am over this accident." Douté sighed. "Indeed, I should speak with him. Can you bring me to him?"

Trying to imagine the dour Guise as anyone's dear family friend, Charles led the way outside and through the infirmary garden's deep summer green, fading to black now in the twilight. They entered the main building by its back door and went to the grand salon, where Charles rang a bell on a side table. Slow steps padded across the antechamber and an elderly lay brother stuck his head around the doorway.

"*Oui?*" he rasped, his bald head shining in the light from a copper sconce.

"*Mon frère,* will you please ask Père Guise to come down? M. Douté would like to speak with him."

The brother grunted, dodged a drip of wax from the sconce, and trudged upstairs. Wanting a glimpse of Guise's relationship with this family, Charles tried to keep up a conversation with Douté, but it was hard going.

"Fernand?"

They both jumped slightly and turned. Guise had arrived behind them as soundlessly as a wraith. He stretched out his hands to Douté.

"I have been giving thanks that my godson is so much improved," he said. "And praying for his brother. I was about to come to you."

Douté held Guise's outstretched hands as though they were a lifeline. "Sebastian, I cannot stop asking myself how all this happened. Have you any more thoughts on where Philippe could be? Lisette is hysterical."

"Of course she is, *mon ami,* she loves them like her own."

Guise gestured a curt dismissal at Charles and led Douté to a pair of high-backed chairs placed against a wall. Ignoring his conscience's lecture on eavesdropping, Charles withdrew to the most shadowed corner of the antechamber, under the stairs.

"This worry over the boys is not at all good for Lisette," he heard Guise say gravely. "Not in her condition."

Douté murmured something Charles didn't catch. Then Guise's voice rose.

"No, no, Fernand, never think so, of course it was only an accident! The other is nothing but an evil story and I am sorry the rector made you hear it. But—forgive me—Père Le Picart is a peasant at heart and he takes the baker's stupid wife at her word. Our poor Antoine simply slipped in the eternal mud of Paris, and that drunken ass rode over him. An accident and nothing more. I have the word of a good honest man as witness to that."

Douté's sad basso murmured interrogatively.

"Yes," Guise said, "this man saw everything and that is what he swears. Of course no one meant to harm the child! You can make yourself easy on that point. Now. Tell me again what you have done to find Philippe, so that my efforts do not waste time by duplicating yours."

"I don't know what more to do, Sebastian! I have spoken or sent messages to all our family and friends here in town. No one has seen the boy. My manservant asked at livery stables round about if Philippe had hired a horse, but learned nothing."

Both voices dropped into antiphonal murmuring until a chair creaked and Douté said clearly, "I pray that he will simply come home. If God will grant me that, and Antoine's recovery, I swear I will never trouble Him for anything else." He sighed like a small bellows. "Now I must go back to Lisette."

"I will come with you. Let me get a candle to light us."

Taking the stairs silently and two at a time, Charles climbed to the staircase landing, where his cassock made him one more black shadow in the darkness. Douté followed Guise to the salon doorway, which was directly beneath Charles, and Guise came into the antechamber, took a candle from the side table, and lit it from a sconce.

"If Philippe is at home when I get back," Douté said, "I will have his miserable hide for causing us this worry. God knows I already have too much worry without breaking my heart over the boys. You know the old Condé is failing. And if he dies— when he dies, God save him—what am I to do? His son will not want me as secretary. And, to tell the truth, I do not want him. A strange man and his temper is foul. I tell you, too, I am at my wit's end with Lisette—she is terrified about this birth. Adeline was never like that." Douté sighed again and the flame of Guise's candle wavered. "But I suppose I must make allowances. Lisette is so young—and her own mother died when she was born, I suppose I must remember that, too. The poor girl badgers me every day to go to Chartres and pray before Le Saint Prepuce for her safe delivery." Douté let out a small bark of laughter. "Can you see me doing that?"

Charles smothered his own laughter. One of his aunts was a fervent believer in the childbed virtues of Le Saint Prepuce, Our Lord's Holy Foreskin. Treasured since His circumcision, it was touted as the only part of Him left behind on earth. Charles had often thought that it must have been of an impressive size, since so many places claimed parts of it. A snippet displayed in a sumptuous reliquary at Chartres attracted droves of pilgrims. Mostly women, of course, but always with a sprinkling of sheepish men, according to Charles's aunt.

Guise had turned from the table with his candle and was facing Douté, giving Charles a clear view of his disapproving expression. "There is no holier relic for childbed than Le Saint Prepuce, Fernand," he said severely. The candle flickered in the breath of his words. "Chartres is not so far away. And is it really so much to ask, to insure the safe delivery of a son—another son?"

"Well, well, I will see about going. There is time enough, she is only in her sixth month." He frowned anxiously. "Or is it seventh?"

"Go soon, Fernand. Children come in God's time."

Douté turned away and Guise watched him for a moment, a mixture of satisfaction and contempt on his face. Then he padded silently after his friend.

Charles climbed to his rooms and lit his own candle. He unlatched the window and leaned out, thinking about what he'd heard and seen. He supposed Guise had met Lisette Douté when he was at court seeing his noble penitents—"confessor to many at court," Guise had proudly informed Charles that first day at dinner. Though why anyone would choose Guise as confessor, Charles couldn't imagine. A breeze brought a faint stench of decay—from nothing worse than the dead cat that had claimed his new skullcap, he hoped—and he shut the window and took his meditations on mortality to the prie-dieu in the corner. Fixing his candle securely in the wall holder, he knelt and gazed at the small painting of the Virgin and Child on the wall in front of him. Then he said Compline and asked the Blessed Mother to protect Antoine, Pernelle, his uncle suffering in the galleys—if he still lived—and all prisoners, captives, and fugitives. Including the silly young idiot Philippe.

Charles stayed on his knees and tried to let the flowing, melting images that filled his mind carry him deeper, into wordless prayer. Instead, they carried him into the past. He saw himself on the June morning nine years ago, when he was still recovering from his war wound, and his father came to his chamber to tell him that Pernelle was married. He watched himself ignore his mother's fussing and go out through the vineyards to climb at a breathless snail's pace up a path yellow with dust. He watched himself take refuge in the cool shallow cave where he and his brother and sisters had played, where he and Pernelle had talked and kissed. He watched his nineteen-year-old heart shrivel and curl in on itself. Then he watched himself go home in the cool of the evening, as dry inside as the sunbaked path, and give all his energy to recovering, watched himself take leave of his parents a month later and go back to the army, resolved to die heroically and as soon as possible.

Even kneeling at the prie-dieu, Charles had to laugh. Instead of a heroic death, he'd gotten near fatal dysentery and been back home within the year, weak as a newborn puppy. During his long and difficult recovery, someone had loaned him a life of St. Ignatius. He'd read it and reread it, and when his strength finally returned, he'd presented himself at the Jesuit novitiate in Avignon.

He started to get up and then sank down again, remembering that he'd missed his hour of private meditation. Grimacing as his knees met the kneeling bench's worn padding, he yawned and set himself to imagine a scene from the life of Christ and then imagine himself into it, as St. Ignatius had taught. He found himself imagining Mary's baby as a little boy Antoine's age, getting in the way in the carpenter shop, bothering his mother with questions, playing noisily in the street with other boys. Had Mary worried that those long-ago streets were dangerous for children? Charles yawned again and the candle flickered. The Virgin's sad eyes seemed to sharpen their gaze. His own eyes closed, and he heard her soft voice.

Philippe is nearly at the river, she said, *run if you want to catch him.* Charles sprinted out of the college and along the rue St. Jacques. The night sky was as brilliant with stars as the sky in his mother's old painted Book of Hours. All of Paris was silent, holding its breath until Philippe was found. Suddenly Charles saw him, running toward the Petit Pont, his yellow shirt shimmering in the starlight. Charles overtook him in a burst of speed and grabbed his shirt. Philippe spun around, laughing behind a half mask. Twisting out of Charles's grip, he flung up his arm and the dagger in his hand flickered cold and bright.

Pain in his cheek woke Charles. He'd slumped down on the prie-dieu and the sharp edge of its little shelf, where his elbows should have been, was pressing into his face. The candle had gone out and Mary and the Child were as black as the wall. He got stiffly to his feet, shed his cassock, and felt his way to bed. As he slid under the covers, he made the sign of the cross against dreams or anything else that might try to follow him into the little death of sleep.

Chapter 9

When the rhetoric class began the next afternoon, Père Jouvancy was still not there. Charles and Maître Beauchamps shrugged worriedly at each other and set the boys to work. While the rest of the college enjoyed Saturday afternoon's rest, the senior rhetoric class rehearsed grimly, still without a Hercules, in an atmosphere charged with unspoken questions over Philippe's continuing absence. Beauchamps hissed scalding corrections through his teeth. The dancers were preternaturally quiet and made more mistakes than usual. At the other end of the room, Charles set the actors to relearn lines that had evaporated from their brains overnight and then stood watching Beauchamps. It was still not the moment to settle the clock problem, but there was obviously never going to be a right moment and he had to do it before Jouvancy returned.

When a pair of dancers finished capering through a piece of buffoonery as misguided Huguenots, Beauchamps gave the cast a short break and Charles beckoned him to the windows. Beauchamps heard him out without moving a muscle. Then he turned his head slightly and glared one-eyed at Charles, like a falcon considering a skinny rabbit.

"No clock? *No* clock? First we have no Hercules—oh, I *had* a new Hercules. A perfect Hercules. M. Louis Pecour, perhaps the most perfect dancer now alive. Who would be a better Hercules than Louis Pecour? No one. Who twisted his cursed ankle and will not be walking for a week, much less dancing? Louis Pecour. Now you say we are to have no clock. Perhaps no ballet master? No ballet?"

"No, *maître*, no, not at all! But I agree with Père Jouvancy that the clock will be too much for the boy who has to wear it. And since you have not even begun working with it yet—"

"It was late from the workshop. Someone smashed the first one. The boy is to begin wearing it today."

"*Maître*—once—at Carpentras—" Charles grimaced inwardly, wishing he hadn't chosen an opening that sounded so much like "once on a time." "We had a beautiful headdress—as your clock is, I'm sure—well, our headdress was for Fortune. A departure from Ripa's design, you understand."

Cesare Ripa's book of characters and costume designs had guided ballet producers for nearly a century, and Charles knew it almost by heart. As Beauchamps certainly did, also.

Beauchamps blinked very slowly. "Really?"

"Yes, our headdress was a wheel." Charles could hear his desperation making the story sound more like a fabrication with every word. "Fortune tried to wear the wheel, but he couldn't manage it—not with the skirt and everything. Well, the headdress crashed to the floor and the audience laughed. And threw bottles, *maître!*" Well, one bottle, and the thrower, when sober, had apologized abjectly and made a handsome contribution to the ballet expenses. But Charles didn't see the need to say that. "So, you see, from my experience at Carpentras—"

"Pardon me. Your . . . experience, you call it?" Beauchamps made the word sound like someone's dirty laundry. "A mere few years, Père Jouvancy told me. In his *Ancient and Modern Ballets*, your own Père Menestrier directs us to force dancers—*force* them, do you hear?——to wear the headdress that goes with the costume! My chiming clock goes with Time's costume and Time will wear it."

"But, *maître,* Time does not even appear as a character in Père Jouvancy's livret——and, you must admit, the minuet he wants for the four seasons would be an easier way for student dancers to show the passing of time——"

"Spare me, Maître du Luc. You well know that we've seen those same damn four seasons a hundred damn times in as many damn ballets! My clock will strike fear into the audience's hearts. With their own ears they will hear time running out for heretics." Beauchamps glared at Charles. "Time. Running out, Maître du Luc. And not only for heretics." He turned on his heel. "Here, you! Time!"

A slender Irish boy named Walter Connor, resting with the others on the floor, jumped to his feet. Beauchamps flung open a three-foot wooden chest his servant had brought and took out a long, bulky parcel swathed in coarse cloth. He unwrapped a perfect imitation of the sort of clock a rich man might have in his salon. Black and gold, solidly made of wire and papier-mâché and fixed to a small leather cap, it was as tall as Charles's forearm was long. Beauchamps placed it tenderly on Time's dark curly head, tied the cap's linen straps tightly under the boy's spotty chin, and stepped back. "Now, M. Connor, as you dance your sarabande, you will tilt your head in perfect time on the first beat of each measure. Like this. A little right, a little left, a little right——you see?——so that the clock chimes. Do you have it? Good. Now."

Connor clutched at the towering headdress. "No, *maître,* wait——"

Beauchamps seized his violin, yelled Time's suite into position, and called the cue. For the first eight measures and their slow, simple steps, it worked. Apart from the look of terror on the boy's face, the effect was impressive. The headdress chimed like the knell of doom. But when the sarabande's steps grew more complex, doom fell on M. Connor. Trying to balance on one foot and wobbling with the weight of the slipping clock, he clutched it with both hands and shoved it upright. Beauchamps growled and kept playing. Charles nodded encouragingly over Beauchamps's shoulder and winked. Connor stared back. Then, with a fleeting grin and a convincing stumble, he clutched at the clock again and one of its straps broke. With an anguished yelp, Beauchamps stopped playing. Feeling that he'd planted a good healthy seed of discord likely to bear the fruit Jouvancy wanted, Charles winked again and left them to it.

At the tragedy end of the room, the Montmorency boy playing Clovis, king of the Franks, was drawing his sword and advancing on his hapless foe and kinsman Ragnacaire.

"Why have you permitted our noble blood to be humiliated?" Clovis thundered. "It were better you should die!"

Whereupon—rather basely, Charles thought, considering that Ragnacaire was shackled—Clovis slew him with a mighty sword swipe. Ragnacaire, played by a languidly handsome son of the Grand Général of Lithuania, sank very carefully to the floor, as though testing an uninviting bed.

"Not like that, you willow wand! Die like a man!" Clovis threw down the wooden sword, clutched his chest, staggered, rolled his eyes, and thudded to the floor like a felled cow.

Ragnacaire sighed and propped himself on one elbow. "Excess is *so* unworthy of a man of taste, Monsieur Montmorency."

Montmorency scowled and swelled, and Charles quickly went to demonstrate stage dying. After several convincing deaths, he

picked himself up, told them to do the scene again, and stood
back to watch. Clovis thundered his line with true conviction.
Ragnacaire died a little more convincingly. Charles nodded to
them to keep going.

Though Jouvancy's Latin was a delight to the ear, Charles
was finding that he disliked the tragedy's story even more than
the ballet's livret. Clovis/Louis waged war everywhere, killing
and looting, regardless of treaties or anything else except his
own will and craving for glory. Then Clovis married a Christian, who was, of course, an allegory for Louis's devout second
wife, Mme de Maintenon. On the brink of defeat in battle,
Clovis—here recalling the emperor Constantine—prayed to the
Christian God for victory, got it, and was baptized, along with
three thousand of his pagan warriors. Thus uniting his realm in
"the most perfect religious and patriotic harmony," as Louis
had supposedly done in revoking the Edict of Nantes.

Charles called a break. The actors broke into small, chattering groups, flinging themselves to the floor to rest or helping
themselves from the pitchers of water standing ready on a table.
Charles answered a few questions, gave suggestions and corrections, and withdrew to the windows. For a miracle, it was another warm day and the courtyard was bathed in sunshine. He
leaned out and, squinting up at the cluster of sundials engraved
on the south-facing observatory tower, figured that the rehearsal
had three-quarters of an hour yet to go. When he looked back
at the courtyard, Père Jouvancy was hurrying across it. Charles
went to the classroom door to meet him.

"Welcome back, *mon père!* Did you have any luck at the college house in Gentilly?"

"None. I have just been with the rector, who has called in
Lieutenant-Général La Reynie. He is the head of our police." A

brief smile lit Jouvancy's tired face. "I have also seen Antoine. Who is ravenously hungry, his usual state, and the best of signs, thank God."

"Thank God indeed!"

"Now. Tell me what you and M. Beauchamps have done here and I will take over. Père Le Picart wants to see you."

"Me? Now?"

"Yes, and you must not keep him waiting."

Charles gave a brief report, ending with the chiming clock situation and leaving Jouvancy stifling laughter. Charles crunched across the gravel's white glare, hoping that this summons didn't mean that last night's eavesdropping had been found out. As he entered the grand salon, off which the rector's study opened, a tall, powerfully built man, no longer young but still an imposing presence, emerged from the study and shut the door behind him. He nodded to Charles and strode across the salon toward the street passage. Charles tapped on the rector's door.

"Come," Père Le Picart called, and Charles stepped into a cool, east-facing room with a high-beamed ceiling and a silky carpet in faded reds and greens on the worn wide-boarded floor. The one small casement of old, green-tinged glass stood open to the courtyard, letting in the sounds of passing feet, an occasional burst of chatter, and the faint noise of street traffic.

Charles bowed. Le Picart rose from the chair behind his desk and gestured Charles to one of a pair of chairs beside the empty fireplace.

"A little wine, Maître du Luc?" He picked up the pottery pitcher on the table between the chairs, poured pale red wine into the waiting cone-shaped glasses, and sat down facing Charles.

"Thank you, *mon père.*"

Though watered as usual, the wine was welcome on a hot

afternoon. As they sipped, Charles studied the rector. Le Picart's lean face was lined and strongly boned, his short thick hair was gray, and traces of peasant Normandy lingered in his voice.

As though he'd heard what Charles was thinking, he smiled over his glass and said, "This time of year at home, we're starting to think of cider. My village is on the edge of Normandy, and my father had an orchard with good Norman apple trees."

"I am fond of cider, too, *mon père*. My mother comes from Normandy."

"Ah. I wondered. Most from the south are dark, but you have the true look of the old North raiders. How did your parents meet?"

"They met at court, at Fontainebleau. My mother was one of the Dowager Queen's ladies and my father was making his brief and only effort to improve his fortunes by gaining the court's notice. When I was little"—Charles laughed—"she used to tease my father, who was shorter and darker, and say that no one would believe I was his child. And he would tease her back, and say, 'whose, then, wench?' And we would all fall down laughing."

"They must have been close, your father and mother! Not many men will be teased in that way."

"Yes, they were close. We all were."

"You were a happy child, then." Le Picart smiled a little sadly. "Children. They should all be happy. Well, at least our Antoine is recovering. But you probably know that Philippe is still missing. The man who left just before you arrived is Nicolas de La Reynie, our Lieutenant-Général of police. I have asked him to search for Philippe. Which is why I have taken you away from your rehearsal." The rector stared into the empty fireplace for a moment and then fixed Charles with a measuring look. "Mme LeClerc has been to see me, Maître du Luc. It seems you left Père Guise out of your story."

Charles sipped his wine to give himself a moment to think. "Yes, *mon père*, I did."

"Why?"

"She obviously dislikes him and—it seemed better to say nothing."

"Describe for me exactly what you saw Père Guise do."

"I saw him talking to a street porter. Mme LeClerc was watching them when I arrived. The porter seemed uneasy. I did not see Père Guise give the man money. Though I was not there all the time they talked."

"Did you speak with the porter yourself?"

"He was gone before I could."

"And what do you think now of Mme LeClerc's story?"

Gazing into his glass, Charles searched his impressions of the baker's wife. "On the whole, I believe her." He lifted his gaze to the rector. "Her anger at the horseman and her concern for Antoine were very convincing. And her bluntness. As I said in the infirmary, I wondered about the mask, though. And about her dislike of Père Guise." Charles smiled ruefully. "Many people are rude about priests, but usually not to the priest's face."

"True. You should know that Père Guise has sometimes taken it on himself to chastise the few shopkeepers who still rent space in our building's frontage for what he considers infractions of our rules. He has also clashed with Mme LeClerc over her small daughter, who has once or twice been found in our stable."

"Ah," Charles said, suddenly remembering the little girl in front of the baker's shop the day Antoine was hurt.

For a moment Le Picart's eyes had what Charles could only call a wicked gleam. "Mme LeClerc is one of the few people who has ever bested Père Guise, at least in volume." He lifted an eyebrow at Charles. "The college is not Eden, Maître du

Luc. Though some of us might think so, if we had only the one serpent."

Charles laughed outright, liking this rector more and more.

"So," Le Picart said. "I called you here because you are obviously taking an interest in what has happened to Antoine and Philippe, and I want you to understand some things. I am going somewhat beyond my writ in what I am about to say. Which you are to treat in the strictest confidence."

"Of course, *mon père.*"

"Père Guise has already been to see me about you. About your heretical views."

Charles went cold. He opened his mouth to defend himself but nothing came out. The rector held up a hand.

"Hear me out. The point—my point here, at least—is not your views, but Père Guise's. He is a brilliant man and a fiercely devoted priest. He is also a bad enemy. His fervor outruns his charity." Le Picart sighed. "The Guise fire from the Wars of Religion still burns hot in him. You know, of course, that his great-grandfather more or less started the wars. And led the Catholic League, paid for its army, and nearly put a Guise on the throne of France. They are themselves royal in a minor way, springing as they do from the House of Lorraine. Sadly—or not, depending on your views—Père Guise is the last male of his house. He pines for the lost Guise glory and seems to offer God a service of white-hot anger. I confess that I often do not know what to make of it. What God makes of it, I cannot imagine."

Charles sipped wine to wet his dry mouth. "And did he convince you my views are heretical?"

The rector eyed Charles. "He convinced me that your views are compassionate. Compassionate to a fault and dangerous. Are there Huguenots in your own family?"

Charles nodded warily.

"That must cause you great pain."

"For many reasons, *mon père*."

Le Picart got up and went to the open window. "We must never forget that we are Jesuits," he said quietly, gazing into the court. "But I have learned to be very wary of *any* man who is sure that he is as right as God."

"For my part, *mon père*, I am sure that cruelty in God's name is wrong."

In the silence that followed, feet ran across the gravel and boys' voices rose in shouts and laughter.

Le Picart turned to face him. "Many devout churchmen would argue passionately against that. And some would argue passionately for it. I do not expect us to settle that question. I do expect you to remember your vow of obedience."

"Yes, *mon père*." Charles began to breathe again.

Le Picart seemed to relax, too, and leaned back against the stone sill. "There is more I want you to understand about this college. Père Guise has no doubt told you that he is confessor to courtiers—I fear he tells everyone at the first opportunity. Although the king shuns Paris, we are only a few leagues from Versailles. This college's links to men—and women—close to the king are, to say the least, intricate. M. Louvois, perhaps the most powerful man in the realm after the king, was educated here. As was the father of Philippe and Antoine, who is now secretary to the Prince of Condé. Condé is a Bourbon, a Prince of the Blood, close kin to King Louis. Now. In himself, M. Douté seems an innocuous man. Well-meaning. A careful secretary, no doubt, but not, I fear, particularly discerning. Witness his choice of a second wife. Nevertheless, he has been close to the old Condé for many years. Though the Prince of Condé appears not to take an active role in the world anymore, his influence has been nearly that of a king. Indeed, it would be a mistake to underestimate it even now. Even though he has long been pardoned, he was one of King Louis's most powerful enemies forty years ago in the nobles' Fronde revolution, as you no doubt know. I say all this, because what has happened to the boys may—just possibly—mean that someone is using them to get at their father—and, through him, at the Condé. M. Douté says that is not so. But I think he would say that, if he were caught in that kind of coil. I have begun to fear that Philippe may have been lured out of the college to be taken and held somewhere. And that Antoine's accident may not have been an accident. Which is why I have called in the head of the police. And why I am telling you to leave these matters strictly alone."

"But, *mon père*—"

The rector stopped him with a look. "When you came to the infirmary after Antoine was hurt, I saw that you are a man who wants to understand events. And you confirm that impression every moment. You are one of those who cannot resist the thread that leads into the maze. But under your vow of obedience, Maître du Luc, let the thread lie. Others will follow it. Others with more understanding of this particular maze than you can possibly have."

"But—"

The rector's eyes turned cold. "I have given you an order, *maître*."

Charles bowed his head and forced the words across his tongue. "Yes, *mon père*."

"Good." Le Picart got to his feet and Charles rose with him. "I look forward to seeing your first Louis le Grand production," he said genially.

"Thank you for your good wishes, *mon père*." Charles made

himself smile politely. "And for all that you have explained to me."

He walked slowly back to the classroom, turning the conversation over in his mind and simmering with frustration. It was true that he didn't have Le Picart's knowledge of the tangled history and connections that might bear on what had happened. But he could put facts together and how could that come amiss to Lieutenant-Général La Reynie, who had the whole city to keep? And whether it came amiss or not, Charles told himself, he was already involved. Philippe was in the ballet and Charles had been sent to find him. And the cut on Antoine's head was still unexplained, and no matter how Charles looked at Guise's and Mme LeClerc's tellings of the accident, they did not match and he wanted to know why. Two such happenings to two brothers, in as many days, was too much coincidence; he wanted to know the truth. But he was a Jesuit and his superior had given him an order.

Partly to give his frustration time to settle, he passed the rhetoric classroom and went through the little archway to the outside latrine. The warmth was opening new blossoms on the thick hedge of old rosebushes, giving a faint sweetness to the air. But the stench inside the latrine nearly made him retch. Holding his breath and wondering when the dung cart had last carried away the waste, he went to the far end of the long bench, lifted his cassock, and started to unlace his breeches. Then he froze, staring into the hole's noisome murk. Something pale was growing there. Something like a five-petaled flower. Only, of course, it couldn't be. Flowers didn't grow in privy muck. Like someone in an evil dream, Charles reached down to pluck at whatever the thing was.

Chapter 10

Charles stumbled out of the latrine and wiped his fouled hand on the grass. Swallowing hard and trying to force his stomach back where it belonged, he relaced his breeches and went to the classroom. Père Jouvancy was rearranging the placement of actors in a scene and Charles let him finish, because what difference could haste make now? When the boys were placed to the rhetoric master's satisfaction, Charles took him aside. The color drained from the older man's face as he listened, and Charles reached for his arm, afraid he was going to faint. Jouvancy shook him off and blundered headlong toward the door, like a badly worked marionette. Hastily, Charles told the oblivious Beauchamps to oversee both rehearsals and ran after Jouvancy.

When Jouvancy had looked into the latrine hole and been sick behind the rosebushes, he and Charles took off their cassocks, rolled up their shirtsleeves, and went back into the shadowy stench. Charles pulled at the seat's front edge. With a protesting shriek of old hinges, a two-holed section lifted, opening a rectangle about four feet by two. When they finally had the body lying on the dirt floor, they were splashed with shit and urine, and swallowing hard. They knelt beside the body. Jouvancy wept as Charles gently wiped Philippe's face with his handkerchief. The young curve of the boy's cheek, where a beard had been just beginning to grow, emerged from the filth.

"Blessed Jesu," Jouvancy groaned, rocking back and forth on his knees as Charles scrubbed at Philippe's chest. "Oh, Philippe, dear child. How could this have happened? Only a very small child could have fallen in—I know that sometimes happens, but—"

"This was no accident," Charles said flatly. He was wiping at the boy's neck, staring at the swatch of discolored skin revealing itself. "Someone put him there."

Against a background of little boys' piping voices from a nearby classroom, they said the prayers for a violently dispatched and unshriven soul. Jouvancy reached out to caress Philippe's face and caught back a sob.

"He looked so much like my sister. He had Adeline's beautiful eyes. And her grace. Always her grace." He used Charles's shoulder to push himself shakily to his feet. "I must go for the rector."

"I will stay with him, *mon père*, and see that no one comes in."

When Jouvancy was gone, Charles stepped briefly outside and found a stick. He used it to stir the latrine's contents where he'd discovered Philippe, but found nothing more. He stood in the doorway, gulping clean air and feeling his grief and anger at what had been done to the boy sharpen into thought. Philippe's body was shirtless. Which made Charles grimly certain that the body had been here all the time, had already been here when someone shoved Charles to the ground and provoked the chase away from the latrine and out of the college.

A small boy hurtled around the rose hedge and stopped, staring wide-eyed at Charles.

"Yes, *mon brave*," Charles said wearily, "I am covered in shit. And no, you cannot come in. Piss somewhere else, please."

"But, *maître*—"

"Somewhere else. Please. Go."

The boy backed hurriedly away, his blue eyes growing even larger as Jouvancy, Le Picart, and two lay brothers carrying blankets came around the hedge. The rector watched the little boy stumble hastily toward a corner of the courtyard, still staring over his shoulder. Shaking his head, Le Picart motioned to the brothers to wait and went into the latrine with Charles and Jouvancy. Le Picart's eyes were wintry pools of sorrow as he signed a cross over Philippe's body. He turned to Jouvancy.

"I am so sorry, *mon père*. So very sorry." Ignoring the filth, he put an arm around Jouvancy's bowed shoulders. "We will take him to the washing room. Below the infirmary," he explained to Charles, "where we occasionally have to prepare bodies for burial—though we have no cemetery here, of course." He gave Charles a long, unreadable look. "Maître du Luc, when the body is clean, I want you to examine it. You were a soldier, you have seen violent death more often than most of us."

He led Charles and Jouvancy outside, where they waited for the lay brothers to wrap Philippe in the blankets they carried and bear him away.

"Will you search, please, Maître du Luc," the rector said, when the body was gone, "for anything in the latrine that seems out of place? It has been too many days, but we must try."

Trying to breathe as little as need be, Charles made his way slowly along the line of seats, scrutinizing the bench and the dirt floor, finding only leaves and grass tracked in from outside and bits of straw from the braided bundles for cleaning oneself that were kept in a wooden bucket beside the door. Eyes still on the ground, he retraced his steps to the corner where he'd found Philippe. As he stood there, staring at the floor and thinking about the yellow shirt and the hands that had shoved him to the ground, his eyes suddenly focused on what they were seeing. With the toe of his shoe he edged a clump of loose broken straw out of the corner and bent to look more closely at it. Its pieces were longer than the pieces that broke off the braided bundles. He picked up his find with his fingertips, sniffed cautiously at it, and carried it outside.

"Père Le Picart, this isn't from a straw bundle for cleaning. It seems to be a clump of stable straw, with traces of horse dung. Do students keep horses in our stable? Would they track this kind of straw into the latrine?"

The rector's eyebrows rose and Jouvancy wiped his eyes and looked at what Charles held.

"No," Le Picart said, "our stable is very small. We keep only our own few horses there."

"Does anyone from the college keep horses nearby?"

"Some of the older students do, mostly at the houses of family. Why would this clump of straw matter?"

"It was in the corner beside the hole where I found Philippe. I wonder how it got there."

Le Picart shrugged dismissively. "The stables are in the next courtyard and this is the nearest latrine. You found nothing else?" When Charles shook his head, Le Picart said, "Go and clean yourselves quickly, both of you, then come to me in the washing room." He looked at them ruefully. "You may have to bathe. But at least the day is warm." Although Jesuit colleges had a reputation for cleanliness, and students were expected to change their shirts every week or so since wearing clean linen was known to keep the body clean, bathing was infrequent and usually regarded with suspicion. Le Picart went the way the brothers had gone with their burden and Jouvancy turned to Charles.

"To the laundry," he said, steadied by having something mundane to do. "They won't be happy about it, but they'll give us a tub of hot water. The only other tubs are the one they'll use for Philippe—" His voice faltered. He cleared his throat and rushed on, "And the one in the infirmary. But if we go into Frère Brunet's domain like this, he will slay us." He looked distastefully at his filthy hands. "Some people say filth makes you ill. I hope not, because if we should be ill from this, Frère Brunet will make us bathe again."

"My mother forced us all into a tub every month or so, winter and summer," Charles said, glad to ease the moment with trivial talk.

"Really! Even though water can soak through the skin and harm the organs? You are not jesting? Well, I must say, bathing does not seem to have harmed you. But there, things are changing, after all. These new lenses—microscopes, I mean—do raise interesting questions. Some years ago, in Germany, our brilliant Father Athanasius Kircher—you know his work, of course—said he saw a little worm in the blood of plague victims that was not there in the blood of healthy people. Some people think the worm generates in dirt and causes plague. I am not so sure, but I did look through a lens once."

"What did you see?"

"Little wriggling things like Père Kircher's worm. I was astonished! And do you know what it made me wonder? Whether we might someday make a lens that allows us to see God! I don't mean any blasphemy, but—if a lens lets us see these things too small for the eye alone, then perhaps, on the other end of the scale, so to speak . . ."

Jouvancy talked on, pouring the balm of words over his raw shock and grief, and Charles found himself thinking of a young marquis who'd kept him from bleeding to death when he'd been wounded in the Spanish Netherlands, in the battle of St. Omer. The boy had stripped off his own shirt, rolled it into a ball, and held it against Charles's mangled shoulder, talking knowledge-ably and desperately about wine while Charles's blood soaked into the linen and the cart picking up the wounded inched toward them.

The lay brothers in the laundry were as little pleased as Jouvancy had said they would be, but they parted with a tub of just-heated water, provided towels, and fetched them clean clothes. Half an hour later, feeling unpleasantly boiled and with water still dripping from their hair, Jouvancy and Charles joined the rector in the room behind the infirmarian's workshop. Philippe's body, stripped and washed, lay on a long table. Now that the body was clean, its youth was even more heartbreaking. Steeling himself, Charles picked up one of Philippe's hands to look for signs of a fight. He found no marks at all on the hands, but the one sign he did find on the body was definitive. The deeply incised mark around Philippe's neck told them beyond doubt that the boy had been strangled. But the mark was oddly varied—several-stranded at the sides and patterned—braided, perhaps—at the throat. With aching tenderness, Jouvancy folded the boy's slender, unlined hands over his chest and pulled the shroud up over him.

His voice shook as he said, "Do you think he was in the latrine all this time?"

"Most likely," Charles said. "The death stiffness has come and gone, and decay looks well advanced. Because of the heat in—in the latrine."

"At least we know now how he was killed. But I would have had the killer use some other means," Le Picart said.

Charles and Jouvancy looked at him in surprise. Then Charles began to nod, but Jouvancy blinked in confusion. "Why?"

"If he had been killed with an obvious weapon," Le Picart said gently, "finding the killer would be easier. Since we forbid all weapons here, a dagger or sword or pistol might be traced to its owner that much more easily. But strangled—every one of us wears something in his clothing that could be woven with other pieces to leave a mark like this."

"Pieces of breech lacing braided together," Charles said, "or even long shoe ribbons might do it."

"Or the cords we string our crosses on," the rector offered.

"The ties that gather shirtsleeves to the wrist," Jouvancy said, "yes, I see. But—"

"And the older among us string our spectacles around our necks," Le Picart went on. He reached into his cassock and brought out his reading spectacles, hanging on a stout length of cord.

"Not to mention all the other kinds of cord and string there must be around the college," Charles said.

"Around the college? But, surely—" Jouvancy's voice trailed off.

"So the question is," Charles went on, "what kind of thing would exactly fit this mark. You can see that the braided pieces are thin, but not too thin. And they would have to be strong. Stronger than ordinary string, certainly."

Jouvancy frowned. "Would there be marks left on whatever was used?"

"There would be blood, the skin on his neck is broken. Though some—maybe even all—of that could be cleaned off, and would have been by now. I don't see any material left in the wound that could tell us what was used."

The rector was shaking his head impatiently. "If you had just strangled someone in a latrine, what would you do next?"

"Weight whatever I had used and drop it in," Charles said promptly.

"Exactly. You seem to be the only one of us without a talent

for murder, *mon père*," Le Picart said to Jouvancy, who was looking at them in alarm. Then the rector frowned. "I rarely visit
that latrine, but I saw today that it is over-full of waste. I will
have to check with Père Montville, but I am nearly certain that
it was supposed to have been cleaned several days ago."

"We could have it cleaned now and look for this cord, or
whatever it is," said Jouvancy.

"But, *mon père*," Charles said, "imagine how many broken
lengths of breeches lacing and other odds and ends of cord
must surely be in there. And with all that they will have soaked
up by now——" he grimaced and shrugged.

"I agree," Le Picart said. "Time will be better spent searching for the killer in other ways. Maître du Luc, the man you
chased when Philippe disappeared—are you still certain that he
was wearing Philippe's shirt?"

"Unless it really was Philippe, and he came back later and
was killed then. Which is possible, but unlikely, I think. The
yellow shirt and the dark hair and the build were enough like
Philippe's that I never doubted it was him I was chasing. But, as
you saw, when I found Philippe's body, the shirt was gone. I
fished for it in the latrine and did not find it. Also, when I went
looking for him that day, someone pushed me to the ground
from behind. I thought then it was Philippe. Now I think it was
the killer, making sure I would give chase and leading me away
from the latrine and the college. Probably so we would not in-
stitute a thorough search here before the body sank in the latrine."

"That seems a logical conclusion," the rector said grimly. He
looked from Jouvancy to Charles. "You understand, I trust,
how essential it is, as we search for this killer, to avoid scandal
to the college and the Society."

"We? Are you not calling in the police?" Charles said, trying to keep the note of challenge out of his voice and wondering just how far Le Picart would go to avoid scandal. "The college of Louis le Grand is still a liberty, then? The king's law does not run here?"

"Of course it does." Le Picart's chin lifted and he drew himself up. "And of course I will ask the help of Lieutenant-Général La Reynie. I had already asked him to search for Philippe. As you know. My point is that we must do everything morally possible to avoid scandal to the college and the Society of Jesus. The decisions that must be made to find the killer will be made by those in authority, Maître du Luc. With regard to your own involvement, I advise you to remember our very recent conversation in my office."

Into the ensuing silence, Jouvancy said, "This is going to kill his father."

"*Mon père*," the rector said gently, "M. Douté is lodging at the Prince of Condé's townhouse. Will you go to him? This terrible news will come better from family."

"Of course, I will go immediately." Jouvancy hesitated. "Do you want me to take Père Guise with me? He is almost closer to them these days than I am, it seems."

"No. Just you, *mon père*."

Jouvancy bowed his head in acquiescence. And relief, Charles thought. But suddenly, the rhetoric master's eyes widened and he clutched the rector's sleeve. "What about Antoine, *mon père*? Could this mean that he, too, is in danger? Though that seems . . . why would anyone . . . after all, it was only an accident . . ." He looked in mute appeal at Le Picart.

"Antoine is safe in the infirmary," the rector said. "And we will all be on our guard. This evening I will gather the faculty, and after them the lay brothers, and find out if anyone knows more about this. I have already told Philippe's confessor and his tutor what has happened. They are coming to take the first watch beside the body. For now, we must do our best to keep this from the students. I do not want it to grow in the telling into some farfetched drama that will only confuse things. Did you recognize the little boy who was wanting to use the latrine when we arrived there, Père Jouvancy?"

"Yes, *mon père*, that was Robert Boisvert. From Rheims. He is new and very shy. I doubt he has told anyone about his vision of a shit-covered professor." Jouvancy gave Charles the ghost of a smile. "I will have a word with him before I leave." The smile fled as Jouvancy laid a gentle hand on Philippe's body. He started to speak, but his mouth quivered and he pressed his lips together until he had mastered himself. "How will we ever find his killer," he said, "with all of Paris to search?"

"Unfortunately, we cannot assume that the killer is beyond our walls," Le Picart said.

Jouvancy stared at him. "But—I can hardly imagine—" He shook his head as if to clear it. "Are you saying, *mon père*, that until this man is found, we must look askance at everyone here—at least at everyone who shares Philippe's height and build and coloring?"

"Yes," the rector said flatly. "Everyone."

Chapter 11

The summer dark finally came, but Charles lay awake, thinking about Philippe Douté, imagining the air growing thick
with prayers around his coffin. Every time he closed his eyes, he
saw Philippe's body as it was when he'd pulled it from the latrine. He flopped over onto his back and distracted himself by
reliving the tense gathering of the Louis le Grand faculty earlier
that evening. Leaving a skeleton staff of proctors to see to the
students, Père Le Picart had called the professors and tutors to
the chapel and told them baldly that Philippe had been murdered. Everyone, of course, had been horrified and, equally of
course, no one had admitted to knowing anything. Père Guise,
magisterial and grim, had risen to ask who had been the last to
see Philippe alive, looking all the while at Charles. Charles had
patiently recounted being sent from the classroom to find the
boy, which nearly everyone already knew. Guise had stood again
to ask how long Charles had been gone on this errand. Twenty
minutes, perhaps a little more, Charles had said. Too long,
Guise had said with ominous quietness. Much too long. Long
enough, perhaps, to strangle Philippe? I did not even know
Philippe, Charles had replied furiously. As they glared at each
other in the charged silence that followed, old Père Dainville
had bounced up with surprising agility, called ringingly for

charity in this most difficult and unprecedented time, and added a tart warning about letting feeling falsify the premises of one's arguments.

At the rector's nod, his assistant, Père Montville, had stood, gestured politely but firmly for Charles and Guise to sit, and shocked the assembly into silence by asking them to rise one by one and briefly state where they'd been at half after two on Monday afternoon, when Philippe left the classroom. Guise was the first to respond, his reproachful baritone filling the chapel as he told them he'd been in the rue Paradis, summoned on family business to the Hôtel de Guise by his aunt. When all who could remember where they'd been had said so, Montville directed the others to come to him privately and then laid out what everyone was to watch for, charging them to bring anything they saw or heard or remembered to the rector or himself. And not to speak of the murder yet to students or anyone else. Then he'd poured political oil on the turbulent waters, telling them that as they thought back to that day, they would surely remember any strangers they'd seen, since the killer, of course, must have come from outside. With a final stern reminder of the danger of scandal to the Society and the college, Le Picart had closed the meeting with prayer.

Charles turned over again and told himself to leave his questions for now and go to sleep or he'd never make it through tomorrow. He was beating his thin pillow into a more comfortable shape when a heavy thump from the little salon made him sit up, listening intently as a vision of Guise creeping toward him rose in his mind. Telling himself not to be an idiot, he gave his pillow a last punch and lay down. And shot to his feet as his door opened a few inches. Mentally cursing the old monastic tradition of lockless sleeping quarters, he heard a soft intake of breath and then the creak of boards as whoever it was retreated.

Charles went soundlessly to the door, looked out, and hastily crossed himself. A small figure, glimmering white in the darkness, was vanishing into Guise's chamber, which was almost directly across from Charles's.

Charles hesitated, then hastily drew on his cassock and tiptoed across the passage. Heavenly messengers wouldn't need to open doors, and the white around this one's head looked more like a bandage than a halo. The lambent light in Guise's chamber was just enough to show him that it was empty and he went softly across it to the adjoining study. Guise wasn't there, but the apparition was.

"Antoine?"

The small white shape whirled away from the far wall where it was standing in front of a tapestry. It stretched its arms out stiffly, took a step, and crumpled to the floor with a loud moan. Hoping that the child hadn't hit his head again in the course of his performance, Charles went to him and shook him gently by the shoulder.

"Get up, it's all right."

But Antoine didn't and Charles was afraid that Guise would come back at any moment. He gathered the boy up and carried him into the passage, shut Guise's door, and hurried down the stairs. As they passed beneath a landing window, Charles looked down at Antoine in time to see the brief bright gleam of an eye.

"Are you all right, *mon petit?*"

The little body went as still as a hunted rabbit.

"What were you doing in there? Where is your godfather?"

Antoine squeezed his eyes more tightly shut and stayed as mute as a rabbit. When they reached the infirmary, Charles put him down on the disheveled narrow bed and spread the blanket over him.

"Frère Brunet," he called. "Wake up, please, *mon frère.*"

The soft snores from the adjoining chamber turned to gurgles and snorts, and the infirmarian appeared in the doorway in his long shirt, blinking and yawning.

"What is it? Is someone ill?"

"It's Antoine Douté. I found him in the main building," Charles said loudly and clearly, watching the child's suspiciously still face. "Sleepwalking, it seemed."

Brunet took the oil lamp from its bracket and bustled over to the bed. He set the lamp on the bedside table, felt Antoine's forehead below the bandage, and lifted one of his eyelids. "Sleepwalking? I didn't know that he sleepwalks. Tsk. He's chilled. But his pulse is steady. You did well not to wake him. Now he just needs to be warmed." He tucked the blanket around Antoine and peered up at Charles. "It's Maître du Luc, isn't it? It's good that you found him, *maître*. I'll sit with him to see he stays put and give him something soothing if he wakes."

"*Mon frère?*" Charles nodded toward the inner chamber. "A word first?"

Brunet spread a second blanket over the child and led the way into his bare little room.

"Does Antoine remember the accident?" Charles ignored his conscience's quick sting at this violation of the rector's order to leave the accident and the murder alone. "Does he remember why he was out in the street?"

"He said something about finding a message—but I didn't pay much attention, he was still not himself."

"A message? From whom?"

"He kept talking about his brother, poor little scrap." Brunet sighed so gustily that his belly shook under his cassock. "He doesn't know about Philippe yet, I hadn't the heart to tell him. I tell you, I dread that moment." Brunet hesitated and leaned closer. "Is it true you chased the murderer?"

"I think so."

Brunet shuddered. "But how did he get in unseen?"

"Perhaps the same way he got out," Charles said, without adding, *if* he got out. "Over the wall beside the stable."

"Still—it's odd no one saw him. The windows of the students' library—that's different from the big new library, you might not know that yet, *maître*—overlook the latrine court. And he'd have to pass the lay brothers' kitchen, there's usually some of us there, and the same for the stable. So you have to wonder . . ."

"Wonder what?" Charles said.

"Whether the murderer was human," Brunet whispered. "Or maybe just invisible," he added judiciously.

Charles grunted noncommittally. Many people, even Jesuits, still believed such things. He did not. Though, when he'd first glimpsed Antoine in the dark just now . . . and God knew, there were enough unexplained things in the world, in spite of the new science.

"The devil uses his own," Brunet was saying softly, gazing intently at Charles. "Witches, *maître*, we all know that. And he uses those poor damned priests who say Black Masses for people who want what the *bon Dieu* won't give—often women burdened with unwanted babes, I'm told. And actual demons, of course," he added matter-of-factly, "we know those are everywhere."

A huge yawn nearly dislocated Charles's jaw and he apologized. Even demons wouldn't be able to keep him awake much longer.

"Oh, dear, *maître*, here I keep talking and you probably haven't even slept yet, have you? Of course not, after finding poor Philippe like that. Would you like a sleeping draught? A valerian tisane? With a drop of poppy in it?"

Charles shuddered at the thought of valerian's musty odor

and shook his head. He wanted nothing to do with anything that smelled stronger than a flower. Then he thought of the roses beside the latrine and crossed flowers off the list as well.

"Thank you, *mon frère*, I think I'll sleep now. God give you and the child a good night."

But when Charles reached his own bed, he lay awake awhile longer, thinking about the message Antoine claimed he'd had. If there really had been a message, Philippe had almost certainly not written it. If Philippe had not written it, then someone had lured the child into the street and the accident had not been an accident. But why had Antoine been in Guise's study? And where was Guise? A trip to the downstairs latrine? But there was a close stool in Guise's chamber. Perhaps he was away for the night. At Versailles, under silken sheets, Charles thought sourly, turning over and wondering if he'd ever get to sleep. He was trying to decide whether it was less trouble to get up and close the window or to wait out a yowling cat, when his body finally relaxed and his eyes closed. Wheels were creaking up the hill toward the college. The untimely dung cart again, he thought vaguely. The wheels ceased their mournful groaning and angry voices rose and were shushed under his window, but Charles was finally asleep and heard nothing.

Chapter 12

"Domine, Iesu Christe, Rex gloriae, libera animas omnium fidelium defunctorum de poenis inferni et de profundo lacu. Libera eas de ore leonis . . ."

The funeral Mass's offertory prayer beat like a muffled bell against the black-draped chapel walls. From where he stood with the senior rhetoric class, Charles could just see Antoine, wearing only a small bandage over his cut now, and sitting rigidly upright beside his father on one of the cushioned chairs placed for the Douté family near the candle-banked coffin. The little boy's shoulders shook as he stared at his brother's coffin, draped with a silk pall so black, it seemed to absorb all the light there ever was or would be. The priest was asking God to "free the souls of all the faithful departed from infernal punishment," from "the deep pit" and "the mouth of the lion." "Lion" meant the devil, and Charles wondered if Antoine was not only grieving for Philippe's death, but worrying because he'd died unshriven.

Charles could hardly believe that it was only the twenty-ninth of July, that he'd been at Louis le Grand only a week and in that week, one of his students had been murdered. And that in barely more than another week, the ballet and tragedy would be performed. He tried to drag his mind back to the Mass as it neared the words that would make God present in the bread and wine. Philippe's cousin Jacques Douté, who was serving as acolyte, blinked away tears, picked up a little cluster of bells, and shook them as the rector raised the round white wafer above his head. The gay frivolity of the sound jarred against the dense funereal black of draped walls and coffin pall, vestments and mourning clothes, cassocks and scholar's gowns.

Charles's students were dignified and quiet, subdued into a preview of the manhood that would soon be upon them. Charles ached for their having to grapple with Philippe's death. Not that death was unfamiliar to anyone, young or old. Death descended on every family and took whom it would. But murder, especially the murder of a fellow student, was more than these boys should have to grieve for yet.

Sunlight streamed through the windows and threw a gold and ruby oriole around Père Le Picart and his assistant priests— Montville, Jouvancy, and Guise—as they moved about the altar. Charles tried not to watch Guise. He didn't want to swallow the Body of Christ into anger, but even if he did, he had to swallow it. Anyone who refused the sacrament today would set everyone else wondering what they had on their conscience.

Everyone communed and the Mass wound toward its end. "Eternal rest grant unto them, O Lord, and let perpetual light shine upon them." As Le Picart reached the "amen," a shrill wail rose from the front of the chapel, as though the soul of the departed were refusing to go anywhere, light or not. But the shrill voice was all too human and Charles wasn't the only one who recognized it. Students stifled nervous laughter, adults exchanged knowing looks, and Charles, hearing Mme Douté's name whispered through the nave, pitied Antoine and M. Douté from his heart. Then the organ burst into life, and it would have taken all the wails of hell itself to cut through the throbbing noise.

The Mass's celebrants and their attendants left the church in solemn procession, and the Doutés were escorted after them through the courtyard door. High-ranking mourners bidden to the funeral feast in the fathers' refectory went next. Resisting the urge to plug his ears that organ music always gave him, Charles waited until the way was clear and led his boys into the Cour d'honneur.

Glare bounced off the gravel, and in the courtyard's center, the little Temple of Rhetoric seemed to sag in the heat. The temple, an aging structure of thin wood and paper-mâché with a plank floor, was the last of the funeral decorations to have been assembled during the three days that Philippe's lead-coffined body had lain in state in the chapel. Charles and the rhetoric class had hastily extracted the structure from a cellar early that morning, and set it up to display poems and alle-gorical drawings (known as emblems) made by students and faculty to honor Philippe. After the funeral meal, the mourners would come to read the elegiac verses and study the emblems. For courtesy's sake—and to keep too many people from crowd-ing into the fragile structure—Charles and the rhetoric class would take turns guiding the mourners through a few at a time, speaking decorous Latin to the men—whether or not they un-derstood—and French to the women.

"What do we do if it falls down?" Armand Beauclaire whis-pered anxiously, as the students and Charles stood in a tight group, looking dubiously at the temple. In spite of all their ef-forts, its thin wood and tired paper-mâché looked what they were, shabby and worn with age.

"If it falls down, we act surprised," Charles said, drawing brief smiles from the somber young faces. "Meanwhile, let's be out of the sun. There's food and drink in the senior refectory—get yourselves something and wait there, I'll join you."

Admonishing them to keep their gowns on in spite of the

heat, he dismissed them to a chorus of groans and watched them cross the court, their scholars' gowns making them look like a flock of dejected young crows. Wishing he could shed his own cassock, he went up the temple's three shallow steps and repinned a swag of black drapery hanging between two pillars. Usually the Temple of Rhetoric was the scene of debate competitions and recitations from heroic tragedy, with laurel crowns handed out to the posturing winners. But today it was a monument to real tragedy.

"A terrible thing." The dancing master Pierre Beauchamps, just emerged from the chapel, stood at Charles's elbow, impeccably turned out in black taffeta breeches, knee-length coat with ebony buttons, and black plumed beaver hat. He shook out a black lace handkerchief and blotted his perspiring face with it. "Terrible!"

"Yes, *maître*, a tragedy," Charles answered, surprised and pleased that Beauchamps's feelings had extended beyond lamenting his heroless ballet to grieving for its dead hero.

"I told them last year to get rid of it," Beauchamps clarified, glowering at the temple. "The thing is a disgrace, it's falling apart."

Charles stared at him. "Hardly the worst thing about this day, *maître*."

The dancing master cocked an eyebrow at him. "You think me heartless? I watched Philippe grow up, from the day he came here. I trained him. He was perhaps the best dancer I ever trained outside the Academies and the professional theatre. Be assured that I will grieve for him. After this ballet is over. If it ever is over. I have found us a Hercules."

"What? Who?" Charles, too, forgot Philippe for a moment.

"A good enough dancer." Beauchamps sighed gustily. "But whether even I can make a hero out of him, Terpsichore, she only knows. Well. I shall be off, not being invited to the funeral feast. Not that I expected to be, of course." His voice dripped honeyed venom. "Though I was Philippe's teacher and nurtured his best talent. But we who are mere practitioners—and not noble theoreticians—know our humble place. Until tomorrow, Maître du Luc."

With an austere smile, Beauchamps stalked majestically toward the street door, pausing to raise his hat to a small plump woman dressed in plain black, who bustled out of the chapel and across his path. Mme LeClerc, Charles realized, as she threw up her hands and hastened toward two children talking animatedly together. As she pulled the little girl away, another woman swooped down on the boy, whom Charles saw now was Antoine. The woman hurried him away and Mme LeClerc made for Charles, towing the protesting little girl behind her.

"Bonjour, Maître du Luc, though a good day it hardly is, the poor young man. Little Antoine is heartbroken. As well he should be. No small thing to lose a brother. Marie-Ange and I stayed a moment in the chapel, praying to the Virgin for him. Ah, well. Make your reverence, Marie-Ange."

Mme LeClerc curtsied and pulled the child forward. Still scowling, the little girl studied Charles, who studied her gravely in return. She was perhaps eight or nine, with her mother's round brown eyes and curly, bright brown hair under her white coif. Her mother prodded her. With a much put-upon sigh, she fluffed her dark blue skirt and curtsied prettily.

"I suppose we shouldn't really be here," Mme LeClerc said, her work-roughened hands fussing with the black scarf loosely wound over her white coif and around her throat. "But we had to come. Antoine and Marie-Ange—"

"Maman, shhh!" The little girl shook her head and her curls danced.

Charles suddenly remembered the rector saying that Mme LeClerc's daughter sometimes strayed into the college stable.

"Maître du Luc won't mind, *ma petite.* Though I know your boys aren't supposed to play with girls," she said to Charles. "But they're just children, and it's only in the shop. That—" Her face darkened and Charles thought for a moment she was going to spit, but she restrained herself. "—that Guise would bring Antoine to buy a treat, or his brother would, and he and my little one took a liking to each other." She stopped for breath.

"Antoine needs friends." Charles smiled at Marie-Ange, who smiled back in surprise. "Especially now. The Doutés are taking Philippe back to Chantilly for burial, but Antoine is staying here."

Mme LeClerc frowned and stepped closer to Charles. "But, *maître,*" she hissed, "do you think that's wise?"

"Wise, madame?"

She looked over her shoulder to be sure no one else was near. "I hardly slept a wink last night," she whispered, "thinking about the poor young man they're burying and wondering if that masked man will try again for Antoine! Have you thought that he is likely the one who killed Philippe?"

The thought *had* certainly occurred to him, and Charles looked at Mme LeClerc with new respect. Her eyes darted warily around the court and she took a step toward the street passage, shooing Marie-Ange ahead of her.

"Will you see me to the postern, *maître?*" They began walking and she said, "One cannot accept it, *maître.* Two brothers attacked in three days? Who can believe in two villains?"

"Madame, you said that the horseman leaned down toward Antoine. Was there anything in his hand?"

She eyed him shrewdly. "Like a dagger, you mean? Not that

I saw. But a dagger would explain why he leaned so far. Nearly out of the saddle the man was. And how else did the child get that gushing cut?"

"When I got there, Antoine was lying on his back. Is that how he fell?"

"Yes, backward. I tell you, *maître*, my heart warns me that we have not seen the last of that man. If only Antoine were going home—anyone would think his parents would want him there at such a time!"

"His stepmother feels that he will be better off here at school than moping at home."

Her eyes narrowed. "Stepmother, is she? Ah. I see. Poor little cabbage. So how do you mean to find that man, *maître*?"

But before Charles could decide what to say, peals of laughter came from the street passage.

"Ah, *mon Dieu*, what is she doing now?" Mme LeClerc picked up her skirts and hurried ahead of him.

Marie-Ange was standing beside the postern door and Frère Martin, the porter, was rocking with laughter on his stool. When he saw Mme LeClerc, he heaved himself up, greeted her as an old friend, and nodded to Charles.

"Do you know what this child said, *maître*? I asked her if she knew her catechism, and she said she could tell me about Adam and Eve and the garden. So I said, 'Yes, do, *ma petite*.' And she said, 'Well, who is in the garden, *mon frère*?' " The brother shook with laughter. " 'In the garden,' she said, 'are *un pomme, deux poires, et beaucoup des pepins!*' One apple, two pears, and a lot of seeds! Seeds of sin, *maître*, get it? A doctor of the church, this one!"

Charles smiled politely at the old joke. *Poire* meant pear, but it also meant fool. Mme LeClerc had gone peony red. Marie-Ange was grinning at her own cleverness and avoiding her mother's eyes.

"I will kill Roger for telling her that," Mme LeClerc muttered as she took her daughter none too gently by the hand. *"Au revoir, maître. Mon frère."*

Still laughing, the brother opened the postern, and Mme LeClerc hurried Marie-Ange away. Charles went back to the Cour d'honneur, squinting in the harsh light and wondering how long the funeral feast would last. A musical peal of laughter made him catch his breath and look up. In a corner beyond the senior refectory, the usually dour lay brother Frère Fabre stood talking with a woman in plain mourning. Her back was to Charles and her head and shoulders were draped in a voluminous black scarf, but her laugh was as bright and full of life as the sunshine. So like Pernelle's laughter that he had to stop himself running across the gravel to see her face. Please God, he prayed, forcing himself to keep his measured pace, let Pernelle have a good life now, a life with laughter in it.

Without letting himself look more closely at the woman, he went into the refectory and scanned the crowd to be sure his students were still there and still gowned. When he saw them, he lifted a hand in greeting and went to the dais, where the food and drink were laid out. To his surprise, Fabre was already there as well.

"I didn't expect to see you back inside so soon," Charles said, as Fabre filled his plate and poured the watered wine. "I saw you in the court just now."

The young brother flushed so red that his freckles seemed to melt together. "It was nothing," he said hurriedly. "Only talk. I was hardly gone at all."

"Softly, *mon frère*, I am not accusing you of anything."

The boy turned away to refill the pitcher. "She's my sister."

Watching him curiously, Charles set his plate on the edge of the table and sipped his wine. He liked this boy, in spite of his prickliness. Or maybe even because of it. "How did you be-come a lay brother, *mon frère*? I am always interested in how men come to the Society."

Fabre gave him a wary glance. "My father is a tanner out by the Bièvre River." He shuddered. "A horrible, stinking trade. I begged our parish priest for schooling." Fabre rubbed at the water beaded on the pitcher. "He taught me to read a little and got me in here as a scholarship student. With a scholarship, you get to live in the college with the pensionnaires. Crowded together in a *dortoir*, but it's a higher place than being just a day boy." His face clouded. "But my reading never got better."

"But why? You obviously have more than enough wit for it."

Fabre ducked his head and smiled fleetingly at the compli-ment. Then he shrugged. "The letters won't stay still for me. They get backward on the page and I can't make out the words. Père Dainville thought I was possessed. He exorcised me, but I still couldn't read much. They said I had to leave, but Père Guise made them keep me as a lay brother."

"Père Guise?" Charles was too startled to cover his surprise.

Fabre turned away and busied himself rearranging a plate of tarts. "He said I would be a good servant."

"And are you content?"

"I am not a tanner." Fabre glanced at Charles, his eyes hard, and started filling plates for the group of boys approaching the table.

Charles joined his students. When a brother came to say that the feast was ending, they drained their glasses, trudged back into the sweltering courtyard, and positioned themselves on the temple steps. After another interminable wait, the guests ap-peared, walking in slow procession. M. and Mme Douté came first, escorted by Père Le Picart and Père Jouvancy. Mme Douté, a head shorter than her none-too-tall husband, walked slowly, her wide black brocade skirts swaying and her coming child apparent even under her long mourning veil. Behind them, red-eyed and tear-streaked, Antoine and his cousin Jacques Douté walked hand in hand. Père Guise came next with a veiled woman Charles had heard was Mme Douté's sister. Père Montville and a thin, gray-haired man representing the Prince of Condé's household followed. To Charles's surprise, the police chief Lieutenant-Général Nicolas de La Reynie, whom he had seen leaving the rector's office the day he found Philippe's body, was also in the line, companioned by a short round man Charles didn't know. The rest of the company, twenty or so relatives and friends, both clerics and lay, stretched behind them.

When the Doutés reached the Temple of Rhetoric, Le Picart and Jouvancy bowed and stepped back to allow them to enter the temple first. Moving at Mme Douté's slow pace, Charles ushered the bereaved couple up the steps. As he guided them through the temple, gently pointing out the compliments paid to Philippe, M. Douté wept openly. With barely a glance at each exhibit, his wife pulled on his arm to hurry him. Halfway through, she stopped and pushed her veil back. She had large brown eyes and fair hair, and would have been pretty had she not looked so fretful.

"I am hot, husband," she said. "And my back hurts me."

"Where is your maid?" M. Douté took a wet handkerchief from his sleeve and wiped his eyes. "Do not grudge me this last glimpse of my son, Lisette."

She reddened and her small pouting mouth opened, but the fat man who had walked with La Reynie appeared at the bottom of the steps that surrounded the open-sided temple, looking like a dark moon in his funeral black.

"Allow me, my dear Mme Douté," he purred. "Leave your poor husband to mourn." He mounted the steps, bowed to M. Douté, and with a severe look at Charles, as though Mme Douté's discomfort were his fault, led her out of the temple.

When M. Douté had thoroughly wrung Charles's heart by weeping over each tribute to Philippe, Charles murmured condolences and turned him over to the rector. For the next half hour or so, Charles kept watch over the student guides and answered questions about the exhibits, especially about the large drawing of Philippe as a fallen Hercules, shown lying gracefully on his cloak in a cypress grove, costumed as he would have been in the ballet. Achilles, Ulysses, Virgil, Homer, Hannibal, Julius Caesar, Apollo, Terpsichore, and Minerva stood weeping over him and a cohort of winged cherubs grasped the corners of his cloak, ready to carry him to heaven, where the Virgin Mary held out her arms to him from a cloud.

When everyone had made their way through the allegories, Charles rounded up his students, thanked them, and dismissed them to their chambers and the comfort of shedding their gowns. He longed to go to his own chamber and do likewise, but too many noble mourners still lingered in slices of shade along the western wall of the courtyard, murmuring and sipping from small glasses of sweet wine that the lay brothers were offering. M. and Mme Douté had already left on the sad journey back to Chantilly with Philippe's coffin.

Charles circulated briefly and then paused in the shade with a glass, watching men reach surreptitiously under their hats to lift their wigs and cool their sweating heads. The few women present stood whispering together, their black fans beating the air like the wings of funereal hummingbirds. Two of them drew apart and the shift of their stiff skirts and tall headdresses revealed Guise, deep in talk with the police chief and the fat man who had escorted Mme Douté from the temple. As though he felt Charles's eyes on him, Guise glanced up. He said something to his companions, who both looked at Charles. Not wanting an encounter with any of them, Charles moved toward a group of departing guests to say his formal farewell. But the police chief and the fat man cut off his escape.

"Maître Charles du Luc?" The westering sun scattered gold over the black plumes in Lieutenant-Général La Reynie's hat as he stopped in front of Charles.

"Yes, *monsieur*," Charles said. "May I help you?"

"I am Nicolas de La Reynie, Lieutenant-Général of Police." He turned to his companion. "Monsieur de Louvois, may I present Maître Charles du Luc?"

The little hairs stood up on the back of Charles's neck and he nearly lost his balance as he bowed. Michel de Louvois was in charge of the king's dragoons, the most powerful man in the kingdom after the king. And Charles had heard, since his first sighting of La Reynie, that the police chief was probably the third.

"You are new here, I understand," La Reynie said conversationally. "Newly come from the south. Nîmes, I believe?"

"Carpentras, *monsieur*." The words came out in a croak and Charles drank quickly to wet his throat, studying La Reynie over the edge of his glass. "You are searching for Philippe's killer, *monsieur*?" he said, hoping to turn the talk away from himself.

La Reynie inclined his head. "A shame that you arrived just in time for this terrible tragedy," he said, studying Charles in return.

"I did not know Philippe, *monsieur*, but I am told he was an honor to the college in every way."

"Did not know him," Louvois said flatly.

"No, *monsieur,* I regret that I did not."

"But he knew you." The war minister's little black eyes glittered with malice.

"Knew me? No, Monsieur Louvois. We met for the first time the afternoon he disappeared."

"Perhaps he knew *of* you, then," La Reynie put in helpfully.

In spite of the heat, a chill was creeping down Charles's back. "I very much doubt it, *messieurs.* I have no fame."

"Oh, I think you are too modest," La Reynie murmured.

Louvois said curtly, "Père Guise says that you were the last to see poor Philippe."

"His killer was the last to see him, *monsieur.* When he disappeared from the classroom, I was sent to find him. I chased someone wearing a yellow shirt, thinking he was Philippe."

Louvois's lip curled. "Though no one else saw this convenient phantom."

"He was no phantom, *monsieur.* And we would only know that no one else saw him if we could question everyone along the route he took. Which is, of course, impossible."

Louvois's eyes narrowed and he stepped closer. La Reynie stepped back, planted his silver-headed walking stick in front of him, and folded his hands over it, watching Charles.

"Père Guise says you were gone too long when you went to find Philippe." Louvois was breathing wine up into Charles's face now. "Far longer than necessary."

"I was gone a little more than twenty minutes. Which Père Guise knows. But perhaps he runs faster than I do."

"Do you think this is a jesting matter?" Louvois hissed. "We know nothing about you. Except that you come from the south. And hold heretical opinions."

A wave of pure fury at Guise broke over Charles. "I beg your pardon, Monsieur Louvois. I am not aware that believing in the love of God is heretical. May I suggest, *messieurs*, that you take your questions back to Père Guise? Unlike me, he knew Philippe well. Whatever led to the boy's disappearance and death, Père Guise is more likely to understand it than I."

Charles bowed and started to walk away, but Louvois grabbed his arm and jerked him sharply back. Charles winced as pain shot through his old injury, and his glass slipped from his hand and shattered on the gravel. He wrenched himself free and what might have happened next fortunately did not, because Antoine burst from nowhere, shoved Louvois aside, and wrapped his arms around Charles's waist, sobbing his heart out.

Chapter 13

W hat is it, *mon brave?*" Astonished, Charles swung Antoine away from the war minister's attempt to grab him and bent over the boy. "What has happened?"

Antoine's eyes darted sideways at Louvois, who was berating him for his intrusion. Charles saw that, in spite of the sobs, the child's dark eyes were as dry as the gravel.

"They've gone," Antoine choked, hiding his face on Charles's cassock and pulling him toward the adjoining courtyard so urgently that Charles nearly lost his footing. "Philippe is gone!"

"Forgive me, *messieurs*," Charles said over his shoulder, "but you see that I must attend to this grieving child."

He walked Antoine across the Cour d'honneur toward the north courtyard as fast as the boy's short legs could go. When they reached the dividing archway, Charles looked back. La Reynie had a hand on Louvois's arm, obviously restraining him, and Louvois was arguing furiously. But La Reynie was thoughtfully watching Charles.

When they were well into the north court, Antoine pulled away. "That showed them!" he said, looking up defiantly.

"Yes," Charles said, caught between laughter and bewilderment. "I think it did. My very sincere thanks, M. Douté. But why such a valiant rescue? We've hardly even met. Except when you—ah—sleepwalked, of course."

"And you knew I wasn't, but you didn't tell on me. And I *hate* old Louvois, he always tells on me and bullies me just like he was bullying you!"

"How do you know him, *mon petit*?"

Antoine scowled. "He comes to our house. And at my stepmother's birthday fête I asked him and Père Guise something and they said I was being rude and telling lies, and my father made me apologize and sent me to bed. And I missed the cakes!"

Charles made a sympathetic face and glanced at the group of boys and tutors talking and reading under a tree on the other side of the court. They seemed to be paying no attention to Antoine or to him. Charles said quietly, "Antoine, why were you in Père Guise's study that night?"

The boy's face closed like a shutter. "I can't tell you. It's a secret." Antoine looked around uneasily, his bravado suddenly gone. "*Maître*—could we speak in my chamber? It's just there." He pointed to the tall stone house on the east side of the court, a venerable survivor of one of the older colleges Louis le Grand had swallowed up, Charles guessed. He hesitated, trying to think of some other place to talk, since teachers were not supposed to go to students' chambers. But this was his chance to ask about the note Frère Brunet had mentioned.

"Is your tutor in your chamber?" Every well-born student had a private tutor—often a Jesuit scholastic like Charles—who supervised him, communicated his progress, or lack of it, to his parents, and oversaw the boy's daily life.

Antoine shrugged. "I don't know where he is."

"All right, then." It was the perfect excuse, since someone needed to keep an eye on the child until the errant tutor returned.

Antoine led him inside and up a staircase. The building was surprisingly quiet; classes had been suspended because of the funeral and some students had gone out with their families.

Though more lowly boarders shared small dormitories, six or eight to a room, Antoine's large chamber was private, as Philippe's no doubt had been. Its casement stood open and a tall lime tree reached companionably toward the stone sill. The bed looked deep and soft under its red wool coverlet, and there was a sturdy oak table, two chairs upholstered and fringed in rich brown, a flat-topped chest with a decorated lock, and a large carved cupboard. A brazier for heat in cold weather stood in a corner, and a small but good painting of the young John the Baptist playing with the infant Jesus hung at the foot of the bed. The tutor's more austere bed stood in a small alcove between the chamber and a half-open door revealing a study with several desks. Politely gesturing Charles to a chair, Antoine sat down on his bed. Charles turned the chair toward the bed and opened his mouth to ask about the note, but Antoine forestalled him.

"I wanted to go with them." The boy smoothed the bed's thick cover as though comforting an animal. "With my father. With Philippe." He looked up, his eyes suddenly blazing, and Charles had an uncanny sense of the older brother looking out of Antoine's black, long-lashed eyes. "My father wanted me to, but she said I couldn't and Père Guise made my father do what she wanted. Did you know Père Guise is my godfather? I wish he wasn't. My father argued, but she started crying about her baby and he gave in. He *always* gives in. I hate her! She said—" His eyes filled with tears, real tears this time. "She said I had to stay here and pray for Philippe, because he's probably in hell. Is he, *maître*?"

Choking on what he wanted to say about Lisette Douté,

Charles took a slow, deep breath. "No, Antoine, he is not," he said flatly.

"But he didn't make his confession before he died."

"That was not his fault. God still loves him, just as He loves you."

The boy looked up from bunching the cover into small red hills. "But Philippe ran away—that was his fault."

Charles stopped himself from saying that Philippe probably hadn't gone farther than the latrine. "Listen, Antoine. People do not go to hell just for being angry. Or scared."

"They don't?"

"They don't."

"Then, if God still loves Philippe, why did He let him get killed?"

Charles sighed. Why, indeed? "That is a very hard question, *mon brave*. Everyone asks it when someone they love dies. But if God reached down and stopped people from doing bad things, even very bad things like killing, then we would just be puppets. Like the marionettes at fairs. God makes us able to choose good or bad. Puppets can't choose anything."

But so many people couldn't choose much about their lives, Charles thought, remembering Frère Fabre. Charles and Antoine were two of the lucky ones. Antoine, who had stopped pulling at the coverlet and listened without moving, suddenly flung himself facedown in a storm of relieved weeping. In spite of the college rules, Charles went to sit beside him.

"I will tell you something else I think, Antoine. Everyone dies, but love never does. Philippe still loves you." He patted the heaving little back. "Just as much as you love him. He's safe with God now. Nothing else bad will ever happen to him. You don't have to worry."

He murmured and patted until Antoine gave a great, shuddering sigh and sat up. Charles handed him a crumpled linen towel from the table and went back to his chair. Antoine mopped his tears, blew his nose, and slid off the bed to kneel at Charles's feet.

"Forgive me, Father," he said, looking pleadingly at Charles. "For I have sinned."

Charles exclaimed in alarm and tried to raise the child to his feet. "I am not your confessor, I am not a priest yet. You cannot—"

"Please, I have to tell someone, *maître!*" the boy said desperately. "It's all my fault Philippe died. And nobody knows and everyone's being kind to me and I don't deserve it!"

For a horrible moment, Charles wondered if Antoine had killed his brother. But that was absurd and probably physically impossible. "Get up, Antoine. I will listen, but not as a confessor. If something needs to be told in that way, you will have to tell it twice, understood?"

The boy nodded and sat down again on his rumpled bed. Further breaking the rules, Charles closed the chamber doors, though the study door refused to latch properly. Wondering what on earth was coming, he resumed his seat.

"Now. What do you want to tell me?"

"After Philippe ran away, he sent me a note," the boy said miserably.

"How?"

"I found it in my Latin dictionary after dinner. It said he needed help and to come to where the rue des Poirées turns and he'd be there. I went, but the accident happened and I woke up in the infirmary. I tried to go and find him again, but you found me instead." He leaned toward Charles, begging him to understand. "Mostly, Philippe thought I was too little to do anything.

But this time he trusted me and I failed him and someone killed him! I meant to go, I tried to—oh, Maître du Luc, I'm so sorry, please don't let God send me to hell, because then I'll *never* see Philippe again!"

Antoine buried his head on his knees and tried to muffle his sobs. Charles opened his mouth, closed it, and gathered the distraught little boy into his arms, rocking him like a baby. But Charles's face was hard with anger. Someone had lured Antoine out of the college to what was surely meant to be his death. Someone had wanted this boy dead, too.

When Antoine had cried himself out and slid off Charles's lap to wipe his face on the already soaked towel, Charles said gently, "Are you sure it was Philippe's writing on the note?"

Antoine nodded and then frowned. "Well—the writing was sloppy. Big and sort of wobbly, but—it would be, wouldn't it? Because something was wrong, that's why he needed me."

"Do you still have this note?"

"It was in my pocket, but Père Guise took it when I got hurt, Marie-Ange saw him, and he won't give it back!"

Charles tried to keep his tone reassuringly conversational. "How would Père Guise know you had the note? And how do you know she saw him take it?"

"I don't know how he knew. But when I woke up in the infirmary, I made Frère Brunet give me my breeches and the note wasn't there. Today, when we came out from the funeral, Marie-Ange told me she saw Père Guise take something out of my pocket after I was hurt. So he *must* have it!"

"Could it have fallen out of your pocket?"

"No! I tucked it deep down. It's the last thing Philippe gave me, Maître du Luc, the last thing he'll ever give me! Please make Père Guise give it back!"

Charles had to take several breaths before he could trust his voice. The note had been the bait. If Guise had known about it, then he had set—or helped to set—the trap. "I can't make him do anything, Antoine. But," Charles said, trying to make his voice bright so Antoine wouldn't see his worry, "you can do something for me, if you will. Something very important."

"Something important? What?" Antoine's eyes lit with hope.

"Promise me that you will not talk about this note. Not even to Marie-Ange. Let everyone think you have forgotten about it. Promise me that, Antoine."

Antoine's face fell. "But why?"

"What are you doing here, Maître du Luc?"

Antoine and Charles whipped around to see Père Guise standing in the study doorway. His black eyes glittered and his face was the color of parchment.

"Get out," he said, "you know you are not supposed to be here."

"Antoine's brother is dead, *mon père*," Charles said evenly. "He is grieving. He doesn't know where his tutor is and he needed company."

"My godson is not in your charge."

Antoine, glowering at Guise with his arms folded tightly across his chest, was about to speak. Charles stood quickly and with his back to Guise formed his mouth into a silent warning. "Sshhh."

"I will be checking on Antoine, *mon père*," Charles said mildly as he turned around. "To see how he does, you understand."

"The rector will hear of your arrogance in exceeding your rank and duties." Guise's lips barely moved. "And of your being here alone with him."

Charles ignored that for the red herring it was. "I know you heard us speaking of Philippe's note, Père Guise. It would be a kindness to return it to Antoine, don't you think?"

"I know nothing about a note."

"Oh?" Charles frowned in apparent confusion. "Then why did you search his clothing after the accident?"

"I did no such thing."

"So many curious contradictions in accounts of the accident. What do you make of that?"

As they stared at each other, Antoine's tutor walked in. Oblivious of the atmosphere in the room, Maître Doissin greeted everyone, then looked more closely at Antoine and put an arm around him.

"Good news on a very sad day, Monsieur Antoine," he said, smiling down at the boy. "I hear there's custard for supper. Your favorite."

Antoine smiled a little and Charles's opinion of Doissin rose. At least he felt some warmth and kindness for the child. Charles reached out to ruffle Antoine's hair.

"I will see you tomorrow, *mon brave*." He nodded to Guise and Doissin, and forced himself to walk sedately out of the chamber. But he felt as though Guise's furious stare were a dagger traveling toward his back.

Chapter 14

The next day was even hotter than the funeral day had been. Charles stood on a ladder, wiping his face on his damply clinging shirtsleeve. Hot air rose, so they said, and it was definitely doing that in the rhetoric classroom. Though he and Père Jouvancy had doffed their cassocks earlier in the rehearsal, Charles licked sweat from his upper lip as he flung another handful of sugar over François de Lille, the Opera stand-in now playing Hercules, who was leading his suite through a raging sugar snowstorm with the pretty lightness of a windblown feather. Beauchamps's pinched nostrils as he sawed at his fiddle did not bode well for Hercules.

"No, no, no, the snow is too brown!"

Jouvancy stormed down the room. Maître Beauchamps stopped playing, still looking daggers at the Opera dancer. The student dancers rolled their eyes at each other. At the ladder's foot, two boys seated on the floor stopped scraping their knives down the tall cone-shaped sugar loaf that stood between them on a plate. Before sugar could be used, for snowstorms or anything else, it had to be scraped from the hard cone it came in and put through a sifter. Trading a conspiratorial look, the two boys put down their knives and began surreptitiously eating the remains of their efforts.

"Whiter sugar," Jouvancy snapped at Charles. "I want whiter sugar! It's supposed to be snow. Not mud oozing from Olympus."

Charles wiped his sleeve across his face again. "*Is* there mud on Olympus?" he murmured and smiled down at Jouvancy. "Shall I get whiter sugar now, *mon père?*"

"Of course not now, don't be absurd." Jouvancy rounded on the new Hercules. "And you, try to dance like a hero, for the love of God! Hercules is not a lovesick girl in a garden!"

De Lille turned helplessly to Beauchamps. Beauchamps abruptly stopped looking as though he wanted to smash his violin over de Lille's beautiful head and bore down on Jouvancy like a sow defending her one piglet.

"*I* am the dancing master, Père Jouvancy, and *I* and no one else will correct him!"

"*I* am the livret's author and I will not see my ballet spoiled by this—this—"

"You only hate him because he is not Philippe!"

"I don't care who he is not, he dances like a lovesick girl!"

Charles yawned and leaned on the top of the ladder to wait out the squabble. He'd lain awake far into the night, wrestling with his conscience and the order he'd been given to leave the murder and the accident to Père Le Picart and Lieutenant-Général La Reynie. It wasn't only Charles's desire for justice that was pushing him to disobey now, but fears for his own safety. His heart had nearly stopped yesterday when La Reynie mentioned Nîmes. Louvois and La Reynie had been in close talk with Père Guise before they accosted him, and Guise had already accused Charles to the rector as a "heretic lover." Charles was fairly certain, though, that Guise didn't know he'd rescued his Protestant cousin. Guise would have trumpeted that knowledge to the skies. But he'd insinuated to the faculty that Charles might have killed Philippe, and yesterday Louvois had virtually accused Charles of the murder while La Reynie had stood back and watched, like someone at a mildly interesting play. If any of the unholy trio started digging for damning information, what Charles had done in Nîmes might well come to light. If it did, reprisals would fall not only on him, but on his family, both Catholics and Protestants alike.

A new thought made him catch his breath. Le Picart had duly turned the murder over to La Reynie. But had he done it planning to side-step the spectre of scandal by making a scape-goat of the "foreigner" from the heretic-tainted south? Charles shook his head involuntarily. However much Le Picart feared scandal, he seemed too honest for that kind of lie. But that didn't solve Charles's problem of the triumverate of Guise, Louvois, and La Reynie and their ominous scrutiny.

At the foot of the ladder, Jouvancy and Beauchamps were still muttering furiously at each other. Except for de Lille, who was happily and obliviously practicing graceful little jumps, the college was dangerously on edge. Too many were relishing Guise's titillating insinuations and looking sideways at Charles. Jouvancy, by all accounts usually the mildest and best loved of teachers, was grieving and exhausted, his temper shorter than Charles's thumb. Half the students were also grieving for Philippe, while the other half were pleasurably frightened over who might be next.

Beauchamps, whose mind was not on Philippe at all, turned abruptly from Jouvancy, ordered de Lille back to earth, and led him away to the windows, pouring a stream of instruction into his ear. Jouvancy snorted in disgust and pushed the remains of the offending sugar cone and its plate toward Charles with a disdainful toe.

"Take this—this"—Jouvancy clamped his lips together and

tried again—"sugar to the lay brothers' kitchen. At least they can get some good out of it."

"Now?" Charles said.

"Of course now!"

Jouvancy stalked back to the silent *Clovis* cast, who stood huddled together like a flock of anxious sheep. Charles, thankful to escape the charged atmosphere, picked up the plate and held it out to the two sugar scrapers, who eagerly took last pinches of sweetness. Everyone needed whatever small comfort he could get just now.

The lay brothers' kitchen and refectory were in the same courtyard as the outdoor latrine and next to the stable court. If he was quick about his errand, he might be able to settle another question about Antoine's "accident." He hurried through the archway between the courtyards, toward the kitchen and the savory smell drifting from its open door. Startling a flutter of sparrows away from a crust of bread, he poked his head into the big room, where a cauldron bubbling in the huge fireplace poured steam into the oven-hot air. Two red-faced brothers with their cassock sleeves folded back to their shoulders were slicing bread at a scarred table, while another brother, whose age had spread an old-fashioned tonsure over most of his freckled scalp, piled peaches onto a tray.

"Trust me, *maître*, you don't want to come into our nice little hell here," the old man called to Charles.

"Not this or any other hell, I hope, *mon frère!*" Charles held out the plate. "Can you use some sugar?"

"But yes, of course, always!" He wiped his sticky hands down his canvas apron and came to the door. "Where did you get it?"

"It was meant for snow. But now Père Jouvancy says it's too brown."

The old brother laughed heartily as he took the plate. "Yes, we usually get a good bit of his snow. Very picky about snow, Père Jouvancy is. We could use some real snow in here today, I'll tell you!"

Still laughing, he went back to his peaches. Charles turned toward the stable court and nearly collided with another lay brother, who danced aside, grinning, and stuck his head inside the kitchen.

"Frère Tricot, one more little one! Come on, *mon frère*, you have Lady Automne's cornucopia there—and it's not even quite August yet!"

A peach flew out the door. The newcomer caught it, nodding enthusiastically, and held up his other hand. A growl from the kitchen followed another peach through the air. The brother caught it, bit into it, and turned to Charles, who had stopped to watch.

"We should always admire the abundance of the *bon Dieu*," the brother said around his bulging mouthful. "Should we not?"

"Nice to be able to accommodate so much of the abundance at once," Charles laughed.

"Ah, I must stretch to it, whenever Lady Abundance deigns to visit me." He dropped the second peach into his apron pocket. "She's a woman, after all, and they always turn on you in the end, don't they?"

"Do they?"

"Mine do."

"Do?" Charles looked pointedly at the short cassock under the man's canvas apron and then added hypocrisy to his mental list of sins for his next confession. Who was he these days to admonish anyone for thinking about women?

"Oh dear, what is wrong with my tongue? *Did* turn on me, I mean, in my far distant past!" The brother's sapphire eyes danced like light on water as he held out his cassock skirt. "But even leaving this aside—and leaving women sadly aside—I suppose I should never predict what anyone will do. Mere sinful men are forbidden to predict the future, are we not?"

Standing at ease, he finished his peach and looked Charles over. Charles was visited by a vision of this wiry, taut-muscled man—who seemed neither to know his place nor care about keeping it—wearing velvet in a grand salon, appraising the company and finding it wanting.

"What is your name, *mon frère?*" Charles said, realizing suddenly that he'd seen the man before. "I saw you juggling in the Cour d'honneur on my first day here."

The brother sketched Charles an ironic bow. "Ah, my one poor talent. I am Frère Moulin, *maître.*" He made an ironic fuss of straightening the regulation high shirt collar just showing above his cassock.

He took three peaches from his apron pocket and began to juggle, spinning them into a golden blur. Charles watched, enjoying the man's skill and thinking that his speech and manner—and juggling, for that matter—consorted ill with the apron and cassock. Lay brothers were the Society's servants, mostly peasants or the sons of poor artisans, as Frère Fabre was. Charles thought that he would eat juggling balls before he'd believe that this Moulin sprang from a peasant's cottage.

"Very impressive, *mon frère,*" he said. "I am Maître Charles du Luc, newly come from Carpentras to teach rhetoric."

"I know." Moulin sent the peaches fountaining higher, spilling their fragrance into the air. "I have heard all about you." He tossed a peach at Charles and caught the other two in one hand.

"All?" Charles plucked the peach out of the air and bit into its warm succulence. "Only the *bon Dieu* knows all, Frère Moulin."

"Alas, too true. Rest assured I will be confessing arrogance next time I go to my confessor. Too true, indeed. 'No man knows even the day or the hour,' so it says in Holy Scripture. But the real truth is, no man knows anything worth a piss. Least of all me." He fixed Charles with a look like a strike of blue lightning and his voice went flat. "Or you."

Then the easy brilliance was back, and with a wide smile and a bow that would have done Versailles credit, Moulin disappeared toward the stable. Charles swallowed the last of the peach and followed. Except for doves pecking around the well, the stable court was empty. Charles stopped in the stable's broad entrance, gazing at the straw-strewn floor and listening to the horse noises—tails switching to keep off flies, soft snorts, the occasional stamp of a hoof, and high-pitched swearing. His eyebrows lifted and he peered into the dimness redolent of hay and dung and leather. No horse he'd ever known swore.

The three stalls on his left were empty. A restless black horse in the first stall on the right thrust its nose over the half door and pricked its ears at him. The next stall was untenanted, but in the third, a stocky little figure astride a placid dappled gray swore steadily as she struggled to kilt her rough brown skirts and blue petticoat above her knees. Her bare legs and feet stuck nearly straight out from the gray's broad back.

"*Bon jour, mademoiselle.*" Charles leaned his arms on the stall's half door. "Where are you riding to today?"

Marie-Ange gave a last tug at her skirts and brandished a wooden sword at him, scowling anxiously. "I am Jeanne d'Arc, going to kill the English! Do not get in my way!"

"I wouldn't think of it," he said, scratching the gray's nose. "Does your mother know you're here, *ma chère* Jeanne?"

She pointed the sword at him again. "What if Jeanne's mother had made her stay home?"

"A very good point," Charles said gravely. "I never thought of that."

She studied him. "I guess Antoine's right about you. He says you're not like grown-ups."

Charles burst out laughing, remembering Jouvancy's assessment of him on his first morning. Overly enthusiastic, perpetually young. Perhaps he should find another wooden sword and join Marie-Ange on the horse. At least then he wouldn't be earning endless penance by covertly hunting Philippe's killer. Or pretending enthusiasm for Louis's allegorical exploits. And he could always use the sword to defend himself if Louvois and La Reynie came after him again.

"You are not listening, *maître!* Maman says you still haven't found that man who hurt Antoine. Why *not?*"

"I am not the police, *ma petite.* It is not easy to find just one man in all Paris."

She sniffed. "Well, you should at least make that old Père Guise give back Antoine's note. Priests shouldn't steal," she added severely.

"What note is that, *ma chère?*" Charles said casually, wanting to hear her version.

"That priest looked through Antoine's pockets, I saw him, and the note Philippe sent Antoine is gone. Antoine asked him very nicely to give it back, but Père Guise says he's imagining things because his head got hurt. But he isn't!"

"Your mother didn't mention seeing Père Guise search Antoine's pockets."

"She didn't see, she was—"

"My queen of victory!" Moulin was marching quickly toward them between the stalls, carrying a shovel as though it were a battle standard. "Here's reinforcements and we'll bury the English yet!"

Marie-Ange drew herself up and pointed the wooden sword at him. "Kneel, Sieur Moulin!"

He planted the shovel martially and sank to his knees.

She pointed her sword at the shovel. "Bury the English devils, because they're all dead. I will marry Antoine and we will be the queen and king of France and you will be our loyal servant!"

Queen and king, Charles noted, grinning, not the other way around.

Humbly, Moulin bowed his head. "I thank you, my liege lady!"

Then he jumped smoothly to his feet, opened the stall door, and held out his arms. Marie-Ange launched herself at him, sword and all. Moulin stepped back into the aisle and swung her around, making her skirts fly. Then he put her down and looked anxiously over his shoulder.

"You must be on your way, my queen," he whispered. "Else your lady mother will find you and we'll be undone before you ever come to the throne. The back gate's open for you." He swatted her smartly on the seat of her skirts. "Off with you!"

She dimpled, ran back into the stall, and emerged wearing sabots and carrying a basket loaded with bread. Leaning to one side to balance the basket's weight, she clomped away toward the gate.

"I didn't expect to see you again so soon, *maître*," Moulin said, shutting the stall door and shaking his thick black hair back from his face.

"I didn't know you worked here. That was a nicely done little fable you played with her. Does she come here often?"

"She loves horses, poor little chit. I let her in sometimes, just into the stables, no farther. She's also quite smitten with our Antoine, you know."

"Does he come here, too?" Charles asked, following Moulin toward the stable door.

The brother looked over his shoulder, wide-eyed with mendacious innocence. "I wouldn't like to get anyone in trouble, now." His eyes darkened. "But yes, he does. I've caught the two of them playing in the hayloft. Nosing. Prying where they shouldn't."

"Surely there's not much to find in a hayloft. And they aren't your responsibility, you won't be in trouble because they misbehave."

"You're right there, *maître*." Moulin gave Charles a brilliant smile. "I won't be. Fair is fair."

"They shouldn't be in the stable at all, but I understand liking horses," Charles said, going to the first stall. "This is a good-looking young fellow. How many horses do we have?"

"These two and one other. Père Guise has that one today. He's off again to Versailles."

"Versailles?"

Moulin's eyes widened. "Where the king lives, *maître*," he said, stepping closer and lowering his voice, as if imparting a state secret. "Very nice house, a bit small for my taste. Full of courtiers, who need a lot of confessing. Our Père Guise does a good business there, you might say. A penitent of his, some noble old lady who's been ill, took a turn for the worse and he galloped off to grab her soul before the devil gets it."

"God defend her," Charles said ambiguously. "What's the third horse like?"

"Another gray. A gelding. Why?"

Charles shrugged. "I suppose I'm a little homesick. But horses are the same everywhere, aren't they?" And none of the three college horses was the rangy roan Antoine's attacker had ridden. Not that he'd thought it would be, but it was one possibility eliminated.

Moulin leaned the shovel against a stall and wheeled a handcart from its place by the door. "I'd better get this place mucked out, or they'll stick me back in that hellhole of a kitchen."

"You like working in the stable, then?"

He flashed Charles a look. "We work where we're needed. No choice for servants." The tone was light but the blue eyes were full of bitterness.

He wheeled the cart toward the stall where Marie-Ange had been and Charles drifted into the tack room. In the sunlight slipping through cracks in the wooden walls and barring the leather-scented shadows with gold, he went quickly over the few bridles, saddles, and saddlebags, noting where there were narrow strips of leather and looking for any place where there should have been such a strip and wasn't.

Chapter 15

The college clock had yet to chime nine the next morning when Père Jouvancy burst into the grammar class where Charles was assisting and spoke briefly with the grammar master, who nodded reluctantly. Jouvancy led Charles out of the room and thrust coins, an old leather satchel, and a hat at him.

"I took the liberty of fetching your hat; it's Wednesday, the markets are open. Now, listen." Pouring out a steady stream of instructions on where and how to buy the perfect sugar, as though Charles were sailing for Martinique instead of walking to the Marché Neuf, he walked Charles at double time to the street postern.

"A companion?" Jouvancy pushed him through the postern. "No time for that, I exempt you. Just bring me sugar—and it had better be white as an angel's wing!"

Charles loped happily toward the Seine. While he'd listened to his students' halting reading, he'd been trying to think how to get out of the college on his own. If this Marché Neuf had blamelessly white sugar and he didn't have to search farther, he should have plenty of time to look for the street porter who'd seen Antoine's accident. Charles reached into his cassock pocket and felt his nearly flat purse with the few coins left from what he'd been given in Carpentras for his journey north. With all that had happened, he'd kept forgetting to give what was left to the rector. He told himself that if his errand was successful, the money would be spent for the good of the college.

His hand was still on the purse when a book display caught his eye. The rue St. Jacques was lined with booksellers and printers, and clots of students and teachers risked life and limb around the display tables in the street. Charles edged among them toward the book he'd seen. The *Itinerarium Extaticum*, by the Jesuit Kircher, was a tale of traveling to the moon, Venus, and the fixed stars in the company of the angel Cosmiel, who showed Kircher that what he'd seen through his telescope, the moon's craters and mountains and the sun's occasional dark blemishes, were real. Charles picked up the battered copy. It wasn't expensive. He'd longed for years to read it. Of course, it might be in Louis le Grand's library, but the Carpentras library didn't have it . . . A boy with his nose in a mathematics tome backed heavily into Charles. The Kircher flew out of Charles's hands and was grabbed by a white-haired man who clutched it to his chest and scuttled into the bookshop.

Charles walked on. If he was lucky, he was going to need his small store of coins. He lengthened his stride, his cassock flapping smartly around his ankles. But his head swiveled from side to side as he gawked like any newcomer to Paris. The glazed windows everywhere surprised him all over again. Even the windows of the gilded, painted carriages were glass. A half dozen black-robed Benedictine monks cut across his path and he craned his neck to glimpse the turrets of the old Hôtel de Cluny, lodging for Benedictine abbots visiting Paris. Nearly colliding with a pair of gowned students debating humanist theology versus the older approaches, he wished he had time to stop and weigh in on the humanist side. But he kept going, dodging a sloshing bucket on a milkmaid's shoulder pole and a double line of small boys pattering in their teacher's wake like duck-lings, who made him think of Antoine. When he'd stopped by the junior refectory after breakfast to check on Antoine, the boy's tutor, Maître Doissin, had come to the door. Using An-toine's grief and proven ability to leave the college on his own for excuse, Charles had urged Doissin not to leave his charge alone. Without quite asking about the funeral afternoon scene in Antoine's room, Doissin had said happily that he would watch the boy with all his eyes and added that anything he could do to annoy Guise would be gladly done.

Bells began to ring from every direction. "Be pleased, O Lord, to deliver me; O Lord, make haste to help me," Charles responded silently, slowing his pace and beginning the prayers for Tierce. Though he wasn't required to say the offices yet, he loved them and they were already carved years deep into his memory. The words came as easily as breathing and made a satisfying counterpoint to his weaving in and out among the hawkers yelling the virtues of milk, scissors, brooms, drinking water fresh out of the Seine, ribbons, and doubtful summer oysters.

The rue St. Jacques ran straight to the Petit Pont and Charles reached the approach to the bridge as he reached the last psalm's end: "The Lord shall watch over your going out and your com-ing in, it is He who shall keep you safe . . ." Flooded with sudden peace, he bowed his head and let the traffic flow around him.

"Go pray in a church, *mon père*, or you'll be praying over your own corpse!"

Charles jumped aside as a string of mules trotted past, their exasperated driver shaking his head and cracking his whip. An-other of the many dangers of religion, Charles thought wryly, and moved into the shade of the ancient bridge's fortified gate for a quick look at the river. The day was already hot, though a narrow ruffle of pearly clouds lined the horizon. Below him, huge barges mounded with goods floated west—downstream— like mammoth turtles. A few boatmen sent their small craft darting among the behemoths as they ferried passengers across the water. Most boats were loaded with goods, like the small barge piled with casks and guided by a huge sweep tiller just passing under the bridge. A flat-bottomed boat full of unhappily bleating sheep was being tied up at the bank below the quay. Other pedestrians stopped to watch as the gilded and carved prow of a noble's open boat came in sight, rowed upriver by thirteen pairs of oars and full of richly dressed men and women lounging on cushions, idly watching Paris pass by. Amid all the waterside busyness, an occasional fisherman sat motionless beside his lines. Charles turned to look upriver, where the towers of Notre Dame soared at the end of the Ile de la Cité. Beyond the cathedral, gleaming mansions lined the newish island called St.-Louis. Real estate speculators had made it, Charles had been told, by linking together the little Ile Notre-Dame and another island where people used to pasture cows.

With difficulty, he pulled himself away from the river's panoply and hurried through the Petit Pont's massive gate onto the short bridge road. Houses, mostly stone, a few still plaster and timber, crowded close on both sides. A shout of *"Gardez l'eau!"* sent him to the other side of the roadway as a girl emptied a chamber pot from an upper window.

"Oh, la! Pardon, mon père!" she shouted, laughing without the least sign of regret.

"You should get a penance for that," he returned, laughing, too. "Chuck it out the back, *mademoiselle*, into the river!"

"Come up and give me a penance, then!"

She leaned her round arms on the windowsill and smiled down at him, as people in the street yelled ribald encouragement. Fighting an unclerical grin, Charles kept walking. A shop sign brought him to a halt. The black sign showed a white skeleton Death being ground under a red apothecary's pestle. Not so long ago, apothecaries had sold sugar. If by some chance this shop still did, he could be done with his errand now, with that much more time for his other business. He ducked through the low doorway and stood blinking in shadow.

"*Bonjour, mon père.*"

At first Charles couldn't locate the treble voice. Then he saw the gleam of eyes peering at him just above the level of the counter.

"Bonjour," he returned, not sure whether he was addressing a monsieur, a madame, or a child. The eyes vanished and a bulky shape clambered onto a tall stool, settled itself, and became recognizable as a tiny old man. He crossed his short arms and legs, tilted his big head to one side, and waited resignedly for Charles to finish realizing that he was a dwarf.

"Now that we've got that over," he said briskly, "what can I do for you, my fine young cleric?"

"I wondered if, by chance, you have sugar, *monsieur*. Very white sugar."

"If your grandfather had come in asking that, or your father, even, the answer would have been yes. But we don't sell sugar now, you should know that." The little man shrugged. "Though I hear your accent and maybe apothecaries still sell it in the south, people are backward down there. But sugar's too common here for Parisians to think it cures anything. And it tastes too good. They could excuse that when it was rare as unicorn's horn and nearly as expensive. But common as mud *and* lovely to eat, who spends silver for medicine like that? Pigeon dung, now, powdered crab's eye, a little urine from a red-haired boy, some dried mouse liver, those are worth money and they'll cure you, sure as saints have halos! Why? Because they're disgusting. And who ever gets well without suffering?"

"*Will* they cure you?"

"People think they will and that's probably just as good. Nothing much cures anything, young man. Oh, oh, yes, prayer, of course. We mustn't forget prayer, must we?" His sarcasm was acid enough to strip the varnish from his counter.

"It sounds as though you don't believe that cures much, either," Charles said.

"One thing cures every ill."

"What's that?"

"Death."

But the dwarf didn't laugh and his eyes were as somber as a funeral Mass. He looked Charles over, enviously but without malice.

"Death will come even to beautiful young men like you eventually, I don't need to sell you that." He jerked his head to the north. "Sugar is across the bridge, at the Marché Neuf."

Thanking him, Charles escaped. As he emerged into the street, a woman brushed past him toward the shop. Her gown and head scarf were unrelieved black, but a surprising froth of rose-colored petticoat swirled under her skirt as she stepped over the apothecary's high threshold. Charles heard the dwarf's voice rise warmly in welcome.

Charles turned away quickly. He didn't need anything more to tell his confessor. He covered the short distance to the Ile de la Cité, turned right onto rue Neuve Notre Dame, realized when he ended up in front of the cathedral that he should have turned left, and retraced his steps. The Ile was the oldest part of Paris, settled even before the Romans came, and the so-called Marché Neuf, the New Market, was old, too, though not that old. This morning it was happy and lucrative chaos, as sellers called their wares, buyers bargained, and sweating jugglers and tumblers vied for whatever coins they could wring from the crowd—deniers, even a few sous if they were lucky, or nearly worthless old copper liards if they weren't. Dogs barked, chickens squawked, and the barefoot children who weren't gathered in front of a marionette show chased each other among the market stalls. The savory smell of roasted meat set Charles's stomach rumbling. Then the deep strong scent of coffee caught him by the nose. He'd tasted coffee and liked it. The Dutch, of course, were mad about it, and had more or less cornered what market there was for it. Paris had coffeehouses, but Charles suspected it was just one more passing craze.

His nose led him to a swarthy man in a purple turban and flowing scarlet robe, sitting cross-legged on a patterned rug. Beside him, coffee simmered in a brass pot on a little stove. Charles nodded politely, wondering how to address a Mahometan. The coffee seller cocked a bright brown eye at him, poured coffee into a pottery bowl, and held it out.

"Coffee of the best, *mon père*, and cheap," he said, revealing himself as Parisian to the bone. "Wakes up the brain, pours heat into the sinews, balances the fluids, practically writes your sermons for you!"

Charles reached recklessly under his cassock and fished money out of his purse. The "Mahometan" whipped the coins from his palm and handed him the bowl. Charles sipped, half repelled by the bitterness, half intoxicated by the smell. And oddly pleased by the buzzing feeling that grew in his head as he drank. Before he knew it, the bowl was empty. Regretfully, he gave it back, refused a refill, and continued on in search of sugar. The buzzing feeling grew as he walked along the aisle between the stalls. Colors seemed twice as bright and he felt like he could walk to Turkey for a coffee tree and be back before dinner.

A splash of glowing red on a grocer's stall stopped him in front of a basket of tomatoes. Tomatoes were common at home, but less so here, it seemed. None had appeared so far on the college table. Charles found himself smiling as he drank in their glowing color, remembering that some people still shunned them as the fruit Eve had given Adam, and what Pernelle had had to say about that. "Well, he didn't *have* to eat it, did he?" she would say, her black eyes snapping. "But, of course, women are always blamed when things go wrong for a man."

"Oh, look, let's get some," the same rich alto voice went on. Charles froze. Could coffee make him hear voices that weren't there?

"Never, child!" an older voice hissed. "They're love apples, they're poisonous, everyone knows that. It's a sin to sell them!"

Very slowly, Charles turned his head. The girl with Pernelle's voice was pretty. But her hair was only brown, not a cloud of midnight. And when she felt Charles's stare and turned to smile at him from under her little cherry ribboned parasol, he saw that her eyes were only brown instead of sparkling onyx.

"*Bonjour, mon père,*" she said demurely, dimpling at his admiration.

He sketched a hasty blessing on the air and moved away to gaze fixedly at a length of badly dyed tawny wool on the next stall. Laughing, the girl called a bold good-bye as her chaperone hurried her away. Blind to the wool's garish color and deaf to the seller's praise for its quality, Charles was seized with longing for news of Pernelle, if she was well, if she liked Geneva, if David's family was kind to her. He closed his eyes, prayed for her, and then walked on, earning a muttered curse from the

disappointed cloth merchant. And another curse when he re-
versed direction and passed by the stall again without stopping.
He'd been so unnerved by the girl, he'd hardly registered the
snowy sugar sparkling on a stall beyond the love apples.

He chose two large cone-shaped loaves and paid for them
with Jouvancy's coins. As the grocer wrapped them, the tower
clock chimed from the old Conciergerie palace. If he kept his
mind on business, he still had enough time to look for the street
porter with the broken nose. He stowed the sugar in Jouvancy's
leather bag and started down the quay that bordered the market,
heading west toward the tip of the island. He soon found the
sort of scene he wanted. Heavily wrapped bolts of cloth, rounds
of cheese, and boxes smelling of cinnamon were being unloaded
from a barge and a small boat, and a dozen or so porters were
securing bundles to the tall carrying frames they wore on their
backs. Charles walked slowly among them, but none had the
nose he was looking for. He reached the quay's end without
finding the man and retraced his steps toward the Petit Pont,
still looking, but with no success. As he came to the bridge, the
tower clock struck the quarter before ten, sending him at a trot
across the river, where he went down the slope and along the left
bank, seeing plenty of porters, but never the one he sought. He
was below the Quay des Augustins, passing small fishing boats
with planks laid so that customers could come from the bank
and buy, when he collided with a woman stepping off a plank
bridge with a basket of eels. The eels went flying and the woman
rained abuse on him as he helped her gather their tangled slip-
periness back into the basket. He straightened and nearly up-
ended the basket again as he came face-to-face with the man
who was trying to step around him.

"*Monsieur*, thank God!" He pulled the startled and protesting
porter to the side of the quay. "Please, *monsieur*, I must talk with

you. About the accident you saw on the rue des Poirées, the little boy—"

"No!" Breathing heavily through his mouth, the porter wrenched his arm away. "Leave me alone!" His long bony face had gone the color of a fish belly. "I told the other one. You've no call to hound me!"

His fingers twisted in the old sign to ward off evil and he tore himself out of Charles's grip and ran, the empty frame bouncing on his long back. Charles started after him, but someone jerked him back by his cassock and spun him around.

"Leave him alone, priest!" His captor had a voice like gravel caught in a sieve, and the face that went with the voice was as expressionless as a wall. He was big in every direction and his four *confrères* were built like the squat, sturdy pillars in a Norman church. The five men closed around Charles.

"I swear by the Virgin, *messieurs*, I mean him no harm," Charles said. "I only want—"

"Are you deaf?" Gravel Voice said, shaking him. "I said leave off. If we cut away the flapping part of your ears, maybe you'd hear better. But there's no sport with your kind. No fight."

The others laughed and Charles breathed onion, garlic, and the stink of sweat. "No, not now," he said evenly, "I swore off fighting a long time ago."

"What would you know of fighting?"

"Enough, after two years in the king's army."

"Where?" the shortest man said skeptically.

"The Spanish Netherlands in '77, for one place. St. Omer."

"You, too?" The short man's eyes lit with interest and he stepped closer and peered up at Charles. "Me, I was there, too, I carried a pike."

"I was a *mousquetaire*," Charles said.

Gravel Voice spat close to Charles's feet. "Why the skirt, then?"

"I was wounded. I had a lot of time to think and decided I didn't like killing people."

"Me, I was wounded, too." The ex-soldier pulled up his patched jacket and showed a jagged scar running the length of his forearm. "But I never thought of being a cleric."

"That randy woman of yours would beat you into a pâté if you did," someone laughed.

"What do you want with Pierre, then, *mon père?*" the ex-soldier said.

"I teach at the college of Louis le Grand, and a few days ago, he saw a little boy from our school ridden down on the rue des Poirées. I just want to hear from him what happened. Only that. He was in no way to blame, he is in no trouble. I would be very grateful and will certainly reward him for telling me what he saw."

The man's eyes narrowed suspiciously. "Why?"

"The boy's father is anxious to know all he can about what happened."

Most of the men grunted, understanding that.

"Would you tell your friend Pierre what I say? And tell him, too"—Charles hesitated, unsure how to put it—"tell him I am not a friend of the other priest who talked to him."

"Good enough for me," the ex-soldier said, ignoring Gravel Voice's protest. "Come back here first thing tomorrow." He pointed across the Seine at the Louvre palace. "You sound foreign, there's your landmark, if you need it. If Pierre wants to talk, he'll be here."

"Thank you, *mon camarade*. Until tomorrow, then."

Slowly, the men stepped back and let Charles through. He

spoiled his attempt at a dignified exit by tripping over the bare feet of a fisherman who was sitting against a barrel beside his pole, so sound asleep beneath his hat that he never stirred. Charles was too excited at having found his man to mind the porters' jibes and laughter.

On the way back to the college, he barely noticed the raucous street life going on around him. If Pierre had seen a knife in the rider's hand as he reached toward Antoine, then the accident was indeed no accident. And if the man confirmed that Guise had paid him for silence, then Charles had a weapon against Guise and his cronies, and Guise had an unpleasant amount of explaining to do.

Charles was reaching for the bell rope beside the college postern when furious female voices reached him from beyond the chapel's west door. Marie-Ange ran out of the bakery with her mother on her heels.

"You will *never* go up there again!" Mme LeClerc shouted. "Never, do you hear me? Do you want to get us turned out? Now be off with you. And come back the moment you've finished. Not like yesterday. I *know* how long delivering bread should take, Marie-Ange."

"But, Maman! It wasn't me that—"

"Go!"

Marie-Ange hefted her loaded basket and her mother went back into the shop. When the little girl was past the chapel, she set the basket down and wiped her wet face on her skirt.

"My lady Jeanne?" Charles squatted down on his heels in front of her. "What has happened, *ma petite*? Are the English winning again?"

Marie-Ange hiccupped indignantly. "I was only trying to help. But grown-ups never think of that, do they, the pigs?"

Charles considered gravely. "No, sometimes we don't."

"Well, it's not fair!"

"I agree. How were you trying to help?"

"We were just—"

"Marie-Ange, go! Now!"

Mme LeClerc was coming toward them, brandishing a bread paddle that could have flattened a horse. With an expressive look at Charles, Marie-Ange picked up her basket and went. Her mother raised the bread paddle to heaven.

"Some days, *maître*, she makes me wish I'd been a nun!"

"Celibacy has its rewards, madame," Charles said dryly. Though lately, he was finding them hard to remember.

"Come in here for a little moment, *maître*, if you please."

She retreated into the shop and Charles followed her. The scent of baking wafted from the ovens and he took a deep, hungry breath.

"Your shop smells so good, madame, a man could eat the air."

"A man may have to, if Roger lets that omelette brain of an apprentice burn my brioches." She bit her lip and her rosy face grew pinched with apology. "*Maître*, this morning Marie-Ange went up your stairs. I am so sorry! I would never have allowed it, but what could I do, I didn't know!"

"What stairs, madame?"

"There." She pointed to a low, arched door in the shop's side wall. "They lead to two rooms above us. In Roger's father's day, the family lived up there. But when Roger inherited the bakery, the college took back the rooms. Since then, we live down here and that door has always been locked. I have not seen the key in an eternity. Now Marie-Ange swears she found it open. *Mon Dieu*, I only hope no one saw her up there!"

"Calm yourself, madame, if someone had seen her, believe me, you would know by now."

"You really think so? Well, that is a relief, but—"

"Beatrice," a male voice boomed from the back of the shop. "I need you!"

Someone else yelped and the voice rumbled angrily. The air was suddenly tinged with the smell of burning.

"Roger! Ah, *Sainte Vierge*, Roger, use your nose if you can't use your ears! He is deaf as a baguette, *maître*. And I wish I were, the way he snores! I tell you, sometimes—Guy, you cabbage head, save the brioches!" Brandishing the bread paddle, Mme LeClerc clattered away, her wooden sabots loud on the stone floor. "Roger, I have told you and told you—"

Hoping that Guy and Roger were fast on their feet, Charles went quickly to the little door and opened it. Narrow, deeply worn stone stairs rose into darkness. He hesitated, then pulled the door shut behind him, abruptly cutting off both light and sound, and began to climb. He felt his way up two switch-back flights, to the level of his own rooms as far as he could tell, and found himself facing another low-arched door. No light showed around its edge. He pinned an ear to the door's planks, heard nothing, and with infinite caution lifted the latch. The door opened soundlessly and then balked, and an eddy of dust made him clap a hand over his nose to stop a sneeze. A length of thick wool hung over the inside of the door. Charles edged it aside enough to see into the room beyond it. He stared at a sliver of a book-littered desk. If he was right about the floor he'd reached, this could well be Guise's study. And he had found Antoine standing in front of a tapestry. He remembered the boy's words: "I tried to go and find him, but you found me, instead." If these stairs led to Guise's rooms, then Antoine's words made sense. He must have been trying to use the stairs to get out of the college and look for Philippe.

Charles quietly retraced his steps. When he reached the bottom of the stairs, he could hear Mme LeClerc's and Roger's voices, but when he peered around the door, he saw that the shop was empty and the voices were coming from the bakery workroom. He realized that this door, like the door at the other end of the stairs, made no sound. He ran a finger over the heavy iron hinges and it came away coated with thick grease. He went quickly through the shop to the street door. Its hinges, too, were newly greased. He had no key to try in the lock, but he would bet that it, too, worked silently. He slipped out of the shop unseen, his mind racing. The stairs changed everything.

Chapter 16

Thick fog blanketed the city, and though it was the first day of August, summer seemed to have fled in the night. Hunched against the chill, Charles slid on patches of slippery grass as he made his way to the water level on the downriver side of the Petit Pont. The weather was no doubt punishment for the lie that had gotten him out of the college, he thought wryly. But at least he had permission to go alone. A twinge in his jaw made him wonder if his excuse of needing a tooth-drawer was becoming reality and part of the list of penances he was earning. He'd come to the river, that much was true. And he was meeting the porter down toward the Pont Neuf, where Frère Fabre had said there were tooth-drawers' booths.

Shouts and grunts were loud in the wet air and the smell of wood was sharp in Charles's nose as he threaded his way through men unloading logs from a barge tied up at the quay. The ghostly outlines of bales, baskets, crates, boats covered with hooped canvas like wagons, boats with masts, flat-bottomed boats poled from their sterns, appeared and disappeared as he walked. Hoping he'd recognize the place where he'd seen Pierre and the other porters the day before, he peered through the fog's shifting veils and caught a glimpse of the Louvre's east end across the river.

This must be more or less the right place. He started whistling a marching song he'd learned at the siege of St. Omer. After a few repetitions, a wheezy voice came back out of the fog, singing the melody's bawdy words.

"Do they know you know that one?" the ex-soldier said, materializing in front of Charles. "Your abbot and such, I mean."

"We don't have abbots." Charles laughed. "But you're right, I don't sing that song much. I realize I don't know your name, *monsieur*," he added politely.

"And I've forgotten yours, if I ever knew it. Better that way. Come on, I'm taking you to where Pierre lives, he doesn't want to be seen talking to you."

"Where?" Charles didn't move.

"Nothing to worry about, I wouldn't do a fellow soldier wrong. Pierre's jumpy, is all."

They moved off into the fog, which seemed to thicken. Charles matched his stride to the man's short legs, but looked warily back over his shoulder, wishing he could see more than a foot or two in any direction.

"Someone after you, too?" His guide cocked an assessing eye up at him. "About this 'accident?'"

"Why?" Charles noted the way the man said *accident*. "Is someone after Pierre?"

"He says so. Following him, he says. But he's drinking a lot, mind you, so it might all be out of his cup."

Charles hoped it was too early in the day for Pierre to be in his cups. They started across the Pont Neuf, turning a little more of Charles's lie into truth. Unlike the city's other bridges, this one bore no houses, just small open shop booths built into its half-round niches, with a raised walkway along them. The booths and the vendors' stalls set up wherever there was room were all doing a brisk business. Fabre had said that on the bridge you could have your dog barbered, hire an umbrella, join the army, buy a mackerel for supper, or a glass eye or wooden leg if a battle or duel turned out badly. Street criers carrying their wares were thick as the fog and Charles glimpsed a wild-eyed man in a tattered scholar's gown standing on a stool and proclaiming the virtues of ancient Greek comedy to a cluster of laughing students. Fog-blinded carriages hurtled across the bridge, making Charles grateful for the raised walkways. The ex-soldier led him off the bridge, past the clanging Samaritaine water pump that drew drinking water out of the Seine, and turned to the left.

"That's it," the ex-soldier said. He pointed at the Louvre's bulk looming fitfully through the fog and quickened his pace. "Where Pierre lives."

Charles stopped abruptly, with an unpleasant vision of yesterday's Gravel Voice and minions waiting for him to walk into a nicely set trap.

"What are you playing at?" he said harshly. "The Louvre's a palace."

The man looked over his shoulder with a puzzled expression. "Of course it is. And Pierre lives there. Him and a few hundred more. They won't eat you. Probably won't even rob you, not with me there. Come on." He vanished around a pile of broken stone and wood, thickly grown with weeds. "Watch yourself," he called back. "The ground's full of holes."

Following the often misunderstood Jesuit teaching that ends must be considered and means appropriately chosen, Charles pulled a long stave of weathered oak from the pile and followed the porter. He found himself in what could have been stage décor for hell. A freshening wind was thinning the fog, revealing pitted and broken ground. His guide led him across hard puddles of spilled mortar, past scattered rotten lumber. The remains of a flat-bottomed cargo boat lay like a skeleton amid the debris. As they neared the long colonnade ahead of them, Charles saw small fires flickering among the rubble and the smells of doubtful cooking assailed his nose. Grimy faces peered sullenly at them through the fog.

"What *is* all this?" Charles asked, keeping his voice low.

"What, never been here? Oh, well, I guess you wouldn't, would you? See that long part we're coming to?"

He pointed to the three-story colonnade that was revealing its full length as the fog blew away. Half of it looked more or less finished, though roofless. The unfinished half was covered with the remains of wooden scaffolding. Neither end of it seemed to be connected to anything.

"What happened was, see, the king started building, wanted to fancy up the place. But in '78, I think it was—around then, anyway—he tired of it. Turned his back on the whole thing and went off and built that Versailles. Just left all this. Which turned out a blessing, really, because a lot of people with no place to live moved into this side. Nice, some of it. Taverns, too. And there's a well. Even a garden, some of the women have."

They reached the abandoned colonnade and Charles saw that the upper halves of the big windows in this south wall of the palace were glassless and boarded over. For warmth, he guessed. In a few places, the makeshift shutters on the lower part of the windows had been set aside to let in what light the morning offered, but oil lamps and candles flickered deep in the cavernous interior. Talk and laughter and arguing echoed as men and women went in and out. Ragged children raced along under the scaffolding, jumping up to hang from pieces of it and laughing uproariously when their rotten handholds broke. A huddle of barefoot women pushed past Charles, carrying hoes and baskets. Their eyes slid sideways at him and quickly away again.

"In here," the ex-soldier said.

They went through a tall doorway without a door, into shadows thick with the smells of too many people in too little space. As his eyes adjusted to the dimness, Charles saw that there were partitions everywhere. These attempts at privacy counted for little, though, as his guide led him through room after makeshift room, one opening into the other. The first two smelled like chamber pots that hadn't been emptied since King Louis left, and Charles's shoes squelched unpleasantly on the floor. Then they crossed a cleaner room with most of a window to itself, where a hollow-cheeked young painter was re-creating Venus rising from the waves on the boards of his partition. In the room beyond Venus, a baby wailed. The ex-soldier beckoned Charles around the painter's partition and then held up a hand.

"Pierre's is next," he said, over the baby's cries. "Wait here, I don't want to surprise him, not the way he's been acting."

He left Charles staring uneasily at the screaming infant lying in a nest of rags beside three women sitting on the dirty parquet, under a slice of the window they shared with the painter. Beside them was a mound of paper. Their jaws worked ceaselessly and, as Charles watched, mystified, two of them spit wads of something into a basket. Then they passed a jug back and forth—vinegary wine, by the smell of it—crumbled some paper from their pile, stuffed it into their mouths, and started chewing again. The youngest, chewing steadily, shoved aside her unlaced stays to put the crying baby to her breast.

"Pardon me—um—*mesdames*," Charles faltered, "but what are you doing?"

The two older women gazed at him like cud-chewing cows.

But the youngest reared her head and glared at him defiantly. Then it hit him. Papier-mâché. Chewed paper. The tatty little Temple of Rhetoric was partly made of it, and so were the heads, hands, and feet of marionettes, so were theatre masks. But he'd never seen it made. He turned at the sound of hurrying feet.

"Come on!" The whites of the ex-soldier's eyes were showing. "We have to get out of here, move!"

"Why? Where's Pierre?"

"See for yourself, if you must! I'm having no more part of this!"

He took to his heels. The papier-mâché chewers followed him with their eyes and then looked back at Charles, as though they were watching a show with puppets they'd helped to make. Charles looked around the partition into the painter's room, in the direction his guide had gone, but the ex-soldier had already disappeared. The oblivious artist was still frowning from Venus to his palette.

Charles went quickly back through the paper chewers' den and into Pierre's room. Pierre lay on the far side of it, on a straw pallet under the uncovered half of a window. His eyes bulged and his face was dark with congested blood. Charles turned in a slow circle, taking in the makeshift brazier, the single dented cooking pot on its side on the floor. He made the sign of the cross, prayed briefly for the violently dispatched soul, and knelt beside the pallet. And froze, staring at the deep, patterned line around the porter's throat, a line that was the twin of the mark he'd seen on Philippe Douté's neck. Charles pulled gently up on the porter's arm. The body was already stiff. Lifting the thin blanket, he saw that the man was wearing only shirt and breeches and looked quickly around the room again. The old leather jerkin and cracked brown boots Pierre had worn yesterday were gone, along with his wooden carrying frame. A simple robbery, then? Not with that mark on his neck.

"You do have a way of showing up in time for murder, Maître du Luc."

Charles leapt to his feet.

"Account for your presence here," Lieutenant-Général La Reynie said. "And if you are foolish enough to use that stave you're holding under your cloak, you will no longer have a presence to account for."

Without taking his eyes off Charles, the lieutenant-général stepped through the partition's opening. A thickset man, with a long, heavy pistol as well as a sword in his belt, came in behind La Reynie, eyeing Charles with happy anticipation. Charles dropped the piece of wood and held out his empty hands.

"I am no threat, *messieurs.* And I know no more of this dead man than you do."

Probably a great deal less than they did, he thought, watching them ignore Pierre's body as though it were old news.

"I somehow doubt that."

"I might also ask what you are doing here, Lieutenant-Général La Reynie."

"Following you, Maître du Luc, what else?"

The words hit Charles like a mailed fist. "I am a member of a religious house, *monsieur,*" he said furiously, "and you have no evidence whatever that I am involved in this! The body is already stiff, he must have been killed hours ago. I have been here only a matter of minutes."

"Yes, but you talked to him yesterday. And whether you spent all of last night on your hard Jesuit bed, I couldn't say. By the time I learned about this body and put two men outside Louis le Grand, you could have been back inside the college. As for threatening me with your invisible little Jesuit tonsure, the king's writ runs everywhere. The old days of immunity for clerics in Paris ended a dozen years ago. Though I get arguments about that," La Reynie added sourly, waving his hand impatiently at the officer hovering beside Charles.

The man grinned evilly. "Turn around."

Knowing that resistance would get him nowhere he wanted to go, Charles turned to the wall. Swiftly, expertly, and impertinently, the man searched him to the skin. He tossed Charles's small purse of coins to La Reynie.

La Reynie caught it. "Now go to the outside door and keep everyone out."

Charles turned around. La Reynie watched his officer out of sight and hefted the nearly flat purse in his hand.

"Did you perhaps rob our friend here, Maître du Luc?"

"Oh, yes," Charles drawled, "there is so much wealth in this miserable stinkhole, I hardly knew where to begin."

"Pity. Then we are back where we started. Why are you here?"

Charles forced himself to swallow his anger. "You know that Philippe Douté's little brother was ridden down in the street. This poor soul saw the accident. I wanted to ask him about it, to satisfy the child's father about what happened. That's all."

La Reynie went to the pallet and looked down at the dead man. "Very interesting that this man was killed in the same way as Philippe."

Charles said nothing.

"Pierre Foret," La Reynie went on thoughtfully, watching Charles. "Quay porter. Sometime pickpocket. Nose smashed in a tavern brawl two years ago, so my sergeant who searched you tells me. Not a bad sort, Pierre, as his sort goes." He suddenly tossed Charles the purse. "On your own admission, you were the last to see Philippe alive and—"

"Except for his killer."

"—and you found his body. And now I find you here, standing over this man who was strangled in the same way as Philippe."

"Search me again." Charles held his arms out at his sides. "I have nothing that would make that kind of mark." He let his arms fall. "But that wouldn't keep you from arresting me, would it? You and Louvois don't need evidence. You destroy whom you please."

La Reynie's brows drew together and his dark eyes flickered. Charles wondered fleetingly if there was a man behind that inscrutable face who minded being feared and hated.

"Have I said that I am arresting you, Maître du Luc?" The police chief's voice was smooth as syrup. "On the contrary, I am offering you a choice."

"What choice?"

"My men can follow you, as they did yesterday. They can watch who comes and goes from Louis le Grand, as they watched you this morning. But I need a fly inside the college, someone to tell me everything there is to know from that vantage point about the murder and the 'accident.' What is being said. And not said. Who—if not you—is the favorite for the role of murderer." He smiled blandly at Charles. "Your good rector is honest as far as his speech goes. But I fear he is telling me only what will not hurt his beloved college and the Society of Jesus. You are not going to have that luxury. There is your choice. Agree to get the information I need, or I will arrest you here and now, on suspicion of that murder and this one and take you to the Châtelet."

He paused courteously, his head on one side as though eager to answer any questions Charles might have. But Charles's tongue was as frozen as the rest of him.

"When we reach the Châtelet, I will summon the war minister. M. Louvois is a ruthless questioner, Maître du Luc. And why? Because his passion is not for morality, but for order. On the whole, a more deadly commitment, I often find. He has few qualms about destroying anyone who brings disorder to the realm. Common criminals, Huguenots, their sympathizers, their co-conspirators. It is all one to Monsieur Louvois. And when you have screamed out your confession of treason in Nîmes, I will use it. Against your college, your Society, and your family."

"Nîmes?" Charles just managed to get the word out.

"Nîmes," La Reynie said genially. "Drunken bishops are so often worth their weight in gold."

Charles closed his eyes and cursed silently. His dear cousin the bishop had never been able to hold his wine. But where in God's name could La Reynie have seen him?

"You didn't know he visited Versailles?" La Reynie said, as though reading Charles's mind. "It was before you came to Paris. Perhaps he was arranging for your new assignment. Or perhaps he was only reminding the king of his existence, since his appointment is still unconfirmed. Thanks to the pope taking his revenge for the church revenue quarrel by refusing to confirm Louis's episcopal appointments. However that may be, Bishop du Luc grew very merry during an evening of court gambling and poured the whole story of the latest du Luc family scandal into the pretty little ear of one of my court flies. Who poured it into mine."

"Flies?"

La Reynie laughed. "As in 'fly on the wall.' Oh, you will be in good company, I promise you. Indeed, you would be surprised at some of my flies. Where was I? Oh, yes. Bishop du Luc was sober enough not to name you, but it was easy enough to guess who his errant churchman cousin was when a du Luc turned up at Louis le Grand. I am aware that teaching assignments there do not normally go to unknown fledglings from the provinces. No matter how talented, of course." He bowed ironically. "You should be very grateful to the bishop." Every trace of amusement was suddenly gone from La Reynie's face. "Choose, Maître du Luc."

Chapter 17

La Reynie's newest fly leaned on the Pont Neuf's parapet, staring at the unlovely face of his cowardice. Refusing the lieutenant-général would have been his death warrant, whether sooner in the Châtelet or later in the Place de Grève or a Mediterranean galley. At least, thank every saint there was, Pernelle was out of La Reynie's reach. Out of M. Louvois's reach, too, and Louvois terrified Charles even more than La Reynie did. And refusing would have unleashed scandal and retribution on the Society, the college, and on the whole du Luc family. God knew, he didn't want anyone else to suffer for what he'd done.

Mostly, though, he didn't want to die. Charles shuddered and closed his eyes, suddenly back at the siege of St. Omer. He heard the din of drums and trumpets and smelled the crazy battle energy, like the air before a storm. He heard the screams of men and horses, saw the blood gleaming on pikes and swords, heard the crack of muskets, and breathed the bitter smell of gunpowder. He'd been as full of battle lust as any man there, secure in the immortality of being eighteen. When the musket ball hit him, he'd thought at first that someone's horse had kicked him. Then he'd seen the bright flower of blood blooming on the shoulder of his padded doublet. The certainty that he was going to die had wiped away his adolescent fantasy of noble death after thwarted love, and he'd thrown back his head and howled—not from the pain, but in grief for his unlived life. He had even less desire to die now.

He opened his eyes and watched the sky shed its last thin veil of fog, watched hunting swallows skim the slow, olive green river, watched a pair of bargemen sprawled on their canvas-wrapped load passing a leather bottle back and forth, watched as though he were going to paint it all. The words of another ex-soldier rose from the depths of memory. "Let it make no difference to thee," Roman Emperor Marcus Aurelius Antoninus had written, "whether thou art dying or doing something else." With a mental salute to the old stoic, Charles straightened. Time to get on with the something else. With being La Reynie's fly, which he wouldn't be if he'd obeyed the rector's order to leave Philippe's murder and Antoine's accident alone. But if he started obeying now, he'd die. La Reynie would see to that. If he kept on disobeying and the rector found out, he'd lose his vocation. Which he preferred to lose by choice, if he was going to lose it. But he wasn't dying, not yet.

He pushed off from the parapet, waved away a man selling cherries from his donkey's panniers, and walked on. He squeezed around a sedan chair, set down beside the mackerel sellers while the lady inside chose her dinner, and hesitated at the end of the bridge. He'd reached the Pont Neuf from the quay, but cutting through the streets might be a faster way back to the college. Paris, like other towns, had no street signs, and he was too new to have a map in his head. But the sun was out now and the college lay to the southeast. How lost could he get?

He set off along the busy street that continued from the Pont Neuf, beside the wall of the Grand Augustin monastery, looking for a southeast turning. As he walked, he set himself to go over everything he knew about the murders and Antoine's injury. He wasn't at all sure of La Reynie's motives, not completely sure that finding the killer was what La Reynie really wanted. It had crossed his mind that La Reynie might be looking for something else inside the college, something Charles didn't know about, and be using the search for the killer as an excuse. But finding the killer was what Charles wanted. That and surviving his indenture as a fly, with minimal betrayal to the Society and his vows. All of which was going to depend on concocting reports that were true as far as they went and went only as far as he wanted them to.

Like an orator making his first point, he held up a thumb. One: The fact that La Reynie needed a spy in the college meant that what had happened was part of something that stretched from Paris into Louis le Grand. Or, of course, the other way around. His first finger went up. Two: According to the ex-soldier who'd taken him to the Louvre, the murdered porter had complained that someone was following him. But the man had been killed before he could tell Charles what he knew, so someone had been following both of them. Charles swallowed and looked over his shoulder, suddenly remembering the menacing gravel-voiced porter who'd stopped him from chasing Pierre. Had the man had his own reasons for trying to keep Pierre from talking to Charles?

His middle finger sprang to attention. Three: The mark on the porter's neck was like the mark on Philippe's. Who knew how Philippe had died? The Louis le Grand faculty and lay brothers. Probably most of the students by now. La Reynie and some of his men. And, no doubt, Louvois, which meant that all three persons of that unholy trinity—La Reynie, Louvois, and Guise—knew about the braided cord the murderer had used.

Charles turned down a lane lined with old houses faced with stone and straightened his ring finger. Four: Guise was the only other person at the college—as far as Charles knew—who had talked to the street porter Pierre. But surely, Charles told himself, if Guise had followed him yesterday, he would have noticed. And he couldn't imagine the fastidious Guise slinking through the beggars' Louvre in the dead of night to murder poor Pierre. But there were the old stairs. If Guise watched his chance in the bakery, he could come and go from his rooms unseen whenever he pleased.

Charles's little finger jabbed the air. Five: Mme LeClerc had witnessed the accident, and had no qualms about talking, yet no one was trying to silence her. The thought of anyone trying to silence Mme LeClerc, however, made Charles laugh out loud, earning him a wary look from a woman with a basket of squawking chickens. So why had the porter been a danger, but not the baker's wife?

The little street dead-ended and Charles stopped, waiting for a clutch of Augustinian monks to pass on the cross street. He turned right and his left thumb stood up. Six: The dead porter, Antoine's story of the note, and the old staircase were all connected, one way or another, to Guise.

Charles's thoughts suddenly jumped their logical track. Guise seemed not to know what Charles had done in Nîmes. Which must mean that La Reynie had not told him. Charles frowned, remembering how La Reynie had watched Louvois accuse him after the funeral, neither contradicting nor agreeing. And then La Reynie had kept Louvois from following him and Antoine. Puzzling over La Reynie, Charles turned east at the next street crossing. But that street curved north and took him nearly back to the river. He stopped, looked around, and held up his next finger. Seven: He was lost.

By the time he found the rue St. Jacques and the college again, the midday meal was half over. He apologized to the rector, slid into his seat, and bolted the boiled beef, brown bread, and cucumber salad, made all the more palatable by the fact that Père Guise ate with his back half turned to Charles, talking only to Père Montville on his left. Père Jouvancy caught Charles on his way out of the refectory to ask solicitously after his tooth. Swallowing guilt, Charles said that his courage had failed him and he'd decided to try medicine before facing the tooth-drawer. Nodding sympathetically, Jouvancy told him to ask Frère Brunet for something to ease the pain. And added an admonition not to be late for rehearsal.

Charles checked to see that Antoine was where he should be, waiting with his class to leave the junior refectory, and went outside, where the quiet recreation hour had started. He sat down on a bench against the refectory wall, pretending to watch a chess game two boys were playing at the bench's other end. When Guise emerged, Charles let him get halfway across the court and then strolled, unnoticed, in his wake. He watched Guise enter the latrine courtyard and go into the building where the students' library was. Assuming the air of a man who wanted only to be alone with his sore tooth and his thoughts, Charles settled on the shady stone bench built into the archway between the two courts and waited, but Guise didn't reappear. Ostentatiously rubbing his jaw, Charles made his way back toward his rooms through an illicitly rowdy game of tag.

Taking the stairs two at a time, he went to Guise's door and listened, then eased it open and went quickly through the empty chamber to the study. Just where Antoine had given his sleepwalking performance, a brown and gold tapestry of Hannibal and his elephants crossing the Alps hung on wooden rings from a pole. Charles slid it aside and uncovered the low, arched door he'd seen from the other side. He tried the latch. The door swung silently inward, revealing the staircase Charles had climbed. As he put his foot on the top step to go and see if the lower door was still unlocked, he heard footsteps climbing the stairs quickly toward him. Noiselessly, he shut the door, pulled the tapestry across it, and raced into the chamber. As he slid out of sight between Guise's bed and the wall, the hanging rattled on its rings and footsteps crossed the study. He pressed his cheek to the floor and saw a pair of spurred boots with folded tops stride quickly across his line of vision. Jackboots the color of burnt sugar, like the boots Mme LeClerc said Antoine's attacker had worn.

Charles burst from his hiding place as the chamber door closed behind his quarry. He scrambled across the bed, yelling at the man to stop, and wrenched the chamber door open. But in the passage, he collided with Père Dainville and had to stop and steady the old man while his quarry's footsteps pounded down the main staircase. By the time Charles reached the foot of the stairs, no one was there but Frère Moulin, coming from the grand salon with a bundle of wet rags in his arms.

"Did you see him? Where did he go?" Charles demanded, nearly falling over a bucket of dirty water,

"Frère Fabre?" The lay brother nodded toward the door to the street passage where Fabre, barefoot like Moulin and with his cassock kilted, was shouldering his way out with a bucket in each hand.

"The man who just ran down the stairs! Quick, which way?"

"We've been cleaning, maître, just finished." Moulin nodded over his shoulder at the salon, whose floor gleamed wetly. "What's wrong?"

Charles strode to the side door and into the street passage. "Did anyone come this way just now?" he called to Frère Martin, the porter, but Martin shook his head. Charles ran into the Cour d'honneur, still crowded with boys playing darts, chess, checkers, reading, and talking. He pushed his way among them, searching desperately for Antoine. The man in the boots was no casual thief, he hadn't searched Guise's rooms and he had known where he was going. If he was Antoine's attacker, if he'd come to finish what he'd bungled in the rue des Poirées . . . Charles went weak with relief when he finally found Antoine in a shaded corner of the student residence courtyard, lying on his belly and frowning over a chessboard. His tutor lay beside him, sound asleep. Charles managed a smile for the child and prodded Maître Doissin hard with his foot. Doissin grunted and Charles pulled him up and walked him out of Antoine's hearing.

"I asked you to watch this child, for God's sake!"

"*Doucement, maître,* softly, sweetly! I am watching him, there he is!"

Remembering the bloody patterned necklace that strangling had left on the porter's neck and Philippe's, Charles said through his teeth, "Do not let him out of your sight. Do you hear me? That means keeping your damned eyes open!"

The tutor spread his arms wide in injured innocence. "He is just there. I am just here. Maître du Luc, your humors must be out of balance—you should ask Frère Brunet to examine a specimen of your water."

Charles turned on his heel and squatted beside Antoine. The other boy, frowning over his next move with his tongue sticking out of the corner of his mouth, paid no attention.

"Remember our talk, *mon brave?*" Charles said in Antoine's ear. "Here's something else you can help me with. Stay close to Maître Doissin. Don't let him nap. Don't let him out of your sight. Even when you go to your grammar class, make sure he stays by the door."

Antoine rolled over and sat up. "Why?" he said eagerly.

"I can't tell you yet. Will you do it? Knights cannot always tell their squires everything, you know," he added, as Antoine began to frown.

"That's true. All right." Antoine glanced tolerantly at his tutor and nodded. "I'll look after him. He needs it." He went back to his game.

Charles went quickly through the rest of the courtyards without finding the man in the jackboots. Trying to search the college buildings by himself was pointless and he went back to the Cour d' honneur. How had the man gone so unnoticed and disappeared so quickly? Charles's head snapped toward the latrine court and he broke into a run.

He ran past the latrine and up the stairs to the students' library, ignoring the bell ringing for afternoon classes. The long, silent library, its walls lined floor to ceiling with book cupboards, with more cupboards set crosswise, making aisles, seemed empty until Guise emerged from an aisle with an open book in his hand.

"What are you doing here?" he snapped. "The bell has rung."

"A student, *mon père*," Charles murmured vaguely, and walked past him into a cross aisle.

"No student has come in here," Guise turned his attention back to his book.

Noting the "no student" rather than "no one," Charles walked quickly through the aisles, searching for other ways out of the single room and finding none. But Guise's lack of concern had already told him the man was not there. As he passed Guise on his way to the door, he glanced at the librarian's open book.

"English?" Charles said in surprise, looking at the crisp new pages.

"A new translation of our Père Bouhours's life of St. Ignatius," Guise said, unbending a little. He stroked the book's calf binding lovingly. "Just published in London," he said, his voice warming. "Thanks to good King James and his open loyalty to the true faith."

"Yes, an interesting situation in England just now. Well. If you're sure no one has come in . . ."

"I have told you. No student has been here, they would all rather play than use their time wisely." The momentary warmth was gone and Guise looked pointedly at the door.

Charles went slowly back to the Cour d'honneur, caught between his conscience and his own needs. In the interest of college safety—especially Antoine's safety—Père Le Picart had to know about the intruder. Which meant that Charles would have to confess his presence in Guise's study and his reason for it. He found Le Picart in the chapel, where two workmen were peering at a crack in the altar's marble. When the rector heard Charles's steps, he looked up and frowned.

"What are you doing here, Maître du Luc?" He hurried down the chancel steps. "Has something happened?"

Charles told him, steeling himself for the inevitable question.

"And how do you know all this, *maître*?" Le Picart's voice was dangerously quiet.

He listened to Charles's answer with a face like thunder. "I will alert the proctors and see to Antoine. And I will see you in my office after supper. Go to your rehearsal and apologize to Père Jouvancy for your lateness."

"Yes, *mon père*."

Charles left the chapel with a heavy heart and the fear that he'd just made sure his first Louis le Grand show would be his last. He hoped Le Picart would be content with shipping him back to the south instead of to some foreign mission. On the other hand, Lieutenant-Général La Reynie was less likely to find him in China or New France. And what La Reynie would do to him if he failed as a "fly" might well be worse than what hostile pagan natives could come up with.

Jouvancy was coaching a sword fight when Charles arrived in the classroom. He waved away Charles's apology and Charles went to the ballet end of the room, where Maître Beauchamps was picking up Time's much-mended chiming clock from the floor at Walter Connor's feet. The dancing master flung it over his shoulder to his servant, who was taken off guard for once and missed it. It crashed to the floor, and as the man stolidly picked up the black and gold pieces, Connor flashed Charles a relieved and triumphant smile. Behind Beauchamps's back, Charles raised clasped hands over his head in a gesture of victory.

It was a long afternoon. Charles and Beauchamps coaxed and threatened the ballet cast through a decent rendering of three of the ballet's four parts. Hercules's suite remembered their steps, François de Lille danced Hercules with more spirit, and Armand Beauclaire knew his left from his right, all of which argued divine collusion between the goddess of dance, Terpsichore, and St. Genesius, patron of anyone crazy enough to be a performer.

But the demons of chaos, expelled for the moment from the ballet, ran gleefully riot in the tragedy. The Montmorency boy playing Clovis jibed once too often at the Lithuanian general's son playing Ragnacaire for dying like a sissy. Ragnacaire's languid patience deserted him and he told Clovis what he could do with his bad acting. Montmorency hit him. Ragnacaire defended his honor while the rest of the cast clapped and cheered. Jouvancy stunned everyone by boxing both combatants soundly on the ears—foreign to his practice and against college rules—and setting them long passages of Virgil to copy out and translate by tomorrow.

When the students had fled and Beauchamps had staggered away, Jouvancy collapsed onto a wooden bench, leaned against the wall, and closed his eyes. Charles slumped down beside him, thinking how much he'd come to like the little priest and how much he wanted to stay in Paris. He turned his head slightly to see if Jouvancy had gone to sleep. The rhetoric master's eyes stayed closed and Charles studied him. Grieving was leaving its mark. Jouvancy's eyes were darkly shadowed and he was noticeably thinner than he'd been a week ago. Charles shook his head and leaned back against the wall. Philippe's murder was eating at the whole college like a canker worm.

He half wished now that he hadn't gone to the rector. He thought now that the man in the boots had likely been on his way to Guise rather than looking for Antoine. He'd used the old stairs, come so confidently through Guise's rooms, seemed to know where he was going. And if the rector used what Charles had told him and confronted Guise, then Guise and the man would both be on their guard and harder to catch. Charles sighed. The chickens were out of the coop. He *had* gone to the rector. And whatever the rector said or didn't to Guise, he was either going to send Charles away in disgrace or discipline him severely for his disobedience.

Which brought Charles face-to-face with the question he didn't want to ask. If he felt so penned by his vow of obedience, what was he doing here? First a soldier, now a Jesuit, why did he keep putting himself into situations where obedience—often unquestioning obedience—was required? *Because I'm an idiot,* he told himself sourly.

True, said the cool-eyed part of him that stood perpetually aside from his feelings, the part that rose up to challenge him when he least wanted it. *But leaving that sad fact aside,* it went on, *you know very well that without obedience there is no order. No justice.*

Perhaps, Charles returned, *yet just a few hours ago La Reynie told me that Louvois is merciless because of his passion for order.*

Does that make all order evil? the cool-eyed part of him asked. *Or is it the man who is evil because he has too much power and too little heart and mostly obeys no one? Because without obedience, you have only yourself. Do you know everything, see everything? Is your own will the right answer to every question?*

No, all right, of course not, Charles thought irritably. *But I'm still an idiot for going to the rector without stopping to think.*

True, the unwelcome part of himself murmured, and left him in peace.

"Is something wrong, Maître du Luc?" Jouvancy was watching him in concern.

Charles felt himself flush, hoping he hadn't said any of his inner argument out loud. "No, *mon père.* Well, yes," he amended. "May I apologize again for being late, *mon père?*" He had no quarrel with courtesy, one of obedience's sweeter fruits.

"If you must." Jouvancy smiled back.

"Thank you."

They went on sitting, listening to a fly buzz lazily in the companionable quiet.

"Cistercians," Jouvancy said into the silence, with the air of a man reaching a conclusion. "On the eighth of August, I shall join the Cistercians."

"What? Why, *mon père?*"

"No children. No Siamese delegation. No theatre."

Charles laughed and then realized what Jouvancy had said. "Siamese delegation?"

"Père La Chaise told the rector that they arrived yesterday at Berny—just outside the city. They will stay there until their presents for the king catch up with them. The king receives them at Versailles on September first."

"But that's not our concern, is it?" Charles said, puzzled.

"I didn't tell you? The Siamese ambassadors are coming to our show."

Charles slid lower on the bench. Just what they needed. Exotic—and no doubt bewildered—strangers from the other side of the world sitting in the front row and mesmerizing the student performers. French Jesuits had been talking for months now about the delegation, which was accompanied by the famous Jesuit mathematician Père Guy Tachard. Siam's King Narai was interested in foreign realms and foreign kings, and King Louis was very interested in elbowing the Dutch out of the center of Siamese trade. Père Tachard wanted to strengthen the Jesuit mission in Siam and make a Christian out of King Narai. If the delegation needed entertainment, Charles had to admit that the Louis le Grand performance was a natural choice.

"I cannot wait to see them!" Jouvancy said, his pique evaporating. "They're said to be little, amber-skinned men. Wonderful clothes, lots of gorgeous silk draped just so. I hear that everywhere they stay, the ladies crowd in to watch them eat their supper." Jouvancy smiled sideways at Charles and raised his eyebrows. "The ambassadors offer fruit to the prettiest ones."

"If our dancers and actors are as fascinated as the ladies, our show is in big trouble."

Jouvancy grunted in agreement. The silence lengthened and Charles fell into a near drowse. "Maître du Luc!"

"What?" Charles shot bolt upright and looked anxiously around.

Jouvancy had turned to face him, his eyes shining. "We can study the Siamese and make drawings, and have a Siamese entrée in next year's ballet!"

But I probably won't be here next year, Charles didn't say. "I thought you were joining the Cistercians, *mon père,*" he said lightly.

"After we do the Siamese entrée."

They both burst out laughing. Glad for even a glimmer of humor in Jouvancy's tired face, Charles shoved away his worry about his meeting with the rector and pulled the rhetoric master to his feet. They went companionably in search of a presupper glass of watered wine.

Chapter 18

Supper was pea soup, seasoned this time with clove and endive, and poured over thick, broth-soaked bread. To Charles's relief, Père Guise continued to ignore him, but even that didn't help his appetite as his meeting with the rector loomed. By the time the refectory was dismissed, dread lay heavy in his belly. And weighed the more when he looked into the junior refectory to check on Antoine, and Antoine wasn't there. As the boy's tablemates filed out the door, Charles grabbed Maître Doissin.

"Where is he?"

"Calm yourself, Maître du Luc!" Antoine's tutor shook his big shaggy head and gently disengaged his arm. "Antoine felt unwell, so I allowed him to stay in his chamber. The kitchen is sending something for him."

"You left him *alone?*" Charles turned abruptly and pushed his way through the press of boys toward the door.

"No, no," Doissin said, following him. "Not alone. Not really alone, the courtyard proctor promised to check on him."

Charles made for the north courtyard, through the evening recreation hour's games of tag and volleys of shuttlecocks. Suddenly Père Guise was in his path.

"To the rector's office," Guise said through his teeth. "Now."

Charles's stomach lurched. Were Guise's accusations of heresy and insinuations of murder going to be part of his meeting with the rector?

"After I find Antoine." Charles started around Guise toward the north court.

"You will not find him there."

"Why? What do you mean? Has something happened to him?"

Guise stalked toward the main building. Charles passed him and burst unceremoniously into the rector's office. Antoine and Marie-Ange stood side by side in front of Père Le Picart's desk.

"Well," Charles said, light-headed with relief, "if it isn't Pitchin and Pitchot." He wanted to throttle Guise for terrifying him. But what were the children doing here? Their fleeting smiles at the names of the folk tale characters vanished as Guise arrived and slammed the door behind him.

Le Picart remained expressionless. "Now," he said, before Guise could speak, "let us clarify matters before we begin."

His voice was flat and dust dry and he was using it, Charles realized with admiration, to soak emotion out of the air like earth soaking away rain.

"The points at issue," Le Picart said, "are as follows. First, Père Guise has just found these children in his study, where they had no right to be. Second, on their own admission, they were searching his belongings. Third, Père Guise seems to feel that you, Maître du Luc, are responsible for this intrusion. Fourth—and attend to me, all of you—" His glance caught and held on Guise "—this conversation will be conducted courteously, or not at all." He eyed the children. "Let us start again, now that Maître du Luc is here. Were you in Père Guise's rooms?"

"Yes, *mon père*." They nodded in unison.

"How did you get into the college, Marie-Ange?"

Charles, standing behind the children, saw Antoine kick her in the ankle. Marie-Ange kicked him harder in return and catapulted Charles back twenty years, to standing hand-in-hand with Pernelle in front of his mother, the two of them charged with some childish misdemeanor, and Pernelle's sharp kick at his ankle bone when he'd tried to take all the blame.

"I went up the old stairs from the bakery, *mon père*," Marie-Ange said.

Guise drew in his breath with a hiss. "How dare you—"

Le Picart held up a hand. "Were the staircase doors unlocked, Marie-Ange?"

"It wasn't her fault, *mon père*," Antoine burst out. "She was only helping me. I wanted to find Philippe's note." He pointed at his godfather. "He took it and it's the last thing Philippe gave me and I want it back!"

"Silence!" Le Picart barely raised his voice, but Guise clamped his teeth together as quickly as Antoine did. "Marie-Ange, answer my question."

"The doors were unlocked, *mon père*."

Le Picart looked fleetingly at Charles. "I see. Now, Antoine. You say that Philippe wrote you a note?"

Antoine recounted finding the note, putting it in his breeches pocket under his scholar's gown, trying to meet his brother, and being prevented by the accident. Marie-Ange said that she'd seen Guise search Antoine's pockets in the street and take something. Guise shut his eyes, slowly shaking his head.

"Did you search his pockets, Père Guise?" the rector said mildly.

"I looked for a handkerchief to stop his bleeding. I had none myself."

"And did you find a note as you searched?"

"I know nothing about a note, *mon père*. I have told Antoine and told him. But he persists in this spiteful fantasy."

Both children turned on Guise. "It is *not*—"

Le Picart slapped his desk. "If you want to be heard, you will obey the rules I have set. Père Guise, what does Maître du Luc have to do with this coil?"

"Though I grieve to say it, *mon père*, he is corrupting my godson. He pays him far too much attention. After the funeral, I found him in the boy's room. Just the two of them." Guise let the words hang in the air until they were loud with what he hadn't said. "He is alienating the child from me, filling his head with lies. He as good as told Antoine that I took this wretched note. How could I even have known such a thing was there?"

"Did you imply to Antoine that Père Guise took this note, Maître du Luc?"

Charles's blue gaze was as wide and innocent as he could make it. "I told Antoine not to bother Père Guise about the note, *mon père*." Charles shook his head. "I regret, Père Guise," he said silkily, "that I was unable to speak with the porter you pointed out, the one who witnessed the accident. Perhaps *he* could clarify this confusion. If we could only find him." Ignoring Guise's look of pure hatred, Charles turned to Le Picart. "Speaking of implying things, *mon père*, I would like to know why Père Guise has spread rumors, in the college and beyond, that I may be guilty of Philippe's murder, when he knows I never met Philippe until the day he died. Does not murder usually have a history and an urgent reason behind it?"

"So I understand," Le Picart said. "I, too, was puzzled by your remarks at our faculty gathering, Père Guise."

"I was overset with grief at Philippe's terrible death," Guise said indignantly. "I hardly knew what I said. But I am not the only one who wonders about du Luc. Before he had been here twenty-four hours, Philippe disappeared. And then this child was run down in the street! What do we truly know of him— besides his dangerous views, of which I have warned you? I will ask questions in the name of God's truth, even if no one else in this college will! Du Luc—"

"He is *Maître* du Luc, *mon père*. And I and his former superiors know quite a lot about him and his views. As I do about you and yours," the rector added, with a benign smile.

Guise went a shade whiter with anger. "Maître du Luc was not ordered to pursue Philippe beyond our walls, we have nothing but his word that he did so. It is common knowledge that he is a heretic lover, and we all know that the evil of those who shield heretics knows no—"

"Common knowledge? You surprise me. Maître du Luc, have you been disciplined for your theological views?"

"No, *mon père*. Père Guise did start a conversation about heretics on my first day here, and I remember saying that our God is a God of love. If he took that as heresy . . ." Charles spread his hands in a helpless gesture.

"I am sure that none of us would take that as heresy in itself," the rector said smoothly. "And did you indeed talk with Antoine in his chamber the day of the funeral?"

"Yes, *mon père*. I broke the rule about being in a student's chamber. He was grieving and did not know where to find his tutor, and I was loathe to leave him alone."

Guise wagged a finger under Charles's nose. "It is not for you to decide what rules to follow!"

Careful not to look at Le Picart, Charles said, "I am very sorry, Père Guise, if you were unable to hear us clearly while you were eavesdropping. I truly did urge Antoine not to bother you about this alleged note."

"And that was well done," the rector said, over Guise's protest. "Now. To continue. Is anything missing from your rooms, *mon père?*"

"I have not yet looked." Guise turned his glare on Marie-Ange. "I am sure I shall find things missing. How this gutter child got a key to the staircase—"

"I am *not* a gutter child! And the doors were unlocked!" Flushed with outrage, her hands fisted on her hips, Marie-Ange looked so much like her mother that Charles had to put up a hand to hide his smile. "*I* don't steal," she spat at Guise. "But you do!"

"You see, *mon père?*" Guise's voice quivered with fury. "You see what she is? She runs in and out of the college, corrupting our boys, who knows all that she does. Maître du Luc encourages her, her presence is *his* fault—"

"Oh, no, *mon père!*" Charles said earnestly, stepping too close to Guise and forcing his attention away from Marie-Ange. "I can tell you definitively that her presence among us is not my fault—indeed, I trust it is Roger the baker's fault!"

Out of the corner of his eye, Charles saw Le Picart's thin shoulders shake with silent laughter. Which vanished as Guise whirled to face him.

"I demand that you discipline this man. He is as insolent as these children!"

"What I will do now is close this discussion," Le Picart said evenly. "If anything is missing from your rooms, Père Guise, report to me. We will consider the staircase doors at a future time." He looked at Marie-Ange. "Whatever is true about this supposed note, child, it is not your business. Have nothing more to do with it." A smile softened his face. "Antoine may visit with you when he comes to your shop, *ma petite*. I think you are a good friend to him. But you must not come into the college. As Père Guise rightly says, it is not a place for girls."

"Yes, *mon père.*" She sighed. More in exasperation than penitence, Charles thought.

"Tomorrow," Le Picart went on, "I will repeat to your mother what I have said to you. And now you may go home, *mademoiselle.* Through the street postern, please."

Marie-Ange eyed the rector as if he were a burned brioche. "Are you going to hit Antoine after I leave? If you are, I'm staying and you'll have to hit me, too, because it was both of us looking for the note!"

The rector pursed his lips, trying to keep a straight face. "Some punishment is in order, but no one is going to hit him. What your mother will do with you, of course, I cannot say."

"Oh, she'll swat my derrière and yell at me." Marie-Ange shrugged. "But she never hits hard."

"Then we wish you a *bonne nuit, mademoiselle.*"

She curtsied to him, and she and Antoine exchanged a furtive squeeze of hands. Then she smiled at Charles, gave Guise her back with all the precise implication of a court lady, and bustled out of the room.

"Sleep well, Jeanne d'Arc," Charles murmured, as the door shut behind her.

"Now for you, Antoine," the rector said, and the little boy drew himself up manfully. "First, I charge you, also, not to talk about or look for this alleged note. Second, you well know that it is a grave wrong to sneak into someone's chamber and look through their belongings. You will say a dozen Paternosters and a dozen Aves before you sleep tonight. Third, before you leave here, you will ask your godfather's pardon."

Antoine's expression turned sullen, but he might have done as he was bidden if Guise had kept quiet.

"Yes, you will certainly ask my forgiveness, Antoine, and on your knees!" Guise pointed a long finger at the floor.

Antoine's chin jutted and his hands closed into fists. "That's not fair. You should apologize to me for taking—"

"Antoine," Le Picart said wearily, "we have finished with that. Do as your godfather tells you. Now."

Suddenly past all restraint, Antoine turned on the rector. "*I* am not finished with it! Why do you always believe him? You don't know the bad things he does, he kisses my stepmother, I was in the tree, I saw him—"

"Liar!"

In a blur of movement, Guise crossed the room and slapped Antoine's face so hard that the boy staggered. Antoine launched himself at Guise, his arms flailing like windmill sails.

"Enough!" Le Picart thundered, leaping to his feet.

Charles grabbed Antoine just before his fists connected with Guise's middle. The boy struggled furiously in his grasp, but Guise stood as though turned to stone.

"Maître du Luc," the rector said through stiff lips, "take this child to the antechamber and keep him there until I call you."

"Come, *mon brave*," Charles sighed, turning the still protesting Antoine toward the door. "This battle is over."

Chapter 19

Charles propelled Antoine across the grand salon and forcibly sat him down on the antechamber's bench.

"I'll kill him," Antoine cried, trying to get up again. "I will!"

"Sit!" Keeping a tight grip on the boy's shoulder, Charles sat beside him. "I wouldn't kill him, you know," he said mildly. "I hear that being hanged is very unpleasant. Even more unpleasant than having Père Guise for a godfather. And the consequences last a lot longer."

Antoine flung himself back against the wall and swore with surprising fluency. Philippe's competent teaching, no doubt.

"I suspect that the rector is as angry at Père Guise as he is at you," Charles said. "But don't go saying I told you that."

Antoine folded his arms and glowered at the three-foot bronze of pious Aeneas on a table against the salon's far wall. But he made no move to get up and Charles felt some of the tension go out of the small body.

"Listen," Charles said, "don't bring more punishment on yourself. When the moment comes, apologize nicely to the rector. And to Père Guise—no, just listen one little moment. Our rules, after all, do frown on attempted single combat with a professor. And one *honnête homme* does not attack another."

"Honest gentlemen have duels! They fight wars!"

"Not in the rector's office. So say the prayers he gave you, take whatever else you get as punishment, and then it will be over. I don't think Père Le Picart will be too severe."

"I don't care," Antoine said sullenly, kicking at one of the bench's legs. "Whoever made the rules didn't know old Guise. And he's not an *honnête homme.*"

Inclined to agree on both counts, Charles let the boy kick. Antoine looked up anxiously.

"Maître du Luc? I didn't break my promise to you. I only promised not to *talk* about the note. Marie-Ange already knew about it and you didn't say anything about not looking for it."

Charles rolled his eyes. "True enough, Monsieur Legalist. I see I should have been more precise. So can we have a civilized gentlemen's agreement not to talk *or* take action about the note?" Charles glanced at the rector's door to be sure it was still closed. "Think for a moment, Antoine. If Père Guise took the note, he will have gotten rid of it long ago."

Antoine looked stricken. "Why?"

Charles frowned at a splotch of blood red in the painting of Alexander the Great on the salon wall and searched for an answer that would satisfy the child without frightening him.

"Well, do you think he would keep it as a memento of Philippe?"

"No! He didn't even like Philippe. He doesn't like me, either, he just pretends to." Antoine moved closer, as though he were suddenly cold, and Charles put an arm around him. "I will do as you say, *maître.*"

"Thank you, *mon brave.* And there's another thing. Stay away from the old stairs. And do not talk about them. Will you promise?"

"Why?"

"Do you always have to have a reason before you obey?"

Antoine returned Charles's stern look. "Don't you?"

Hoist with his own petard, Charles gazed down at the fierce little face. Truth deserved a measure of truth in return. "Remember where those stairs lead, Antoine. Do you really want to make Père Guise any angrier?"

Antoine shivered involuntarily and shook his head.

"Then, *monsieur*, will you do me the honor of giving me your word, as one *honnête homme* to another?"

Antoine stood up. "I give you my word, *mon père*," he said gravely and bowed like a courtier.

Charles rose, bowed in return, and they both sat back down. Feeling as though he'd come slightly scathed through a duel of words, he fought the urge to question the boy about Guise kissing Lisette Douté.

"You think I lied about him kissing her, don't you?" Antoine said, as though he'd heard Charles's thoughts.

"Did you?"

"No! He kissed her and they laughed and he kissed her some more."

Charles struggled briefly with himself and lost. "When was that?"

"At her birthday fête. The thirteenth of July. In our garden in Chantilly."

"But, Antoine, everyone gets kissed on their birthday."

Antoine shook his head so hard that his fine dark hair flew over his face. "Not like that! It was like when my father thinks they're alone and kisses her. Long and"—he wrinkled his nose with distaste—"they wiggle and make noises. Ugh!"

Wiggling and noises? Charles's eyebrows climbed almost into his hair. "How did you see all this?"

"I didn't mean to. It's base to spy and I wasn't!"

Charles winced. Yes, it was indeed base to spy. "Where were you?"

"Philippe had chased me and I'd climbed a big tree beside the garden path. Then Père Guise and Lisette stopped right under me. They didn't know I was there and I didn't want them to, so I was very still."

Guise came out of the rector's office with a face like marble and disappeared toward the back of the house. Antoine followed him with angry eyes.

"At least he didn't kiss old Louvois," the boy muttered.

"What?!"

"M. Louvois was there, too. The fat pig."

"The M. Louvois who is the minister of war?"

Antoine nodded. "After Lisette went away, Père Guise walked on down the path, and I was climbing down, but I saw Philippe coming and I threw some gravel I had in my pocket at him, and he climbed up to get me back. But then Père Guise came back with Monsieur Louvois. So we stayed in the tree because we didn't want to talk to them. They stopped on the path beside the tree and argued for a while. Later I asked them about something they said and they said I was lying. And they were angry that I'd listened in the tree and my father sent me to bed before the cakes, like I told you after Philippe's funeral. But I wasn't lying! I didn't mean to listen, but I couldn't not hear them, could I? All I wanted was to know about dragons because they'd said that even if there aren't any here, there might still be some in England!"

Charles stared blankly, trying to make sense out of that. Then his lips tightened as he realized that Antoine had probably heard Louvois talking about soldiers, his cursed dragoons. Charles smiled at Antoine. "Yes, I suppose there might be some dragons still in England." When he was Antoine's age, he, too, had explained France's sad lack of dragons by deciding that they'd taken refuge in England, a heretical country where St. Michael and St. Mary Magdalene might not be able to fight them effectively. Suddenly another thought struck him.

"Did you tell Philippe about this kiss you saw?"

"Yes, on the way back into the house. He got angry and said he didn't care who kissed her. She'd been trying to get Philippe to kiss her all day, but he wouldn't." The boy sighed. "He was angry a lot of the time."

"What about?"

"Oh, about her. And other things. He was angry about the treasure, but that was after the fête."

Charles twisted on the bench to see Antoine's face, wondering if they were back in the land of dragons. "Treasure?"

"Will you keep it secret if I tell you?"

"If keeping it secret won't hurt anyone."

"Oh, it won't." Antoine wriggled closer. "Marie-Ange and I found it," he whispered. "In the stable hayloft. A real treasure, a knight's treasure! Marie-Ange cried, it was so sad—jewels and a scarf and a little portrait and some golden ribbons, all from the knight's dead lady! And we weren't trying to steal it! I was climbing out onto a rafter and the box was wedged between the rafter and the wall and it fell out. The latch part with the lock was so rusted it broke open. We were looking at the things when Philippe came looking for me and climbed up, and Frère Moulin came with him. When they saw the box, they were so angry that Marie-Ange was scared, but I wasn't. I'm so tired of everyone being angry at me!"

"Another good reason to stay out of the stable," Charles said, wondering if the sad little box of memories was poor

Frère Moulin's. If so, it was prohibited for a lay brother to have, but illicit or not, Charles was certainly not going to interfere in another man's struggles with what he'd had to leave behind.

Heavy footsteps sounded and Guise re-entered the salon, followed by Maître Doissin. With a hangdog look at Charles, Doissin went into the rector's office. Guise swept past Charles and Antoine as though they were furniture and climbed the stairs.

Antoine leaned his head against Charles and yawned. "Will you come and see me tomorrow?"

"I'll at least look in at your refectory door."

"That's all?" Antoine sighed and kicked halfheartedly at the bench.

By the time a very chastened Doissin came out of the office with Le Picart, the boy was nearly asleep. Charles shook him gently and he scrambled up from the bench. Charles hauled himself to his feet, wishing that this was the end of the day's events. But his own session with Le Picart was still to come. Doissin smiled apologetically and shrugged at Charles, who stared back accusingly.

"Antoine," the rector said, "Maître Doissin will take you to your chamber now. Where I expect you to apologize to him for lying and saying you were sick. Before you go to your bed, you will complete the penance I gave you. Tomorrow morning after Mass, Maître Doissin will bring you to my office and we will consider the rest of the matter." His expression softened and he tilted the boy's chin up gently. "Do not trouble too much about it for now. God grant you a peaceful night, child."

Blinking with exhaustion, Antoine let Doissin lead him away. Charles tried a tentative step toward the stairs, but Le Picart gestured him curtly to the office, where he shut the door and pointed him to a chair beside the empty fireplace.

"Not the evening any of us wanted," he said, going to the

tall oak cupboard beside the desk. "And you and I have still not talked."

Charles swallowed. Here it came. "No, *mon père*."

He watched in confusion as Le Picart put glasses on the table between the two chairs, set a small brown pitcher beside the glasses, and sat down. He poured a wine dark as plums and held a glass out to Charles, who took it with wary thanks.

"You are thinking that wine—especially unwatered wine—does not usually accompany a rector's chastisement." Le Picart drank and smiled tiredly. "You are correct. It has been a very long day and I am indulging myself." He drank again and set the glass down. "Now for the chastisement. I ordered you to leave finding Philippe's killer and Antoine's attacker to others. You have disobeyed me repeatedly. Why?"

Charles put his wine down untasted. "Because Philippe was my student, however briefly, and I was sent to find him. Because I found his body. Because I have been virtually accused of killing him. Because I think that Antoine is still in danger. Because I hate killing."

"Did you not kill men as a soldier?"

Charles nodded.

"Under obedience to your commander."

Charles nodded again. The silence stretched until he wished Le Picart would tell him to pack his things and be done with it.

"And now I am your commander," Le Picart said softly. "But you refuse to obey me. Why?"

Charles groped for the right words and ended up saying bluntly, "Somewhat because I feared you wanted to avoid scandal more than you wanted to find the killer. More because I can no longer obey if it means ignoring evil."

"I dread scandal, yes. As no doubt you will, if you come to a position of responsibility. But I grieve that you think so ill of me. Do you really think yourself the only man in Paris who can do what is needed in these affairs?"

"Of course not, *mon père*. And I do not think ill of you. But I must do what I can do, if I am to live with myself. I am sorry—" Charles broke off and rubbed his hands over his face. "No, I am not sorry. But I do sincerely ask your forgiveness for disobeying you."

"Why did you become a Jesuit, knowing that obedience to superiors would be required?"

Charles's mouth quirked. "I suppose I didn't think there would be killing."

"That was naive of you. Evil is always killing good, one way and another. Or trying to."

Charles stood up.

"Where are you going, *maître?*"

"You have told me I have no business as a Jesuit. And you are right, because I cannot obey your order."

"Sit down."

"But—"

"Sit *down*. I suppose you can do that much without offending your conscience?"

Charles sat.

"I have not told you that you have no business as a Jesuit. Drink your wine. You have not even tasted it. It's good, better than usual."

Bewildered, Charles tasted the wine, which was indeed better than usual.

"Maître du Luc, this afternoon I was very angry. And perhaps it *will* turn out that you must leave the Society." He lifted his shoulders slightly. "And what I am about to say may mean that I will be on your heels. But I am not telling you to leave, and my own superior is not here to tell *me* to leave. St. Ignatius said that his men must not obey any ill order. I do not believe that I gave you an ill order in telling you to leave the murder and the accident alone. But I am not God. Perhaps your conscience sees farther, by God's grace, than I can. Obedience, ultimately, is to God's will. Mediated, we believe, through the ordered ranks of our superiors. But any man, no matter how exalted, may be wrong." He drained his glass and filled it again. "If you obey the order I am about to give you, I suspect that you will find more than sufficient penance for whatever was not of God in your failure to obey me so far. What human action, after all, is completely free of sin? My order is this: Find Philippe's killer, and find the man who attacked Antoine. If they are two different men."

Charles stared at Le Picart like the Israelites might have stared at the dry path opening before them as the Red Sea drew back.

"What is your answer, Maître du Luc?"

Flinching at the unwitting echo of La Reynie's words earlier that day in the Louvre, Charles said, "My answer is yes, *mon père*. I will gladly obey your order." This time he meant it.

"Then you are excused from your morning class, though not from your duties surrounding the ballet and tragedy. Those must be carried out absolutely, no matter what else happens." He looked at Charles over the rim of his glass. "Always excepting, of course, your own demise."

"Which would be very thorough penance," Charles returned dryly.

"It would. In the meantime, you have my permission to come and go from the college, alone and at will. If anyone challenges that, refer him to me. You will report to me and you will tell no one else what you are doing. And when this is over, you will make a thirty-day retreat during which you will examine yourself very seriously with regard to the vow of obedience and your future as a Jesuit."

Charles bowed his head. "Yes, *mon père.*"

Le Picart suppressed a yawn. "We both want our beds. But first, I must hear all you know and suspect. Did Antoine really receive a note from Philippe?"

Charles drank down half his wine in an effort to pull himself together. "I think he is telling the truth about the note. It explains his being out in the street. But when I asked him if he recognized Philippe's writing, he said the writing was 'wobbly.' I think someone wrote the note after Philippe was already dead, to lure Antoine into the street for the 'accident.'"

"But you could be wrong about whoever ran from you wearing the yellow shirt. It could have been Philippe. He could have come back and left the note."

"But why ask an eight-year-old for help? Wouldn't Philippe more likely turn to someone at least his own age—his cousin Jacques, perhaps?"

"Unless he was asking for something only Antoine would know or could do. Though I admit, it is hard to think what that might be."

"And there is also the question of why Philippe left the classroom in the first place, *mon père.* He watched the windows that day, to the exclusion of nearly everything else. I think he was waiting for a signal to go and meet someone. And when it came, I think he went directly to his death." Charles leaned forward in his chair. "Antoine told me more about what he saw between Père Guise and Mme Douté. Philippe didn't witness the kiss, but Antoine told him about it, and Philippe was angry. Antoine is too young to understand what he saw, but Philippe would have understood it all too well, especially since the woman was apparently trying to entice him, too. Hearing that

Père Guise welcomed her advances might have been the last straw for Philippe—I think he would have been outraged on his father's behalf. What if he taxed Père Guise with it, and Père Guise killed him in fear of exposure?"

"No, no, after you and Antoine left, Père Guise told me what lay behind Antoine's accusation. He apologized for striking him, but what the child said embarrassed him so deeply, he lost control of himself. It seems that, a year or more ago, before she was married, Lisette Douté developed an unfortunate passion for him. He was her confessor while she was at court and, well, as I am sure you know, these things do happen with young girls. He admitted that that was why he'd introduced her to M. Douté in the first place. He thought marriage had solved the problem, but then she threw herself at him that day in the garden. He had no idea Antoine was there."

"As Antoine tells it, Père Guise did his share of the throwing."

"How long have you been in the Society, *maître*?"

"Seven years, *mon père*."

"Long enough, then, to know that God does not conveniently remove the sexual organs at first or even final vows. An oversight on His part, one is often tempted to think, but there it is."

"Remove them?" Charles involuntarily recrossed his legs. "I wouldn't go that far, *mon père*. After all, even St. Augustine prayed that the gift of chastity might be delayed."

The rector's gaze was uncomfortably speculative. "But he did pray for the gift. Père Guise would not be the first priest to have mixed feelings over the attentions of a pretty girl. That is between him and his own confessor. No, Maître du Luc, the situation with the girl is a small thing. As for Philippe's anger at Père Guise, people are constantly angry at him." He sighed. "I often am, myself. And even if we entertain your theory, it immediately becomes impossible. Père Guise says he was with his aunt the Duchesse when Philippe disappeared, and the brother who was keeping the door that day confirms that Père Guise left by the postern immediately after dinner and was gone all afternoon."

"But the old stairs make the doorkeeper's statement meaningless. Père Guise could have returned to the college and left again unseen. Strangling doesn't take long, *mon père*."

The rector's eyebrows lifted. "I will not ask how you know that—I am beginning to suspect that you learned much as a soldier that I have no wish to know. Yes, Père Guise could have used those stairs, but so could any one of us. You will not be of use to me—or to the truth—if you let your dislike of the man blind you."

Charles bowed his head in acknowledgment. "Forgive me, *mon père*."

"I wish we had blocked that staircase when we took back the rooms above the bakery," Le Picart said, "but there was no money. No one is supposed to have the key to the doors but myself and the head proctor."

Charles looked up, his gaze sharpening. "The head proctor?"

"Frère Chevalier is seventy-three, the soul of honor, and too arthritic to climb stairs."

"But could Père Guise—or someone else—have taken his key and copied it?"

Le Picart frowned. "Frère Chevalier doesn't see as well as he used to. I will ask him, but—could anyone really come and go through the bakery without being spotted? Or heard?"

"I did." Charles drained his glass. "The door hinges have been greased. You have only to watch your moment, when the LeClercs are in the back of the shop, and then be quick. I think it could be done even at night, if you had a key to the bakery door. And I would wager that Père Guise has one. The baker is deaf, his wife says. Though she certainly is not! *Mon père*, even without the Mme Douté complication, we come back again and again to Père Guise. He searches for the note, the hidden stairs lead to his rooms, he is close to the Douté family, he—"

"He could have been looking for a handkerchief, as he says. When Mme LeClerc came to see me, she said nothing about his searching the boy's clothes."

"Marie-Ange says her mother was talking to the street porter and didn't see."

The rector rubbed his forehead as though it hurt. "The street porter. Do you think you could find the man and talk to him?"

Charles put down his glass. "I found him. This morning."

"This morning? Ah, yes. I trust your toothache has miraculously recovered," the rector said dryly. "What does the porter say?"

"Nothing. I found him strangled in the beggars' Louvre. With the same marks on his neck that we saw on Philippe."

Le Picart jerked his head back as though Charles had struck him. "Jesu, have mercy." He crossed himself.

"The porter's friend told me that Pierre—that was the dead man's name—thought he was being followed. He ran from me yesterday, but—"

"Yesterday?"

"I originally found him on the quay yesterday when Père Jouvancy sent me to buy sugar, *mon père*."

"Go on."

"Pierre's friend arranged a meeting for this morning. I think that someone saw our encounter yesterday and silenced the porter before we could talk."

"And you feel his death cannot have been a private matter, or part of a simple robbery, because he was marked in the same way Philippe was."

"You have it."

The rector shook his head sadly. "God keep the poor man's soul. Do you have any thought of what he might have said about the accident?"

"A bare guess, yes. Mme LeClerc said that the horseman leaned far down toward Antoine. Père Guise insists that the man was trying to push Antoine out of the way. But the cut on the boy's head was made by a sharp edge. As I said the day it happened, I went over every inch of the street where he fell and saw nothing that could have made that cut. It's possible, as Frère Brunet said, that the horse's hoof could have caught him. But such a wound is usually more bruised and leaves a worse head injury. I think that the horseman was trying to stab Antoine. The porter may have seen the knife, and been bribed to keep quiet about it. The one thing he did say yesterday before he ran was 'I told the other one. You've no cause to hound me.'"

"'The other one.' The other Jesuit?" Le Picart said reluctantly.

"That was my thought."

"But—you found this man dead in the beggars' Louvre. Can you really imagine Père Guise going there to kill him?"

Charles shrugged. It wasn't easy to envision. "But if someone is helping him? The man whose boots I saw today knew how to find the stairs to Père Guise's rooms."

"But *why*? Why any of it?" Le Picart closed his eyes and pinched the bridge of his nose as though his head hurt. "I think you are being too quick to accuse Père Guise. I already told you that what has happened to these boys might be tied—through their father—to the old Prince of Condé."

"Could Père Guise be acting for the Condé?"

"I doubt that. The Prince of Condé was the king's enemy forty years ago in the Fronde revolution, fighting on the side of the rebels, and the very mention of the Fronde still makes Père Guise froth at the mouth. Even worse, the Condé has a long reputation as a free thinker. Though he's become a good Catholic again in his old age. No, I was thinking more of someone in the Condé's household who might be trying to use the boys to force their father to something—Monsieur Douté keeps some of the Condé accounts, which means he has access to a great deal of money." Le Picart emptied the wine pitcher into his glass. "I want the truth of these murders and the accident. But neither the college nor the Society can stand a public scandal. People still remember Jean Châtel, our deranged student who tried to kill Henri IV at the end of the Wars of Religion. And that a Louis le Grand professor who had taught him was hanged and burned and the Society banished from the realm for years. Part of my reason for laying this task on you is selfish, in that the faster the killer is found, the less damage there will be to the Society of Jesus and Louis le Grand."

"And if Père Guise turns out to be . . . involved, shall we say?"

"Then we will endure what we must endure."

"Until we know, can you confine him to the college?"

"Perhaps. I will think on it."

Charles opened his mouth to argue and then closed it. "I am also very worried about Antoine's safety, *mon père.* Can you not send him home till this is over?"

"I could. But I think he may be safer here, where there are more of us to watch him. After what we heard and saw tonight, if anything further happens to Antoine, Père Guise will be the first person you and I will think of. He knows that. I have also spoken sternly to Maître Doissin. A good enough man, but lazy. And I will see that others also keep an eye on the boy." Le Picart frowned, fingering the rosary hanging from his cincture as he gazed at Charles. "Has anyone told you of our house east of town, *maître*?"

"No, *mon père*."

"Our Père La Chaise, the king's confessor, often uses it. Because he guides the king's conscience, he has to know what is afoot in the world and what the powerful are saying about it. To that end, he frequently hosts gatherings of influential men. He is holding one of his soirées tomorrow evening, and I want you to go. Père Guise has been invited, and someone from the Condé house here in town usually attends as well. Fall into conversation with the Condé's representative; see if you can find out the gossip in his household. And see who Père Guise talks to. I know that the thought of spying on a brother Jesuit is distasteful. But if he is—involved—I want to know it first."

"How am I to spy in a salon?" Charles said in dismay. "And on a man who knows me!"

"It will be a large gathering, you will be just one more Jesuit there. I will tell Père Guise that you are doing an errand for me and paying your respects to Père La Chaise." Le Picart smiled. "Your official errand will be to take him the plan I have made for our reception of the Siamese. I am gambling on your acting being as good as your dancing, Maître du Luc. Oh, yes, I heard all about your classroom gigue. I wish I had seen it myself." He stood up and Charles rose with him. "I will give you a letter of introduction to Père La Chaise. He knows what has been happening here. And now, bed."

"How do I get to this soirée, *mon père*? Shall I take a horse from our stables?"

The rector frowned, thinking. "They may be spoken for. I will tell you tomorrow and give you directions." He looked up, suddenly just a tired, worried, aging priest. "May the Holy Virgin protect you, Maître du Luc. If what you are doing for me becomes known, you will look to someone like Nemesis. Do not forget that for a single moment."

❧ *Chapter 20* ❧

Charles stood beside the well in the stable courtyard, waiting for his hired horse and looking anxiously at the sky. If the flying clouds erased tonight's moon, he would have to find his way back in the pitch dark. Hoofbeats clopped along the lane behind the college. He opened the gate and Frère Fabre reined in a big black horse and slid to the ground. The horse rolled an uncertain eye at Charles.

"He seems all right," Fabre said dubiously, handing over the reins. "But watch out for cats. One ran in front of him just now and he shied like he had a poker up his ass."

Charles eyed the horse. "Oh, good. And stray cats are so rare in Paris. But thanks for the warning. What's his name?"

The brother shrugged. "You need to be introduced?"

"I've ridden horses that thought so." Charles gave the horse's nose a scratch and swung himself up.

"When you get back tonight, *maître*, put him in the stable here. I'll return him tomorrow." Fabre raised an admonitory finger. "Now remember. Cross the river on the Pont de la Tournelle, not the Petit Pont—"

"Père Le Picart made me memorize the directions. St. Anthony must have told him how lost I got coming home the other day. My thanks for fetching the horse, *mon frère*, and a peaceful night to you."

"And to you. If you stay away from cats."

Charles clucked to the nameless horse and rode away down the lane, thinking that cats were going to be the least of his worries. But the sky seemed to be clearing again, that was something. And when the lane met the rue St. Jacques and he turned toward the river, he saw that the wind had dropped enough to let the long shop signs hang quiet on their poles. The Latin Quarter's shops and the ramshackle vendors' booths scattered along side streets were closing. Belated shoppers darted like rabbits, seeking things forgotten earlier, their demands for cheap end-of-the-day prices—and complaints when their demands were refused—shrill above the rumble of carriage wheels. Charles's eye was caught by a sign painter on a ladder, finishing a silver spoon on a scarlet ground.

"Pewterer or roast shop, *mon ami*?" he called out.

"Best roast shop in Paris! We open tomorrow, come and try the garlic mutton!"

Charles's horse shied in protest as an onslaught of released day students pelted down the hill from Louis le Grand, Plessis, Cambray, and Gervais. Their game of stealing each other's hats grew into armed conflict as one group of scholars fired a volley of gutter refuse at its rivals. Charles ducked and reined his horse aside to avoid a flying bunch of rotting carrots, and the horse's hooves just missed a stack of small gleaming boxes outside a joiner's shop. The joiner's shock-haired apprentice ran out, yelling abuse, and belatedly gathered up his master's wares.

Glad to escape the fray, Charles turned into little rue Galande, past the ancient church of St. Julien the Poor. A clutch of the modern poor darted from the shelter of its doors, proffering bloody bandages, sores, and a sleeping swaddled infant. Charles suspected that the bandages and sores were works of art, not nature, but the thin, vacant-eyed woman holding the baby wrung his heart. Praying that Pernelle and Lucie were not in want, he gave her a handful of copper gros from the purse Le Picart had given him to use if he needed. For expenses, Charles supposed. Or bribes. Le Picart hadn't said.

He was nearly at the Pont de la Tournelle when he rode into a tiny square and found himself in one of those spaces of quiet all cities hold. The cacophony of Paris faded and a cascade of song poured from an open window, somehow deepening the hush. "Thick forest," the singer lamented, "you cannot conceal my unhappy love . . ." Doves cooed from a walled garden and Charles breathed in the scent of flowers. It came to him that all this—the city, being on his own with money to spend, no vow of obedience, nothing to curb his choices—could be his ordinary life if he left the Society.

Not money to spend, he corrected himself. Since their father's death, his older brother, René, had run the family land, selling the olives, wine, and figs, collecting his seigneurial dues, even overseeing his small seigneurial court in person, which was somewhat unusual these days. But prices had fallen and the land barely kept René's family and Charles's mother in modest comfort. If Charles left the Society, he would be on his own. He supposed he could support himself teaching. Though Paris schools expected their teachers to be, if not clerics, at least single. And he might not stay in Paris. Or stay single . . . Turning away from where that thought tried to take him, he told himself he could earn a living as a dancing master. If he could find students who liked the wailing of amorous cats, which was what his violin playing sounded like. Or a theatre company might take him on. He'd proved that he could still dance, and his heart leapt at the thought of performing. He was old, though, to turn professional; and his shoulder was permanently stiff, outright painful if he overused it. But he also acted well enough, and acting would be easier on his shoulder . . .

His imaginings carried him across the Pont de la Tournelle to the Ile St. Louis—the Ile Notre Dame, as some still called it—where wooden cranes and piles of stone and lumber testified to the ongoing lure of this island, created for the rich. As he reached the Right Bank, the slowly fading light recalled him to his evening's business. He would have to get himself presented to whoever was representing the Prince of Condé. But he was increasingly sure that the key to the murders was in Paris, not away in Chantilly. His main goal tonight was learning as much as possible about Guise's life outside the college. Though how to do that with Guise's gimlet stare following his every move, he didn't know. His spirits sank abruptly as he turned along the wide rue St. Antoine. What skills did he really have for this? His mother had often said that he could talk the horns off a brass goat when he wanted to. And he could act. Fighting, dancing, and directing had taught him to read bodies and their intentions—a useful skill when facing angry men, but he was going to an urbane soirée in a Jesuit house, not a street fight. So acting and talking the horns off a brass goat would be tonight's weapons of choice.

A tall fountain in the middle of the street made him shove his worries aside and look eagerly for the Society's new church of St. Louis. Just by St. Catherine's fountain, Le Picart had said, and there it was. Charles slowed his horse to a walk, drinking in the pale honey stone facade, craning his neck to follow the graceful curves soaring into the evening sky like a Mass's Gloria. Patterned after the Jesuits' great Gesù in Rome, St. Louis was exuberantly carved, painted, niched, and scrolled. Even the enormous clock over the church porch was gorgeous, its face surrounded by a golden sunburst. Charles was suddenly as glad to be brother to those who made such extravagant beauty for God, as glad to be making his own small contribution to such beauty in the ballets, as he'd been just moments ago to imagine himself uncassocked and his own man in the way of ordinary men.

Mentally throwing up his hands at his own inconstancy, Charles nudged the horse to a trot and left the church behind. *What do You want*, he demanded silently of God. *I feel more like a shuttlecock every day. Is that what I am? A toy for You and the devil to knock back and forth between you? And which side is Yours? Is it better to walk away from the Society and its sins of power? Or to stay and try for some power myself and hope to lessen the sins? Or is it better to leave the sins to You and get on with the good the Society does? I cannot just tell myself piously that all things work together for good and leave off thinking!* He waited, but this time his sparring didn't deepen into prayer.

The sunset reddened behind him and the ancient bulk of the Bastille loomed ahead. No longer in the mood for sightseeing, he passed it unheeding. He rode through the medallion-encrusted Arc de triomphe that had replaced the St. Antoine gate, across the stinking sewage ditch running along the line of the old wall, and took out his feelings in riding harder than he needed to through the gathering dusk. When he turned east and left the ditch behind, he pulled the horse to a trot. He was in real countryside now, passing canvas-sailed windmills, a tiny village, fields ripening toward haying, patches of woods. The road rose gently and he rode into the spacious courtyard of a stone house whose windows shone yellow against a sheltering hill.

A chorus of loud voices and laughter from the stable suggested a lively game of dice among grooms and escorts passing the time until they were needed again, and beside the stable door, two men nearly as tall as Charles, with pistols at their belts, stood talking. The unfamiliar cadence of their words thudded against Charles's ears as he dismounted. English, he thought in surprise, and handed his reins to the stable boy who came to meet him.

Charles dug his formal three-pronged Jesuit hat from the saddlebag, stowed his outdoor hat, and crossed the forecourt under the assessing stare of the Jesuit waiting at the top of a flight of handsome stone steps, beside the house door. The doorkeeper asked his name and led him into a long salon glowing with candlelight, whose wide casements stood open to the evening, letting moths blunder in to singe themselves in the candle flames. The salon's plain white plaster walls and bare wood floor contrasted sharply with the men who filled it. The curls of their full-bottomed wigs clustered on their blue, green, gold, and tawny shoulders. Snowy lace and lawn rippled down the fronts of their full-skirted coats and foamed from their foot-wide cuffs. Rings twinkled and ribbons fluttered on high-heeled shoes as they gestured and bowed to one another, and their busy eyes missed nothing.

Charles followed his guide through the crowd, past the richly dressed men and the Jesuits quietly offering them wine in plain, cone-shaped glasses like those that graced the college tables. The plangent sound of recorder and lute wove through the buzzing talk, and Charles finally found the musicians reflected in a gilt-framed mirror. It was the room's only decoration besides a half-life-size and brightly painted crucifix on the wall toward which his guide was leading him. As they passed the mirror, it also showed Charles three Capuchin monks, their signature pointed brown hoods hanging down their backs. A Capuchin had been Cardinal Richelieu's spymaster in the previous reign and Charles wondered if the order offered similar services to Père La Chaise, the king's confessor. To his discomfort, he realized that he was only half joking. His guide stopped in front of a sixtyish, fleshy-faced Jesuit standing before the crucifix.

"Père La Chaise," the doorkeeper said, bowing, "may I present Maître Charles du Luc, from the College of Louis le Grand?" He gestured Charles forward and retreated.

"*Bon soir, mon père,*" Charles murmured, bowing low.

La Chaise inclined his head and turned to the tall, fair-haired man in a russet coat and breeches who stood beside him. "If you would excuse us for a moment, *mon ami?* College business. Often banal, I fear, but it must be done."

A shadow of annoyance passed over the fair-haired man's big-boned face, but he nodded politely. Surprised at not being introduced, Charles watched him withdraw toward the windows.

"*Mon père,*" he said, remembering his manners and taking the rector's two letters from his inside pocket, "I bring you these from Père Le Picart."

La Chaise looked briefly at the letter about the Siamese, pocketed it, and unfolded the second. As he read, Charles studied him. The king's confessor had fine dark hair that curled a little around his skullcap, a high forehead, a long straight nose, and a doubling chin. The lines around his mouth were good humored and the look in his eyes was at once wise, weary, and tolerant. Charles supposed that after eleven years confessing King Louis XIV, a man would have to either look like that or be a crabbed, bitter cynic. La Chaise refolded the letter introducing Charles and looked up, smiling.

"You are most welcome, Maître du Luc. To Louis le Grand and to this house." He lowered his voice and spoke just on the edge of hearing. "If I can help you, you have only to ask. We must make sure that these sad events at the college damage us as little as may be."

"And we must make sure that the guilty are found, *mon père*."

"That goes without saying. What do you need here this evening?"

"I was told to meet whoever is representing the Prince of Condé's household, *mon père*."

"Ah. Unfortunately, I have been told that the Hôtel de Condé's chaplain, who usually comes, has sent his regrets. I trust you will still be able to make good use of your presence, *maître*."

"I trust so, *mon père*," Charles said, thinking that now he was free to concentrate on Guise.

La Chaise reached under his cassock, drew something out, and peered at it. He opened his hand and showed Charles a tiny clock in the shape of a skull. "My timekeeper. Spiritually as well as temporally useful, as you see. I must seek someone else now, if you will excuse me. Come to me for whatever you need."

Charles bowed his thanks and waited courteously for La Chaise to walk away first. Then he went to find the circulating drinks. Sipping the disappointing but thoroughly Jesuit vintage, he scanned the room for Guise and listened to the conversation around him. A few feet away, a bantam-sized young man in lushly purple velvet was holding forth on the philosopher Spinoza.

"—and I assure you, gentlemen," he was saying, "I have the very best authority for my opinion: my illustrious confessor, the devout and learned Père Guise."

Charles moved closer, gratified to see that the name made some of the listeners look as though they'd swallowed vinegar. This looked like his cue to start talking the horns off a brass goat. He surveyed his goat a moment longer, assumed an expression of polite interest, and joined the little circle.

"I say it again, this Jew's god has no divine plan," the goat pronounced, as the circle made room for Charles. "The god of Spinoza feels nothing, judges nothing, he is as cold and useless to the soul as a triangle." The young man looked around the circle, preening himself.

"Earnestly argued, *monsieur*," Charles said, with a smile and a bow. "But—cold as a triangle? I find your argument flawed."

"Indeed, *mon père?*" The goat blinked. "I am surprised to hear a Jesuit say so."

"Please, I am a mere *maître, monsieur*. Not *père*, not yet. Maître Charles du Luc, newly at Louis le Grand. As for your surprise, this Spinoza sometimes echoes Jesuit teaching."

An older man eyed Charles with respect and nodded, but the rest looked puzzled.

"Allow me to quote from our gentle Jew's *Ethics*." Charles assumed ballet's fourth position, the rhetorician's stance. "'There cannot be too much merriment.' And 'Nothing save gloomy superstition prohibits laughter.' And again, 'To make use of things, and take delight in them . . . is the part of a wise man.' The Society of Jesus teaches that we must make learning pleasurable. And that whatever is good and innocent of itself is worthy of Christian attention and delight and can be used to the glory of God."

The young man swelled with offense. Teetering on his very high heels, he tried to make himself seem taller as he faced Charles. "How can you possibly compare infidel maunderings with pious Catholic teaching?"

"Oh, dear. Do you mean that we are to reject *all* Jewish writing?" Charles frowned and looked around the circle as though for help. "But, *monsieur*, the Jews gave us the Old Testament, which speaks of a Savior." He threw out his hands in supplication. "And, think, I beg you—if we got rid of the Old Testament, Holy Scripture would lose fully three-quarters of its volume. Would that be wise? If Holy Writ weighed so little, ordinary people might want to carry it around. Even read it and interpret it for themselves! Like the Huguenots," Charles said in a shocked whisper. "And then where would good Catholics be?" Besides better educated and less credulous, he added silently, as several of his listeners snorted with laughter.

"I am not speaking of Holy Scripture," the young man said stiffly. "Spinoza was a Christ killer trying to lead good Christians astray. I trust you do not allow his work at Louis le Grand."

"Oh no," Charles said in a horrified tone. "Père Guise would never stand for that."

"Certainly not! A more ardent and orthodox Christian does not exist."

Charles looked vaguely around. "Where *is* Père Guise? I have not yet seen him."

"He is here. On important business." The disciple glanced over his shoulder and beckoned the circle closer. "Business that will bring glory to Holy Church." He put a hand on his chest, as though to still his bounding heart. "I must go now, *messieurs*, to play my own small role." He bowed and withdrew.

Into the silence he left behind, someone said thoughtfully, "His grandfather was a butcher in Rouen."

"Ah, yes," someone else purred. "He is a little like Madame of the Moment, then."

Everyone laughed. Mme de Maintenon, the king's new wife, had also risen from the lower orders. Because her surname sounded like "*maintenant*" or "right this minute," her enemies never tired of calling her Madame of the Moment and hoping that her pious influence at court would last no longer than that. Charles laughed with them, but his eyes followed his goat. As the circle's talk wound itself somehow from Mme de Maintenon to England and what James II's open Catholicism meant for English religion, the goat stopped beside the man who had been standing with La Chaise when Charles arrived. The two of them moved purposefully across the room, and Charles bowed to the circle and followed them.

At the salon's far wall, the goat looked around furtively, failed to see Charles watching him, and hurried his companion through a door. Charles drifted toward the wall. With his back to the door, he set his glass on a side table and benignly surveyed the company as he felt behind him for the latch. When, as far as he could tell, no one was noticing him, he lifted the latch and stepped backward.

Chapter 21

All Charles could tell at first was that he had walked into near darkness. He stretched out his arms and his fingers touched plaster on both sides. A passage, then. As his eyes adjusted, he saw that light leaked thinly under the door he'd just closed and that a line of light showed under another door on his left. He moved closer. Someone was talking, but the voice was too muffled for him to make out words. He put his ear to the door. The voice came more clearly; not a French voice, though its French was passable.

"You already know something of my purpose," the voice said. "But now that M. Lysarde here has made us known to each other, I will put my plea before you in my own heartfelt words. I truly believe that God led M. Lysarde to visit King James's court. We met at Mass, as he has told you, and later I had the pleasure of presenting him to His Majesty. I met M. Lysarde often after that to talk of our devotion to Holy Church. As you know from Père La Chaise, I am one of King James's Catholic advisors. Unofficial—he will deny knowledge of me, if necessary—but close to him. It is in that capacity that I have accompanied our young friend here to France. To ask your help on King James's behalf in ridding England of heresy, as you have so efficiently rid your own realm of it."

Charles went rigid against the door.

"Our king desires to emulate your great Louis and wipe away England's Protestant stain," the man went on in his accented French. "The moment is ripe, if only you will help us seize it."

"Eloquent, *mon cher* Monsieur Winters," Charles's goat said fervently.

"You are too kind, Monsieur Lysarde," the voice murmured.

"Exactly what do you mean, Monsieur Winters?" The unpleasantly familiar voice was that of Michel Louvois, the war minister.

"Why, I mean dragoons, Monsieur Louvois. The dragoons that you deploy so successfully here, to teach our English troops the methods of conversion you have perfected."

Charles bit blood from his tongue to keep his silence and told himself that it would be suicide to burst into the room.

"Then your errand is in vain," Louvois replied stiffly. "Do you not know in England that King Louis has officially forbidden dragonnades?"

"Of course. And like everyone else, we know that he was only placating our too tender-hearted pope. Rulers so often cannot afford to let their right hand know what their left hand does. Let me congratulate you, *monsieur.* As minister of war, you have been a most effective left hand."

The room was suddenly full of a silence whose discomfort Charles felt even through the door.

"Monsieur Louvois? How shall I interpret this silence?" Winters hesitated. "You are his left hand, are you not? Or— dear God, dare I say it—has someone continued these dragonnades without your king's knowledge? But who values his life so little as to poach on King Louis's vaunted authority? No, no, that is beyond belief."

"You continue to puzzle me." Louvois's words were silky

with danger. "Your King James seems bent on toleration for all—Anglicans, Anabaptists, Quakers. Even Jews, I hear. Just last spring, he released twelve hundred Quakers from your jails. Why would he suddenly want dragoons?"

"This 'tolerance' is but a mask, the face James shows to England in order to secure the throne and forestall rebellion."

"Of course it is," a new voice said reprovingly.

Guise. Charles pressed his ear closer to the door and held his breath.

"Since the hell-bound Henry destroyed the true Church in England, its throne has been a precarious seat for a Catholic monarch," Guise declaimed. "As you well know, Monsieur Louvois."

Louvois ignored him. "Why do you not carry some token from King James, Monsieur Winters?"

"Is it not enough that I am here, in this sacred Jesuit house, vouched for by your king's confessor? And by M. Lysarde, of course. Safety lies in anonymity." Winters's voice grew hard. "I am, of course, wholly dispensable, but King James cannot risk his plans becoming known. I will tell you, though, that even now he has fourteen thousand soldiers gathered at Hounslow. Soldiers led by Catholic officers, who hear Mass in a chapel the king has built for them."

"These soldiers," Guise said eagerly, "are they ready to move?"

"They wait only for your dragoons."

"Then they will wait until hell freezes, *monsieur*," Louvois said flatly. "There will be no dragoons."

"I—I am shocked, Monsieur Louvois," Winters said over Guise's recriminations. "My king is guided by his Jesuit confessor, Père Edward Petre, as your king is guided by our noble host. Père Petre and Père La Chaise have prayed—and more—for years to restore the true Church in England. Are you prepared to take the eternal consequences of flying in the face of such holy hopes? King James looks to the king of France as to a father, he pleads with him for aid. The moment he knows that you will send soldiers, the restoration of Holy Church will begin in our long-suffering island."

"You move me inexpressibly, Monsieur Winters." Guise's voice vibrated with fervor. "God and His saints are truly calling us to this. We will lay this request before King Louis at the first opportunity. As soon as—"

"You forget yourself, Père Guise." Louvois sounded like he was choking on swallowed fury. "Dragonnades are forbidden. And your Anglicans and Quakers and such are not swarming across the Channel to attack us, Monsieur Winters, but the Holy Roman Emperor and this new Augsburg alliance are very likely to do so. French troops will go east and north and nowhere else."

"All our troops need not be sent there," Guise snapped.

"I am minister of war and I say they will be. Even setting aside other objections, who would pay for dragoons in England? The English king indeed relies on King Louis as a father when it comes to money."

"Money? Is that what really concerns you? Why, Monsieur Louvois"—Winters laughed—"you sound more like a Dutch merchant than France's war minister and a true son of Holy Church."

"I will pay, *messieurs!*" Lysarde, the goat, cried. "With my last sou, if necessary!"

In spite of his horror, Charles wanted to laugh. Lysarde sounded like a student actor playing doomed Roland refusing to surrender.

"Dutch?" Louvois said, ignoring the would-be hero. The war minister's voice was heavy with irony. "A *Dutch* merchant? A very interesting choice of comparisons, Monsieur Winters."

"A common enough turn of phrase, I believe," Winters said lightly. "But forgive my jest, if it offends you. Well, *messieurs*. I can see that you need time to consider what I have put before you. I beg you to think—and pray—long and well about King James's request. Discuss it, of course, with those you most trust. And when you put it to your king, lose no time in letting me know his answer. Sadly, the English court swarms with heretic spies who have deep pockets for bribing royal couriers. It will be safest to send letters through the two men whose names are written here." There was a rustle of paper. "They are both known to King James and will protect our correspondence with their lives. Now, I thank you from my heart for this audience and bid you adieu, in the hope of hearing very soon that the great King Louis will aid us in the service of Holy Church."

Charles reached the deeper darkness at the passage's far end just in time. Light spilled across the floor. As Winters and Lysarde hurried down the passage and slipped back into the salon, Charles realized that Winters was the man he'd seen standing with Père La Chaise when he arrived. Someone inside the room the men had left pulled its door shut and Charles crept back to his listening post.

"How dare you, Monsieur Louvois? I am ashamed of you." Guise was spluttering with fury. "You will feel it in penance. If I had not heard you with my own ears, I would not believe it! After your education at Louis le Grand, after all my own guidance, to see you spit on God's chosen time and the true faith as you have just done breaks my heart."

So Louis le Grand had not only educated the war minister, Guise was his confessor. Charles remembered Le Picart's warning that the college, the court, and the government hung in the same web.

"*Mon père*, when you first mentioned this meeting to me in

M. Douté's garden during the birthday fête, I feared that Winters was a fraud," Louvois said. "I said so, but no, you were bent on receiving him. And now that I have seen him, I am certain he is a fraud. I will take my oath that he lied from start to finish. That was a direct threat, his wondering so innocently if someone has usurped the king's authority to run dragonnades. And why come to us? Why not go straight to Versailles, if he really comes from James? Official or unofficial, Louis would have received him."

"You heard him, James must do this as quietly as possible so that no rumor leaks out and lets the enemy prepare!"

"I heard him. And if we don't take Winters's heart-rending "plea" to Louis, the cur will make good on his threat."

"Threat?! It is certainly not—"

"Threat, Père Guise! If we don't do what Winters asks, he will send a storm of rumor and gossip about our dragonnades straight at Louis's head. Half of the court will pretend to be unbearably surprised that dragonnades go on and will whisper that Louis's absolute authority is no longer absolute. It will be as though we've cuckolded him! He would probably mind less if we had truly cuckolded him. Meanwhile, the other half of the court will titter that of course we *haven't* cuckolded the king's authority, because everyone knows he never meant the dragonnades to stop. And Louis will then be very publicly caught. Because he swore to the pope he'd stopped the dragonnades. I tell you, Louis will be caught, but he will see that the vise closes on us!"

Charles tried to take in what he was hearing. His eyes widened. Dragons. Dragons in England. Antoine had told him and he'd thought the child was just being a child. From his perch in the tree, Antoine had heard Louvois and Guise talking not just about dragonnades in France, as Charles had thought, but, God forbid, about these proposed dragonnades in England. No wonder that when Antoine asked to hear more about "dragons in England," he had been sent to bed. His questions would have told Guise that he and Louvois had been overheard, which was a much more believable reason for murder than witnessing an illicit kiss. Antoine had told Philippe about that kiss. Had he also told him about the "dragons?" Had Philippe died because he'd understood what that meant?

"I warn you," Guise hissed. "If you reject this chance to restore the Church in England, you will walk to Rome on your knees."

"We are caught, I tell you! Do you really want to go to Louis and make him talk about dragonnades? Not dragonnades in Huguenot rat holes so far away that he and the pope can fail to notice, but blazingly public dragonnades across the Channel that would scandalize all Europe! Including Rome and the Protestant Augsburg states!"

"Holy Church—"

"I tell you, we are caught! If we go to the king and the slightest whisper leaks out of the audience chamber—as you know it will, the court's very air gossips—it will start a fire trail of rumor that will flash from Versailles to London to Rome. 'Have you heard? King Louis is about to unleash French dragonnades on Anglicans.' 'What?' the pope will say. 'The same King Louis who solemnly forbade dragonnades five years ago?' His Holiness will seize this new excuse to grow even more adamant in his quarrel with Louis over church revenue and bishops. And the Augsburg alliance will grow even more determined to contain French power! And in England, James will have revolution on his hands and we will lose our Catholic ally there. Which is exactly what this Dutch Winters wants! Dutch, Père Guise! Could you not hear the accent under his appalling French? The man doesn't want dragonnades, he wants destabilizing rumors to help his master William of Orange to the English throne!"

"Calm yourself, *mon fils*, he is not—"

"If we do this, King Louis will have only two choices! To admit that he lied to the pope about stopping the dragonnades—which he will never admit—or to take the only other way out. To quickly "discover" that you and I have, as Winters so elegantly put it, poached the king's authority. Louis will cover himself by accusing us of usurping his sovereignty. He will swear that anything to do with dragonnades is against his will and without his knowledge, and he will charge us with treason. *Us.*" Louvois spit the word out like a piece of bad meat. "Even your name will not save you, Père Guise."

"You dare threaten me?" Guise thundered.

"For the good God's sake, I am trying—"

Wood grated over stone. Charles reacted a heartbeat too late as a hand was clamped over his mouth, an arm tightened around his throat, and someone dragged him backward.

Chapter 22

Charles fought as though his last battle had been yesterday. But his assailant, with two good shoulders, surprise on his side, and no cassock skirts, had him through the open door and belly down on the terrace in the space of a few breaths. Straddling him, the man pulled Charles's head up sharply to expose his throat. A dagger gleamed in front of Charles's eyes and the man laughed. Charles twisted, threw the man onto his dagger hand, and rolled free. He got his feet under him, but the man was up and rushing him, thrusting for his heart. Charles threw himself sideways and backward over the terrace balustrade. The man kept coming and landed half on top of him. Charles grabbed his assailant's dagger wrist, brought his other elbow up under the man's chin, and hurled him aside.

Then he was on his feet and running. As he ran, some detached part of him wondered what had seemed wrong about his pursuer's face. He needed to see the man in the light, but without dying for the privilege. The man fell behind as Charles's long legs ate up the ground. Charles was running now through a formal garden, jumping low hedges and flower borders in fitful moonlight. The garden was long and narrow, bounded by stone balustrades like those around the terrace, but beyond them on his left, trees showed against the night sky. Leaping over a gravel path and its betraying crunch, he vaulted the railing. And fell farther than he'd wanted to, onto tree roots. Swallowing a grunt of pain, Charles kilted his entangling skirts with his cincture and made his way deeper into the trees, thankful for soft, tended turf underfoot instead of last year's crackling leaves.

He stopped and listened. Running feet slowed and he saw his pursuer outlined against the sky, standing halfway down the garden and slowly turning his head as he searched for his quarry. Feeling his way among the trees, Charles followed the line of the balustrade toward the far end of the garden, where a massive chestnut tree filled the angle of the balustrade's turn across the garden's end. With the chestnut's trunk between himself and the man, Charles climbed silently back into the garden and stood invisible in the tree's inky shadows.

A little more moonlight filtered through the clouds and showed him his pursuer walking toward the tree. The man was middling tall and hatless, and his head was curiously smooth. Bald, perhaps, or shaven, Charles thought. Then moonlight poured through a rip in the clouds and he saw what had seemed wrong about the face. Its upper half was masked, not with an ordinary half mask, but with a mask that covered the top and back of the head, almost like the mask executioners wore. Which was fitting enough, Charles thought grimly. The silvery light shone on the knife in the man's hand, splashed into the high folded tops of his boots, and then dimmed before Charles could tell the color. But Charles would have bet his life—maybe was about to bet his life—that the boots were the color of burnt sugar. And that under a hat pulled low, the mask would look like the half mask Mme LeClerc had insisted Antoine's attacker had worn.

The man was nearly at the tree. Charles crouched and gathered himself, waiting for his moment. A night bird called, a gust of wind flurried the branches, and he used the sounds for cover as he launched himself low at his quarry and knocked him off his feet. He brought his fist down like a hammer on the man's knife wrist, and the numbed fingers relaxed and dropped the knife. Charles meant to gag the man, tie him, take him to La Reynie. But certainty that this was not only his own would-be killer, but Philippe's and the porter's, certainty that this was Antoine's attacker, boiled into rage. His hands reached for the man's throat, trying to find skin under the padded doublet's high collar.

The moon hid its face. The two men thrashed together like desperate lovers, rolling over and over in the grass. Through the bloodlust singing in him, Charles felt his enemy's life going. Then the heavens intervened. Laughing, talking men surged out of the house, and their noise and the light of their approaching lanterns cut through Charles's rage. His grip loosened and his victim rolled away retching, staggered up, and was gone. Charles struggled to his feet. The oblivious newcomers at the garden's entrance were pointing upward, too engrossed in the sky and their chattering to notice him, a black shadow among shadows. Muffling his panting breath, he slipped over the balustrade again.

"Ah, there's one!" he heard someone say. "And another!"

"Magnificent! How often do the astronomers say these showers happen, did you say?"

Charles looked up through the trees and saw a shooting star streak across the sky. Giving thanks for this bright deliverance from the murder he'd nearly committed, he stumbled toward the stables. The grooms and men at arms had taken their dice elsewhere and the stable was quiet. As far as he could tell, only the boy who looked sleepily over the loft's edge saw him lead his horse out of the stable and ride away.

Now that he wished the moon would stay hidden, it shone steadily. He kept glancing over his shoulder, expecting to see the killer behind him, but the road stayed empty. Charles rode as quickly as he dared, but the tree shadows were deep as pools and his horse was unsure on the rutted surface. He tried to make sense of the attack. The man must have jumped him because he'd found him listening outside the door. But why had he been allowed to listen so long? Guards needed to piss like anyone else, the explanation might be that simple. When the attack came, it had been in earnest. And with what he'd heard, he doubted he'd be left alone just because the first attack had failed. He had to get to Père Le Picart, and quickly.

He reached the St. Antoine gate with no sign of pursuit. But there would be tracks through woods and fields a horseman could follow to the city. He decided that the Petit Pont was his best way to the college, rather than the way he'd come. Crossing the river, with no side streets and nowhere to take cover, would be his most vulnerable point, and the Petit Pont was short. After it, he'd have only a brief ride up the rue St. Jacques to Louis le Grand.

Half of Paris seemed to be out enjoying the fitfully bright night, going from tavern to tavern or just strolling in the small streets and lanes. His horse stepped over snoring drunks, and a pair of loud prostitutes emerged from a doorway to grab at his cassock. A few streets over, he heard the night watch making its noisy passage north, away from the river. He was nearly at the Hôtel de Ville and beginning to relax when galloping hooves sounded behind him. He jerked his horse through an opening between houses, a gap so narrow his toes grazed the walls. Cornering like a madman, he rode for the Petit Pont, trying to keep a course that paralleled the river. A shot cracked past him and slammed into a wall. Charles kicked the horse harder and flattened himself on its neck. Praying that the pistol had only one barrel and that the man would have to fall back to reload, he kept on through the lanes. His horse skidded on rubbish and as it regained its feet, another shot ripped through the night. Pain seared Charles's ribs. Behind him, a horse screamed and a human cry turned into curses. Lying along his horse's neck, Charles made for a church tower gleaming above house roofs. He thought the other horse might have gone down, but he wasn't sure, and another accurate shot would be the end of him. If he could find grass, it would muffle his horse's hooves and let him put silent distance between himself and the shooter.

Luck was with him. The churchyard gate was open and the ground was uneven but soft going under old trees as he picked his way around the edge of the little enclosure. There was no sound behind him now. He reached back cautiously to feel his left side and tried to gauge how bad his wound was. Gritting his teeth, he pulled his cassock tight and was twisting it into a knot against the bleeding when something white flashed between his horse's hooves. A cat yowled and the horse jumped sideways and broke into a frenzied gallop.

Charles hauled uselessly on the reins and quickly decided that his only hope was to hang on. The terrified horse plunged out of the churchyard and along a winding street. Then it was running over rough ground, slowing and stumbling. Fighting weakness, Charles hugged the horse's neck. His hip was wet with blood now. A man ran toward him through the moon shadows and he tried desperately to turn the horse before the man could take aim. Then he was falling, trying to pray before he died, and then there was nothing.

"*Morbleu, mon père*, wake up, you have to walk, come on, now!"

The face looming over Charles disappeared. Strong hands gripped his armpits and hauled him to his feet, and an arm went around him. He groaned as it brushed against his wound.

"I know, I can feel it," the man gabbled, "you're bleeding, but we'll both do worse than bleed if you don't walk! I heard the shot, and the devil that fired it can't be far away, that's right, keep walking now . . ."

"My horse," Charles mumbled.

"I'm leading your horse, never mind, just keep putting one foot, then the other, that's it. We're not far."

The voice and the hillocked, rubble-strewn ground seemed familiar, but Charles couldn't remember why. His side felt like someone had sharpened a dagger on it. After what felt like days, he was allowed to collapse facedown on straw.

"I can't see your side," the man said. "We have to get your priest gown off. It's either rip it, which you surely don't want, or it's flip you and untie your belt."

There was an unpleasant interval in flickering candlelight before the voice faded into dark and painful dreams. Then the thin light of early morning was seeping into the room and someone had an arm around his shoulders and was holding a cup to his mouth. He opened his eyes, gasped at the face looking down at him, and choked on the sour wine.

He was dead and this was an angel. A dirty, bedraggled angel whose eyes glittered like wet onyx with unshed tears. Greasy black curls hung over her tired face and she was beautiful beyond words. His bewildered gaze strayed around the ramshackle room. Heaven couldn't be this filthy. Though hell might be. But hell had no angels. Especially not Provençal-speaking ones.

"Softly, now, softly, slowly. The wound is not deep, but you bled like a pig and you're weak." The angel settled herself beside him on the floor and gently stroked his hair back from his forehead. "I was just as surprised to see you, believe me."

Charles stared, wine dribbling down his chin. "Pernelle?"

Chapter 23

Hello, Charles," Pernelle said gravely, easing him back onto the thin pallet.

He groped for her hand, feeling with dismay how thin it was. "In God's name, Pernelle, what—how did you come here?" Wherever here was. A baby began to cry and she withdrew her hand and turned quickly toward the wailing.

"Lucie?" he croaked, realizing as he said it that the baby sounded too young.

The crying stopped abruptly and she turned back, shaking her head. The slowly growing light glazed her jutting cheekbones and showed him the gray shadows under her eyes.

"Where is she?" he said, speaking Provençal to her and realizing how much he'd missed it.

"Safe, I pray God every moment. Oh, Charles, I thought we'd never get anywhere, at the rate the widow's coach traveled. We were weeks on the road and when we reached her house, we had to stay a little because Julie was unwell. Then a soldier caught me as we were fording a stream in sight of Switzerland. Julie and Lucie were on the horse and they got across and away." Her mouth trembled. "I pray they are in Geneva." She looked down, smoothing the skirt of her stained blue gown and trying to steady her lips.

"I pray so, too. But how did you get *here?*" He looked around at the dirty floor, the makeshift brazier, the thin partitions and half-boarded window and realized that "here" was the murdered porter's room in the beggars' Louvre and he was lying on the dead man's pallet.

"I will tell you, Charles—but then it will be your turn to explain what *you* are doing here! Me, I was packed into a coach with seven other women and sent here. To a penitential convent over the river. I escaped two nights ago."

"How, in the name of God's holy angels?"

"Out a third-floor window, along a ledge, down a tree, and over a wall. Thank God men always underestimate women. The back garden was unguarded."

"Male stupidity is good for something, then," he tried to joke. But the risk she had taken turned him sick. "And you ended up here."

"Barbe brought me."

"Who is Barbe?"

"The mother of the crying baby." Pernelle nodded toward the partition. "When I saw you last night, I thought I had finally gone mad with worry and was seeing things. I still half believe I'm seeing things." She fixed her black gaze on him and waited.

"I was reassigned to the Society's college here."

"Yes? And you gave so much Latin translation that your students chased you here and shot you?"

Pernelle's tartness could have cured olives, and Charles felt himself smiling foolishly. It was one of the things he'd always loved about her. "The perils of teaching," he quipped back. "Some robber took a shot at me as I was riding back to the school. Who brought me in here last night?"

"Henri. A porter. He said he'd brought you here once before. At least I think that's what he said—understanding these people is far harder than reading my French Bible! If he did say that, your new teaching assignment must be very unusual, Charles." Her moth-wing eyebrows rose and she waited for an explanation.

A little more fog cleared from Charles's brain. Henri must be the ex-soldier who'd brought him to see Pierre yesterday—no, the day before yesterday it must be now. "Where did he find me?"

Pernelle smiled slightly. "He was on his way here last night to sleep—he says his wife found him with a girl and won't let him into their rooms—and he saw you fall from your horse and recognized you. By the time he got you inside, you'd lost so much blood, you were only half conscious."

Suddenly Charles remembered his nameless hired horse. It would be worth a fortune to anyone here. "Do you know what happened to my horse?"

"I saw Henri nearly throttle a man who tried to steal it. He's put out the word that if the horse isn't bothered, you'll buy free drinks for everyone at the tavern. The women have it tied out by the garden to get the good of the dung. And they're all armed with hoes." She studied him gravely. "Charles, were you sent north because of what you did for me?"

He sighed. Another thing he'd always loved about Pernelle was that she was impossible to fool.

"The Society doesn't know about it. But you know how our family gossips. Our pious cousin the bishop found out."

Pernelle's eyes widened in horror and her hand flew to her mouth.

"It's all right, he's also pious about family. And you were always his favorite heretic. He settled for calling in favors and getting me reassigned as far as possible from his new diocese."

Charles tried to raise himself to reach for the wine cup and grunted with pain. Pernelle tsked at him and held the cup to his lips.

"So now," he said, trying to smile as he eased himself down again, "we have to start again with getting you to Geneva." He grinned suddenly. "Those nuns' habits got you and Julie out of Nîmes. I could borrow another one and be Sister Charlotte and escort you the rest of the way." He hoped the joking hid his surge of longing to go with her.

Her full lips thinned with reproach. "Is there nothing you can't jest about, Charles? Even if you were serious," she said, softening, "I wouldn't let you risk everything again."

"Listen, Pernelle—"

She wasn't listening. "Charles, there are—we call them Huguenot highways, people who help us get out of France. There are one or two in Paris, but I don't know their names. All I know is that one of them is a Jew. If I could find him—"

"A Jew? There are no Jews in Paris, hardly any Jews in France, not for hundreds of years! All right, a few, but—"

Her eyes were suddenly black ice. "Is that what Jesuits teach? No more Jews, just like there are no Huguenots left in France?"

He felt himself flush. "No. I mean—but even if this Jew is here, why would he help you?"

He reached out a hand to try to close the distance that had opened between them, but she clasped her hands tightly in her lap.

"Why would he help me?" Her expression was incredulous. "I cannot imagine what it must be like to be you, so secure, so—think about it, Charles! Who knows better than a Jew what it is to be hated and pursued and tormented? And who would know better how to hide and escape? Don't you realize that my life is far more like theirs than like yours?" She looked around the sordid room. "I'm even starting to feel a little at home here."

She sighed. "And people like these are starting to feel at home with me. Barbe has taught me how to beg. Do you know what else she does to live, Charles? Besides showing her baby and begging? She and her mother and another old woman are paper chewers. For papier-mâché. The two older ones are so fuddled with wine most of the time, poor things, they're hardly there. Dear God, it terrifies me what poor women have to do to live!"

"I saw them—three women chewing paper—the other time I was here," Charles said. "I couldn't tell if they were only fuddled, or simple."

"Barbe is far from simple," Pernelle said. "There's nothing wrong with her except hunger and living like this. And the poor will put on any act to keep people like us—well, not me, now—from paying real attention to them. Except for getting alms, being noticed usually means trouble." Her eyes flashed. "And I've learnt *that* lesson from being a Huguenot. The less you notice us, the less we suffer."

Charles flinched at the "you" and the "us." She was right, but the words made him feel as battered inside as he was outside. He wanted to turn over on the moldy straw, lose himself in oblivion, and wake up in a less brutal world. A movement at the edge of the partition made them both look up.

"Come in, Barbe," Pernelle said in careful French, and held out her hand.

The girl moved a few steps into the room, her eyes darting between Pernelle and Charles. Her ragged bodice—a man's ancient doublet—was open, and she held a baby who had fallen asleep at her breast. Her eyes finally came to rest on Charles.

"I saw you before," she said hoarsely. "After he got killed. There, where you're lying."

Pernelle's eyes widened. "Who got killed?"

"I remember you, Barbe," Charles said. "Did you know the porter? Pierre?"

Barbe squatted down beside the pallet. Charles tried not to draw back from her smell and felt ashamed when Pernelle reached out and took the swaddled baby, who was giving off more than its share of the stench. Pernelle bent over the infant, her lips moving, and Charles knew she was praying for Lucie.

Barbe stretched her thin arms and sat on the floor. "Pierre was that one's father."

Charles stared. "Oh. Well. I—I'm sorry," he stammered.

The girl shrugged. "He was all right. He gave me food. That man that killed him was an idiot, though, he left all Pierre's things. I sold the boots. I would have sold the jerkin, except some bastard stole it first. The idiot that killed Pierre had his own boots," Barbe said, sticking to what mattered in the story. "Good ones. But he could have taken Pierre's and sold them. Awful to be that stupid."

Charles picked the jewel out of the midden of Barbe's words. "You saw who killed Pierre?"

She bent sideways and scratched under her skirt. Over her head, Charles and Pernelle traded glances.

"What did the idiot who left the boots look like, Barbe?" Pernelle said casually, picking up her cue.

"Big hat. No feather." She shrugged. "I only saw his back."

"It was night," Charles said, watching her closely. "How could you see him at all?"

"Had a lantern, didn't he? The light woke me when he went by. You sleep too sound in here, you maybe don't wake up. Something—I don't know—made me crawl over to the partition and see what he was up to. I watched him."

"You watched him kill the baby's father?" Pernelle said, aghast.

Barbe looked from her to Charles. Her eyes were the cloudy green of Charles's shaving mirror. "I know what you're thinking. But what was I going to do? Get killed, too?" She glanced at the baby. "Then who'd feed him?"

Charles lurched painfully onto his elbow. "Barbe, how did the man kill Pierre?"

She shrugged, scratching again.

He struggled to keep his voice level. "Please. Tell me everything the man did."

She sighed like someone who had long ago stopped expecting other people's wants to make sense. "He walked in here, went to Pierre's pallet. He put down the lantern and got something out of his pocket and leaned over. Lately, Pierre went to bed drunk most nights, so he didn't hear anything. Then he yelled out— Pierre, I mean—and kicked, but the man kept on bending over him till he quit."

"Then what, Barbe?"

"Nothing."

"What did the man do then, I mean?"

"He sat on the floor and did something to his boots. I couldn't see. Like I said, his back was to me. Then he got up and I curled up like I was dead asleep and he left."

Absently watching a cockroach busy in a corner's rubbish heap, Charles thought about what she'd said. The man had taken something from his pocket and strangled the porter. Then he'd sat down, done something to his boots . . . *By all hell's devils! So that* was *what he had used!* Charles struggled to get up.

"Charles, no!" Holding the baby in one arm, Pernelle tried to keep him on the pallet. "Lie down!"

"Help me, Pernelle," he said through his gritted teeth. "I have to get back to the college. Where's my cassock?"

"Are you crazy? You've bled too much, you can't go riding across Paris!"

His eyes fell on the pallet's small pillow and he saw that it was his rolled-up cassock. "Hand me that. Please. I need the horse. I have to get to my rector."

In eloquently disapproving silence, Pernelle gave Barbe the baby and held the cassock out to Charles. "And I stay here?" Her words were angry, but her eyes were full of fear.

"Of course you can't stay in this—" He saw Barbe looking at him and dropped his voice. "If the police raid this place, they'll be looking for you."

But where Pernelle could stay, he had no idea. If he didn't wear his cassock, she could ride behind him back to Louis le Grand. What to do after that escaped him, but at least he could get them both that far. He pulled the rector's purse out of his breeches pocket.

"For you and the baby, Barbe," he said, holding out a handful of sous. "For what you've told me."

A smile lit her face as she took the coins and, for a moment, Charles saw beneath the dirt and bitter difficulty of her life. He took out more coins.

"Two more for you if you'll bring my horse to the door. And the rest for Henri and those drinks in the tavern. Will you see that he gets his share?"

She scowled, then shrugged and laughed. "He'll get them." Holding the baby close, she hurried away, light-footed with her good fortune.

The ride across Paris was a nightmare for Charles. The morning was already hot, and his head throbbed. His side burned and ached, even though Pernelle tried to hold herself steady behind him without touching it. The tired horse walked at a snail's pace, not pleased at carrying two people. As they went, Charles tried to think of what to do with Pernelle, but he'd come up with nothing when the horse stopped at the college postern. Mme LeClerc was standing at the bakery door surveying the street. When she saw Charles, she let out a shriek and hurried to take hold of the horse's bridle.

"Dear Blessed Virgin, *maître*, what on earth has come to you? And where have you been? Poor Frère Martin says you never came back last night, he's been sticking his head out the door looking for you every minute!"

Staring round-eyed at Pernelle, she steadied Charles as he dismounted. Pernelle slid down and stood beside him.

"Robbers, eh? That lieutenant-général of police is good for nothing!" She tsked at Charles's blood-stained shirt. "You look terrible! And you, *mademoiselle*, are you hurt? No, well, thank the Virgin for that. No, no, I ask no questions, we're only young once and he's not even *père* yet, and if we did as the church says all the time, there would be no children, if not worse, look at all the days, seasons, even, when you can't even think about it! Well, take the famine with the feast, that's what Roger always says. Roger's my husband, *mademoiselle*, and now, would you like to come with me? Because you certainly can't go with Maître du Luc. I can give you a place to lie down and something to eat. You look as tired as he does, poor thing. We live plainly, we're bakers, but our bread is the best, you'll see. Now, *maître*, why are you still standing there, go in before you fall down, and what Père Le Picart will say—"

Charles caught Pernelle's eye and saw that she was on the edge of hysterical laughter.

"Madame LeClerc," he said, "this lady is Madame Pernelle. She is—" He stopped himself from saying she was his cousin. Better no one knew that. Though the moment Pernelle opened her mouth . . . But he was too exhausted to think his way through that problem yet. "May she stay with you for a day or two? I can pay you for her lodging."

"But of course she can stay! How you two will manage, though, I don't know. Now go and look after yourself, I'll see to your young lady. And this horse, too, the apprentice will take it around to your stable." She shooed him toward the postern and bustled Pernelle ahead of her into the bakery.

Charles dragged his torn and stained cassock from the saddlebow, rang for the doorkeeper, and leaned against the wall to keep himself upright. A street fool, in motley with a mirror strung around his neck, danced by. Juggling a half dozen bright colored balls, he called out, "Not all the fools are in the streets, come out and see the fool!" Charles's eyes followed the fountaining balls—blue, crimson, green, gold, rose—until the postern opened and a horrified Frère Martin pulled him inside.

The brother was trying to take him to the infirmary when Frère Moulin came into the passage, hurried to help Martin hold Charles up, and added his voice to the urging. But Charles insisted on going first to Le Picart. The disapproving brothers helped him to the office and left him there. Charles told Le Picart almost everything about what had happened at Père La Chaise's and after, only leaving out that he'd nearly murdered his attacker. And of course leaving out that he'd encountered Pernelle and brought her back with him.

"The man who attacked me at Père La Chaise's gathering is our killer and Antoine's attacker, I am sure of it. Last night he wore a mask like the one Mme LeClerc said the horseman wore. His boots were like the horseman's and like the ones on the man who came up the old stairs. And, *mon père*, someone in the beggars' Louvre saw the porter killed. From what she said, it seems almost certain that the man was strangled with a long spur garter." Spur garters were lengths of leather or chain, wrapped either once or twice around the wide ankle of a man's boot, to which spurs could be attached. "And a braided leather garter could certainly have made the kind of marks that were on the porter's neck. And on Philippe's."

"Did the boots you saw last night have such garters?"

"They were gartered, but I couldn't see the garters clearly."

"Do you think the man who attacked you at Père La Chaise's house is the same man who shot you?"

"Unless Père Guise and Louvois have more than one killer working for them."

"Of Louvois I would believe anything. But can we be sure of Père Guise's part? There is still nothing that absolutely proves his involvement in the murders and the attack on Antoine. Circumstance, suggestion, yes. Proof, no."

"We have proof that he is deep in the dragonnades and this hellish English plot. We have proof that the man in the boots walked fearlessly up the old stairs and through Père Guise's rooms as though he'd done it often. And last night, *mon père*, it was Père Guise urging Louvois on, not the other way around."

The rector's face was ashen. "You realize that this English plot could be the end of the Society of Jesus in France. Blessed Jesu, dragonnades in England are the last thing King Louis wants! He needs a Catholic king there, with the northern Protestant alliance growing against him. And James is his cousin! If this thing happened, James would not keep his throne a week. If this plot becomes known, whether or not it is carried out, even his illustrious name will not save Père Guise. And nothing will save us."

"What will you do?"

"For now, I can find pretexts for confining him to the college. Then I will have to see Père La Chaise and the head of our Paris Province for advice. You say that Louvois, thank God, is digging in his heels about England. So there is at least a little time. I will take extra measures for Antoine's safety and you must be vigilant on your own behalf, *maître*. Though I don't think Père Guise would risk anything—anything more, God help us—here in the college."

"And Louvois? What will you do about him?"

"Nothing. No one but the king can do anything about M. Louvois."

Chapter 24

Charles woke to sunlight streaming through the infirmary windows, groggy from whatever was in the tisane Frère Brunet had forced on him at intervals yesterday after Pére Le Picart delivered him to the infirmary. His wound hurt less, though the rest of him felt as though he'd been in a fight and fallen off a horse. Which, of course, he had. When he had eaten, Brunet smeared salve on his wound and rebandaged it.

"That's better," he said, patting the freshly tied bandage. "You're much better this morning, *maître*. All you young men need is sleep and you're good as new!"

Charles smiled wanly. Not quite that good.

Brunet put down his scissors. "Your wound will take some time to heal, but it's no great matter, bar your loss of blood. St. Barbara gave the rogue poor aim, thank God." He helped Charles into the shirt Frère Fabre had brought. "There is no infection I can see, but come back tomorrow after Mass for more salve and a fresh bandage."

"Yes, *mon frère*. Thank you."

Fabre had brought Charles's old cassock, and Charles was tying the cincture around it when the rector came in.

"*Bonjour, maître,*" Père Le Picart said warmly. "You look much improved."

"Oh, he is," Brunet said cheerfully, looking around from his supply cupboard in the corner. "He'll do very well now."

Charles tried for a less wan smile and put his skullcap on.

"We thank the Blessed Virgin for your well doing, Maître du Luc. Frère Brunet, the bursar sends his apologies for disturbing your Sabbath, but he must see you about the infirmary accounts."

"Oh, oh. I knew he'd query the extra poppy." Brunet bustled out the door.

"Lieutenant-Général La Reynie is here to see you," Le Picart said quietly, when Brunet was gone. "He already knew you were shot—the man's spies are everywhere."

Charles willed himself not to redden with guilt.

"Tell him nothing about Père Guise or this English plot," the rector said. "You can tell him where you were—he knows about those soirées, he's gone himself. Say that someone tried to rob you on your way home, if you like. But nothing else. Not yet."

"You have great faith in me, *mon père*, if you think I can lie convincingly to M. La Reynie."

"Lie? No, mislead, rather."

Charles became absorbed in shaking a tangle out of his rosary cord to give himself a moment to think. He felt like a deer with hounds baying at him from both sides. And he still wasn't sure how far he trusted either hound. He kept remembering Guise and La Reynie and Louvois with their heads together after the funeral. And he was increasingly unsure of how far Le Picart's desire to protect the Society and the college might go.

"*Mon père,*" he said at last, "I understand that you need time to consider what to do about all that I told you yesterday. Have you decided whether or not to confine Père Guise to the college?"

"I have told him that I feared he was in danger because of his connection to Philippe and Antoine Douté. He acquiesced without a murmur. And I gave the same order to Père Jouvancy, to make it more believable."

"Will you also block the old stairway? That would—"

"Père Guise has given me his key to the stairway doors. Both doors are now locked. Enough, Maître du Luc. We must not keep the lieutenant-général waiting longer. Remember, tell him only that robbers attacked you."

"*Bonjour*, Père Le Picart, Maître du Luc."

They turned sharply. Lieutenant-Général La Reynie was in the doorway, straightening from a bow.

His bright dark eyes went from one startled face to the other. "Forgive me, if I have come in too soon. But the door was a little open and I heard you talking." He smiled broadly. "So I took it on myself to join you."

"Please do, Monsieur La Reynie," the rector said, his tone delicately tinged with irony. "As you see, Maître du Luc is better. Allow us just to finish some college business and then you may talk with him. No, no, stay. We have no secrets." He turned his back and grimaced at Charles. "You remember, I trust, Maître du Luc," he said, pitching his voice so that La Reynie heard him clearly, "that although it is Sunday, you have a rehearsal this afternoon. Since the performance is only four days away."

Sighing inwardly, Charles nodded. He hadn't remembered. And he wanted to go and see how Pernelle was faring. But Wednesday and the performance were nearly upon them.

"Père Jouvancy wants you there, even if you only sit and watch. I have said you are injured because your horse threw you. No need for more hysterical gossip." He turned to La Reynie. "I will leave you in private. I beg you not to tire Maître du Luc, as he must work this afternoon."

La Reynie bowed the rector out the door. He waited a few moments in silence, opened the door quickly, checked the passageway, then closed it again and walked back to Charles. "If you were injured in my service, *maître*, please accept my regrets." He lifted his dark blue coat skirts out of the way and sat down on a bed.

"In Père Le Picart's service as well as yours, *monsieur*," Charles said curtly, sinking carefully onto the bed he'd occupied.

La Reynie rested his crossed hands on the silver head of his walking stick. "So you are ordered to tell me robbers attacked you. Now why would robbers risk drawing the watch's attention by shooting, Maître du Luc?"

"And where *was* the watch, anyway?" Charles said irritably. "They're never there when you need them."

"So I often hear. Who attacked you?"

"I never saw the man who shot at me."

"You had been at Père La Chaise's soirée?"

"You know that because one of your flies was also there?"

La Reynie smiled wolfishly. "Of course—you were there."

"Père Le Picart sent me to deliver messages and pay my respects."

"And did you meet the visiting Englishman? Or Dutchman, as I'm told some thought him?"

"I saw a visitor who was said to be English," Charles said, thinking that there really had been another fly at Père La Chaise's soirée. "We were not introduced."

"A pity." La Reynie scratched with a fingernail at a patch of tarnish on his walking stick's silver. "How did you end up in the beggars' Louvre?"

Hoping that La Reynie had learned that from the rector,

Charles said, "When the attacker shot at me the second time, my horse bolted and fetched up near the unfinished colonnade." Charles shrugged and grimaced with pain. "I fell off and a Good Samaritan found me and dragged me inside."

"And who is the woman who tended you there and spoke your southern language with you?"

A cold hand closed on Charles's gut. He shook his head as though baffled. "There was a woman, one of the beggars. She had a thick accent, but—" He shrugged. "She was very kind and I gave her some coins. I never thought to get her name. I hardly remember even being there, *monsieur*, let alone any delirious nonsense I uttered. I had bled a great deal." He closed his eyes and tried to look pathetic.

"Why did your attacker not pursue you there and finish you?"

Charles opened his eyes. This he could answer truthfully. "I think his horse went down and he lost me. We were going at demon speed through streets hardly wide enough for a man on foot to pass."

"I hear that a young Huguenot woman escaped from the New Converts convent last week. Did she end up at the Louvre, Maître du Luc?"

"Possibly," Charles said indifferently. "Since she would have no coreligionists to go to."

"Oh, there are Huguenots in Paris," La Reynie said softly, watching him. "Not many, but some. Most are artisans. But a few are men of wealth, whom the king needs. Do you not realize that one reason the dragonnades are always far from Paris is because the Huguenots here are more or less protected?"

"By whom?" Charles said, startled out of his verbal fencing.

"By me. And, in his way, by Monsieur Louvois."

"But he runs the—" Charles pressed his lips together, cursing himself.

"Of course he runs the dragonnades," La Reynie sighed. "He is the war minister. *Mort de ma vie*, are you really so innocent? Everyone knows he runs the dragonnades, there's no trouble in that. So long as you don't say so to the king. I repeat, the king needs some few Huguenots. In case it has escaped you, France is struggling and money is scarce. The countryside is poor, the king is poor, I am poor, even the Jesuits may be poor, for all I know, though I doubt it. Only the New World and the Huguenots are rich. Sometimes the king needs their money more than he needs their conversion."

"I cannot believe that Louvois protects Huguenots, however rich."

"*Mon cher maître*, Louvois is responsible not only for war, but for some part of the realm's finance. And as I told you in the Louvre, he loves order the way other men love mistresses. Especially order in Paris. The absence of order usually means the absence of money. In the interests of the king's treasury, he helps me protect some few Huguenots here for the sake of civic peace."

"And what is your own reason for protecting them?"

"The king tells me to, Maître du Luc, why else? Just as he sometimes tells me to help convert them—oh, not by torture. I am to do them favors. And have little—theological conversations."

Charles stared. "*Theological* conversations?"

La Reynie nodded and rolled his eyes, looking almost sheepish. It was Charles's first clear glimpse of the man behind the public role.

"You can believe me, *maître*, when I say that I do not care whether your Huguenot cousin is in Paris. My interest is in you. I forced you into spying for me because I need your help. I watched you carefully when Louvois accosted you after Philippe's funeral. You are, like many of your Jesuit brothers, intelligent beyond the ordinary. I knew beyond doubt that you were looking for answers to the attack on the child and to his brother's murder when I found you standing over the dead porter. Now someone has tried to murder you on your way home from Père La Chaise's soirée. I heard your rector order you not to tell me something. And, indeed, you are telling me nothing. In spite of the threats I still hold over you. Was I wrong about you? Are you going to help your rector shield your Society instead of the Douté child? Make no mistake, Maître du Luc, this tangle has Jesuit intrigue written all over it but I am going to untangle it and you are going to help me. Unless you prefer the alternatives."

Mislead him, Le Picart had said of La Reynie. Charles thought that men who had misled the lieutenant-général must be few and far between.

"Who attacked you?" La Reynie's voice cracked like a whip and Charles jumped.

"I don't know."

"I think you do. It was a Jesuit and you are shielding him."

"I assure you, I like my life too much to shield anyone who wants to kill me." Charles stirred uncomfortably on the bed. His attacker had certainly not been Guise, because Guise had still been inside the room arguing with Louvois. And Charles doubted that Guise would deign to take the role of common assassin. But most Louis le Grand Jesuits had grown up learning how to ride and use weapons. Even the poorest lay brother knew how to use a knife. "I do know what was used to kill Philippe and the porter," Charles said, partly to redirect La Reynie's attention.

La Reynie's gaze sharpened and he leaned forward. "What?"

"Someone in the Louvre saw the porter's murder," Charles said. "This witness never saw the killer's face, but did see the man take something from his pocket and strangle Pierre with it, then sit on the floor and do something to one of his boots. I think the killer strangled the porter with a spur garter and put it back on his boot. As he did with Philippe. A long, partially braided leather garter would fit the marks on both bodies."

"Well done," La Reynie said, in surprised approval.

"A woman who saw Antoine's accident said the man who rode him down wore burnt sugar–colored jackboots. On Thursday afternoon, I saw a man in the college wearing boots like that. I tried to catch him, but he eluded me. I told Père Le Picart, and we have taken extra measures to protect Antoine."

"Were the jackboots you saw gartered?"

"Yes."

"Too bad you let the man elude you. Now tell me what your rector forbade you to say this morning."

"I have given you what I know."

The lieutenant-général brought his walking stick's iron tip down sharply on the floorboards. Charles jumped.

"You have given me what you choose to give me. I know that you are caught between me and your rector, but that is your own affair. Your agreement with me stands, or you had better hope it stands. I have something to tell *you*, Maître du Luc, and perhaps it will help loosen your tongue. Early this morning, two of Père La Chaise's Friday evening guests were found floating in the river. Stabbed. One M. Lysarde and one M. Winters. The visiting Englishman. Or Dutchman."

Charles swallowed. "Did the watch find them?"

"Interestingly enough, no. The report was brought to me by one of M. Louvois's men. One of M. Louvois's servants, out on an early errand, I'm told, found them near the Ile St. Louis, where Lysarde lived. The other man was staying with him. They never came home on Friday night. Lysarde's servants claim to know nothing. Lysarde was an avid member of the Catholic League and one of Père Guise's penitents. But I think you already know that."

Charles crossed himself, unable to keep his hand from shaking as he remembered Louvois's fury at Winters. The war minister's rage—and fear—had been palpable, even through the door. Poor Lysarde, poor posturing little goat, whose greatest crime was stupidity. And poor Charles, perhaps, because by now Louvois and Guise had to know that Charles had overheard them.

"I ask you again, Maître du Luc, did you meet those two men? Did you talk to them?"

"I briefly met Lysarde. We discussed Spinoza."

"So it is simple Christian compassion that makes your hand shake and has you looking more ill than when I came," La Reynie said dryly. "Now hear me. You were attacked on your way back from Père La Chaise's soirée. Two other men were murdered after that same Jesuit-hosted evening. On your own admission, this booted horseman had previously come to the college. What did he come to do? Who did he come to see? Did he deliver a message? To your rector, perhaps? Your rector is well known in Paris as an astute politician. Or was the message for Père Montville, his almost equally astute assistant?" La Reynie's eyes bored into Charles. "Or was it, perhaps, for the illustrious and fervent Père Guise? I put it to you that what your rector so urgently wants you not to tell me is that all these murders are in the service of a Jesuit plot." He rose and looked down at Charles. "Find out who the booted man came here to see. And why. And who he is." La Reynie bared his teeth in what might have been a smile. "And now, I wish you a good day. By the way, I always come to the Louis le Grand show. Be sure I have a good seat."

Chapter 25

Dinner was garlic mutton. Charles wondered if it was as good as the sign painter's. Whether it was or not, it tasted like sawdust, since he had to eat it cheek by jowl with Père Guise. Once, as he reached for the bread, he caught Guise staring at him and the hatred in the man's eyes nearly knocked him off his chair. But, as Père Le Picart had said, surely Guise wouldn't risk another death in the college. When the meal ended, Père Dainville accosted Charles outside the refectory. His papery old face was grave, but Charles couldn't hear what he said. While he'd been in the infirmary, the Cour d'honneur had become a chaos of lumber, canvas, and rope, echoing with the hammering and the shouts of workmen and lay brothers constructing the outdoor stage. Like Charles, they were working on Sunday afternoon because time was short. Dainville put his mouth next to Charles's ear.

"Please come with me to the fathers' garden," he said in a quavering shout. "I have something to ask you."

Charles started to plead his injury as an excuse, but Dainville was already making for the garden and didn't hear him. Exasperated, Charles followed. Seeing Pernelle would have to wait.

Dainville led him across the little expanse of turf drowsing in the sunshine and sat on a stone bench in the lee of the age-blackened west wall.

Charles exclaimed and pointed at the north wall, where ripening grapes fattened on a gnarled vine in what sun Paris had to offer. "Vines here, *mon père?* Do we make wine?" He had glanced into this garden in his search for the boots, but he hadn't seen the grapes.

Dainville laughed. "Frère Brunet tries. But he gets only a drop. Though a venerable drop, as that vine descends from Roman vines, you know. There are still vines like that one all over St. Geneviève's hill. Sadly, our winters are too cold for them to flourish. I think the old Romans brought Italy's warmth with them when they settled here, and took it away when they left. And now, *mon fils,* for what I must ask." He peered earnestly at Charles. "I saw you come out of Père Guise's chamber a few days ago. When we collided in the passage."

Charles nodded warily.

"Another man left the chamber just ahead of you. I happen to know that Père Guise was not there, he was in the library. I must ask what the two of you were doing, my son."

In his excitement, Charles gripped Dainville's hand. "Did you recognize him, *mon père?* Who was he?"

Dainville snatched his hand away and stared at Charles in consternation. "You do not even know who he was?"

"No, and I must. Please, *mon père!*"

"So brazen in your sin?" Dainville crossed himself, shaking his head.

Charles suddenly realized what the old priest was saying. With so many men and boys living together, confessors worried constantly about the danger of unnatural affections. And Guise might well be spreading rumors about finding Charles in Antoine's room.

"*Mon père*, be assured that there was nothing sinful in what you saw," Charles assured him. "More than that I am under obedience not to say. But I must know who you saw in the passage."

"Under obedience to whom?" Dainville said suspiciously.

"To Père Le Picart. I swear it by all the saints."

The old priest frowned and then slowly nodded. "All I can tell you is that the man was dressed as a lay brother. Not a big man, certainly smaller than you. He ran past me, and that passage is always dark. I fear I do not see so well as I used to. But he wore an apron and a short cassock. And boots, so he must have been about to ride somewhere."

So La Reynie was right, Charles thought, trying to keep his horror off his face. The killer was a Jesuit. Or a senior student in lay brother's clothes? Hardly stopping to thank the perplexed Dainville, Charles hurried out of the garden as fast as his aching body would let him. The rector was in his office, in the act of rising from his prie-dieu. Before Le Picart could even speak, Charles launched into what he had to tell.

"—but Père Dainville only saw his back," Charles finished. "*Mon père*, it is critical now that Antoine's tutor—or someone— keeps the boy always in sight. Always!"

A cascade of falling metal came from the courtyard, accompanied by ripe curses. With a mild oath of his own, Le Picart slammed the casement shut. Charles started to speak, but the rector held up a peremptory hand.

"Let me think, for the love of God!" Le Picart stood utterly still, staring at the floor. "I can replace Maître Doissin. I should have done it before now. And I will have the lay brothers' dormitory searched—I will say there are rats or something. When we find the boots, we will find the man. If we find nothing, I will have the students' quarters searched as well."

"And when La Reynie makes the man talk, we will have Père Guise," Charles said ruthlessly. "Is there any lay brother Père Guise is especially close to?"

The rector sighed. "He has sponsored one or two. That young redhead—Frère Fabre. That was a sad case, the boy is barely seventeen. He owes much to Père Guise."

Charles's stomach felt hollow. Fabre had told him that and he'd forgotten. "Why did Père Guise want to keep him?"

"He *is* capable of simple benevolence," the rector said angrily. "Whatever you may think!"

"Forgive me, *mon père*." Charles bent his head in outward apology and kept his thoughts behind his face.

The rector cast a harried look toward the courtyard as the college clock chimed. "Go to your rehearsal, *maître*. I had overmuch to do and now I have more."

Charles picked his way through the maze of construction, wondering if it was one of the half dozen lay brothers wielding hammers and saws who had tried to kill him. His steps slowed as he studied the rapidly rising stage. It would cover most of the court's east side and reach to the top of the second-story windows. The stage floor was already in place against the rhetoric classroom's windows, with space beneath for the ropes, capstans, and the massive wooden gears that worked the stage machinery and trap doors. In spite of everything, excitement about the upcoming show surged through him.

Rehearsal hadn't started, but the rhetoric classroom was a whirlwind. Two boys, in outsized papier-mâché masks with open mouths and knobby features, clung to the ladder Charles had used for the sugar snowstorm. The ladder was teetering dangerously and Maître Beauchamps was trying to steady it. A third boy was picking up pieces of his mask from the floor. Charles recognized the three masks as those portraying the ballet's hubris-crazed giants trying to climb into heaven, allegories for the Huguenots.

"Hold on, lean out, balance each other," Beauchamps yelled to the two on the ladder. "Ah, *morbleu*, jump then, but don't let the other two masks fall!"

The boys landed on their feet and Charles lowered himself toward a bench and then had to stand up again as Jouvancy called everyone together for the opening prayer. Then Jouvancy took the actors through the tragedy with no stops while Charles and Beauchamps did the same with the ballet. In spite of the workmen hammering, shouting, swearing, and spitting sawdust just outside the windows, the dancers did so well that Charles forgot his fears and his aching body and grinned from ear to ear as he softly counted measures. Jouvancy called a break and came to sit beside him.

"Whoof! Excellent! I think we are going to make it after all! Today, tomorrow, Tuesday, and then we're on, can you believe it? They'll finish the stage tonight and tomorrow morning the machinery will be in place. The Opera craftsmen showed me the finished Hydra yesterday and I tell you, it is glorious, painted the most deliciously horrible green and orange and purple!" Jouvancy hugged himself in anticipation. "Tomorrow afternoon is our first rehearsal on the stage. Cast, costumes, machines, musicians, everything. It will be a disaster, it always is. My only comfort is that this year we're not putting the musicians in trees." He suddenly focused on Charles. "How are you, *maître*? I was so very sorry to learn of your injury. I have never trusted horses! You must not tire yourself," he added vaguely, and stood up, clapping his hands and shouting for everyone's attention. "We will begin again, alternating the tragedy acts with the ballet parts, as we will on Wednesday. Place yourselves!"

Everyone—actors, dancers, and the presiding theatrical saints and goddesses—more than rose to the occasion. On Wednesday the closing Ballet Général would end with the philosopher Diogenes, played by Père Montville, descending on a painted cloud with his famous lantern to find the boys receiving the annual school prizes and bring them to the stage. Today it ended with Charles, Jouvancy, and Beauchamps kissing each other on both cheeks and Beauchamps bursting into a spontaneous gigue as everyone stamped and clapped and yelled. Charles was clapping and yelling, too, his aches forgotten, when he saw Frère Fabre at the door. Watching the brother warily, Charles pushed his way through the crowd of boys.

"Are you looking for someone, *mon frère?*"

Fabre stared mutely at Charles, his eyes wide with shock.

"Mon frère?" Fear clutched at Charles's heart. "What is it?"

"He's dead," Fabre whispered.

"Who?" Charles shook Fabre roughly by the arm. "Who's dead?"

"Maître Doissin," Fabre finally got out, his voice shaking.

Charles stared in bewilderment. "Was he ill? I didn't know. What happened?" And in the next breath demanded, "Antoine—is he all right?"

"Yes, he didn't—he was in the little study, he—"

"Wait here."

Charles pulled Jouvancy out of the jubilant crowd and told him what had happened.

"Go to Antoine," Jouvancy said grimly. "I'll follow as soon as I can."

Charles shepherded Fabre out of the building. "Tell me the rest as we go."

"It was *gaufres*," the lay brother whispered, still staring at Charles.

"What? Do you mean those little sweet wafers?" Charles pulled Fabre out of the way as a pair of workmen hauled on ropes to raise a joist. "Start at the beginning!"

"Someone left them—a package of them—with the porter. For Antoine."

"Who left them?"

Fabre shrugged. "Frère Martin just gave me the package to take to Maître Doissin. Since gifts go first to the tutor and—"

"I know. When was the package left?"

Fabre shrugged again.

"Did Maître Doissin seem well when you gave him the package?"

"He was just as usual. We started talking and he unwrapped the *gaufres* and ate one. He offered me one, but I said no. They had syrup on them and I don't like them like that, thank St. Benedict!" St. Benedict, once the target of poisoning, was everyone's protector against it.

Charles crossed himself. "Thank St. Benedict indeed. What happened then?"

"We talked about candles and sheets for the chamber." Fabre's voice was shaking and Charles could hardly hear him. "Things like that. Maître Doissin kept eating the *gaufres* and then he started spewing. Then he couldn't breathe. He just—collapsed. Antoine and the other boys ran in from the study, but I made them go back. Then I yelled out the window for help. A proctor came and then Frère Brunet arrived with his medicines. But by then, Maître Doissin couldn't swallow anything. Before God, *maître*, if I'd known anything was wrong with the *gaufres*—"

"You couldn't have known. It wasn't your fault." They were almost at the door of the building where Antoine lived. "Go and find out everything Frère Martin can remember about who brought the package and when, every detail. And find out—" Charles caught himself. Find out where Guise was, he'd been going to say. But he couldn't ignore the fact that Fabre owed his escape from the tannery to Guise. "Never mind. Just talk to Frère Martin."

"But he already told me he hardly saw the man—"

"Ask him again, talk him through it, he may remember something. Then come and tell me. Go on, hurry!"

Stifling a sob, Fabre stumbled back the way they'd come. At the top of the stairs Charles could hardly make his way through the excitedly appalled tutors and lay brothers blocking Antoine's chamber door. Doissin lay on the floor in pools of vomit and Frère Brunet was on his knees beside him, closing his bulging eyes. Golden *gaufres*, shining with syrup, were scattered over the floor like giant's coins, their sugar and vanilla sweetness strong even under the smells of death. The death that would have been Antoine's, if this poor hapless man hadn't been so greedy. Charles leaned down to Brunet.

"Was it poison, *mon frère?*" he said quietly.

The infirmarian looked up. "I think so. Most likely in the syrup. Aconite, perhaps, though a few others could act as fast. Those *gaufres* should be picked up, *maître*, but keep the syrup from cuts or scratches, it could kill you."

Out of the corner of his eye, Charles saw a gawking elderly lay brother lean into the room and pick a *gaufre* off the floor.

"Leave it!" He slapped it out of the man's hand. "Unless you want to die like Maître Doissin."

The brother's dull eyes were full of offense as he rubbed his slapped hand. "Why? He was possessed. I always thought so, the way he fell asleep all the time. A demon killed him, why shouldn't I take a *gaufre?*"

"Why not, indeed?" someone said sardonically, and Frère Moulin's face appeared, looking over the old man's shoulder into the room. He grimaced and shook his head.

"Mon frère," Charles said quickly, "will you see that our brother here washes his hands, and thoroughly?"

Moulin grunted assent, and Charles shut the chamber door and went into the study, closing that door, too, before the boys' avid eyes could see around him. Antoine's companions traded frustrated looks and slumped on their benches, but Antoine ran to Charles, who put an arm around him. One of the boys snickered and Charles shot him a look that made him bury his face in his Cicero.

Antoine looked up at Charles. His wet eyes were huge in his pale face. "Maître Doissin is dead."

"Yes, *mon brave,* he is. I'm sorry." Charles *was* sorry, and not just because an innocent man had been murdered. For all his laziness, Doissin had given Antoine warmth and kindness, and Antoine had liked him.

The other boys erupted in questions. "Why? How? Was he sick? That old lay brother said it was demons!"

Deciding that a modicum of truth was better than demon rumors, Charles led Antoine back to his desk, sat him down, and addressed them all.

"Maître Doissin was suddenly very sick and died of it."

Antoine whispered, "We should pray for him, *maître.*"

Charles led them in prayers for the suddenly dead. Then he waited a moment and said, "You are all to stay here until someone comes for you. I see that you have books and work to do, yes?"

All four of them looked with distaste at the quills, paper, Ciceros, and Latin grammars in front of them.

"Good," Charles said briskly. "To your books now."

The other three made at least a show of settling to work under Charles's stern eye, but Antoine sat motionless.

"Maître?" His voice was so small that Charles had to squat on his haunches to hear him. "Did he die because of me? Like Philippe?"

Charles took the boy's cold hands. "Look at me, *mon brave.*"

The child brought his eyes up fleetingly and then looked down at his desk again, studying its scarred and initialled surface as though it were an examination text.

"Philippe and Maître Doissin died because a grown-up person did evil things," Charles said softly. "None of it is your fault. Do you understand?"

A tiny nod—in which Charles did not believe at all—was all his answer.

"Your uncle Jouvancy is coming for you, *mon brave.* You won't be left alone."

Charles patted his shoulder, murmured stern encouragement to the others, and went back to the chamber, where Brunet was praying beside the body. Charles took a towel from Antoine's cupboard, covered his hand with it, and collected the spilled *gaufres.* As he laid them on the thick paper they'd come in, he wondered whether, if he'd killed the booted man in Père La Chaise's garden, Maître Doissin would be alive. And whether, in the divine economy of sin, one outcome would have been better than the other.

Chapter 26

Père Jouvancy arrived a few minutes later and led Antoine away, holding his hand as though he would never again let the child out of his sight. Frère Fabre returned, and he and Charles spoke at the head of the stairs, empty now of gawkers. Fabre's freckles stood out sharply against his blanched skin as he tried not to look at the rewrapped package of *gaufres* in Charles's hand.

"What did you learn from the porter, *mon frère?*"

"He—he said—maybe a woman left them. Maybe an hour ago. He didn't see her face because she wore a long veil. Or a big shawl, maybe. *Maître*, it could have been a man dressed in woman's clothes."

"Did she—or he—sound young or old?"

"Young. But some people sound young when they're not. She—he—just said that the package was for Antoine."

"Did the porter say anything else?"

"The *gaufres* might have come from the bakery next door. He said the little girl brought him one yesterday."

Charles's heart sank. If the LeClercs had sold them, the rector and the police would descend on the bakery, which was the last thing Pernelle needed. Not that he thought for a moment that the LeClercs had poisoned the *gaufres*. The bakery wasn't even open today, it being Sunday, but the *gaufres* could have been bought yesterday and then poisoned. But what poisoner would be stupid enough to buy the *gaufres* next door?

"Do you have any cuts or scratches on your hands, Frère Fabre?"

The boy gaped at him. Charles grabbed one cold clammy hand and then the other. Finding stage scenery paint stains but no grazes, he thrust the package at Fabre.

"Stay here and give these to the rector when he comes. Do not put them down or give them to anyone else. Tell the rector to keep them wrapped. Frère Brunet will tell him the rest. Then wash your hands. Thoroughly. With soap. I'm going to see Mme LeClerc. I'll be back as soon as I can."

Leaving Fabre holding the package at arm's length as though it might explode, Charles went to the street passage. The porter got up from his stool.

"Frère Martin," Charles greeted him, "tell me again about whoever brought the *gaufres*."

"I told it all to the boy. Poor cabbage, you'd think he'd never seen death." Martin repeated his story, but it wasn't quite the story Fabre had told. Martin was certain that the person under the mourning veil was a woman. Small, he said, and by the voice, young.

"Little hands, *maître*. Gloved. Hot weather for that, but carrying poison, that explains it."

"Who else has come and gone in the last hour or so? Professors, students? They may have seen something, if I can find them."

The porter shook his head. "No one at all. Did young rooster head tell you those *gaufres* maybe came from next door?

Little Marie-Ange brought me one yesterday. But it wasn't poisoned, as you see!" He laughed heartily as he opened the postern for Charles.

Life, Charles thought sourly, *was much less harrying for the unimaginative.* To his relief, the bakery door stood open, no doubt to let out the strong smell of burned pastry that met his nose. Mme LeClerc, arranging cream cakes behind the counter, whirled when she heard him and her hard, unwelcoming expression stopped him in the doorway.

"Oh, it's you," she said, with a relieved smile. "But you should still be resting, *maître!*"

He managed a smile. "I'm well enough. Forgive me for startling you, madame." His eyes went toward the back of the shop, where he heard Pernelle's voice.

"Yes, *maître*, she is there, helping clean up our ass-brained apprentice's mess. Roger would insist on letting him practice pastry on Sunday. Are you come to see your lady?"

"One small moment. Madame, did you sell *gaufres* yesterday to a woman in a mourning veil?"

"I did not. Why?" She finished arranging the cakes on their wooden tray and stepped back to look critically at them, her head on one side.

"But you did make *gaufres?*"

She looked up. "How did you know?"

Not wanting to get Marie-Ange in trouble, Charles didn't reply. Instead he said, "We've had another tragedy in the college. Someone left poisoned *gaufres* for Antoine."

"Mon Dieu!" She pressed both hands to her mouth. "Is he—?"

"He didn't eat them, madame, he's well. Sadly, however, his tutor did. And died."

"St. Benedict protect us! As I hope for salvation, *maître*, I never poisoned any *gaufres!*"

"Calm yourself, madame, I never thought you did. But I wondered if someone might have bought them here and then poisoned them."

"Poison?" Marie-Ange burst out of the workroom, towing Pernelle behind her. "Who is poisoned?"

"Marie-Ange, no, I told you to keep mademoiselle out of sight!" Madame flapped her apron at them and Pernelle stopped, smiling at Charles. Marie-Ange ran to him and pulled anxiously at his sleeve.

"Is it Antoine, *maître*?"

"Not Antoine, his tutor," Charles said. "Antoine is fine."

The little girl's worried frown relaxed. Pernelle ignored Mme LeClerc's clucking and walked quickly down the shop to him.

"More murder? You look terrible, Charles."

"More murder, yes." But he was smiling. The shadows under her eyes were gone and the pink in her cheeks contrasted prettily with the shabby gray kirtle and bodice she wore, which were clearly Mme LeClerc's. A flour-dusted apron bunched the wide gown in thick folds around her waist, and the skirt barely covered her white-stockinged calves.

"Veiled, you said, *maître*?" The baker's wife was frowning and staring at nothing. "I *did* see a woman in mourning pass by today."

"When? Are you sure it was a woman?"

"An hour or two ago. I assumed it was a woman. But those mourning veils hide most everything, don't they?" She shook her head scornfully. "Those veils! If you're so much in mourning you don't even want to see where you're going, then why be out in the street? Why not stay home with the shutters closed and black bed hangings and all? Unless you just don't want to live anymore and you're trying to get run over, sin though that would be, though it's so easy to be hurt in traffic, it's hardly fair to count it as sin. But losing loved ones takes us all different ways, I suppose. Still, in that flaunting petticoat of hers, she can't have been all that deeply mourning, now can she?"

"Was the woman you saw carrying anything?" Charles asked, not daring to look at Pernelle, who was openly laughing at Mme LeClerc's observations.

Before Mme LeClerc could answer, someone coughed politely and they all turned toward the street door. A solidly built man in brown breeches and jacket stood there. He was smiling at them, but most of his smile was landing on Pernelle, who caught Marie-Ange by the hand and disappeared into the workroom. Mme LeClerc moved briskly around the counter. Taking his cue from her hurry, Charles smiled affably and stood between the man and the back of the shop. The newcomer was wigless. His hair only reached the nape of his neck and he wore both a sword and a pistol on his thick leather belt. Everything about him said police.

"Monsieur? Back again?" Mme LeClerc said sharply, demanding the man's attention. "I told you before that we are not open."

"You did, madame," he said, with an easy smile. "But if you sold me a little cream cake, I think no one would know." He nodded toward the workroom door. "For not being open, you have a lot of help today. From far away, as I could tell from the young woman's voice when you gave me that magnificent brioche a while ago."

Charles tensed. So much for La Reynie's lack of interest in the Provençal-speaking fugitive in the beggars' Louvre, damn the man. His flies there must have told him she had left. Of course he would start searching at the college door. Charles moved closer to the man.

"I always have plenty of help," Mme LeClerc said tartly. "And my niece will not thank you for calling her a foreigner." She waved away the man's sous and handed him a cake. *"Adieu, monsieur."* A pointed "good-bye" instead of the shopkeeper's hopeful "see you soon." She walked purposefully out from behind the counter and toward the street, forcing him backward. As he went, he studied Charles as though memorizing him. Then the man dodged among carriages and riders to lean against the bookshop wall across the street, nibbling at the cake and watching the bakery through the traffic.

"Police," Mme LeClerc said flatly, slamming the door and shaking her head. "He keeps trying to see Mademoiselle Pernelle."

"And you let her speak to him?" Charles demanded.

"Of course not!" She dropped the bar across the door. "I should have barred the door before, but I thought that would only convince him we had something to hide. When he walked in the first time, I had just called out to the back room that I wanted the work table scrubbed and she was answering me. The man's master had been here earlier."

"What? Lieutenant-Général La Reynie?"

"Himself. Pretending he was only making sure we were not selling when we shouldn't. Your Pernelle was in here helping me scrub these counters. And since then, his man"—she glanced pointedly across the street—"has been making me nervous as a wet hen. I don't like it. I'm sure she's done nothing that's police business, nor you, either!"

Ignoring that, Charles went to the door to the old stairs and tried the latch. It was locked, as the rector had said. "Your key is lost, I hear, madame?"

"And our back door is bricked up. If your young lady needs

a sudden way out, the only way is through a little back window into your courtyard. Unless St. Anthony takes pity and finds our key to the stairway door."

"Madame, I fear," Charles said slowly, "that Mademoiselle Pernelle must disappear. Can you borrow your apprentice's other set of clothes for her? Cut her hair, blacken some teeth with soot. She can be a mute so she doesn't have to speak. If the worst comes to the worst and you have to send her through the window, tell her to go to our porter and ask for me. It's the best I can think of."

"It's well enough and well thought. We will do it. And who would expect you to think, *maître*, with people being poisoned?" She glanced across the street. "Wait, I'll give you a reason for coming here." She clattered into the back and reappeared with a round loaf, dark with rye, tossing it from hand to hand. "If *he* asks, you can say it's a gift and I forgot to send it to you yesterday. It's hot, be careful!"

Charles wrapped it in a fold of his cassock. "Thank you for this, and for everything, madame. I will think of somewhere else your—ah—new apprentice can go. If you need me before tomorrow, tell the porter. And pray!" He went out into the street, a desperate urgency at his heels. He had to get Pernelle away from here and on the road to Geneva. Wishing he could find the entrance to her Huguenot highway, he put up his hand to ring the postern bell and froze. The policeman was still across the street, talking with another, even larger armed man and pointing at the bakery. Charles turned hastily back to warn Mme LeClerc, but two more men, one on foot and one on horseback, closed on him from both sides.

❧ *Chapter 27* ❧

"M*on père*, my master—"

"Silence, fellow!" The man on horseback raised an imperious gloved hand. "*Mon père*, a word!"

Tensed for assault, arrest, or both, Charles looked from the boy in servant's livery to the middle-aged, red-faced man on the horse. Far from laying hands on him, the two were jockeying for his attention like courtiers accosting the king. Realizing that he was holding the wheel of bread in front of him like a shield, Charles shifted it to one arm and smiled at the youngster. Then he turned to the horseman, who was slapping his tawny wool covered thigh impatiently with his riding crop.

"How may I help you, *monsieur?*" Charles said, smiling insincerely. The sooner well-dressed self-importance got its way, the faster it departed.

The man frowned and squinted at him. "I don't know you. But you are a Jesuit, surely you know who I am."

Beyond the rider, Charles saw the two police agents walk away. In tones of heartfelt relief, he said, "I have not the pleasure, *monsieur.*"

The man drew a long, offended breath. "Your accent tells me you are not from Paris, so perhaps that excuses you. I am

Monsieur Jean Donneau de Visé, editor of the *Nouveau Mercure Galant*. Are you attached to the college?"

"Yes, *monsieur*. I am Maître Charles du Luc," Charles said, groaning inwardly. He had seen the *Mercure*, a weekly gazette reporting theatre and social news for the court and the wealthy. De Visé would no doubt be writing up Wednesday's performance. If Charles offended this well-known journalist and playwright, Père Jouvancy would probably scalp him and use the results to fix the mangy blond wig. "I sincerely hope, Monsieur de Visé, that we will have the honor of your presence on Wednesday."

"That is why I stopped when I saw you. You can carry my request and I will not have to waste time going into the college. I want a better seat than I had last year. I could hardly see and couldn't hear a thing. And make sure I am well away from the edge of that damned awning. Rain sluices off it and I will *not* risk wetting my good beaver hat. Good day."

Not bothering to raise the hat in question, he turned the horse and trotted away. Charles turned with relief to the boy.

"And how may I help you?" he said.

The boy dragged his eyes away from a pretty maidservant who was smiling at him and sending an extra sway of hips his way.

"I was sent from the Hôtel de Sully, *mon*—I mean—*maître*, I heard you say?"

"Yes. And your errand?"

"The duke reminds the college to be sure a poster for the tragedy and ballet is put at our gate. You forgot last year and he didn't like it. Will you carry that message for him?"

"A lot of people didn't like things last year, it seems." Charles's wry face made the boy grin. "Yes, I will see that you get a poster. You may tell your master that the printer says we'll have them Tuesday morning."

"Thank you, *mon père*." The boy sketched a bow and made off after the girl.

A lay brother Charles didn't know opened the postern. Charles thrust the bread into his arms and asked him to send it to the kitchen. Then he went to Le Picart's office. Looking as though he was barely holding himself together under the news of this latest death, the rector was talking to Frères Brunet, Martin the doorkeeper, and Fabre. Brunet and Martin were listening tensely, but Fabre was staring at the floor.

"You have been very helpful," Le Picart said to them. "For now, if anyone asks you, say only that Maître Doissin was taken suddenly and violently ill and died. Lieutenant-Général La Reynie is coming. When he gives permission, we will have a quiet funeral mass and burial across the river at St. Louis."

He dismissed them and turned to Charles. "So now we have poison. And from outside the college."

"*Mon père*, Mme LeClerc saw a woman in a mourning veil pass by an hour or two ago. And, as Frère Martin no doubt told you, the *gaufres* were brought by someone in a veil."

"Would a woman do this thing? Who in God's name can she be?"

"My first thought was that it might be Antoine's stepmother, *mon père*. She *is* in mourning. But Mme Douté went back to Chantilly with Philippe's body. Didn't she?"

"I—yes—I believe so. I didn't see her go, but—" Shaking his head, Le Picart felt for his chair and sat down heavily, like an old man. "Until we get to the bottom of this, Antoine will be either with Père Jouvancy or Frère Brunet. He will not go to classes and he will sleep in the infirmary." The rector sighed. "You were right, I was too complacent, and now I have Maître Doissin's death heavy on my conscience."

After supper, Charles's much-tried body overruled his frantic mind and he lay down on his bed. Compline bells woke him. He hauled himself up and went to kneel in front of the painting of Mary and the infant Jesus. But before he could bow his head to say the office, his gaze caught and held on Mary's patient face. *Show me how to find the killers,* he whispered. *Before more people die.* He waited, every nerve stretched to listen beyond hearing and see beyond seeing. The evening light went on dimming, noise from the street hushed toward its night level, and that was all.

He resorted to bargaining. *Help me, Blessed Mother, and I will put my questions aside and serve you as a Jesuit all my life. Help me crush them. Guise and his hatred, Louvois and his cruelty.* The strength of his desire turned the knuckles of his clasped hands white. Mary's gaze seemed to darken. *Justice? Or revenge?* Her questions were loud in the stillness. Charles bowed his head and prayed for forgiveness. Prayed to want justice and not vengeance.

Slowly, heartbeat by heartbeat, the room's quiet filled with the Silence that came to him sometimes. He lifted his head. The painting was dim now. Mary's half-hooded eyes veiled her thoughts. She was so often like that in paintings. Pondering things in her heart, he supposed, as Scripture said. Worrying, probably, about those three ominous gifts to the baby. Gold, frankincense, and myrrh. The myrrh especially, that bitter funeral spice, must have haunted her as she suckled her fat, happy baby. The painter had put a little window in the wall behind her. Its curtain was pulled back and its casement stood open, showing green hills dotted with tiny white sheep. The hills were suspiciously rounded and matched in size, like green breasts. Charles wondered confusedly if the painter meant to say that Mary had to suckle all the world's poor stupid human sheep.

"Holy Queen, mother of mercy," he prayed, imagining himself sitting beside her and talking quietly while evening filled her little room. "Hail, our life, our sweetness, and our hope. To you do we cry, poor banished children of Eve; to you do we send up our sighs, mourning and weeping in this vale of tears. Most gracious advocate, turn your eyes of mercy toward us . . ."

As he reached the "amen," he looked again at the painting and noticed that the curtain at the painting's window was red. Blue was the Virgin's color. Did the red stand for blood? That funereal myrrh again? This red wasn't a scarlet, flaunting red. It was more rose, such a feminine color, rose . . .

Charles was on his feet and out the door, words of thanksgiving tumbling from his lips as he pelted down the stairs two at a time, hardly feeling his wound. The antechamber at the stair foot was shadowed in twilight, and he nearly didn't see Fabre at the side table, stopped in the act of putting a new candle in a copper candlestick.

"What's happened now, *maître?*" Fabre said anxiously, putting the candle down.

Charles didn't slacken his pace. "I just remembered something, that's all."

"It's after Compline! Where are you going?" Fabre grabbed at Charles's sleeve, but Charles shook off his hand and disappeared into the street passage.

Chapter 28

Frère Martin was just locking the postern. He opened it again and Charles made for the river, but once through the bridge gate's torchlit passage, he slowed. The Petit Pont's narrow roadway with its tall old houses was in deep twilight and he didn't want to miss the shop. Voices and occasional music floated through open windows, a descant to the rougher music of the light traffic's wheels, hooves, and feet. Charles stopped under the apothecary's sign. No light showed in the shop or anywhere else in the house. He pounded on the door, waited, and pounded again. As he stepped back to see if a light showed in any upper window, the door grated over uneven stones. A candle flame wavered in the crack between the door and its jamb, and the barrel of a long pistol gleamed below it. Charles stepped hastily aside.

"What do you want?" the dwarf's high-pitched voice demanded.

"Only to speak with you, *monsieur*. I am a cleric and unarmed."

"Stand where I can see you."

"I do not wish to speak with your pistol, *monsieur*."

"And I do not wish to be robbed and murdered."

But the gun barrel was lowered and Charles moved warily

into the dwarf's line of sight, holding his hands pacifically open in front of him.

"Ah. The beautiful young man looking in the wrong place for sugar. So now you are shopping in the dark?"

"We must talk, *monsieur*," Charles said.

"I am here. Talk."

"Do you want to discuss your poison selling here in the street?"

"You are the one who wants to discuss." A sigh came out of the darkness and the door opened a little wider. "Come in, then."

"And your pistol, *monsieur*?"

"I am not going to shoot you unless you give me reason. And I am not going to stand here all night."

Charles took a cautious step toward the threshold. The dwarf's small hand closed like a vise on his wrist and pulled him inside. The little man shut the door, locked it with a key as long as Charles's foot, and picked up the candle from a low chest.

"I am working in the back, there is light there."

Seeing that the pistol was now pushed into the back of the dwarf's belt, Charles let himself be led. He could overwhelm his captor by sheer size and weight before the man could get to his weapon. All Charles's senses were alert. The shop's dry warm air was full of the competing odors of herbs. But the dwarf himself smelled of sulfur. As demons were said to smell. Charles's mind had doubts about demons, but his body suddenly declared traditional opinions and he found himself pulling back against his guide. Who only gripped him tighter, towing him like a small horse pulling a boat along a towpath.

The house was utterly silent. They crossed a large, beamed kitchen, where the outline of a sleeping cat showed beside the banked fire. The dwarf let go of Charles to open a door and soft light spilled across the worn stone floor of the kitchen.

"In here."

"After you."

"What do you think I am going to do, my dear young man, lock you in?"

Thinking exactly that, Charles waited out of reach. With a shrug, the little man disappeared through the door. Charles followed cautiously and found himself in a large room with a vaulted stone ceiling, perhaps a storeroom when the old house was built. Candles burned on a low wooden table and flickered in sconces, picking out the signs of the zodiac painted on the windowless plastered walls. The apothecary was an alchemist, then, which probably explained the stink of sulfur. It was a common enough combining of crafts. The dwarf tied an apron over his black jerkin and breeches and glanced into a trio of crucibles bubbling on trivets in the small fireplace. He blew more life into the coals with a pair of bellows and plucked a pair of spectacles from the littered the table.

"So talk to me," he said.

"What poisons do you sell?"

"The ones everyone sells. Look for yourself."

As though his visitor no longer concerned him, the dwarf blew out the candles on the table and picked up a small clay pot. Charles started slowly around the room, looking for aconite. Between the zodiacal paintings, wooden shelves overflowed with brown, green, and clear glass bottles and beakers, stoppered clay pots, and brightly glazed jars. The contents of the jars were written in their glazes. "Aethiopis Mineralis," Charles read on a yellow and green one, and remembered his mother telling him it was black sulphide of mercury, good for constipation, toothache, melancholy, and childbirth. Another jar held "Laudanum," opium in wine, God's gift for easing pain. There was "Elixir Salutis," a stomach purge, as he knew to his sorrow. And "Ens of Venus," "Salt of Sylvie," "Crocus Saturn," "Bezoar Orientalis," "Aqua Tofani." He stopped. "Aqua Tofani," arsenious oxide, was an Italian poison. Infallibly deadly, as of course it would be, since—as everyone knew—Italians were the world's arch-poisoners.

"You sell Aqua Tofani?" Charles said.

The dwarf looked up from whatever he was doing to a sliver of wood. The narrow circles of horn that held the lenses of his spectacles made him look like an irritated owl.

"A little of something, that's medicine. Too much, that's poison."

"And what would you sell 'a little' Aqua Tofani for?" Charles said acidly.

"A little rat."

"Of course." Charles bent to peer at a squat round jar of clear glass with muslin tied over its top and stepped quickly back. Leeches. He stared in frustration at a blue glazed jar with "Vanilla" blazoned on it, thinking that if he tried to read every label, he would be here till morning. Following his gaze, the dwarf said, "Oh, now I see. You want a love potion and are too embarrassed to say so."

Charles's eyebrows rose. "Vanilla?"

"A fine aphrodisiac, yes. Very popular with priests."

"I am not yet a priest," Charles said dryly. And thought, *I definitely do not need an aphrodisiac. The contrary, if anything.*

He finished his circuit of the room, past a stack of firewood, a huddle of small unlabeled barrels standing oddly in the middle of the room, and a tier of shelves crammed with books, including the Jesuit Athanasius Kircher's *Sphinx Mystagoga*, in Latin with Egyptian hieroglyphs. He came back to the little fireplace.

"When I was here before," he began, but a brilliant flash of light and a harsh stink of sulfur sent him cowering back against the wall.

"When you were here before, what?" the dwarf said, as though nothing had happened.

"What in the name of all hell's devils did you just do?" Fear made Charles's words sharp with anger.

The apothecary turned, holding up another sliver of wood. "You see this common match," he said, assuming a lecturer's tone. "A piece of wood with a little sulfur on the end to make it light when you hold it to a flame." He held up a piece of paper. "On this paper, I have smeared phosphorus. From that jar. An Englishman has found that this phosphorus burns as soon as it touches sulfur, so that the match lights instantly. And burns brighter. If I draw the unlit sulphur-tipped match through the phosphorus-treated paper—"

He did and produced another small burst of fire. He extinguished the burning sliver in a bucket of water beside the table and tipped the jar toward Charles. It was full of an eerie white light that made Charles hurriedly cross himself.

"Phosphorus, not demons," the dwarf laughed. "I made the stuff myself."

"How?" Charles said, fascinated in spite of himself, but still unsettled by the glow. "Is it poison?"

"It looks like it should be, doesn't it? Would you believe I made it from piss? An ungodly lot of piss, you have no idea. Long, nasty process. My books say piss will eventually produce gold. They're wrong, it produces fire. Think about that the next time you're watering a wall."

"*Monsieur*—" Charles walked around the table and faced the apothecary. He suddenly realized he didn't know the man's name. "What are you called?"

"Called? I am called Monsieur Rivière."

"Well, Monsieur Rivière, a man died this afternoon at the college of Louis le Grand. I think he died from poison you sold. The day I came asking about sugar, a woman came in as I left. A young woman. She wore a black veil and gown, but with a rose-colored petticoat under it. You greeted her as though you knew her. Who is she?"

The dwarf was carefully examining his pieces of wood and sorting them by size. "Do I remember everyone who comes through my door? *And* their petticoats?"

"You are required by law to keep a register, with the names of all who buy poison and the reason they give for buying it. You are also required to sell poison only to people you know."

"And why should you think this rose-petticoated woman bought poison? Are you certain you do not wish a love potion, my beautiful cleric?"

"Are you certain you do not want me to return with Lieutenant-Général La Reynie?"

The apothecary sighed and took off his spectacles. "Always such a fuss about death," he murmured, rubbing his eyes. "So much death, always, and no one gets used to it. Isn't death the only way to your heaven? You'd think—"

Your heaven? Charles decided he didn't have time for whatever that meant. "I heard you greet her, *monsieur*, you know her. Give me her name." He stepped closer, forcing the little man to crane his neck back and look nearly straight up. "If you can't remember, go and get your register. If you keep a register."

The dwarf moved away and rubbed his neck. "I think you mean Mademoiselle La Salle." His deep brown eyes were full of the sadness Charles remembered from his first visit. "She is a servant in the Place Royale."

"The Place Royale? You're sure?"

"The silly chit brags about it. She makes it sound as though the close stools are solid gold and her mistress shits rubies. She goes on about how high and great and rich the woman is, and says that soon she will be rich, too."

"Who is her mistress? Which house is it?"

The apothecary shrugged. "She told me once that she watched a duel in the Place from her window. But I suppose you could do that from any of those houses."

"Did she buy aconite?"

"She often buys it. Her mistress uses it to make a salve to ease backache, the girl says. I make the same salve myself, it's a perfectly good reason for buying aconite. Dangerous to handle, but I tell them how to be careful. Now may I see you out and get back to my work?"

Charles's inheld anger flared like the phosphorus match. "By all means, *monsieur*. And as you get on with your work, pray for the soul of Maître Doissin. Dead from your aconite. Which wasn't even meant for him. Mademoiselle La Salle meant it for an eight-year-old child."

He left the dwarf standing there and felt his way through the dark house. Behind him, the dwarf's voice rose in a strange, minor-keyed lament, sad enough to mourn all the world's dead, past and to come. Charles shivered as the despairing music coiled around his heart.

Chapter 29

L a Salle. La Salle. The name beat in time to Charles's foot-steps like a funeral drum. Who was she? If La Salle was re-ally her name, which he doubted. Whoever she was, what was her connection to Antoine Douté? She had a connection, of that he was certain, though his certainty was irrational and fragile, woven from glimpses of her petticoat: red, rose red, bloodred now in his mind's eye. It was full dark now and the streets were as close to quiet as Paris streets ever seemed to get. Someone's Nemesis, Le Picart had called him, and Charles felt like Nemesis as he descended on the Place Royale and strode through the south gate beneath the Pavillon du Roi. A carriage rolled in front of him along the gravelled roadway that divided the arcaded, nearly identical houses from the square's garden. In the garden, a few murmuring, laughing strollers still crisscrossed the paths around Louis XIII's statue. An outburst of coarse laughter made him turn to see an obvious *fille de joie* dart from the ground-floor ar-cade and run like the wind toward the square's ungated north-west corner. Her bare-scalped customer pounded behind her, yelling for help and pointing to his long, expensive wig, which the girl carried aloft like a trophy.

Charles left them to it and walked along the roadway, past

the arcade's closed shops and the lanterns burning by house gates. He descended abruptly from tragedy to farce: Nemesis didn't know which house held the poisoner. Or what she looked like, except that she was small and wore a gaudy petticoat. Hoping for inspiration, he kept on doggedly around the square, looking up at the big windows glowing with candlelight and watching the gates. He supposed he could ring at every house, but a strange Jesuit asking for a servant girl would raise a flurry of questions, maybe warn his quarry and give her time to escape by a back way. His frustrated sigh was answered by a gasp from a dark stretch of arcade.

"Who's there?" he demanded and immediately felt his face grow hot. A gasp in the dark could have reasons that were none of his business. A stifled sob followed the gasp.

"Who's there?" he said more boldly. "Is something wrong?" Offering help was certainly his business.

Frère Fabre emerged from the arcade, his red hair shining in the light from the windows. His face was a mask of misery.

For a moment neither of them moved. Then Charles grabbed the boy, twisting his cassock into hard knots. "You followed me. Why?" Fabre turned his head away and Charles shook him. "*Why?*"

"When you went out, *maître*, I was afraid you knew, but you went into that house on the bridge. I came here, anyway, but I didn't warn her, I swear it! I meant to, but I couldn't!" The boy covered his face and sobbed in earnest.

"Didn't warn who?"

"Agnes." Fabre tried to wipe his face on his cassock skirt and Charles released his hold. "When I got here, I kept remembering Maître Doissin. And that it might have been Antoine. And I—" He shook his head wordlessly.

"Frère Fabre, who is Agnes?"

"My sister. My half-sister, her surname is La Salle. She's Mme Douté's maid."

Charles stared at him, bereft of speech.

"You saw her at Philippe's funeral, *maître*. I was talking to her."

"Yes," Charles managed to say, "I remember. I didn't know she was Mme Douté's maid."

Fabre nodded at the nearest gate. "She's been here most of the summer with her mistress. The house belongs to Mme Montfort, Mme Douté's sister."

"Mme Douté didn't go to Chantilly with Philippe's body?"

"She said the journey was too much for her. She made M. Douté leave her here."

"So you knew it was your sister who had left the *gaufres*. That's why you were so upset and tried to confuse what Frère Martin said."

"Forgive me, *maître!*" Fabre's face was full of anguish. "I told myself it had to be an accident, a mistake, she couldn't have meant to do it!"

"You saw her leave the package?"

"Not leave it, no. I'd just polished the handles and the knocker on the big doors. For Wednesday's performance. I took most of the cleaning things inside and when I came back for the rest, Agnes was turning away from the postern. Her back was to me and she had on a mourning veil, but I knew her by her red petticoat. She had her overskirt lifted away from the street." He laughed unsteadily. "She wouldn't put off that red petticoat if she was mourning a husband, let alone her mistress's stepson. I didn't call out to her because I didn't have time to talk—once you get Agnes started, you're stuck." He looked pleadingly at Charles. "Why would she want to hurt Antoine? *Maître*, she couldn't have known the *gaufres* were poisoned!"

"She bought the poison herself," Charles said. "I talked to the apothecary who sold it to her."

"He's lying! Or wrong. He must be, please, *maître*—"

"You saw Maître Doissin die, Frère Fabre. A hard death. You saw your sister leave the postern just after the poisoned *gaufres* were left. Agnes must at least explain herself. Will you go for the police? Ask someone where the nearest commissaire lives and bring him, or one of his men."

It was the best he could think of. He couldn't leave Fabre here to warn Agnes. And if Fabre didn't come back—well, that would be information, too.

The boy gave the gate a last anguished look and wiped his eyes on his sleeve. "I'll go."

To Charles's relief, Fabre returned quickly, bringing a man in the night watch uniform of plumed hat and blue jerkin laced with silver. The man was built like a bull, with hard eyes and a mouth like a trap.

"This is Monsieur Servier," Fabre panted. "He is—"

Servier cut across the social niceties. "What's going on?"

"I am Maître Charles du Luc, from the College of Louis le Grand, *monsieur*. A tutor died there this afternoon. From poison. Which you may already know, since our rector notified your lieutenant-général. The tutor ate poisoned *gaufres* intended for a little boy, Antoine Douté. The woman who left the *gaufres* is Agnes La Salle, maid to Mme Lisette Douté. Mme Douté is the boy's stepmother and she is staying here with Mme Montfort, who is her sister. I want you to question the maid and the stepmother. The maid was recognized just after she left the cakes, and I know where she bought the poison."

Servier's eyebrows rose as he eyed the gate. "You know Montfort's related some way to the Guises," he growled.

"The king's law runs here, not the Guises', *monsieur*. And God's law runs everywhere."

"Just so you know whose broth you're stirring. The commissaire's not going to like this. He's already had a murder tonight—an apprentice did for his master and they're all in his house, witnesses, widow, accused, you should see it." Serious offenders and witnesses were usually questioned first by the neighborhood commissaire, no matter what the hour.

Servier hitched up his belt, which supported a light sword and a small pistol, and took the pieces of a heavy wooden baton from under his cloak. He assembled them into a long, thick weapon, pulled the Montforts's bell rope, and followed up the pull with a volley of baton blows on the gate. Running feet approached and a grille slid open.

"Tell your master that M. Servier of the watch wants to see Mme Douté and the woman Agnes La Salle."

"My master is not at home."

"Then tell your mistress. But first open the gate."

The man started to bluster and Servier lifted his baton in front of the grille and slapped it loudly against his open palm. The grille slammed shut, bolts were slid back, and the gate began to open. Servier wrenched it wide and strode into the cobbled yard, Charles and Fabre behind him. The servant's eyes grew round when he saw their cassocks.

"Please," he said, "wait here." He backed toward the tall, beautifully carved house door across the court.

"We'll wait inside, if you please," Servier said. "Or if you don't."

With a helpless gesture, the man hurried ahead of them to the door of the beautiful brick house, whose upper floors made three sides of the court. The lower floors housed stables and outbuildings. A lantern beside the open stable doors raised gleams from the paintwork of a coach standing inside. They followed the servant into an anteroom at the foot of a curving staircase.

"I beg you, wait here!" The man held his hands toward them as though warding off a pack of dogs and ran upstairs.

"Come on," Servier said over his shoulder to Charles and Fabre. "But if you make a noise and the women get away, I'll arrest you both instead."

They went soft-footed up the gleaming stairs, toward the sound of women's voices exclaiming and arguing. The voices grew louder as the servant emerged from a door carved with fruit and garlands.

"Who's in there?" Servier demanded, over the man's protests.

"I am." The woman who had come out of the salon put enough ice into the two words to freeze the Seine from Troyes to Rouen.

The servant stepped hastily aside and walked to the head of the stairs, blocking their path. Charles made a pretense of rubbing his chin to make sure his mouth was closed. She looked like one of the goddesses cavorting on the painted ceiling above her head. Her pale hair, gathered up behind and dripping ringlets around the perfect oval of her face, was silvery in the candlelight. Little golden pears hung trembling from her ears and her low bodice spilled creamy flesh and ivory lace. One dimpled hand held up shimmering gray satin skirts. Her eyes were the blue of pond ice. Her cold gaze settled on Charles.

"*Mon père?* What is this about?"

"Madame Montfort?"

She nodded fractionally.

"I apologize for this intrusion, madame. I am Maître Charles du Luc, from Louis le Grand. I beg you to hear what M. Servier has to say."

"I must speak with the maid Agnes La Salle," Servier growled. "And her mistress."

"Her mistress is unwell and is seeing no one. Why do you want her maid?"

"Because these good Jesuits have laid evidence that she poisoned a man this afternoon."

The heavy skirts slipped from Mme de Montfort's hand. "That is absurd! She has been with Mme Douté all day. You are mistaken."

"I don't think so, madame. But others will decide that." Servier started to climb the few remaining stairs.

"No! Wait. I will bring the maid out, you can speak to her downstairs. Her mistress, my sister, knows nothing of this. She is very near her time. It's her first and your coming here has already upset her more than enough."

Servier and Mme de Montfort locked eyes. He smiled at her bosom and withdrew a short way down the stairs, forcing Charles and Fabre down behind him, stopping where he could still see the salon door. When she saw that he would go no farther, she went back into the salon. Voices clamored briefly and she returned with a delicately built girl a few years older than Fabre. The tendrils of hair escaping from her white coif were as red as her brother's. Watching her over his shoulder, Servier descended to the anteroom. She had not yet seen Fabre, who had withdrawn with Charles into the anteroom's shadows. When Servier turned around, the girl checked sharply at the sight of his baton, but Mme de Montfort forced her down the last few steps. With an assessing glance at Servier, the girl lowered her dark lashes and folded her hands at her tiny waist. Her breath came fast, swelling her plain black bodice.

"Yes, *monsieur?*" she said softly.

"You are Agnes La Salle?"

"Yes." Her lips parted over small even teeth, and her voice grew breathy. "Is there—something—anything—I can do for you?"

"You left poisoned cakes at the college of Louis le Grand today. A tutor ate them and died. I am arresting you for murder, *mademoiselle.*"

Agnes sprang away from him and clutched at Mme de Montfort. "No! I've done nothing, tell him, madame!" Then she saw Fabre. "Denis?" she faltered. Emotions chased each other like clouds shredding and forming across her face. "Tell him, Denis," she shrieked, flinging herself into his arms. "I am innocent!"

"It's all right," her brother said, holding her tightly. "You didn't know they were poisoned. But I saw you at the college, and—"

She reared back in his arms. "What do you mean, you saw me?"

She wasn't surprised at the mention of poison, Charles noted. Only at having been seen.

"I saw you leave the postern," Fabre said. "You had on a veil, but I still knew you." He smiled a little. "I saw your red underskirt." His eyes pleaded with her to be the sister he'd always known. "The porter gave me the package to deliver and—it was terrible, Agnes. Antoine's tutor ate some of the *gaufres.* I saw him die."

She tossed her head and pushed him away. "Other women have red petticoats. And what does it have to do with me? Even if I brought the child some cakes, as my mistress told me to, it's hardly my fault if some old man is ill and dies!"

"Antoine?" Mme Montfort's face was rigid with horror. "The poisoned cakes were for Antoine?"

"*What* poison?" Agnes stamped her foot, as though they were all thickheaded. "The baker must have poisoned them!"

"Where did you get them? When?"

"Yesterday. From a shop on the Place Maubert."

"But you bought poison, Mademoiselle La Salle," Charles said quietly. "You bought aconite from the dwarf on the Petit Pont. You bought it more than once."

"You lie! Everyone knows Jesuits lie, what you say means nothing!"

"I saw you go into his shop. M. Rivière, the apothecary, has your name and your purchases in his register." If there was a register. But that was another matter.

She shrugged indifferently. "My mistress sends me to buy it." Her calculating gaze flicked from face to face. "Talk to her."

"Oh, we will, *mademoiselle*," Servier said. "We will talk further with both of you. At the Châtelet, I think, since the commissaire is so busy." He grinned evilly. The Châtelet was notorious for its torture facilities.

Agnes screamed and slammed her hand into his face, catching him in the eye, and plunged toward the door. Charles caught her and swung her around. Blinking furiously, Servier grabbed her and pinned her arms against her sides.

"It was her, it was my mistress!" Agnes screamed, writhing against his hold. "She set me to it, I won't die for her and her brat!"

"That's good enough." Servier gave Charles a satisfied nod. "You hear that?" he said to Mme Montfort, who seemed to have turned to stone. "Your sister's accused of murder. You say she's expecting and ill. Keep her here. I'll be back shortly and if I find her gone, madame, I'll take you instead."

Agnes threw back her head. "You'll burn, Lisette," she screamed at the dispassionate divinities on the ceiling. "Tell them, you bitch, it was you, not me!"

Stumbling on her skirts, Mme Montfort fled up the stairs. The manservant, who had been listening from the upper floor, rushed down with a cloak and Charles draped it around the now-sobbing Agnes. Fabre stood frozen, his face wet with tears.

"Judas," Agnes spat at him, as Servier pushed her over the threshold. "You had your chance to get away from the godforsaken tannery. This was mine! Damn you to hell, you stinking Judas!"

Chapter 30

The cold stone and stooping shadows of the Châtelet did nothing to quell Agnes La Salle's fury. She stood at bay in a small chamber lit only by a lantern that the watch officer, M. Servier, had set on a scarred table. Servier stood at the table's end and Lieutenant-Général La Reynie, Père Le Picart, Frère Fabre, and Charles all sat behind it on a bench, watching her. Like judges, Charles thought uncomfortably. La Reynie had sent a carriage for the rector, and ordered Servier to stay for Agnes's questioning. When it was over, La Reynie and Servier would take what they'd learned back to the Place Royale to question Mme Douté.

"It's not my fault," Agnes insisted sullenly. "Mme Douté told me to deliver the package." She looked at them from under her lashes. "Because of what M. Louis told her."

"Who is M. Louis?" La Reynie asked sternly.

"Her astrologer. He told her the first wife's brats would kill hers to get all of old Douté's money."

The three Jesuits crossed themselves. La Reynie's face was rigid with anger. In the anteroom, the rector had told Charles that La Reynie was still haunted by the notorious poison trials ten years ago, when it seemed that half Versailles and Paris had poisoned someone or had been some poisoner's target. And that now he was merciless toward mountebanks who preyed on the ignorant.

"Where did she go to meet with this man?" La Reynie demanded.

Agnes smiled slyly at the Jesuits. "He calls himself Louis in honor of your St. Louis church. He lives by the old city wall that runs behind it."

"Describe him," La Reynie said.

"I'll tell you if you let me go."

"Oh, you'll tell me, mademoiselle." La Reynie sighed. "One way or another. For your own good, I suggest you tell me here rather than in the chamber beyond that door."

The whites of her eyes showed as she glanced at the heavy planked door. "Young," Agnes said sullenly. "Not tall." Slowly, her lips curved and her eyes took on a faraway look. "Blue eyes and a voice you could listen to forever. He always wore his hood up, I never saw his hair. He wore a beautiful blue robe—I always wondered what he had on underneath." Her dreaming tone grew venomous. "He's the one should be here, not me! It was his idea, his and Mme Douté's, never mine!"

"When did she first consult him?"

Agnes thrust her lower lip out and turned her head away. Servier started toward her. "The end of June," she spat, before he could touch her. "And twice after that."

"But why, Agnes?" Fabre burst out. "Why would you help her poison a child?"

She held out a fistful of her plain skirt and shook it at him. "I am a servant. Like you. I do what I am told, I didn't know what was in the package, how could I?"

"You knew," Charles said. "You knew what the astrologer had said. You bought the poison. And you disguised yourself in the veil. Your mistress's mourning veil, wasn't it?" His voice hammered at her. "You left the *gaufres* at the college and said they were for Antoine. What did your mistress promise you that was worth his life, and your own damnation?"

"Nothing *you* would understand, you bloodless Jesuit!"

"You said it was your way out of the tannery, Agnes," Fabre said, begging her to show them they were wrong. "But you've been gone from it four years, you're in good service, what could you need so badly?"

"You always were an idiot, Denis. Do you think I am content to be a mealymouthed servant all my life, like you? Do you think I am content to be talked at, ordered around from morning to night, hit if anyone feels like it? I won't be beaten, ever again! And don't tell me you don't remember the beatings, I know you do!"

"I remember," Fabre whispered. "When he tried to make you marry Jules. But—"

"Yes, damn your father's ugly soul! He beat me till I couldn't stand and when you tried to make him stop, he beat you, too."

Fabre looked at Charles. "There was an old tanner—my father tried to make Agnes marry him, to get control of the tannery when the old man died."

"I was fifteen, even still a virgin, if you'll believe that." Agnes rushed to the table and leaned across it, staring into her brother's eyes. "What do I need, Denis? I need a rich husband, I want a soft living, just like you do. And that's what she promised me! Don't look at me like that, you're no better than me, you damned little hypocrite!" She grabbed up the lantern and swung it at his head. Fire spilled onto the table and kindled the papers in front of La Reynie. The men jumped to their feet, and Charles smothered the flames with his cassock skirt, as Servier wrenched the lantern away from Agnes.

The rest of them fled the cell. Fabre's cheek was livid where the hot edge of the lantern had caught it, but he seemed to feel nothing. Charles sat him on a bench and asked a guard for water while La Reynie and the rector talked hurriedly. Servier came out of the cell and La Reynie spoke quietly to him.

"Yes, *mon lieutenant-général*," Servier said smartly, and clattered away down the echoing stone stairs.

La Reynie went into Agnes's cell, and Le Picart sat down on the other side of Charles and dropped his face into his hands.

"God help us all," he muttered. "Lisette Douté? I can hardly make myself believe it."

"Nor can I, *mon père*," Charles said.

The rector sat up, shaking his head. "She's seemed to me barely capable of tying her own hair ribbons. Dear God, poor M. Douté."

The guard brought a cup of water and Charles dipped the edge of Fabre's cassock in it and held the wet fabric against the burn. The boy heaved a shuddering sigh. After what seemed a long time, La Reynie came out of the cell and locked the door on Agnes's sobbing.

"Père Le Picart," he said, "one of my men will see the lay brother back to Louis le Grand. I would like you and Maître du Luc to come to the Place Royale. I think you should be there while we question Mme Douté."

Grimly, the rector agreed, and the three of them went downstairs and through the arcade that separated the prison side of the Châtelet from the law courts, to La Reynie's waiting carriage. But when they reached the Place Royale, they found Servier taking the Montfort house apart, room by room. Lisette Douté was gone.

Chapter 31

Monday afternoon's first chaotic rehearsal on the new stage was blessedly over, and Charles and Père Jouvancy were in the rhetoric classroom, checking costumes for damage and putting them ready for tomorrow's dress rehearsal. Charles picked up Time's stiff-skirted black tonneau and straightened quickly as a seam ripped in his too-small, borrowed cassock. His wound ached and last night's events still swirled in his tired brain. Lieutenant-Général La Reynie and M. Servier had questioned Mme Montfort relentlessly, but she'd sworn on her hope of salvation that she didn't know how Lisette Douté had escaped the house and hadn't helped her. Nor, she said, did she know where Lisette had gone. La Reynie had left Servier to watch the house in case Mme Montfort was lying. He had also said he would send a man to Chantilly at first light, in case she'd gone there, and to break the news to her husband.

Charles spread the tonneau neatly over a bench and picked up three long glass vials full of colored water, "poison" from the secret store of three-headed Cerberus, the hell-dog. The ballet *would* have a poison entrée, he thought with distaste. The entrée's *actualité*—its real-life reference—was the poison plots that had rocked Paris and Versailles a decade ago. But for Charles, and Jouvancy, and even more poignantly for Fabre, who had been part of the stage crew today, the poison entrée's *actualité* could only be what had happened yesterday. Charles had gone below stage to correct the timing of Cerberus's emergence through the trap, and found Frère Moulin juggling a chalk ball, an apple, and a knot of rope in an effort to cheer Fabre, who had stared blankly at the flying miscellany without seeming to see it. But it had been a kind thought on Moulin's part. Praying that Fabre's misery was only for his sister and not because he had had any part in her act, Charles put the "poison" vials away in their box and picked up a soldier's helmet.

"Maître du Luc?" A lay brother put his head around the door. "The porter wants you at the postern. There's a strange boy asking for you."

The boy was backed defiantly into the street passage's darkest corner, a folded paper in his fist, and Frère Martin was standing over him.

"Slipped in like an eel and held up that note with your name on it. Won't say a word."

The youth, whose dirty face was half hidden by an oversized leather hat, glowered at Charles from under its tired brim.

"Perhaps he'll talk more easily without an audience. Come on, you." Charles led the way to the chapel, checked to see that no one was at their devotions, and went to a dark side altar dedicated to France's heroine, Jeanne d'Arc. He knelt and pulled his charge down beside him. "What happened?" he hissed. "And fold your hands. If we look like we're praying, we're less noticeable." He reached up and pulled off the hat.

Pernelle snatched it back and jammed it over her hair, which had been raggedly shorn. "It hides my face."

"The dirt hides your face. What happened?"

"The head of the Paris police came back to the bakery this

morning and wanted to see me. Madame LeClerc said I'd gone back home—to St. Denis, she said, she has family there—and he left. But we thought I'd better leave for real."

Charles leaned his elbows on the altar rail and rested his head on his clasped hands. "All right. Help me come up with a story, my wits are far past working. Why you're here, who you are, why you can stay. And where, God help us."

When she didn't answer, Charles raised his head. She was gazing with distaste at the chapel's pink and gold veined marble, its glowing paintings, the lapis and gold glinting under the altar's sanctuary lamp. With a slight shudder, she turned from the richness and looked up at the armor-clad statue of the Maid of Orleans, the *bon Dieu's* blessed scourge of the English.

"Hmph," she grunted. "If I believed in your saints—"

"She's not a saint."

"Well, she's dead and she has an altar. Anyway, if I believed in your religion, I'd think she might look kindly on us. She's not exactly wearing womanly finery, either, is she? Is she supposed to help people with something?"

A grin spread across Charles's tired face. "Some people think she has a soft spot for those who must go against the church's authority for a good cause."

"Amen," Pernelle returned piously. She stretched up to whisper in his ear. "I'll stay in your chamber, Charles."

"You can't—"

"Are you all right in there, *maître?*" a voice called from the courtyard door.

"Yes, Frère Martin." Charles shot to his feet and stood between the brother and Pernelle. "I'll see the boy out through the chapel's street door."

"Ah. Well. All right, then."

Martin backed out of the courtyard door and trudged toward the neighboring court's latrine. Charles sped to the small porter's room off the street passage and grabbed the canvas apron kept there on a peg for the porter's use. He shoved it under his cassock and went back to the chapel.

"Put this on," he said, handing it to Pernelle. "And wait here." Forcing himself to walk unconcernedly, he went to the rhetoric classroom and came back with the gown of one of the ballet's goddesses. "Hold this in your arms, high, so it froths up and hides your face and stay behind me."

They crossed the deserted Cour d'honneur, made it to the street passage and into the main building, only to find themselves face-to-face with Frère Moulin. His eyes went from the "boy" carrying the costume to Charles, but Charles kept walking and Moulin passed them without comment and disappeared into the street passage. Before Charles's heart could stop thumping, Père Montville came out of the grand salon.

"Something wrong with the costume, *maître?*" he said, stopping.

"Just delivered back from being repaired, *mon père,*" Charles said easily, willing Pernelle to stay behind him and keep her head down.

"Good, good. Oh—about Frère Fabre, *maître,* you probably noticed that he's been reassigned to the stage crew. We thought he should have something new to think about, poor boy. But he won't be seeing to your rooms the next few days, you'll have to see to yourself."

"Good, yes, very thoughtful," Charles gabbled, thinking that Jeanne d'Arc or someone was surely watching over them. How to deal with Fabre's morning visits had been the next problem waiting for him.

When they reached his rooms, Charles pushed Pernelle

through the door, shut it, and dragged the heavy carved linen chest in front of it. They collapsed onto the chest and wiped their sweating faces.

"I can't believe we're doing this," he said in her ear. "Listen, this isn't a busy passage, but you can't let yourself be heard. When you have to talk, murmur, whisper."

Pernelle nodded, dropped the costume on the floor and took off her hat with shaking hands.

Charles got wearily to his feet. "If anyone tries to come in—" He measured the bed's height with his eyes. "I think you can squeeze under the bed. It's not long till supper. I'll bring you something. There's water in the pitcher there." He picked up the costume. "I'll take this back to the classroom."

Pernelle stood up, too. "It will be all right, Charles." She smiled at him and the knot of fear in his chest suddenly didn't matter.

When Charles reached the refectory, he saw that Père Guise, who had not been at dinner, was also not at supper. And immediately began to wonder where he was. *No*, he admonished himself. He had, as the rector had kept warning him, let his dislike of Guise lead him astray. Let La Reynie do his own work now, at least until the show was over. Charles turned his attention resolutely to the beef stew and when he was finished, wrapped bread, cheese, and a peach in his napkin and slipped it into the bosom of his cassock. On his way out of the refectory, Le Picart stopped him. For an anxious moment Charles thought he was going to be questioned about the stolen food.

"Is all well with the show, *maître?*" Le Picart said loudly, and drew Charles aside to the wall. Without waiting for an answer, he dropped his voice and said, "You saw that Père Guise has not been at meals today. In case you are trying to make too much of that, I want you to know that I had a message from him. He was called to Versailles early this morning. To confess a very ill woman who has been failing for weeks now."

"Ah." Charles nodded, remembering Moulin's acid portrait of Guise galloping off to save the soul of a sick old penitent at court. "Is there any news of Mme Douté?"

"None. M. La Reynie was here this morning to ask if I had heard anything. He is beside himself over her escape."

"Well, I pray God—" Charles stopped, thinking of the unborn child and M. Doute and Antoine. "I hardly know what to ask of God, *mon père.*"

"Nor do I." Le Picart crossed himself.

Charles followed suit and made his escape.

He found Pernelle safely in his chamber, gazing pensively out the window. When she had eaten, he pointed to the bed.

"You have that, I'll make a bed in the study. No, don't argue."

"We'll take turns with the bed."

He felt himself go hot at the thought of both of them in the same bed, even if not at the same time. "Fine." He took his cloak and the extra blanket from the chest. "The pot is under the bed. I'll use the latrine downstairs if need be."

"Good night, Charles." Her dark eyes gleamed in the shadows falling over the room.

"Good night."

The Compline bells rang out, Charles said his prayers, and quiet settled over the college. But the prayers didn't bring their usual peace and he lay awake far into the night, listening to Pernelle's soft breathing from his bed.

-◦❦H Chapter 32 H❦◦-

Tuesday dawned gray and still, the air thick with damp. Charles roused Pernelle at first light and got her safely out to the stage. Père Jouvancy was already there, fiddling with his beloved seven-headed Hydra, and Charles introduced the "boy" as Jean, Mme LeClerc's stage-struck nephew—mute, but with good ears and wits—who wanted to learn to build stage machinery. Well disposed toward anyone who would take an interest in machines like his beautiful Hydra monster, Jouvancy said that since Mme LeClerc would be watching Antoine during tomorrow's festivities, indulging her nephew was the very least they could do. So far, no one had given "Jean," still enveloped in the flopping hat, a second glance. So far, so good, but Charles was finding the strain unnerving.

By late morning, he was supervising the last stage details, fanning himself with his list of things to do as he watched Frère Moulin crawl out of the Hydra and hand the clanking tool bag to the listless Frère Fabre.

"You did well," Moulin told him, "I didn't check all the mouths, only the last two you worked on. No offense, but I've been at this stage business longer than you."

"Good, I thank you both," Charles said, going to the front

its mouths, forced open wider now,
over the audience.

pped through the trapdoor to the un-
otted Pernelle, coiling rope around a
rang out and the rest of the stagehands
ay brothers' refectory. When everyone else
was gone, ...nt below stage and found her sitting cross-
legged against a huge coil of rope.

"All's well?" he asked softly.

"Well enough." She smiled and flexed her sore arms. "I never
knew making theater was so much physical work!"

"I'll bring you some dinner."

"Good! I could eat a horse."

"We don't run much to horse, thank the *bon Dieu*—and the
bursar—but I'll do my best."

By the time dinner ended, the humid heat trapped under the
huge canvas awning felt like a foretaste of hell. By dress rehearsal
time, sweat runnelled the actors' makeup as they took their places
and stung the musicians' eyes and made them miss notes in the
overture. In the prompt wing, Charles moved a little away from
a taut-faced boy in painted canvas armor. If God sent them a
breeze tomorrow, he hoped it wouldn't blow the costumes' ripening scent straight up the audience's nose.

The overture ended and Charles and the soldier traded
nervous grins as heels clacked on the other side of the curtain.
Jacques Douté spoke the prologue, and Frères Moulin and Fabre,
hidden from the audience, parted the halves of the curtain to
reveal a forest whose green leaves seemed to flutter in the shadows cast by the candles fixed to the side flats. Jacques's blue satin
back shimmered in the candlelight as he bowed in the direction
of the audience and swept offstage. Charles sent up a prayer
that all would go smoothly below stage, where Pernelle would

be leaning manfully into the gear wheels that moved the stage machinery.

Clovis conquered his way through the first act and the ballet cast took over. De Lille–Hercules had surprised everyone but Beauchamps by evolving into a thoroughly convincing hero. He slew the Nemean lion with panache, cut through the obstacles of three more entrées, and arrived triumphantly in the Hesperides. Clovis and his minions returned and Charles hissed occasional prompts from the tragedy script and scribbled frantic notes, licking his quill's end when it threatened to dry, spattering ink as he dipped it in the little inkwell on the stool beside him.

As the next ballet entrée began, he thrust his head around the flats to see how Maître Beauchamps was faring. Wigless and bowing a full-sized violin, the ballet master directed his musicians with furious swings of his head, his flying silvery hair making him look like he was playing in a cyclone. Charles drew back into his downstage wing. The music, the dancers' passion burning their movement into the air, the actors' voices rolling Jouvancy's beautiful Latin off their tongues—the beauty of it all wiped everything else from his mind and filled him with a piercing happiness.

When the ballet's last entrée began, everyone was riding high on a wave of success. On cue, the trap opened and the gloriously horrible seven-headed Hydra rose towering from hell. Glistening black and poison green, it rolled downstage toward its foes, red smoke belching from its yawning mouths as the lay brother crouched inside blew mightily up a cluster of long pipes. But only six mouths were belching smoke. Charles frowned and made a note. As he looked up, a pipe poked a hole in the monster's canvas neck and a puff of smoke drifted toward Charles. The dancers didn't notice. Feet flickering like hummingbirds, they bounded around the beast and thrust their spears at it. As

Hercules balanced on the ball of one foot, his spear poised for the final blow, a pair of boots fell from the smokeless mouth and landed at his feet.

He ignored them like the professional he was, but Charles dashed onstage, ducked under the spear thrust, and snatched them up. Clutching them to his chest, he retreated to his wing and gaped at them in disbelief. They were the color of burnt sugar. Ungartered, but faint lines in the leather showed where garters had been. Their tops were high and folded. Charles stowed them between his feet and stood over them like a bird with one egg.

The finale ended triumphantly and everyone rushed onstage, applauding and congratulating and whooping. The rector, who had watched from a lone chair in the middle of the court, applauded with them. Notes in one hand and boots in the other, Charles praised and congratulated everyone, and tried to keep an eye on Fabre and Moulin. Armand Beauclaire and two other boys made a three-man pyramid and Beauclaire somersaulted from it, landed in front of the astonished de Lille, and made him a wildly elaborate bow. De Lille blushed with pleasure.

"We'll use that next year, Armand, don't forget how you did it!" Jouvancy called, laughing.

The crew came up from the understage and down from the loft, and the musicians perched on the edge of the stage. Pernelle sat beside the trap in her hat, silent and watchful. Fabre stood with Moulin in the cluster of stagehands. Jouvancy and Beauchamps dispensed praise, followed by fearsome threats should anyone—performers or crew—slack off tomorrow on the strength of today's success. They gave their last-minute notes and corrections and then it was Charles's turn. Charles put the boots down beside him and looked at his notes, but before he could begin, Le Picart, who was standing near the musicians, nodded toward the boots with a questioning look. Charles gave him a small nod and tackled his short critique of the performance.

"And one more thing," he said, as he finished. "Most of you didn't see that there was a problem with the Hydra. One mouth was blocked and the smoke couldn't get out. The smoke pipe dislodged the blockage." He held up the boots. "Whose are these?"

Everyone jostled, peered, disclaimed, and shrugged. Frowning at the thought that someone might play fast and loose with his precious Hydra, Jouvancy took the boots and examined them closely.

"Mmm—no," he said, "not ours. They're good boots, though," he added wistfully, always covetous of discards for costumes.

"Me, I'll take them, if no one else does," someone joked.

"Give the rest of us a chance!" Moulin pushed his way to the front. "They look a good fit for me."

Charles handed him a boot. Moulin took off his shoe, tugged the boot on over his stocking, put his foot down, and winced.

"My poor big toe is folded in half. Oh, well, too bad." He pulled the boot off. "Just my luck. Anyone else? You, Frère Fabre, you could use some good news and your dainty foot looks the right size!"

Laughing students and brothers pushed Fabre forward. He shook his head and tried to draw back, but Moulin leaned down and picked up the boy's foot, making Fabre grab his shoulder for balance. Moulin pulled off the shoe, shoved on the boot, and set Fabre's foot firmly on the floor.

"There." He felt Fabre's toes and tugged up the boot's top. "A perfect fit, *mon frère*, this is your very lucky day!"

"They're not mine." Fabre started to pull the boot off.

Moulin stopped him, laughing. "But they can be yours now." He made a half bow to Jouvancy. "If no one minds."

Charles leaned down to feel the boot's fit. "Put this one on, too, *mon frère*," he said pleasantly. "They really do seem to fit you. Wait here one little moment."

Looking at his notes, as though he'd just remembered an important question, he hurried to Le Picart and drew him a little distance away, talking low and fast.

"You're sure they're the same boots?" the rector said, gesturing at the scenery, as though that were their subject.

"As sure as I can be, though the spur garters are gone. Frère Fabre worked on the Hydra's mouths this morning. Frère Moulin checked what he'd done, but he only checked two of the mouths. *Mon père*, Frère Fabre tried hard to mislead us about who left the poison for Antoine, and now his sister stands accused. And the boots of the man who attacked Antoine and tried to kill me fit him perfectly."

"But he can't be the man you chased, not with that hair!" Le Picart looked at Fabre, who was staring miserably at his feet, hardly seeming to hear his confrères' teasing. "But yes, what you say is damning enough. I will question him. And I will have Père Dainville look at him in the passage upstairs. If it was Frère Fabre he saw coming out of Père Guise's chamber, I will send for La Reynie."

Le Picart and Charles crossed the stage and stood on either side of Fabre. Jouvancy rapped for silence and brought everyone back to the last-minute business of where to be tomorrow before the performance and when. When he finished, Le Picart picked up Fabre's discarded shoes and said something in the boy's ear. Fabre seemed to protest, then subsided and followed him dejectedly across the court.

Hoping against hope that Dainville would say it hadn't been Fabre he'd seen, Charles forced himself back to the job at hand and went below stage to help with the damaged Hydra. Pernelle was holding a glue pot for Jouvancy.

"I suppose an Opera workman did it," Jouvancy was saying as he brushed glue carefully onto the canvas skin where the patch would be. "Hid someone's boots for a joke."

"At least," Charles said, "they fell out today and not to-morrow."

Chapter 33

I took another two hours to finish the last-minute stage details. When all that could be done had been, Charles left Pernelle hidden under the stage—getting her back to his rooms
was impossible until everyone was at supper—and went to find
Père Le Picart. Père Dainville couldn't say, the rector told him,
if it was Frère Fabre he'd seen that day. If he'd seen the flaming
hair, the old man said, he would be sure, but the passage had
been dark and whoever it was had worn the regulation broad-
brimmed outdoor hat. Fabre, in tears, had fiercely proclaimed
his innocence, but Le Picart had sent for Lieutenant-Général La
Reynie. When La Reynie got no further with Fabre, he'd tried
to take him to the Châtelet but had finally agreed to Le Picart
keeping the boy under the college version of house arrest for
now. An agreement reached only after a pitched battle, Charles
surmised, reading between the lines of the rector's account.
Fabre was shut into a small room, decently provided for, with a
large, incurious brother posted at the door.

That was news enough, but Le Picart had saved the real
news for last. When La Reynie had come to the college yesterday, the rector had told him, as he'd told Charles, that Père
Guise was gone to Versailles. But this afternoon, after questioning Fabre, La Reynie told the rector that he'd sent a man to

Versailles to make sure Guise was there. The man had returned to say that Guise was not, and had not been seen there. La Reynie now had two men watching the Hôtel de Guise, which was his best guess as to where Guise might be. La Reynie had also gotten a female spy inside the Guise house as a new kitchen maid, to listen to gossip.

"It may be," Le Picart said to Charles, "and M. La Reynie obviously thinks so, that Père Guise has helped Mme Douté to escape. I suppose she could have sent a servant to him after Frère Fabre's sister was taken away. And she could have bribed her sister's servants to keep quiet about her disappearance. But even if Père Guise helped her, I think we will find that he is as devastated by what she has done as the rest of us. Remember, he used to be her confessor, it would be like him to try to bring her to penance before she is turned over to the police."

Charles listened, but kept his thoughts to himself—admonishing himself the while for lack of charity—and agreed with Le Picart that whatever the truth was, the college's priority now had to be tomorrow's performance. The rest could wait on God's good time.

On his way back to the stage, Charles found Père Jouvancy supervising brothers who were setting up rows of benches in the courtyard. Seizing his chance, he made a show of being on his last legs, not needing to put much acting into it.

"*Mon père*, do you think the kitchen might send me bread and cheese or something in my chamber? Enough for tonight and the morning, too?"

"Of course, Maître du Luc, of course," Jouvancy said apologetically. "I am so sorry, I forget that you are still recovering from your wound. You have been working like a Trojan."

When the supper bell emptied the courtyard, Charles walked Pernelle into the street passage, as though seeing "Jean" out. They slipped through the main building's side door and made it to Charles's rooms without meeting anyone. As he closed the door and dragged the heavy chest across it, his sigh of relief became a groan because Pernelle demanded washing water. The eccentric desire to wash ran in the family.

A lay brother brought a bucket of hot water, Charles filled his shaving basin, and Pernelle emerged from the study and made for the water like a peasant making for a side of beef.

"Out, Charles, go and pray, or whatever you do!" She untied the neck of her shirt.

Schooling his eyes like a novice nun, he retreated to the study. "Leave some for me. While it's still warm!"

"Soap?"

"Under the towel beside my shaving mirror."

Trying to ignore the blissful sighs from his bedchamber, he began to say Vespers. But his head was soon on his arms and he was nearly asleep when Pernelle dashed into the room, holding her shirt around her and clutching a dripping towel.

"Quick," she hissed in his ear, "get wet."

As he gaped at her, she wrung the towel out over his hair and face.

"Where do you want this, *mon père?*" a voice called from the bedroom.

Supper, Pernelle mouthed.

Charles waved her behind the door and grabbed the towel. "Coming, *mon frère!*" He went into the chamber, mopping his head and face.

"Thank you," he said, as the elderly man squeezed the laden tray in next to the basin. "This is most appreciated."

"Why are you keeping that chest in the middle of the floor like that? Someone will break a leg." The brother eyed the basin and bucket. "Ill, are you?" He backed away.

"No, no, just tired and dirty."

"St. Firmin preserve you," the brother muttered as he fled, invoking a saint known to be effective against plague.

Charles dragged the chest back across the door, dipped the towel in the warm water, and scrubbed at his face, sniffing hungrily at the savory steam rising from the dishes.

"Wait your turn!" Pernelle whispered from the doorway.

He threw her the towel and went back to his desk. Watching dusk fall outside the window, he tried not to think about how much he was enjoying the camaraderie they'd settled into in their close and illicit quarters.

"Charles?" Pernelle came in, dressed in the LeClerc apprentice's oversized breeches and one of Charles's clean shirts, which hung to her knees. Her skin glowed from its scrubbing and her wet hair was a mass of short curls. "Why did those boots matter? Are they to do with the murders?"

He told her about Philippe and Antoine and Lisette Douté.

"Those poor children!" Her eyes glistened with tears. "How could she, standing in the place of a mother to them? She must be mad!"

"For her sake, I hope so."

Pernelle hugged herself. "Sometimes I think that if I don't find Lucie again—if anything happens to her—I will go mad."

Charles clasped his hands tightly to keep from taking her in his arms. "You'll find her. It will all turn out, you'll see."

"Turn out, yes," she said shakily. "Everything 'turns out,' idiot, one way or another. But *how* will it turn out?"

"When this show is over, we will get you on your way to Geneva again. Where Lucie will grow up and you will grow old in blessedly dull safety." He pushed himself to his feet.

Pernelle summoned a smile and took a book from the top of the leaning pile. "Nothing more exciting than Tacitus?"

"The banned books are under the bed," he said, straight-faced, and went into the chamber. The water wasn't very warm anymore, but it ran over his tired body like a blessing. Even his wound felt better. He put on his last clean shirt and the same dirty breeches, his only pair, and called Pernelle to eat. What Jouvancy had sent was more than enough for two: lentil stew, bread, cheese, half a roasted chicken, salad, and a pitcher of wine. They saved the bread and cheese for morning and made short work of the rest. Then Charles dragged himself to his feet and went to the chest for his extra blanket.

"No," Pernelle said firmly, plucking it out of his hands. "You sleep in the bed." She pushed him gently toward it and he saw that she had already turned down its covers. "Get in. You look half dead. And you have to shine tomorrow." She added his cloak and her own to the blanket and hefted them under her arm. "Good night, dear Charles." She went into the study.

Charles lowered himself, groaning, onto the bed and plummeted into sleep. He woke long before the morning lightened, feeling more human than he had for days. Blessing Pernelle for giving him the bed, he stretched, rose, and made his way to the indoor latrine downstairs. On his way back, he stopped at one of the small salon's windows and looked down into the courtyard. The stage, rows of benches, and shield-sized allegorical drawings and poems about heroes that hung around the courtyard were invisible in the darkness. Below him, a door thudded and feet hurried over the gravel. He opened the casement and leaned out. Père Jouvancy, carrying a lantern and followed by two boys in their long sleeping shirts with buckets and brushes, was making for the stage. Going to repaint the patched Hydra, at something like four in the morning, Charles realized. Unaccountably moved, he shut the window and went back to his rooms.

The air was fragrant with Pernelle's sweet scent. He stood in the study doorway, listening to her breathing, facing the fact that he had to get her out of his rooms. And out of his life. Either that or go with her.

"Pernelle. Wake up."

"Mmmmph. Still dark."

"Barely, and we have to get you to the stage and say you've come early to help. I won't be able to get you downstairs later. Up."

She roused, grumbling, and he set out the bread and cheese and the mouthful each they'd saved of last night's wine. Pernelle came in yawning and running her hands through her hair. She took a piece of bread from the tray and they ate standing.

She was fully dressed, but Charles had to gaze out at the slowly graying street to avoid devouring her with his eyes. "Are things going all right below stage?" he said, around a mouthful of cheese.

"I think so. I play mute and do what they tell me. When something's too heavy, I act stupid and they shove me aside and lift whatever it is. But every muscle I have is screaming."

"If you'd slept in the bed—"

"Hush! It did you good, you look like a different person this morning."

"Tonight the bed is yours."

"I'll take it gladly!" She swallowed a mouthful of cheese and said, "Tell me about the brother called Moulin."

Charles looked around in surprise. "He's amusing. He can juggle, of all things. And he's bright. I think he's like poor Fabre, bitter over what life has offered him."

"Yes." She poured her share of the wine. "The thing is, he flirts with me."

"What?" Charles's heart sank. "He knows you're a woman?"

"If he doesn't, then he likes boys."

"Moulin definitely likes women. This is all we need. Stay away from him. As much as you can, anyway. Pick your nose, spit, scratch, make yourself disgusting."

"I can do that."

"I doubt it," he said under his breath, and turned back toward the window. Outside, August the seventh's sun was gilding the Sorbonne roofs. "Come on, boy, the day of reckoning is upon us."

Chapter 34

The clock chimed the quarter before midday. Uncomfortably aware of dinner swallowed too fast, Charles was alone in his rooms, wiping a linen towel over his face and hands and doing what he could to tame his hair, which curled like young vines in the humid warmth.

The morning had been all too short. Ignoring the courtyard chaos of students and faculty practicing for the Siamese reception ceremony, Charles and Père Jouvancy had checked and rechecked props, costumes, and the slowly drying paint on the Hydra's patch. As Charles went back and forth from stage to understage, he'd seen that Pernelle was holding her own acting the awkward boy quick to learn in spite of his muteness. To his relief, Frère Moulin had been nowhere in sight.

The only news from Lieutenant-Général La Reynie was that his kitchen maid spy at the Hôtel de Guise had heard a woman screaming somewhere in the house. And that Fabre, still held at the college in close confinement, was now refusing to speak to anyone.

Charles pulled his wrinkled shirt down smoothly over his black *caleçons*, his knee-length underpants. Today he wouldn't be teaching and demonstrating, so he had no reason to wear breeches. Just as well in the heat, he thought, taking the tight-across-the-shoulders cassock the clothing master had given him from the hanging rail. He pulled it on, tied the cincture, made sure his rosary hung straight down, and put on the three-pronged formal hat. His mouth was as dry as an over-roasted turkey, the way it used to be when he performed as a student. *Terpsichore, St. Genesius, St. Vitus,* he prayed, *give wings to the dancers' feet. Make the actors' words stick to their memories like Paris mud. Don't let the giants fall off the ladder. Whisper "right" and "left" in Armand Beauclaire's ear.* The clock chimed twelve. At a quarter past, the Siamese were coming. Charles hastened downstairs.

It was a little cooler than yesterday and less humid, and the awning made a pleasant shade. A breeze fluttered around its edges and rippled the stage curtain into a blue velvet lake. Lay brothers were making a last check of the benches and straightening the rows. Nearly all the windows below the awning and with views of the stage were open. The women in the audience would sit there, as though in box seats. Straight across from the stage, the third-floor windows of the little salon, where Charles had stood before daylight, were hung with swags of red drapery and three high-backed armchairs were drawn close to the sills. The Siamese would sit there, with a perfect view of the stage and high enough above the crowd to satisfy their notions of honor. In Siam, Jouvancy had said, honor meant being placed well above the ground and social inferiors. The ambassadors' letter from King Narai to King Louis, treated as if it were Narai himself, had apparently created endless confusion on the journey from the coast to Paris, since no one could be housed higher than the room where the letter lay in its elaborate casket.

In the center aisle between the benches, the student linguists were gathering to welcome the ambassadors in twenty-four languages. Their scholars' gowns had been brushed, their hair was unnaturally neat, and their hands had been scrubbed. The inseparable pair of twelve-year-old Chinese boys stood a little apart, black eyes flashing as they talked excitedly and pointed at the red-draped windows. Père Montville, the ceremony's director, burst out of the main building, slammed the door behind him, and was nearly flattened as an allegorical emblem the size of a small table crashed to the ground.

"Help!" he yelled to the lay brothers. "You have ten minutes to get that back in place." He rolled his eyes at Charles, who had come running. "We'll get through it. We always do. And tomorrow we'll be looking forward to next year. That's because we're insane, and you seem to fit right in, *Maître*. *Bonne chance* this afternoon!"

The clock chimed a quarter past twelve.

"Ah, *mon Dieu*," Montville implored, casting his eyes up at the canvas awning. He bore down on the linguists. "Form up in your line and stay there!"

He hurtled back through the rear door, Charles on his heels. When they reached the grand salon, Montville made his way through the crowd of excited Jesuits to stand on the rector's left, under the archway between the salon and the antechamber. The king's confessor, Père La Chaise, stood on the rector's other side. Charles slid along the salon wall and worked his way to a vantage point behind La Chaise's right shoulder. A strip of thick carpet patterned in red and gold ran from the rector's feet across the antechamber's patterned stone floor to the street doors. The college's most noble students, dressed in satin and lace under their scholar's gowns, were ranged along both sides of the carpet, fidgeting and whispering. The five boys nearest the double doors—the natural son of the late Charles II of England, and the sons of the Grand Généraux of Poland and Lithuania—had lent their personal carriages to bring the Siamese from Berny, two leagues south of Paris, and would escort the ambassadors into the college. Le Picart clapped his hands to call everyone's attention.

"Remember," he said sternly, "this visit is supposed to be incognito, since the ambassadors have not yet made their formal entry into the city. We do not want to draw a crowd, so you must get them out of the carriages and inside as quickly as courtesy allows. Do not let them stand in the street and look at everything. The music should help to draw them. I hope."

The muted sound of slowing horses and carriage wheels drew all eyes to the doors. The boys stood like statues, in perfect fourth positions. Le Picart signaled the trumpeters hidden in a side alcove and a deafening processional made Charles flinch. Two lay brothers opened the great double doors. Charles II's son, eleven-year-old Charles Lennox, swept through them and opened the door of the first carriage, which had his coat of arms blazoned on it. He bowed deeply as the chief ambassador, Kosa Pan, descended from the carriage. The ambassador was resplendent in a long-sleeved tunic, curiously draped breeches, and a tall, narrow hat with a small brim, all of heavy gold silk covered with intricate gold stitching. His brilliant black eyes darted everywhere with lively curiosity, but he meekly allowed young Lennox to lead him inside. His two attendant Siamese nobles and M. Torf, a Frenchman who had accompanied the entourage from Siam, followed them. Kosa Pan bowed to Le Picart and the attendant nobles knelt with their noses in the carpet and their silk-clad rumps in the air. Before the desperately straight-faced students could give way to giggles, a new trumpet blast announced the next carriage.

In spite of Lennox's efficiency with Kosa Pan, an excited crowd was gathering in the street. Elbowing each other, they watched the other two ambassadors, a glum elderly man in blue silk embroidered with gold flowers and a young man in green silk and a fur-trimmed hat, alight from the carriages. As the last of the entourage trailed through the college doors, there was a pause in the music and a child's piercing treble voice rose from the crowd.

"*Maman*, they are just like monkeys!"

The great double doors swung shut. Charles hoped the Siamese didn't have enough French to understand the remark, but Kosa Pan's dancing eyes and brief snort of tolerant laughter told him otherwise. As the ambassadors' servants began laying brocade-wrapped gifts at the rector's feet, Charles faded back along the salon wall and retreated to the courtyard.

Half the linguists had abandoned their line and most had their gowns nearly off their shoulders. Charles chivvied them back into order just as Montville and two of the trumpeters emerged into the court and placed themselves below the red-draped upper windows, facing the long line of students. A blasting fanfare from the third-floor salon, answered by the courtyard trumpeters, signaled that the ambassadors had reached their red armchairs. The first linguist stepped smoothly forward. He bowed to the open windows, delivered greetings in French, bowed again, and exited around the outside of the benches. The second boy welcomed the guests in Siamese, and if his pronunciation made the ambassadorial mouths quiver, it also brought wide, appreciative smiles for the effort. Twenty more languages followed and finally the Chinese boys advanced, red silk flashing under their gowns. They delivered a brief antiphonal Chinese oration, expressing the college's joy in welcoming honored Mandarins from the East.

They withdrew and a longer fanfare announced Père La Chaise, escorting the king's German sister-in-law Liselotte, Madame, as she was styled by her royal title. She and her bevy of ladies acknowledged the ambassadors, who rose and bowed in return. Then Madame was shown to the middle chair of three upholstered in blue cut velvet, set between the benches and the stage. As she arranged her billowing lemon satin skirts around her, Père La Chaise sat down on her right. Her ladies claimed the first bench, their white linen headdresses, called fontanges, standing up on their ringleted heads like half-folded fans.

The other benches began to fill, as the boarding students not in the performance took their places. Charles saw Père Montville showing the *Mercure* editor to a good place near the front, and Beauchamps and the musicians emerged from the senior refectory, their tiring room, and arranged their music on stands. The mothers, aunts, and sisters of the students filled the windows, their jewels and gowns gleaming even in the subdued light, and their men, equally dazzling, flowed into the courtyard. Members of religious orders began arriving in a flood of black, brown, and white: Augustinians, Cordeliers, Carmelites, Jacobins, and Celestines.

With a last look at his audience, Charles slipped through the door to the understage, where Pernelle, cheeks flushed with excitement, stood beside her assigned gear wheel. The flirtatious Frère Moulin was still not in evidence, and the other brothers were too busy to pay her any attention. Charles smiled at her and went up through the trap and through the rhetoric classroom windows into a simmer of anticipation. Pale under their makeup, boys were dressing, muttering lines, practicing steps, and discovering that, once dressed, their churning insides needed the latrine. Père Jouvancy, calm and eagle-eyed, was everywhere at once. The clock chimed the quarter before one, preliminary music began in the courtyard, and a hush descended on the classroom.

"A good time to pray, *messieurs*," Jouvancy said to the students happily. "Keep your headdresses on, God will understand."

They gathered around him. Jacques Douté bowed his head, closed his eyes, and fell over his feet. Charles caught him and murmured, "Good, you got that over with in here."

Jouvancy glanced sideways at them. "Dear Lord," he prayed, "you took a body like ours, and our bodies are glorified in You. Please make us all, actors and their words, dancers and their movements, musicians and their music, stagehands and their work, instruments of Your truth. Let all we have made together be to Your glory." He paused. "And, dear Lord, extra courage wouldn't come amiss." The "amen" was full-throated and garnished with laughter. *Clovis*'s opening actors scrambled for last sips of water, smoothed tunics and straightened helmets, and streamed through the windows to their places. Charles followed and settled himself and his thumping heart in the prompter's wing.

The overture ended and Jacques Douté, blessedly sure-footed and commanding, spoke his prologue. Two lay brothers Charles didn't know drew the curtains apart and revealed the shadowy green forest, and the stage magic began to work its will. The audience grew quiet and attentive, as though the tragedy's sonorous Latin cast a beneficent spell. The robust swordplay drew cheers. Roars of laughter greeted the antics of comic characters. And if the tragedy cast a spell, the ballet wove a deep enchantment. The Siamese, who had watched the tragedy in polite bewilderment, came alive when the dancers appeared. Crowded close to the windows, they laughed and pointed and applauded.

When Hercules and his suite celebrated winning the Hesperides with a gravely joyous minuet, in a garden of golden fruit under a pink and gold and purple sunset, the audience breathed a collective sigh of contented wonder. Disaster threatened briefly when Armand Beauclaire went beautifully right, instead of correctly left. But, to Charles's amazement, Beauclaire realized his mistake and pirouetted smoothly out of harm's way. When the treasure-hunting Argonauts sailed their ship across the stage, the sea of billowing blue ribbons was so realistic that Charles saw a face or two in the audience turn faintly green. When the big-headed giants tried to scale heaven and fell thudding back to earth, even severe Carmelites held their sides laughing.

Holding his three-foot hourglass, Walter Connor danced Time's sarabande with majestic menace. As the sparkling sands of time and life drained visibly away, people blanched and shrank back in their seats. As Hercules slew the smoke-breathing Hydra, the audience leapt to its feet, applauding and cheering. Even the sober-faced German Madame smiled and nodded happily as the red smoke drifted over her head.

And when the exuberant Ballet Général began, Charles was half afraid the audience would surge onto the stage and join in. Hercules's long chaconne was a tour de force. Applause drowned the creaking of his pink cloud as Diogenes—Père Montville—wobbled to earth. Holding his lantern high, he brought the students receiving prizes onto the stage. To Charles's delight, Antoine Douté won the lower grammar class's prize, a fat Latin tome that he hugged proudly to his skinny chest. Finally, the trumpets accompanied Madame and her ladies from the courtyard and the Siamese down from their aerie. Royalty, ambassadors, and nobles went to the reception in the fathers' refectory, and the cast and less exalted remainder of the audience surged together, hugging, kissing, bragging, and congratulating.

Giddy with relief, flooded with happiness at the beauty he'd helped to make, and moist-eyed with pride at the students' achievement, Charles gave—and received—exuberant congratulations. Mme LeClerc made her way toward the stage, holding Marie-Ange and Antoine both firmly by the hand, and Charles jumped to the ground to greet her. He congratulated Antoine on his prize and both children forgot their manners and hugged him. Mme LeClerc was so excited that she forgot to reprove them.

"Your show was miraculous," she cried, throwing up her hands. "The saints must be dancing in heaven!" Under cover of giving him a smacking kiss on the cheek, she said in his ear, "Is Mademoiselle Pernelle all right, is she with you?"

He jerked his head at the stage. "Below. All is well, madame. After you sent her to me, did the police return?"

"No, thank the Virgin! She can come back to us, if you think it's safe."

Charles hesitated. "I—no, she'll be leaving soon." Though how, he still had no idea.

Seeing Père Jouvancy and Maître Beauchamps bearing down on Charles, Mme LeClerc curtsied and took the children's hands to steer them through the crowd. Jouvancy stopped to congratulate his nephew and speak briefly with Mme LeClerc. Then he and Beauchamps rained praise on Charles, who shoved away his worry about Pernelle and praised them fulsomely in return. The three of them linked arms and went to make their appearance at the rector's reception, feeling like heroes indeed.

But before they reached the fathers' refectory, Lieutenant-Général La Reynie appeared seemingly from nowhere, detached Charles from Jouvancy and Beauchamps, and drew him into an empty antechamber.

"I didn't see you in the audience," Charles said pleasantly, but his stomach lurched at the lieutenant-général's expression.

"I was at the Hôtel de Guise—outside with the two men I've set to watch. The Duchesse de Guise is seeing no one and the footman who answers the door insists that Père Guise is not there and that no one there knows where he is. The only way I can get in without bringing more trouble on myself than I want is with an order from the king. Which I doubt he would give me against a Guise, with only the evidence that I have."

"What will you do next?" Charles said.

La Reynie glared at Charles. "I came here to take Frère Fabre into custody, but Père Le Picart will not give him up. I will not force him in the presence of his guests. But tomorrow I will have Fabre, one way or the other. And you will help me get him, if it comes to that. I want an end to this."

"He may not be guilty—"

"I will have him, and find out whether or not he is guilty. You are still my fly here, Maître du Luc. Hear me. If Fabre conveniently flits as the other two did, you and you alone will answer for it. Your ballet is over, get back to work. Convince your rector that if he doesn't want scandal, he'd better give me his prisoner."

He stalked away, leaving Charles fallen from the heights of his triumph to cold, hard earth.

Chapter 35

Dusk had fallen on the empty Cour d'honneur. Festive torches burned at the entrance to the street passage and beside the archway into the north court, where voices and laughter sounded from the parties in students' rooms. Charles, who had volunteered himself and "Jean" to put away costumes and props, sat on the empty stage, dangling his feet into the open trapdoor. The front curtains had been taken down, and the flickering torchlight was just enough to let him see Pernelle, standing in the understage, and licking crumbs of a tart he'd brought her from her fingers. Her hat was on the floor, her hair was tangled, and her shirt was stained with sweat, and she looked happier than Charles had seen her since before their lives diverged.

"You did well down there," he said, trying to ignore the catch in his voice.

"I liked it. Oh, and that Moulin who was bothering me? He wasn't here—no one seemed to know where he was. You should be very pleased with your show, Charles. It was magnificent."

"I thought you'd hate all the Protestant-baiting and Louis-gilding."

"Oh, I did. But it didn't ruin the boys' triumph. Or yours. You're very good at what you do, I didn't realize how good."

"Thank you." He shook his head in amazement. "Who would ever have thought we'd work on a Jesuit performance together?"

Her eyes danced. "Shall we do a Huguenot ballet next?"

"In which King Louis can be hubris-crazed and fall off the giants' ladder!"

They laughed and then a silence fell between them. The court was nearly dark now and the sounds of revelry from the student receptions were growing louder. Charles sighed, reluctant to leave their refuge and face all that waited for them. "We should escape upstairs before the students' guests start heading for the postern." He picked up a scholar's gown from the stage floor and tossed it down to her. "Put this on—someone left it on a bench. If we meet anyone, keep your head down and look like a boy caught over-reveling." He stood up and stretched. "I took more food from the reception up to my rooms, so we—"

"Du Luc!"

The voice's rage jerked Charles sharply around, automatically feeling for the sword he hadn't worn in years. A disheveled and haggard Père Guise strode out of the street passage into the torchlight.

"Hide," Charles barely had time to say to Pernelle, before Guise was at the foot of the stage. Charles pushed his astonishment aside and said mildly, hoping to quiet the man, "What is it, *mon père*? Where have you been?"

Guise vaulted onto the front of the stage with a ferocious ease that made Charles back up quickly and reassess his own danger.

"I beg you, *mon père*, calm yourself," Charles said soothingly, as though Guise were a threatening dog. He edged upstage toward the rhetoric classroom windows. "What has angered you?"

"You," Guise bellowed, matching him step for step. "You

hell-born bitch spawn! You heretical piece of garbage! I should have killed you the first day I saw you."

"Why should you want to kill me?" Charles kept his eyes on the priest's hands. He doubted Guise had a weapon, but the man seemed insane with rage. "What have I done?"

"You dare ask me what you've done?" Guise threw his head back and his voice boomed and echoed beneath the awning. "You killed my son, you devil from hell! My son, my only son."

Charles shook his head in bewilderment. "What—but how—what do you mean, your son?"

"He lived only a few moments." Tears streamed down Guise's face. "You killed him. If you hadn't terrified her and made her flee, he would have lived!"

A blaze of revelation brought Charles to a halt, and instantly Guise had him by the throat. Charles thrust his hands between Guise's arms and tried to hook the priest's feet from under him. Guise fell and Charles twisted free, throwing himself across the man's writhing body.

"Get help," he yelled toward the trap door, "I can't hold him!"

Other hands shoved Charles aside. There was a grunt, a cry, and then the hot metallic smell of blood. Charles struggled to his feet, staring in horror at Frère Moulin sitting astride Guise's back and holding him by the hair. Neatly avoiding the spreading pool of blood from Guise's throat, the lay brother jumped up and wiped his knife on his gaping cassock, whose cincture had come loose in the struggle.

"Frère Moulin? Dear God, what—" Charles made himself breathe, searching for words. "Dear God, did you have to kill him?"

"You'd rather be dead yourself?" Moulin moved closer. "You're not hurt, *maître*?" He peered anxiously at Charles.

"No. I—but—" Charles shook his head. "Thank God and

all his saints that you were here. But could you not have—"
Charles looked at Guise's body and tried to regret that the man
was dead.

"No, I couldn't. He was crazed, *maître*. I heard him yelling
and came running."

"He said there was a child—his son, he said. A newborn
child."

"His woman birthed his babe a little while ago and like he
said, it died. So did she."

"His woman?" Charles whispered, staring at Moulin.

"Lisette Douté. I can see that's what you're thinking, and
you're right."

"How do you know all this?" Charles said, trying to make
his shocked mind work.

"He sent for me this morning. From the Hôtel de Guise,
where he'd hidden her. And now all his plans are undone. Clas-
sic tragedy," Moulin said, with a bitter laugh. "You could make
something of it for your show next year."

Charles started to reprove Moulin for his jest, then didn't.
Moulin had just killed someone—to save a life, but still, Charles
knew what that did to men. "What do you mean, his plans are
undone?"

Moulin put a shaking hand on Charles's sleeve. "He had
great plans. But he was stupid and mad! And the Douté woman
was stupid and greedy. But neither of them—"

"Frère Moulin, please—" Charles took a few steps away
from him, toward the stage's edge.

Moulin followed him. "Let me speak truth for once! Neither of them was as stupid as old Douté. Thought he was the
prize bull, getting her pregnant so fast. But that was Guise's
work. Couldn't marry her himself, of course, so he made a quick
match with Douté. Insane about blood and dynasty, Guise was.

God, he wanted that babe! No Guises left now but him and the old duchesse. She has brats by a lover, I heard—but it seems they don't count as Guises. This babe couldn't be a real Guise, either, being a bastard, but he was going to be the Jesus Christ of a bigger and better Catholic League—maybe that's why Guise wanted him born in the old League chapel—"

"The chapel? Surely not," Charles said, horrified, but Moulin ignored him.

"The Duchesse Marie couldn't leave her money to Guise, right? Him being a Jesuit. So to finance his League, he had to be sure his son would inherit all the Douté money. *Exeunt omnes*, as we say on the stage, don't we, exit the first Douté wife's two brats. And that mealymouthed Fabre helped him."

"Are you sure?"

"Sure as shit. He's next to me in the dormitory, I know all about him."

Charles felt sick. "If you'd told someone all this earlier," he said angrily, "fewer people might have died!"

Rising wind made the courtyard torches flare, and Moulin's eyes gleamed blue. "I was afraid, *maître*," he said, so close that Charles could feel his breath. "Guise was mad but powerful, and I'm only a servant."

"Go and find Père Le Picart, *mon frère*," Charles said wearily. "We need him here." They did need the rector, but Charles had also remembered that Pernelle was still hiding in the understage. He had to get her away before the stage was overrun by all the people this latest death would bring.

Moulin, quiet now that he had purged himself of his terrible knowledge, had turned to look toward the street passage. As he turned toward Charles, the torches flamed brightly in the wind and teased a brilliant yellow gleam from the shirt beneath his gaping cassock. Charles's eyes widened. Time seemed to stop and his heartbeat with it. The hair rose on his neck. He raised his eyes to Moulin's and what he saw there turned him faint.

"You," Charles breathed. He wanted to run, but couldn't move. Moulin's crow of laughter slapped him back to Père La Chaise's terrace, where the man who'd tried to slit his throat had laughed exactly the same way.

"Had you going, didn't I, feeling so sorry for me! Philippe's shirt becomes me, don't you think?" Moulin had darted between Charles and the edge of the stage and was bouncing happily on the balls of his feet, tossing his knife lightly from hand to hand. "That was fun, making you chase me out of the shithouse and over the wall that day!"

Moving with the infinite caution terror bestows, Charles took a small sideways step, trying for a clear path around Moulin. "You did Guise's killing for him. You, not Frère Fabre." If he kept Moulin talking, the brother might not notice what Charles's feet were doing.

"Fabre winces when he crushes fleas," Moulin scoffed. "Guise couldn't risk the street porter saying he'd been paid to keep quiet about seeing the knife in my hand, could he? And I couldn't risk it, either, could I!"

"How did you know I'd found the porter?" Charles slid his feet another few inches aside.

"You tripped over me on the quay, you clumsy piece of shit! But you're wrong about Philippe. I did Philippe for *me*, not Guise. The little cock saw my box of souvenirs and was going to be the lily-white boy and get me thrown out for thieving. Or womanizing, he couldn't quite make up his mind which. Insufferable little shit, even mealymouthed Fabre scolded him once for the way he talked to me! Pride goeth before a fall, they say, don't they? His went."

"Souvenirs?" Charles gained another half an inch. "The box Antoine and Marie-Ange found in the stable loft?"

"The same. Mementoes of my dead sister."

"But—surely no one would blame you for keeping those!"

Moulin chortled. "My *very* dead sister. And *much too* dear, most people would say. Oh, no, that killing's still remembered. I couldn't risk my treasures being seen, so—exit Philippe. Told him that if he'd meet me by the latrine, I'd explain where I got the things in the box and he could do as he thought best." He shrugged a shoulder. "You could say my past is even more checkered than the pasts of most noble younger sons. And Guise knew where the bodies were buried. Literally, I'm afraid, and held what he knew over my head. That's why he gave me a new name, sponsored me as a lay brother, and in turn got himself a humble servant for his little projects. In exchange, I got entertainment, money, and a new identity. Speaking of bodies, you never would have found Philippe's if the shit collectors I paid to take it away and dump it hadn't gotten cold feet." Moulin's voice turned sullen. "Killing Philippe should have made Guise grateful, since he'd planned to do it anyway, but did it? No, I was just the servant, never anything more, no matter if I'd brought the bastard the Holy Grail!"

"Why should he have been grateful?" As Charles risked a lightning glance at the stage edge, measuring the distance, he thought he saw shadows moving slowly along the right-hand wall of the courtyard. But he couldn't be sure in the light and dared not take his eyes from Moulin long enough to look again.

"Don't you listen? Guise was planning all along to get rid of the Douté brats, and when Philippe turned up missing, Guise took it as a sign from God. Had me go ahead and try for the other one. But the little snot-nose was too fast and I missed him."

Moulin caressed his knife as though to comfort it. "Then Guise had Lisette try, but Doissin ruined that. I told Guise the poison scheme was trouble. When he listened to me, his projects turned out, but when he didn't—see where it got him?"

They looked at Guise's body. The reek of blood from the priest's throat hung over the stage. Suddenly, out of the corner of his eye, Charles saw a brief flash of torchlight on metal where he thought he'd seen shadows moving.

"I'll tell you about one of his projects, knowing how much you'll hate it." Moulin's eyes gleamed in a windy flare of torchlight and he leaned closer, smiling wolfishly. "Dragonnades! Not the silly English plot. The ones Guise and Louvois have been running for our saintly king. I've been their messenger to the *very* well-paid military couriers who pass orders to provincial officials. Want to know where the next one is? Metz." Moulin lunged playfully at Charles and pricked the end of the knife through his cassock and shirt. "Don't worry, however— you won't grieve when it happens, because you'll be dead."

"Why go on killing?" Slowly, Charles bent his knees to leap for the edge of the stage. "You could still confess and do penance, instead of damning your soul—"

"You think God cares about any of this? If he did, would the world be such a shithole? No theologian's ever explained that one and some of them are almost as smart as I am. Sorry. But I am leaving Paris." Moulin jerked his head toward Guise's body. "Tidying up before I go. Too bad you saw my pretty shirt."

He sprang with part of the sentence still in his mouth. As he knocked Charles to the floor, flipped him onto his belly, and straddled him, gunfire echoed off the courtyard walls.

Chapter 36

Charles lay rigid, not knowing who had fired the shot or which of them had been its target.

"Charles, oh, dear God, Charles, don't be dead!" Pernelle fell to her knees beside him. And jumped up with a smothered sob as someone vaulted onto the stage.

The light from a swinging lantern made Charles blink. Shoes crossed his line of vision and Moulin's weight was rolled off his back. A large hand framed in lace reached down.

"Are you hurt?" Lieutenant-Général La Reynie pulled Charles up and holstered a pistol with his other hand.

Feeling at his wound to see if it was bleeding again, Charles shook his head. Pernelle had withdrawn to the edge of a wing, a hand pressed to her mouth, her eyes enormous in her white face.

A man with a bloodied bandage around his arm held the lantern over Moulin's body.

"That's him." The words were full of grim satisfaction.

La Reynie nodded. "Go back to the Châtelet, let them see to you," he said to the man.

Charles stared at what had been Moulin, trying to pray for the man's twisted, violently dispatched soul and failing utterly. He looked up. "I owe you my life, M. La Reynie."

"It was one of my men who shot him."

"How did you know to come here?"

"When Guise left the Hôtel de Guise, two of my men followed him. This Moulin must have been watching the Guise
house, too, because he followed my men. One of my officers
realized he was there and doubled back to question him. Moulin
killed him for his trouble and wounded the one who just left,
but that one got word back to me at the Châtelet. I guessed
Guise would come here and thank God I guessed right." La
Reynie gave Charles an appreciative nod. "You did well to keep
Moulin talking. Did you know we were in the courtyard?"

"I knew someone was. You heard what Moulin said?"

"Most of it. Enough."

Hurrying footsteps made them turn.

"*Maître!* Thank God!" Père Le Picart rested trembling hands
on Charles's shoulders. "You are not hurt?"

Charles shook his head. "It's finished, *mon père*," he said gently.
"It's over." He nodded toward the bodies. "Frère Moulin was behind it all, not Frère Fabre. But he was working for Père Guise, as
was Mme Douté."

Briefly, Charles and La Reynie told the rector what had happened and what they'd learned.

"It is not finished," Le Picart said into the quiet that fell
then. "Not for their souls." He looked from Moulin's splayed
body to Guise's, lying in a glistening pool of blood. "I failed
them. I was their superior, I stood as their father in religion. I
should have known, I should have seen . . ."

"They made their own evil, *mon père*," La Reynie said
brusquely.

"As do we all." The rector knelt between the bodies and
began to pray for his lost "sons."

Lieutenant-Général La Reynie went down into the courtyard

to talk to his men and Charles went to find Pernelle. She was sitting in the dark corner of a wing with her face in her hands.

"Are you all right?" He touched her shoulder. "I'm sorry you had to see this."

A sob caught in her throat. "I thought you were dead."

"So did I for a moment." Charles held on to a side flat, thinking that he might still die from sheer exhaustion. "Can you stay hidden a little while more? La Reynie seems to have forgotten you and I want to keep it that way. I'll get us away as soon as I can."

A sudden beam of light sent Charles's heart into his throat.

"Emotional, isn't he, your young friend?" La Reynie stood behind Charles, holding the lantern high and looking at Pernelle. "As emotional as a girl. From the south, too, I hear in his voice. An unusual coincidence."

"I'll see him home shortly." Charles started back through the narrow passage between the wings and La Reynie had to retreat in front of him. Charles stopped close to the wings, so as not to disturb Le Picart, who was still praying. As a distraction from Pernelle, but also because he wanted to know, Charles asked, "Is it true, Monsieur La Reynie, about the child and Mme Douté? Are they dead?"

"I've sent someone to find out for certain."

Charles looked at the rector, bent low as though the deaths Guise had caused hung on his own soul, and thought about the other deaths, Huguenot deaths, that Guise had helped to cause. "Monsieur La Reynie," he said abruptly, "you told me that you protect the Huguenots still in Paris."

"What of it?" La Reynie said warily.

"You heard what Moulin said about the dragonnades? French dragonnades, I mean."

"I heard."

"You can use what you heard to stop them."

Le Reynie looked pityingly at him. "I cannot."

"Why not? Do you want more of this?" Charles gestured angrily at the bodies, the priest, the blood.

La Reynie did not respond.

"Oh, I see." Helplessness rose in Charles's throat like bile. "I beg your pardon. I should have known. After all, I first saw you talking to Guise and Louvois. An unholy trinity, I thought you were then. I had come to think differently, but you are telling me I was right the first time. Death does not trouble you."

La Reynie's eyes blazed red in the torchlight and he struck Charles a blow on the cheek that sent him crashing into a wing. Two of La Reynie's men, stooping to lift Guise's body onto a board, started toward Charles, but La Reynie shook his head and they held where they were. For a long perilous moment, he and Charles faced each other, both their faces dark with anger.

Then the lieutenant-général shut his eyes and turned his head away. "I watched my first wife die." His shaking voice was a thread of sound for only Charles to hear. "And three of my children." He opened his eyes and stepped close to Charles. "You are a celibate, you will never know the pain of any of that! You may be very sure that death bothers me. I see death most days. And of course I have a part in the dragonnades. So do you and every other faithful Catholic, if you choose to look deeply enough. You blind innocent, I will spell it out for you. And if you talk, you may well find yourself dead. Our war minister Louvois has become too powerful for the comfort of many highly placed men. Many of whom not only hate him, they fear him. And his ambition." La Reynie's softly furious words sounded like grease spitting in a hot pan. "Everyone knows that Louvois keeps the dragonnades going for Louis. But few know that Guise was Louvois's confessor. Which means that Guise knew Louvois's secrets like no one else, and Louvois's secrets are not only legion, but potentially perilous to Louvois. When I learned that he was Guise's penitent, I began to wonder if I might get some hold over Guise and trade with him for some threat I could use to curb Louvois's power. Then someone— and I was sure it was someone in your college—started killing. And I recruited you. Now, thanks in great part to you and your rector, I have this English plot to hold over Louvois's head."

"What about Lysarde's murder and the Dutchman's—or whoever he was? When you told me those two were dead, I had the strong feeling that you assumed Louvois was responsible."

"No doubt. But there will be no proving it."

"What about the dragonnades, then? You can prove those, you can stop them!"

"How can they be stopped when officially they do not occur? The man who makes Louis admit they go on at all is finished."

Charles shook his head in disgust. Louvois had said exactly that to Guise. "And so we are back where we were," he flung at La Reynie. "You will not risk your comfortable position."

"Oh, very comfortable," La Reynie said wearily. "If you could hear anything other than your own emotion, you might be in better case, Maître du Luc. I have used my power to draw a fragile circle of peace around Paris. And Versailles. I have done what I can do."

A soft rustle of cloth made Charles realize that Pernelle had crept closer and was listening just out of sight. "Why did you have men watching the LeClercs's bakery?" he said.

The lieutenant-général watched his men carry away Moulin's body. Softly, more to himself than to Charles, he said, "To keep Louvois's men away from her. He has flies in the Louvre, too."

"To keep Louvois's men away?" Charles said, to be sure he'd heard right. That couldn't mean what it seemed to mean. But if it did . . . As he stared at La Reynie, an insane thought—or a fragile hope—reared itself in Charles's mind. When La Reynie's men were gone, the thought and the hope were still there. Charles began cautiously feeling his way. "Forgive me for insulting you, Monsieur La Reynie."

La Reynie nodded slightly without looking at him.

"You have said that you are indebted to me, *monsieur*," Charles said.

Another nod.

"I think you are a man who pays his debts. Even to self-righteous innocents."

Now La Reynie was looking at him. "I pay my debts."

Praying that his hunch was right, Charles nodded toward the wings. "My young friend needs to go to Geneva." He heard Pernelle stifle a gasp. "Will you pay your debt, Lieutenant-Général La Reynie, by helping him on his way?"

It seemed to Charles that all three of them stopped breathing for longer than should have been possible. La Reynie looked into the darkness where Pernelle stood.

"Come here," the lieutenant-général said.

Pernelle stepped into the lantern's light.

"Take your hat off, boy," La Reynie said gruffly.

She looked at Charles. He nodded and she slowly removed her hat.

A soft sound escaped La Reynie. "I thought so." His voice caught in his throat and he swallowed. "When I saw you in the bakery, you ran to the back so quickly, but I thought so. You could almost be my Marguerite's—" He smiled at Pernelle "—brother, shall we say?" To Charles's astonishment, he drew himself up, swept his hat off, and bowed low to her. When he straightened, he was Lieutenant-Général of Paris again. "Be at the college postern before first light, boy. Accept my apology for striking you," he said stiffly to Charles. Then he went to deal with the dead and the fragment of peace their dying had restored to his city.

Chapter 37

As Lieutenant-Général La Reynie reached the edge of the stage, the man he'd sent to the Hôtel de Guise came running back across the courtyard, spurs clanking. Charles went closer to hear the man's report. He'd seen the female spy working at the house, the officer told La Reynie, and it was true that a woman had given birth there a few hours ago. In the Guise chapel, he added, with avid relish. Neither the woman nor the child had lived. Gossip in the house had it that the child was full-term.

Charles crossed himself and said quietly, "Her child was due in October, I heard."

"So M. Douté no doubt believed," La Reynie returned. "I suppose she would have prepared him to welcome a surprisingly large and healthy early-born babe."

Behind them, the rector groaned. They turned around as he crossed himself and got to his feet. "May God forgive her," Le Picart said sadly. "May God forgive us all. Monsieur La Reynie, I must call brothers to take charge of the bodies and prepare them for their graves. Will you wait in my office? We can finish saying what needs to be said there. And you, Maître du Luc, go to your bed. You and I will talk tomorrow. You have done more than enough for us today."

"Thank you, *mon père*. Will you release Frère Fabre now? Tonight?"

"Immediately. And you will see that boy of Mme LeClerc's home?"

When Le Picart and La Reynie were gone, Charles went to get Pernelle, who had withdrawn again into the stage wings. He wanted to have her gone before the lay brothers came for the bodies.

"Is it really true?" she whispered, grasping his hands. In the torchlight, her face was white with shock. "I thought you had gone deranged. Am I really going, and so easily? Can we trust him?"

"Yes." Charles wasn't sure he liked La Reynie, but he had misjudged him badly. "We can trust him."

"I can never thank you for what you've done, Charles."

"Seeing me through the show was thanks enough." His effort at lightness was a failure. His insane gamble had succeeded and she was going. He cleared his throat and dropped her hands. "Go back to Mme LeClerc tonight, Pernelle. It's safe. I'll meet you outside the postern before first light."

She looked almost as though he'd struck her. "Is that what you want?"

"You'll be more—" He couldn't force the lie through his tightening throat. "Please."

She studied him for a moment. Then she drew his face down and kissed him, spun quickly away, and ran across the stage and jumped to the ground. When Charles heard the porter open and close the postern, he sighed out what started as relief and ended as desolation.

In his rooms, he shed his cassock without bothering to light the candle. He went to the window, opened the casement, and leaned out, remembering his first Paris night. There were fewer candles now in the windows up and down the street. Schools were closing for vacation, as Louis le Grand shortly would. He lifted his face to the damp air and clouded sky and wondered if there would be rain before morning. Think of rain, weather, the tragedy, the ballet, he told himself. Even of the real tragedy, whose final act had played out tonight on the stage. Think of anything but Pernelle.

He felt his way to the prie-dieu, groping like a blind man, but not because of the dark. He sank to his knees and prayed for the Doutés, living and dead, for Lisette's dead child, for her maid Agnes waiting for her trial in the Châtelet, and the porter and the tutor. He even brought himself to pray for Guise and Moulin, because guilty and innocent alike had been brought to ruin by greed and hatred and the love of power. He turned then to giving thanks for the preservation of his own life and for La Reynie's unexpected humanity. Finally, he prayed for Pernelle's safe journey and that she would find her daughter and sister-in-law waiting for her. But those last prayers cost him dearly and his heart overflowed with the pain of her going. These last few days, even with their danger, exhaustion, and worry, had been so full of the happiness he'd always felt in her presence. Just knowing she was there, at Mme LeClerc's, even when he hadn't seen her, had lit a small, bright fire in his heart. *What will I do now*, he asked the Silence. Finish the school term, make my yearly Jesuit retreat, and during it make my decision about the Society? He dropped his head onto his arms. "Tell me," he begged aloud. "I love her. What do you want of me?" The Silence held its peace. Some quality in the air, or maybe it was only his misery, made Charles feel that It was holding Its breath.

"Charles?" The door closed softly and Pernelle's feet moved lightly across the ancient floorboards.

Charles raised his head. "What's wrong? How did you get here?"

"Shhh." Her fingers were warm on his lips. "Nothing's wrong. Mme LeClerc found her stairway key; it was in a flour barrel." She withdrew her hand and he waited, like a man in a trance. "She said spending my last night down there was a terrible waste. She said it wasn't fair. To either of us."

"And what do you say?" he said in a choked whisper. "What's fair to you?"

"I am here," she said simply. "David is gone, I am not breaking any vow."

"But I would be."

"Not a final vow."

"That's hair splitting."

"Well, that thing Jesuits do—casuistry, isn't it called? Don't you teach that the end justifies the means?"

"It's much more complicated than that." Suddenly he was laughing. And thinking that any man who thought body and mind had no commerce had never loved a brilliant woman. "Is it the custom among Huguenots to discuss theology when considering—um—?"

"Considering bedding together? It has been known," she said gravely, but he could hear her smile even though he couldn't see it. "But it is not required."

"What is the end the means might justify, Pernelle?"

"Whole-heartedness."

"Whose?"

"Ours. But especially yours."

"Expound, my learned *maîtresse*," he said laughing softly.

"We loved each other, Charles. We meant to marry. When they pulled us apart, I thought I would die. But I learned to love

David and he loved me. My heart grew into one whole piece again. But I think yours has not been able to. You need a whole heart to give to God." She put her hand on his cheek and a small yearning sound escaped her. "Make love with me, Charles. For both our sakes. If we go through this last door together, then perhaps we can go on apart."

Her fingers fumbling at his neck to untie his shirt stirred him into fire. He rose to his feet, untied the cloak she wore, and pushed her shirt—his shirt—off her shoulders. He held her against his naked chest, his face buried in her hair, and felt like every lost creature who has ever found its home again. The Silence, or the air around him, or maybe just he himself, released a long-held breath.

Hours later, when he woke, it was deep night and rain was blowing against the window. For a moment, he thought he was a boy at home again and his brother was taking up most of the bed. Then his heart nearly burst with thankfulness as he realized that the knees in his back and the arm across his waist were Pernelle's. He wriggled closer to her, and she stirred and kissed his spine.

"Good morning," he said.

"Not morning yet, but very, very good!"

He rolled onto his back, hardly feeling his wound, and pulled her on top of him. "My joy, my heart, my love." He was nearly singing. "Thank you. For your wisdom, for your great gift. I kneel at your feet, I—"

Laughing, she covered his mouth with hers and then pulled away. "That's all very pretty, but get to business, sir."

So he did.

When he woke again she was sleeping soundly. Her head was on his chest and he breathed in the sweet scent of her hair.

He hoped he hadn't been repulsive, still wearing his day's sweat. But she hadn't seemed repulsed. His smile was broad enough to light the dark. But dawn was coming. His arm tightened around her. Before dawn, she would go. He tensed against grief's assault, but it didn't come. *But I love her with all my heart,* he said to the Silence, appalled at his lack of feeling.

Yes, Something said very distinctly in the dark. Charles froze, feeling like Adam discovered with Eve after they'd shared the apple, and everything else. Pernelle sighed in her sleep and put a warm hand over his heart. Light too bright to look at seemed to come from nowhere and flood everything, every smallest piece of him. And he finally understood, though he also didn't understand at all. She would go and he would love her. And he would love many other things, though not any other woman. *Yes,* the Silence said.

Darkness still held Paris in its arms when Charles and Pernelle went hand in hand to the street passage. The college was sleeping and the porter hadn't yet come to his post. Pernelle was in her boy's clothes, wearing her cloak and with the last of the rector's pouch of coins in her pocket. Before they reached the postern, the bell rang beside it. They stopped and turned to each other. Charles put down his lantern.

"Go with God, beloved heart," he whispered, and kissed her. "Always."

Her dark eyes were silvery with tears. "Always."

Charles unbarred the postern door and Lieutenant-Général La Reynie, booted and cloaked, stepped out of the darkness.

"Quickly," he whispered.

Pernelle's hand rested briefly against Charles's heart. Then she turned to La Reynie and Charles closed and rebarred the door. He listened to the two pairs of feet walk toward the river and when he could no longer hear them, he went to the chapel. He meant to go to the Virgin's altar, but he found himself instead standing in front of the statue of Jeanne d'Arc, the Maid of Orleans. He knelt where he and Pernelle had knelt just a few days before, and waited for the blow of her leaving to hit him. Instead, an emptiness grew inside him. Not a grieving emptiness. A waiting emptiness, he thought, gazing uneasily up at the Maid. She stared over his head, as though she were waiting, too, waiting for the English army and knowing, against all the odds, that she would prevail.

"But they killed you," Charles said out loud. The statue calmly studied the horizon. "They burned you," he said. But only after she had saved France. His breath began to come short. "I have no power," he protested, "no power at all!" But neither had she, only belief in her truth. They could take her mortal life—and they had—but God had held her soul's life. So she had clung to nothing but God; her enemies had had nothing she wanted. She'd had no price. That was her power. Charles stood up. Or something pulled him upright.

Chapter 38

The servant who opened the Hôtel de Louvois's gate was as brusque as the war minister himself. He waved Charles across the cobbles to the house door and disappeared into one of the ground-floor outbuildings. Charles picked up the iron fist that served as a knocker and let it fall.

"I am Maître Charles Matthieu Beuvron du Luc," he said to the surly footman who answered, putting several generations of Provençal noblemen into his voice. "Please tell M. Louvois that I must speak with him. About last night's events at the college of Louis le Grand."

"Wait here."

He waited in an antechamber done in rich red, listening to the early-morning stirrings of the household. The footman returned as quickly as Charles thought he would and led him upstairs to a large room whose glowing parquet was an expanse of eight-pointed golden stars. Across the room, in front of long windows, Louvois sat writing behind a massive black desk. *Ebony*, Charles thought. The room was so padded and plump with luxury that Louvois's plum brocade house robe and turbanlike head wrapping made him seem like just one more piece of costly decor.

"*Monsieur*." Charles nodded to him slightly.

Louvois glanced up. "What do you want? It is barely day."

"You will have heard, I think, in spite of the hour, of last night's deaths at the college."

"Of course," Louvois said, still writing. "It is all over Paris. Père Guise was my confessor," he added accusingly, as though Charles were disturbing his mourning.

"Before Père Guise and Frère Moulin died, they talked."

Louvois's hands stilled. "I did not know this Moulin."

"On the contrary, Monsieur Louvois. Last night Frère Moulin talked much about his usefulness to you. As your errand boy for the dragonnades you and Père Guise have run these last years. I know the king knows about them. I know he wants them to go on. I also know that if they are forced publicly on his notice, you will be the scapegoat. He will accuse you of usurping his authority and you will likely die a very public traitor's death to save his face."

"The man who forces such knowledge on Louis will also die," Louvois said, purple with fury. "He will see to that, make no mistake."

"Nevertheless, I am here to give you notice, *monsieur*, that if the dragonnades continue, *I* will force all that on the king. The next dragonnade is planned for Metz, I understand."

Louvois's eyes bulged. "You are insane. You are a rogue Jesuit. Do you expect me to believe that Jesuit policy toward heretics has changed?"

"I expect you to believe that I will do what I have said."

Louvois surged to his feet and bellowed for his servants. Charles ran. Halfway down the stairs, he straight-armed a man over the banister and into the path of more men coming behind him. Charles gained the front door, covered the courtyard in a few long strides, and was through the gate, just opened for a carriage coming in. He took a twisting path away from the rue de Richelieu and when he passed the open door of a tiny church, he ducked inside.

Hidden in a corner's shadows, he gasped for breath, sweating with fear and holding on to the wall because his legs threatened to collapse under him. What in God's name had he just done? Had he truly gone insane? A priest came out of the sacristy and started toward him, and Charles went back outside, wary and watchful, but no one paid him any attention. He walked toward the river, gulping rain-washed air, still asking himself what he'd done. As he crossed the Petit Pont, the utterly simple answer came: He had done what he could.

He had also guaranteed that he would be looking over his shoulder for as long as he lived. As long as Louvois lived, anyway. Rogue Jesuit, Louvois had called Charles. In a way, he supposed he was. Yesterday he had helped Louis le Grand to a public triumph. But this morning he had kissed his lover goodbye. Just now, he had struck a blow against what many Jesuits applauded. And before any of that, he'd already had penance coming. For the lies that had bought him time to solve the murders, for acting as La Reynie's spy, for breaking his vow of chastity. But not for loving. Never for loving. If that made him a rogue, then rogue he was.

Dodging the rivulets of mud sliding down the rue St. Jacques, he climbed toward the college. When he reached it, he stopped in the street and looked up at the words carved over the double doors. *Collegium Magni Ludo.* The College of Louis the Great, the king's college. But not only the king's. It was also Le Picart's, Jouvancy's, Dainville's, Fabre's, God's . . .

"God's thorn bonnet, *mon père!*" A cart driver pulled his horse nearly onto its haunches to keep from hitting Charles. "Are you going in or out? Make up your mind!"

"In," Charles said. "I'm going in."

Epilogue

The last dragonnade in France took place in August 1686 in Metz.

In 1688, when the Catholic King James II fled England, rumors that French dragoons were poised to invade and dragonnade the Anglicans helped to bring about his fall. The English throne went to his Protestant daughter Mary and her husband, William of Orange.

Marie, Duchesse of Guise, died without heirs in 1688. In 1700, the Hôtel de Guise passed to the Prince of Soubise, in token of Louis XIV's gratitude for the illicit favors of the Prince's wife.

According to St. Simone, orders for the Minister of War François Michel Le Tellier de Louvois's arrest and permanent imprisonment in the Bastille were issued on July 16, 1691. On that day, before he could be arrested, Louvois died suddenly at court, of apoplexy.

❦ Author's Note ❦

The past is a patchwork of what we know, what we may guess, and what we can never know. As others have said, the writer of historical fiction often works where the known joins the unknown, and I worked in that way in this story when I imagined a reason for the end of the dragonnades in France. I also used what we do know: deliberately created rumors of English dragonnades did help to topple King James from the throne, but I have imagined how they were created. The sixteenth-century Wars of Religion and the bitter fruit they bore in the seventeenth century were also real.

The college of Louis le Grand was much as I have presented it. Now a state *lycée*, it still stands on the Left Bank's rue St. Jacques. Until the early 1770s, when the Society of Jesus was suppressed by the pope, the Jesuits produced drama, ballets, and even opera in their schools as part of teaching rhetoric, and many ballet programs survive. The August 1686 performance, with the Siamese ambassadors in the audience, is historical.

Many of the story's characters are real people. Lieutenant-Général La Reynie is sometimes called the first modern police official. Michel Louvois, Louis XIV's feared minister of war, directed the dragoons and much else in France. The great Pierre Beauchamps was the Louis le Grand ballet master and Père

Joseph Jouvancy was a renowned rhetoric master at the college at the time of the story. The House of Guise and its Catholic League played pivotal roles in the Wars of Religion, and in Charles's time, Marie of Guise had her "court" in the Hôtel de Guise in the rue Paradis. Père Sebastian Guise, her nephew, is imaginary.

Charles and Pernelle are also imagined, but the du Luc family was real. Charles Gaspard du Luc was bishop of Marseilles and later archbishop of Paris—though his actions in this story are invented. Two boys named Antoine and Philippe Douté are listed as student performers in a Louis le Grand ballet program, though their names are all I know about them. A Père Le Picart was the college rector in 1686, but beyond his name, he, too, is my creation.

Why do these seventeenth-century people, real and imagined, fascinate me? One reason is that they live with one foot in the fading medieval world and the other foot in the emerging modern world. Paris was still in many ways a medieval city, though its walls were going down, "modern" buildings were rising, and what we would call urban renewal was taking place. It was possible to believe whole-heartedly in demons and alchemy, while keeping abreast of the latest developments in telescopes, microscopes, and anatomy, and speculating about extraterrestrial worlds.

I have tried to make the story's people true to their own century, and not just us in costumes. My hope is that their humanity reaches out and touches the reader, so that the reader can touch the past.

READERS GUIDE

*The Rhetoric
of Death*

DISCUSSION QUESTIONS

1. Discuss the significance of the arts, especially dance and the art of communication, as a vital part of education during this period in France's history. Though Charles came from a family of minor nobility and his education prepared him to take an important place in the secular world, why do you think he ended up where he did, first as a soldier and then training to be a priest?

2. Being new to Louis le Grand, and with a checkered past he'd rather keep hidden, Charles had much to lose by investigating Philippe's death. What do you think his reasons were for involving himself in the investigation?

3. Discuss the devious characters in the novel. How do some use their duplicitous nature for good, and others for evil?

4. When Charles finds the hidden staircase above the bakery he thinks, "The stairs changed everything" (page 173). What do you think he means by this? Do you think Philippe's murder could have been avoided had the staircase not existed?

5. This time period (the late 1600s) in France straddled the beginning of modernity and the end of medieval times. How do you think this time of great transition affected the characters and their actions throughout the novel? What seemed especially different to you from what might happen now in similar circumstances?

6. Religious persecution and power are main themes throughout the

course of the novel. Discuss why religion, government, and education were so tied together.

7. After ordering Charles to leave the murder investigation to others, Père Le Picart summons Charles to his chamber and orders him to find Philippe's killer. Why do you think Le Picart changes his mind? When Le Picart asks, "What human action, after all, is completely free of sin?" (page 215), what do you think he means?

8. Charles has participated in untoward acts in his past, but has chosen a life of service to God and the church. Do you think, based on his character and actions throughout the novel, that this is a true calling for him? Why or why not?

9. When Pernelle is hiding in Charles's chamber, Charles says his prayers but they do not bring him his usual peace, as he listens to Pernelle's breathing deep into the night (page 320). Do you think it is because he is questioning his calling as a priest?

10. Jealousy runs rampant throughout the novel and is the reason for several characters' demise. Discuss how the time period might have spurred those feelings.

11. Do you think Charles's love for Pernelle takes away from his love for God?

12. Toward the end of the novel, when Charles sees the Jeanne d'Arc statue, he realizes that belief in personal truth is better—and maybe stronger—than worldly power. Do you think this idea has been forming in him throughout the novel and influencing his dealings with the power structures of church, college, social class, and government?

13. Do you think the Society of Jesus and the Roman Catholic Church were like the other power structures in France at the time?

14. Do you think Charles will stay with the Society of Jesus and become a priest?

———

Charles and his Paris will return in late 2011—for updates and details, please check the author's website at www.judithrock.com.